Harry's Game

Blue Skies & Tailwinds

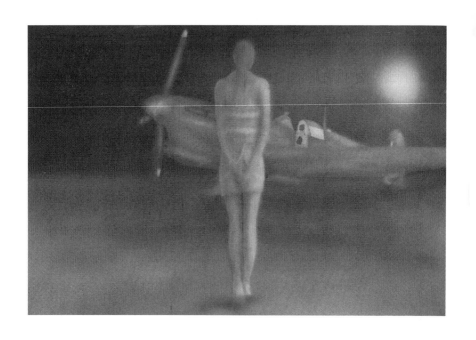

Harry's Game

Blue Skies & Tailwinds

Karl Jackson

Alpaca & Goose
2021

Book design & Illustration by Karl Jackson

First published – July 2021 by Alpaca & Goose

www.alpacagoose.com

First Edition

ISBN 978-1-9162651-4-1

www.harrysgame.com

'Friends'

Dedicated to Malta, the Ohio, and the PRU

Chapter 1

Down To Earth

"OK, Black Sheep Squadron, keep your eyes open and watch each other's backs. Stay in your pairs, and if you get one on your tail that you can't shift, drop to the deck and run back to the airfield. Pull them past the anti aircraft guns, if you can, but don't try and land, or they'll have you!" Harriet said over the radio, as she pulled her loosely gathered formation of Spitfires into line, and led them in a steep climb as they turned for the Malta coast. "And for God's sake, stay away from the Grand Harbour, or the gunners will knock you down quicker than the Luftwaffe can!"

"Understood, Black Sheep Leader," came one reply after another, as the collection of newly arrived pilots who'd only been in Malta long enough for their Spitfires to be rearmed and refuelled, checked in. Having brought a swarm of desperately needed Spitfires across the Mediterranean from their aircraft carriers, Harriet and her fellow pilots were told they'd be relieved by experienced Malta pilots, who were going to get the Spitfires up right away to greet the anticipated welcome raid by the Luftwaffe. That was exactly what happened, for all except eight of the newly arrived Spitfires, Harriet included. Their relief pilots had been shot up by a marauding fighter sweep that hit the airfield shortly before their Spitfires arrived, leaving eight very valuable Mk V Spitfires sitting on the ground, making perfect targets for any incoming raid. Harriet immediately rounded up a group of volunteers, including the Wing Commander who'd commanded the relief operation. She led them up and to the west to gather height before turning back in to meet the incoming Germans, who she could already see in the distance. Hundreds of tiny specks turning the northern sky black as all the other Spitfire squadrons raced to intercept.

"Shadow, this is Black Sheep Leader. We're coming in over the west coast, where do you want us?" Harriet called, while checking left and right to make sure her Spitfires were still with her. She got a nod of support from the Wing Commander, who'd volunteered to fly as her number two, and she waved confidently in reply. "Come on, Shadow!" she bellowed furiously, feeling irritated at the delay. She knew from bitter past experience that every second counted when fighting over Malta, and delays coordinating the battle got pilots in a bad position at best, and killed at worst. "I can see them from here!"

"Stand by, Black Sheep Leader," came Cas' calm and collected reply. She felt herself smile instinctively at the sound of his voice, which even at the most stressful of times had a way of soothing, in a way that she couldn't fathom. "Shadow Leader, vector zero seven zero and make angels two zero. We've got some trouble causers sneaking in over the sea and heading for Grand Harbour; you can't miss them."

"Wilco, Shadow. Black sheep, make zero seven zero, and climb to angels two zero." Harriet said as her heart started to race, and the familiar dryness returned to her mouth. She'd been in combat over Malta so many times, and she had so many memories, but she didn't have time to think of them; she needed to focus. If nothing else, she knew that combat over Malta was more deadly than anywhere else in the world, and she needed to be sharp. "There they are!" she said as they levelled out. Racing towards Grand Harbour from the northeast were twelve Junkers Ju 87 Stukas, the strikingly effective and frequently devastating two seat dive bombers with distinctive upturned gull wings. Above them were a dozen of her old adversaries, Messerschmitt 109s. Her mind raced as she formed a plan. The Stukas were slow, but their rear gunners could be deadly at close range. They were easy targets for Spitfires, but she knew that as soon as she started the attack, the 109s would drop on them. "B Flight, stay up here and keep those 109s busy, and don't let them split you up. I'll take A Flight down and get among those Stukas; hopefully we can break up their attack and stop them getting through to the docks." She looked over to the armada of incoming bombers approaching from the north, and hoped that the Spitfires would be able to hold them off, and no stray fighters would slip through and add to her problems. "OK, here we go, A Flight. Get stuck into the bombers, but stay away from the harbour. The anti aircraft box will cut you to pieces. Tally Ho!" She flipped the Spitfire to the right and into a steep, turning dive, feeling the g forces pinning her to her seat as she swallowed hard, desperate to get some moisture into her throat. The other three Spitfires of A Flight followed closely behind, with the Wing Commander quickly taking his place on her wing, and the other pair over to her right. "Hit them on the first pass, go straight through, then come back up and hit them from underneath. Watch for their tail gunners!" She set her sights on the leading Stuka, then pulled back on her stick a little to drift the sight slightly ahead while calculating her dive speed, the Stuka's speed, and the trajectory of her shots, then she narrowed her eyes and put her thumb over the centre of the fire button as she waited for the right moment. "Number twos have a crack too, but watch your leader!" The four Spitfires raced down at the neat formation of Stukas, which were flying in tight diamonds of fours, fitted together into one large diamond. "Here goes!" The rear gunners started to fire from the Stukas, sending up a mesh of glowing tracer rounds that zipped all around Harriet's Spitfire. A little closer, and as her target filled her gunsight, she fired. Guns and cannons let rip in unison, sending long white streaks of white smoke trailing after the rounds as they cut through the Stuka's cockpit, spraying it red as the crew were cut to pieces. Job done, she rolled to her right as the dead Stuka shuddered and slumped into a nosedive. She continued her dive past the formation before pulling up in a sweeping turn, ready to come back for a second go. "How are those fighters, B Flight?" She yelled as the g forces greyed and narrowed her vision.

"Don't worry, we've got them chasing their tails!" came the confident and almost jovial reply. She smiled as she steadied herself, and the g forces eased, letting her see and think properly and focus on the job at hand. The formation of Stukas had broken apart, and there were trails of smoke spiralling through the air as aircraft plummeted downwards. She quickly spun her head and counted up; all the Spitfires were there, and all still in the fight. She picked a Stuka that had started a spiralling dive towards the docks and had a snapshot at it, rattling its right wing enough to make it wobble and level out below her, heading north and out of danger. She gave it a moment's thought, but she knew she'd rip her own wings off if she tried to turn tight enough to catch the Stuka before it got away, so she made the decision to leave it alone. The objective was to stop the raid, not risk her neck for a kill. Besides, a glint of sun on Perspex gave a pair of Stukas away. They were already diving at a ship in Grand Harbour, and they had a good head start. She opened her throttle and pushed her stick forward, determined to give chase and stop them getting through. The harbour's anti aircraft barrage had already opened up with their welcome, filling the sky over the harbour with balls of black smoke and raging flames. She'd seen it enough times before to know how dangerous it was and how deadly accurate the gunners were, but she also knew that the bold and the brave, or the lucky, could sometimes find their way through the barrage; she'd done it herself the last time she was in Malta. She was dripping with sweat, it was streaming down her spine and soaking her armpits, and to her relief, it was running down her cheeks so she could lick at it to moisten her throat. She closed on the Stukas, getting ever closer as their rear gunners started to take shots at her. She slipped gently left and right, expertly avoiding their tracer streams, until she was scared out of her skin by a stream of tracer that glanced off her cockpit and sparked off the airframe as it passed from behind. She glanced into her mirror and cursed herself for neglecting it as she saw a 109 closing. Before she had the chance to respond, it burst into flames and rolled away to reveal another Spitfire.

"Sorry about that, skipper. I won't let the buggers get that close again!" the same jolly and cheerful voice shouted. "Your tail's clear; carry on."

"Good shooting!" she replied, then returned her attention to the Stukas, just as one of them was blown apart by an anti aircraft shell. It exploded in a ball of flames, throwing wreckage and body parts in every direction, including hers. Leaving her windscreen smeared in oil and blood as she passed through the unavoidable horror and fixed her sights on the remaining Stuka. It was too late to pull out; she was in the box. The air around her was black with smoke, lit up by flash after flash of explosions that sent shrapnel and splinters in every direction, rattling off her Spitfire like hailstones. She closed her eyes tight and tensed her stomach. "Come on, come on," she desperately repeated, then there was light. Not the flash of an explosion, but constant, brilliant light. She opened her eyes to see a large merchant ship sitting in the deep blue waters of Grand Harbour below her. Between her and it, the Stuka was preparing to release its deadly load. She couldn't wait any longer, and didn't have time to find the perfect firing position. She hit the fire button and let everything go, cannons and guns, and kept her thumb on the gun button and used the white smoke trails to guide her shots on target, snaking her fire through the air until it rattled the Stuka. She held firm and emptied her ammunition into it, and as her Spitfire fell from the sky, guns and cannons silent, a ball of orange flame coughed from the Stuka. She looked into the eyes of the rear gunner; he'd stopped firing when her bullets found home. She didn't know if he was hit or hurt, but his eyes said he was still alive. He nodded in salute, or it could have been resignation, and the Stuka hit the water, sending up a huge white plume of spray that enveloped Harriet's Spitfire as she pulled out of her dive and skimmed across the surface of the water, following her previous path towards the breakwater and out towards the open sea. Some of the air defence machine gunners were eager and fired up by the attack, and one after another took shots at her as she opened the throttle and pushed through the gate to get the maximum speed from her engine. She flew so low that she whipped up a wake behind her as she ran for safety. She pulled up as she passed the harbour walls, letting the seaward gunners see her markings and hoping they wouldn't take shots at her. Once she was sure she wasn't going to be shot down by her own side, she checked her gauges. Everything was where it should be, the engine was a little warm, but otherwise, things were fine. She throttled back a little to take the pressure off the engine, then quickly looked around as she started her climb. Her wings had a few holes in them, but otherwise, she couldn't see anything worth worrying too much about, so she continued to gain height enough to turn safely. She knew her guns and cannons were empty, and she wouldn't be heading back into the fight, but she still had to make a run across the island during a heavy raid to get back to the airfield, which was just as deadly as combat at twenty thousand feet, especially with 109s marauding over the island looking for easy prey to dive on.

After rechecking her instruments and searching the sky in every direction for signs of trouble, she rolled the Spitfire onto its side and turned back towards the island. She appreciated her blue and white silk scarf sitting snug around her neck; it stopped the skin rubbing raw as she spun her head left and right, up and down, searching for the enemy as she crossed the coast and roared across the arid sand brown ground, crisscrossed with white stone walls, and sparsely scattered green cacti dotted around the otherwise desert like landscape. She dropped low, relying on her aeroplane's camouflage to hide her from anyone watching from above, and followed Malta's curves, buzzing small villages and outposts, passing so low that the people on the ground instinctively ducked as she sped by. She pulled up a little as she saw Mdina on its hill, then she caught sight of Takali airfield sitting below. She'd made it, but this was the tricky time, getting in without being caught in the act. She scanned the sky again, high and low, and just as she pulled around to get into position, she noticed something shimmering low in the haze, lower than her and moving fast. She blinked and focused, and her heart squeezed as she recognised the familiar outlines of a 109 skimming the contours of the earth over to her right, not fifty feet off the ground. She followed its trajectory forward and noticed a Spitfire lining up with the runway, descending with undercarriage down. The perfect target. There was no time to think, and with no ammunition, Harriet knew exactly what she had to do. Instead of calculating the perfect deflection shot to fire a stream of bullets for the 109 to fly into, she opened her throttle as she worked out exactly where she needed to put herself. Her heart raced as she dropped to the deck, almost at cactus height, and nudged her rudder pedals gently to swing the nose of her Spitfire as she cut through the air so low, she left a trail of dust behind her. It took just a few seconds of racing at full speed for her to be exactly where she needed to be, and her calculations had been perfect, as she knew they would be. She took a deep breath, then pulled back on her stick and put her Spitfire right in front of the 109's nose, while closing her eyes in anticipation of the collision that didn't come. Instead, the 109 pulled up to avoid her, while Harriet climbed high and right. The 109 pilot had exposed himself. Harriet didn't have any ammunition left, but the airfield's anti aircraft gunners did. The 109 was rattled with heavy machine gun fire, and came down in a cloud of dust seconds later. Harriet smiled between gasps of air, then pulled open her canopy and tried to slow her breathing and slow her heart, which was beating so loud she could hear it thundering in her ears as she swept the horizon for any more trouble. Nothing stood out, so she slipped into line with the airfield and lowered her undercarriage and flaps, then immediately dropped onto the rough runway, which shook her in her seat as she bounced through the cratered and debris strewn airfield. She dodged a couple of the larger holes in the runway, the ones she'd seen when she'd first landed after her trip from the aircraft carrier, then followed the signals of the ground crew guiding her in, and rolled to her designated pit where she spun the Spitfire into position before applying the brakes and shutting down the engine. A team of soldiers were quickly surrounding her and pushing the Spitfire backwards into the relative safety of the blast pen, the walls of which were made of fuel cans stuffed with sand and stones, and stacked high enough to protect the inhabitants from all but a direct hit.

She pulled off her flying helmet and leant her head back on the rest as she composed herself following the morning's exertions. She'd been up long before dawn, and launched from the deck of an aircraft carrier hundreds of miles away as first light started to brighten the horizon. After a long and fraught trip to Malta, which tested her navigation and confidence to the limit, she'd thrown herself into battle against what seemed like a massive incoming raid. For the second time in her life, she'd flown through the anti aircraft box above Grand Harbour, one of the more stupid things she'd ever done, and for the second time in her life, she'd lived to tell the tale, somehow. She smirked. It was either that or pass out in a heap, and as tired as she was, she had no intention of sleeping in a Spitfire cockpit. She'd been in one almost continually since dawn, except for fifteen minutes when she stretched her legs by running to a rocky outcrop to relieve her bladder while her Spitfire was refuelled and rearmed, and she was sore. Though her bladder was no longer an issue, she was so dry she could drink a lake, which experience told her wasn't the best condition to be in when in Malta. Especially as the heat was already cooking her as she sat in the cockpit. She'd forgotten how warm Malta could be.

"Good hunting, Ma'am?" Chalky asked as he appeared above the cockpit and looked down at her with a big smile. His teeth were brilliant white, almost glowing against his baked mahogany skin. He was darker than she'd remembered, and leaner, his body lithe and sinewy, and his mop of blond hair almost the colour of golden straw.

"Chalky?" she asked, letting her smirk turn to a smile.

"Yes, Ma'am!" he replied proudly. "Welcome home; it's good to have you back!" He reached into the cockpit and offered his hand, which she happily took, and with a pull was she was standing on her seat.

"It's good to be back, Chalky." He guided her out of the cockpit, then jumped in to replace her.

"Anything I should know about?"

"She's flying well, but I took a bit of flack over the harbour, so you'll probably need to check nothing important has been damaged."

"Will do, Ma'am."

"Oh, and I pushed the engine at maximum for a bit. Not too long, and the temperature didn't rise too much, but it's probably worth checking all the same." He nodded and smiled, and quickly went about checking the instruments and switches.

"Ma'am," he said, as she turned to walk off the wing. "Your kit is next to mine under the petrol cans at the back of the pit."

"Thanks, Chalky." She smiled, then jumped down into the dust, quickly getting herself out of the way so the team of airmen and soldiers could go about their business. A line had formed, and petrol cans were being passed hurriedly to the nose, where an airman was straddling the Spitfire and pouring the petrol into a large funnel sticking in the tank. She made her way to the back of the pit, where she found a large bench made of petrol cans. When she couldn't find any other petrol cans, other than those making the walls and the others filling her Spitfire, she lifted the board on top of them to reveal a dark store cupboard where her kit bag and small day pack had been stored. She pulled them out, then pulled a small chocolate bar from the pocket of her flying jacket and slipped it into Chalky's backpack before replacing the board. Smiling to herself, she pulled her things together, then dodged the line of bronzed, shirtless soldiers as she left the pen.

"Ma'am," Chalky shouted from the cockpit. She turned to see him standing and pointing in the direction behind the pens. "Over that way." She nodded and waved, then smiled as she walked off. She knew Takali like the back of her hand, or at least she had before she'd left the island over a year earlier, and a lot had changed. Blast pens were scattered everywhere, and the airfield itself was littered with burned out aircraft and vehicles, either left where they'd met their end, or dragged into position to stop German gliders from landing in an assault. Everything seemed to have a lot more holes in it, too. The ground, the buildings, even the rocks. It seemed there wasn't a thing

16

that hadn't been hit or damaged in some way. She paused for a moment as she walked, and watched as Spitfire after Spitfire came into land, while a pair of Hurricanes buzzed around in circles above, keeping watch as the main force came into land. She felt a brief sense of relief. The number of Spitfires returning suggested that casualties weren't too bad, and the battle can't have gone too badly. She continued walking as she made her way to what was her old office, the stone dispersal hut not far from the runway. It was undoubtedly in worse condition than she'd left it. There wasn't a window to be seen, and that wasn't the worst part. The roof was half gone, replaced by a damaged parachute and a sheet of wriggly corrugated tin, the walls were peppered with bullet and shrapnel holes, and the door was nowhere to be seen. It felt like home, in a way, but a home that had been long neglected, and wasn't particularly nice to be coming back to, though at that moment, she was more than happy just to be alive. Malta hadn't got any less dangerous since she'd been gone, but it had certainly got a lot hotter. Her sweat stained shirt had already dried out, and the heat was baking, reminding her how thirsty she was. She stepped into the shade and relative coolness of the dispersal hut, and blinked as her eyes focused. There was nobody to be seen, but there was a large water flask, though no cups. She held her cupped hand under the spout and hoped the contents wouldn't be hot when she decanted them. Much to her relief, it was lukewarm water. She filled her hand and raised it to her parched lips, then sucked the water into her mouth. She had tried her hardest to forget the taste, and she wasn't quite ready for the salty petrol aftertaste that filled her mouth after she swilled the water around a few times, before swallowing it down and feeling her throat ease. She coughed a little and gasped, and quickly decided that one mouthful would be enough for the time being. She gathered her things again, as she wondered what she was supposed to do next, now she was back. There wasn't anyone around to greet her or point her in the right direction, and there was nobody to report to.

"The Luftwaffe aren't going to be happy that you're back in town," a familiar voice said from behind. Harriet quickly turned, excited to match the voice with the picture in her head, and she wasn't disappointed to see her friend Kit Robbens standing in the doorway.

"Robbie..." Harriet said with a big smile.

"Welcome home, Harry," Robbie replied, as she walked into the hut and gave Harriet a tight hug. Harriet dropped her bags and wrapped her arms around her friend, she hadn't thought she'd see her again, and she was happy to know her friend was alive and well, if not a little emaciated. She could feel Robbie's ribs through her blouse; she was as wiry and tanned as everyone else Harriet had seen since she'd been back in Malta.

"I wish people wouldn't keep saying that to me..." Harriet protested mockingly, deciding not to mention Robbie's bones. She broke the hug and stepped back to look at her friend. Her cheeks were drawn, and her chocolate brown hair had been lightened by the heat, but she was still the glamorous young woman she remembered.

"Why, what's wrong with being welcomed home?" Robbie asked with a frown.

"Home implies I live here..."

"Well, you did spend quite a lot of time here in the past, and you do seem to have returned quite unannounced and made yourself at home. You've even started fighting with the neighbours, right where you left off. If that's not home, I don't know what is."

"I'd rather home didn't involve being shot at."

"You definitely picked the wrong job if that's your forte!"

"You're telling me..."

"You're certainly the bundle of joy and happiness I remember; at least some things haven't changed. Come on, we can't stand around gassing all day." She picked up Harriet's kit bag and headed for the door.

"Where are we going?" Harriet asked as she hurried behind Robbie.

"Valletta. You've been summoned..." Robbie looked over her shoulder as they stepped outside into the burning sunlight, and gave

Harriet a mischievous wink. She led them to her waiting truck, which looked more beaten up and bedraggled than Harriet remembered, and Robbie quickly had them bouncing along the track and away from Takali. "You're looking pale; England's weather doesn't agree with you." Robbie teased.

"Thanks..." Harriet frowned in reply, as she looked at her forearms and legs. She was golden, California golden, and in her short time back in England, people had commented everywhere she went on how healthy she looked. She then looked at Robbie. Her friend always had a healthy tan, she'd seen that much when they'd been swimming and sunbathing together, but she was a much deeper brown than before, so much that the whites of her eyes sparkled. In comparison, Harriet looked very much the pale English rose, regardless of how much time she'd had under the Californian sun, which, in contrast to that which was beating down on her now, felt like a cold day in Hull.

"I don't remember it being so hot here..."

"It wasn't when you were last here."

"Excuse me?"

"You arrived in late autumn and left before summer even got started. You've never experienced a proper Maltese summer."

"So it seems..." Harriet frowned a little, then looked around as they entered the outskirts of the urban centre of the island. Buildings here and there were damaged, and every now and then, there was a pile of rubble where a house, or a large wall, had been blown down. People stopped their daily business and waved as she passed, making her feel a little embarrassed, especially as things didn't appear to be great for them. Her discomfort grew the further they drove. First, they entered Floriana, the once beautiful district where Robbie had her apartment, and where Harriet had joined her relaxing and sunbathing on her balcony, or on the roof of the tall apartment block which overlooked Grand Harbour. The area had been devastated. Whole apartment blocks had been ravaged, and there were bomb craters and mounds of rubble everywhere the eye could see. All the

19

colourful doors and balconies had been muted by a thick layer of dust, as had everything else in the area, making it look every bit the war zone. "Has it really been that bad here?" Harriet asked as she looked around at the devastation.

"Worse, at times," Robbie replied with a forced smile. "The Germans just keep coming and coming, and we've been running out of places to hide."

"It looks like hell."

"It has been, but we're still here, still holding on. Something we'll be able to do all the better now we have those Spitfires you brought in this morning."

"Seeing all this, it doesn't feel like enough."

"Trust me, it's more than you think. With Spitfires we have a chance, and we can keep holding them off. Every single one of them is worth their weight in gold, and you brought us almost seventy of them!" She smiled excitedly, making Harriet force a smile of her own, despite her increasing distress at what had happened to Malta.

"What have you been doing since I've been gone? Still looking after the Squadron?"

"No, I moved up to Headquarters a while ago, and run things in there instead. Logistics, mainly."

"Obviously..."

"Well, it's my natural skill set. You've got to play to your strengths."

"Of course, though it does seem a little careless putting the poacher in charge of the livestock, don't you think?"

"And what's that supposed to mean?"

"I seem to remember you being the centre of Malta's black market operation... Putting you in charge of the island's logistics seems counterintuitive."

"Nonsense... Besides, isn't it better to have a poacher on the gamekeeper's staff? They know all the tricks and what to watch for, after all..." She winked again, as they descended the hill and came to a halt in the car park long familiar to Harriet.

Chapter 2

Welcome Home

"What on earth are you doing back here?!" Cas demanded as he stood from his desk, while Harriet stepped past Robbie and into the very small office he was occupying in the underground tunnels at Lascaris, where the island's defences were being coordinated.

"Charming..." Harriet replied with a frown, as she looked him up and down. His uniform was baggier than she remembered, and though still as smart as it could be, it was a little ragged around the edges. He was tanned, and his eyes sparkled in the dim artificial light as he fixed her in his gaze.

"I'll leave you two to say your hello's," Robbie said with a roll of her eyes. "Some of us have work to do."

"What's that you were saying?" Cas asked Harriet.

"What?" she replied with a frown.

"What?" he responded.

"Oh, stop it!" she said in frustration, a feeling that grew as she watched him smirk. "I see you haven't got any less annoying since I've been gone."

"Nice to know I've been missed... Anyway, I see you haven't got any less single minded and careless in your absence."

"What are you talking about now?" she sighed.

"It was reported that a Spitfire chased a pair of Stukas into the air defence box over the harbour in the last raid."

"So..." She felt a blush start to burn her cheeks as he talked, and instinctively tried everything she could to fight it, which experience told her made her look all the more guilty.

22

"So, the pilot flew so low after shooting down the last of the Stukas and saving the merchantman tied up in the docks, that the gunners got a very good view of them, or her, as it transpires."

"If they got that good of a look, they should probably have stopped trying to shoot me down!" she snapped.

"I've missed you..." Cas said with a warm smile.

"Well, I haven't missed your teasing!" she said firmly, crossing her arms and frowning defiantly as he walked around the desk. Without warning, he wrapped his arms around her and gave her the type of hug she'd been craving for months, which made her instantly melt and wrap her arms around him and squeeze tight.

"You'll have to forgive the smell down here," he said as he pulled away, leaving her smiling. He leant against his desk and pulled out a battered pack of Navy issue cigarettes, which even Harriet knew tasted like a mix of dust and manure. "We've managed to run air ducting throughout the tunnel system, most of it recovered from ships that have been sunk in the harbour, but we have so little fuel on the island that we can only run it occasionally to recycle the air, the rest of the time we have to put up with sweating our days and nights away below ground. The only thing that improves the smell is cigarette smoke, and you with that Chanel you're wearing..." He gave her a wink, and she found herself blushing again, as she remembered giving herself a small spray after landing, from the bottle she'd squeezed into her kit bag. She'd done it to try and hide her own smell, aware that she'd been in a Spitfire cockpit all morning and sweating her way through combat. She didn't want to give a bad impression to those on the ground, though that was increasingly becoming less of a concern, it appeared.

"Wait..." she said, then put her kit bag down and quickly rummaged in it, before pulling out a tin of the best cigarettes she'd been able to buy in London's West End. They were part of the stock she'd bought with the intent of bartering, wherever she ended up, which she hadn't imagined would be Malta. "Here, I brought you something."

"My God," he gasped as his eyes opened wide at the sight. "Where did you get those?"

"Harrods," she said with a cheery smile.

"You've made an old man very happy..." He opened the tin, almost hungrily, and took out a cigarette, which he held under his nose for a moment while he inhaled. "Heaven!" He quickly lit it and took a long draw, then closed his eyes and sighed as he exhaled a cloud of blue smoke. "Harriet Cornwall, you've saved my life," he said as his eyes twinkled.

"Well, that's just great, isn't it?!" She frowned again.

"What have I done now?" he protested.

"The cigarettes got a better welcome than I did!"

"Oh, don't be like that, Harry."

"It almost makes me think I shouldn't give you the other thing I have for you."

"What other thing?" he frowned at her.

"If all I am is a delivery girl, I'm not sure I'm going to tell you..."

"Harry..." he sighed. She smirked, her eyes sparkling a little, then she pulled out the ornate caddy of tea she'd picked up in Fortnum's and waved it teasingly in front of him. "Proper tea..." he gasped.

"Proper tea..." she replied.

"Hand it over." He reached out, but she snatched it away before he could grab it.

"What's it worth?"

"What do you want?"

"What have you got?"

"I'll pay you..."

"I have enough money, thank you."

"Then what?"

"I haven't eaten since before leaving the aircraft carrier this morning. Take me out for lunch, and it's yours."

"You're on!" he said confidently, as he stood straight and grabbed his hat from his desk. She threw him the caddy, which he opened, sniffed, then locked away in his desk cupboard, along with the cigarettes he couldn't squeeze into his silver cigarette case. "Come on!" He opened the door.

"Now?"

"Can you think of somewhere else you'd rather go?"

"Not really..."

"Then what are you waiting for? Leave your bags in here; they'll be quite safe." He led them through the humid, strong smelling stone corridors until they broke into daylight again. Harriet gasped in the warm dusty air, which to her relief didn't have an undertone of human sweat to it. They walked up the hill and into town, past the rubble and buildings pockmarked with bullet holes, and along the streets with the previously busy shops and businesses boarded up; it looked almost derelict to the way Harriet remembered it. Even in the toughest raids she'd witnessed, Malta had kept going, and when the raids cleared, the shops and bars reopened, and Valletta came back to life; but now it was almost like a ghost town.

"What happened to all the shops and bars?" she asked as they walked.

"Many went out of business, others only open at certain times of the day, mostly because of rationing. Stocks of almost everything have dried up since you've been gone, and there's nothing much left to buy or sell. Then, when the fleet left for Alexandria, the bars that could still get booze went out of business too, as they had nobody to sell it to."

"I see..."

"The only oasis in a sea of misery," he said as he showed her to a small bar, which was scattered with a number of RAF uniforms, a few civilian women, and a few well dressed civilians. "The owner still gets his hands on good booze, though your guess how is as good as mine, but I doubt either of us would be surprised if it didn't involve a certain brunette we both know. Anyway, he has the good stuff, and unlike anywhere else on the island, his prices are the same now as they were last year, which makes it a popular spot."

"Mister Cas!" The Maltese owner said warmly, as Cas and Harriet stood by the bar. "And this must be the great Harry?" he looked at her for a moment, seeming intrigued, but nowhere near as intrigued as she was to know how he knew her.

"Indeed it is," Cas said. "Two Horse's Necks, and if you can lay your hands on a couple of cheese pastizzi, we'd be eternally grateful. Harry's just brought in a load of new Spitfires, and she's ravenous!"

"Spitfires?" His eyes lit up with excitement. "This is reason to celebrate!" He quickly disappeared into the back room.

"I don't think I remember him?" Harriet said to Cas, after the owner had left.

"You wouldn't. You didn't come into town that much when you were last here. As I remember it, you spent most of your time in the sky irritating Germans."

"Somebody had to do it," Harriet shrugged. At that, the owner returned and poured their drinks, Horse's Necks, a tall glass of brandy and ginger ale, then presented them before disappearing into the back again.

"Anyway, it's fair to say you have one or two fans on the island." He held up his glass. "Cheers?" Harriet raised hers and clinked it against his, then took a sip.

"Cheers... That's good," she muttered, as it washed away the stink of the tunnels and the bitter after taste of the water she'd drunk after landing. The owner returned and presented each of them with a small pastizzi.

"Thanks, old man," Cas said, as he pulled out his wallet.

"No," the owner said, almost insulted.

"Let's not get into this again, if you don't take payment, you'll go broke like everyone else around here, and if we don't have you to serve us the good stuff, we're all buggered."

"My gift," he nodded at Harriet, who was already blushing again at the conversation.

"At least let me pay for mine in that case." The owner nodded, and Cas paid, settling the debate and letting the owner smile warmly, before running off to serve another customer.

"Why on earth do I have fans?" Harriet whispered.

"Because the Maltese like standing on rooftops and watching our fighters take on the enemy, and there's something of an urban legend doing the rounds about a pair of young women who swept the skies of Malta clean, and kept the island safe from invasion."

"Sounds a little far fetched if you ask me."

"I said the same, but there's no changing people's minds when they start believing in fairy stories." He smirked, and Harriet jabbed at him with her elbow, then bit into the pastizzi. It was thick and doughy, as she remembered, and tasted great, but it was so small she didn't dare rush it, so savoured it slowly. "How is Nicole?"

"She's fine," Harriet replied casually. "She's in Yorkshire with Archie, teaching pilots how to fly the new Mosquito Fighter Bomber."

"Nicole's teaching people?"

"Yes..."

"God bless them. They'd better get it right the first time..."

"I know, I never thought it would be something she'd have the temperament for, but she's loving it, and staying out of harm's way."

"Speaking of staying out of harm's way, it seems America agreed with you."

"I loved it there," she replied with a warm and genuine smile. "The people, the country, the food, everything about the place is just incredible. Even with a war going on, they're making it work. You should go some time."

"Oh, I did, a while ago. I enjoyed it, too. You managed to stay away from the war, I hope? You spent some time in Hawaii?"

"Oh, yes. I spent most of my time teaching British girls how to fly in California." She brushed over her Hawaiian exploits, thinking it was neither the time nor the place to discuss the hell she'd witnessed.

"What on earth were British girls doing out there?"

"Learning to fly."

"Yes... I got that part. Why?"

"The RAF decided to round up a group of WAAF volunteers to send over to America as part of the Arnold Scheme to train British pilots. They're good. Their American instructors put them through their paces in all sorts of different aeroplanes; they'll be great additions to the war effort when they're finished."

"I have no doubt. Was AP with them? Or Wilson?"

"No... Sadly not. They went through a course in Scotland, apparently. The Americans wanted a full class of girls to put through together, and AP and Daisy had already started. The ATA girls trained separately, too. Archie tells me they were doing well."

"And how is Archie?"

"He's a Wing Commander in charge of the Mosquito Operational Conversion Unit."

"He's done well for himself."

"He has, so has Max. He has one of the American squadrons, and I think Lexi is there with him, or so I heard."

"Lexi?"

"Really?"

"What?"

"You're going to pretend you don't remember the glamorous golden American who poured herself all over you every time you met?"

"Oh, that Lexi..." He shrugged casually, and quite unconvincingly.

"You know, you're not as funny as you think... Anyway, how're things here? How's Sully?" He looked at her for a moment in silence. Her heart sank immediately, without him needing to say a word.

"How?"

"Truthfully, we don't know. He got stuck into a whole swarm of 109s out over the sea north of Gozo. He got two of them, we know that much, but he never came back."

"I'm sorry..."

"Me too; he was a good man. Sadly, that doesn't count for much over here. Good, bad, or indifferent, we've been critically outnumbered for as long as I can remember, and even the best go down sooner or later, as we know." He gave her a warm smile. "How is the shoulder?"

"Better than it was."

"Good. You had us worried for a moment."

"What was the final score with that raid we bumped into earlier?" Harriet asked, quickly trying to change the subject to something more positive. "I saw plenty of Spitfires coming back in, so can't have been half bad."

"Half bad? It was the best result we've had all year!" He smiled. "The last lot of Spitfires we had were wiped out almost as soon as they landed, most were caught on the ground, and those that got up had so little experience over Malta that they were knocked down in minutes. We lost them all in forty eight hours. That's why we wanted to get everything back up as soon as it landed today. We knew the Germans would be waiting for us. Timing their raids to try and catch us on the ground again, but this time we were waiting for them. So far, we have verified claims for forty two enemy bombers and fighters knocked down, including the two you took care of..."

"Forty two? That's incredible!"

"There's more to come. The score will be higher when we get done counting up."

"Losses...?" Harriet asked, dreading the reply.

"None..." Cas replied casually.

"Excuse me?"

"Not one aeroplane lost. A few holes here and there, but everyone came back. This just goes to show we were right all along. Give us Spitfires in numbers, and we'll more than hold the line; we'll win!" Harriet found herself smiling. She'd been part of it, but more than just the fighting, she'd been drafted in to bring the Spitfires safely to Malta, and while she'd initially been unhappy about it, she was now very proud of the part she'd played. She was even happy to be back in Malta, despite her initial fears. "Well, we can't stay and yap all day, unfortunately. Some of us have work to do." Cas finished his drink and stood.

"Where to?" Harriet asked as she finished hers.

"Back to my desk."

"What about me?"

"We'll find out when we get back; come on." He took a handful of his new cigarettes from his case and waved the owner over, then reached over the bar and pressed the cigarettes lightly into his hand. "Fresh from London." He gave the owner a wink, then they left and headed out into the dusty, war ravaged street. They took the long, almost scenic route back to the tunnels, walking along the narrow streets, then along the Upper Barrakka Gardens overlooking Grand Harbour. It was different to the last time Harriet was there. The docks were devastated, and the rabbit warrens of residential streets in the three cities across the water were a mass of rubble and smoke, making it impossible to believe that some people were still living there. The Germans had made a mess of Malta, there wasn't a building unscathed, and it was heartbreaking to see what had been done to such a beautiful island and such warm people.

"Bloody good show we put on this morning, Cas," the AOC said as he met Harriet and Cas outside Cas' office.

"Yes, Sir. No losses on our side, I believe."

"Not one! Thank God for Spitfires!"

"Absolutely, Sir."

"Who's this?" the AOC asked as he looked past Cas' shoulder, despite his apparent best efforts to stand between the senior officer and Harriet, almost entirely hiding her from view.

"Who?" Cas asked, almost comedically, then turned to reveal Harriet. "Oh, sorry, yes. This is Squadron Leader Cornwall; she led in the relief Spitfires this morning.

"Fantastic effort, Cornwall! We couldn't have been any more desperate for those Spitfires, and you got them here in the nick of time. Really first class, well done!" He waved his cigarette holder at her confidently as he spoke, as if directing an orchestra. "The blighters will think twice about coming back in a hurry!" Harriet nodded and smiled politely, while feeling her cheeks ache and glow with yet another blush. "Right, better get on." He continued past them in the corridor. "Oh, Cas?"

"Sir?"

"Drop by my office this afternoon, would you? When you get a minute, no rush. I've got something I want to run past you."

"Yes, Sir..." Cas opened his office door and gestured Harriet inside, then quickly closed it after her.

"What's wrong?" she asked, as he hurried around his desk and picked up his phone. He waved at her to take a seat, then perched on the desk, looking very pensive.

"Robbie, get down here as quick as you can." He put the phone down then looked at her while taking another cigarette from his case and lighting it nervously.

"You're making me feel as nervous as you look..."

"What? No, sorry, it's nothing," he laughed it off. "I just have an idea what the AOC's got in mind, that's all. Anyway, I thought it'd be nice while you're here if you got up to Mdina to meet your old landlord and landlady. Robbie will run you over there, maybe take a few hours off and enjoy the company?"

"You still haven't told me what I'm going to be doing now I'm here..."

"That's because we didn't know you were coming, so we didn't have any plans for you."

"I'm not sure how to take that."

"As it's meant, I hope? Your turning up here has been the single most wonderful thing that's happened to me in a long time, but that doesn't change the fact that we weren't expecting you, and don't have a plan for you."

"I'm a Spitfire pilot, and the last time I looked, Malta needed all of those it could get."

"You're also a Squadron Leader, and we already have lots of those... Look, we're getting caught up on details. I have a few ideas swimming around upstairs, so you get across to Mdina and leave it with me to sort something. Don't worry, I'll have it worked out by the time Robbie collects you later."

"Well, I suppose if anyone can sort it, you can."

"Happy we agree." He gave her a reassuring wink, which made her smile, then the door opened, and Robbie stepped in.

"What's happening?" Robbie asked.

"I wondered if you'd take Harry over to her old digs in Mdina? She's at a loose end, and I need to do some work for the AOC, so I thought it would be good for her to spend some time catching up with old friends. If you don't mind, of course?"

"Not at all. I needed to go down to the seaplane base at Kalafrana anyway, so I can drop her off on the way."

"Good show! Right, see you both later; I'd better get on." He smiled warmly, and Harriet took her bags and followed Robbie out along the corridor.

"He's behaving strangely," Harriet said as they walked.

"How so?"

"He was fine until we met the AOC. After that, he seemed a little tetchy."

"You met the AOC?"

"Yes... The one with the cigarette holder, but no cigarette, right?"

"That's him."

"Why, what's wrong with him?"

"Nothing, he's been fantastic for the island's defences since he got here around the time you left. He's a good man and a good leader. He even had me walk down the runway with him during a raid once. His theory was that if the men saw their senior officer and a woman walking about during a raid, they'd be less worried and less likely to hide unless a raid was right on top of them, and therefore more productive."

"Did it work?"

"It seemed to. The lads can't be seen to be scared when a girl isn't, you know how it is..."

"Weren't you scared?"

"Absolutely petrified."

"Did he still have his cigarette holder?"

"Right through it."

"Cigarette?"

"None to be seen."

"What a curious habit."

"Yes, he has lots of those." They climbed into the truck, and Robbie soon had them rolling out of Valletta and away from the destruction. The small villages weren't as badly damaged as the cities, but they'd clearly had their fair share, with shot up or bombed out buildings here and there, and wreckage strewn around the fields. They talked about how life had been on the island, and how rationing had been a curse that had blighted all, which explained the emaciated state of virtually everyone Harriet had seen, to the point where her slender athletic build put her among the more generously proportioned people in Malta. They talked about nicer things too, and how Robbie's grandparents were still doing well, and still as defiant as ever. The garden wasn't as it once was, thanks to the lack of fresh water, and because most of the trees had been cut back to nothing for firewood during the previous winter. They were still happy, though, and more confident than ever that Malta would pull through. They made Harriet happy, their confidence strengthened her resolve, and despite her very matter of fact stoic attitude, it seemed that Robbie took comfort in their beliefs too. Harriet was dropped at the house where she rented a room, and Robbie waited outside in the truck, just to make sure Harriet wasn't left out on the street if nobody was home. She didn't have to wait long. The door opened, and seconds later, Harriet had Lissy wrapped around her shoulders, hugging her emotionally. Robbie smiled and waved, then rolled the truck down the narrow street and on to her next destination, the sea plane base which, while largely deserted these days, still had the occasional visitor, who Harriet assumed would be bringing in what Robbie had taken to describing as 'logistical inducements'.

"Anj!" Lissy yelled as she pulled Harriet into the house. "Anj!"

"What is it?" he replied, as he walked into the kitchen to meet them.

"Our girl is home!" Lissy said excitedly.

"I can't believe my eyes," he said equally as excitedly, then quickly joined Lissy in hugging Harriet. "Welcome home," he said warmly.

"She looks so well, doesn't she?" Lissy added.

"Remarkably! You can tell she's been away. When did you arrive?"

"I came in this morning," Harriet replied, feeling excited to have her Maltese family so happy to see her. "With the Spitfires."

"I told you!" Lissy said. "I told you, didn't I?"

"She did," Anj conceded with a shrug. "She said you'd bring the Spitfires we needed."

"Sit!" Lissy demanded. "I'll make tea... Though I should warn you, what passes for tea in Malta these days may not be what you remember."

"Oh...?" Harriet put her kit back on the table and rummaged in it, then pulled out another tin of Fortnum's tea, feeling very grateful that she'd stocked up on treats and trading goods when she had the chance. "Here, use this." She handed Lissy the tea.

"We can't accept this," Lissy said with eyes wide open.

"You're family, it's my gift," Harriet said with a smug smile, then put her bag on the floor and took her seat, while Lissy measured a small amount of tea into the teapot before sealing the tin again and trying to hand it back to Harriet. "It's yours. My thanks for looking after me when I was last here."

"Do you need your room again?" Anj asked.

"I don't know," Harriet shrugged.

"If you have somewhere else, we'll understand, though the room is there if you want it."

"I do want it; I just don't know what's happening yet."

"What do you mean?"

"Well, I was sent here at the last minute. Everyone else who arrived with me knew they were coming. They all had jobs waiting for them. Nobody quite knows what to do with me just yet, though Cas assures

36

me he's working on it, so until I know what I'm doing, it would be rude of me to take your room."

"Nonsense," Lissy said. "As you told us, you're family, so your room is your room. Use it for an hour or a year. It's always yours."

"What about the rest of your family? How are they? Do they still live here?"

"They do, but the house is big, and they are well, so the room is yours."

Harriet instantly felt relaxed, like she'd never left, and she enjoyed the tea as they talked and caught up. She told them about her trip to California, and the different way of life in America. They asked so many questions, and she did her best to answer them all, before taking them up on the offer of the room for a while so she could freshen up. Water was limited, and she didn't want to abuse their generosity, so she filled a small bowl and had a strip wash to remove the sweat from the flying, and make herself feel more presentable. The room was no different from when she left. The family hadn't taken any other lodgers since Harriet and Nicole had left. They said the heartache of seeing their girls broken was too much to bear, so the room was as it was left, even down to the silk parachute blanket on the bed. Harriet smiled to herself and took what remained of her tea out onto the rooftop terrace, and stood against the wall while surveying Malta. She had so many memories, and they all came flooding back at once, good and bad. She'd been so scared to return because all she remembered was the fear and the death, but there was so much more. The bad times were intense, but so were the good. Malta was an incredibly special place for her, and being back had reminded her how special. It wasn't Malta that had almost killed her; that was the Luftwaffe, the same Luftwaffe that had tried to kill her in France and England. It was Malta that had saved her life, though, and it was Maltese people that pulled her from a church roof in the middle of an air raid and kept her alive. She was happy to be back, and maybe everybody else who'd greeted her already knew what she'd been too blind or stubborn to see; she was back home, and that was OK. She smiled as she sipped her tea, then laid in her old deckchair, which sat where she'd left it under the tattered old parasol, and dozed as she thought of all the happy times she'd had.

The afternoon drifted slowly as Harriet slept off her morning of flying, and when she woke in the light of early evening, it was to the sound of a truck's engine rumbling down below, and a horn being sounded. She leaned over the wall and looked down into the street, where Robbie was standing in her truck and looking upwards.

"Have you ever heard of knocking?" Harriet shouted down.

"Don't have time," Robbie shouted in reply. "Grab your bags; we're leaving." Harriet nodded and ran back into her room. She quickly gathered her things, then ran down the stairs to where Lissy and Anj were waiting at the front door, both looking confused.

"You're leaving?" Anj asked.

"Apparently," Harriet replied.

"Where?"

"I've no idea..." She handed him another tin from her collection, the fruitcake she'd bought. "For you and your family." She ran out of the house and threw her bags into the back of the truck, then climbed in beside Robbie, who immediately revved the engine. "Thank you!" Harriet called, as Robbie drove them away at speed through the narrow winding streets of Mdina, the high walls of the tall houses trapping the roar of the truck's engine as they rolled. "What's the hurry?" Harriet asked, as they passed through the city gates.

"Cas wants you down at Luqa airfield about five minutes ago."

"What? What's going on? Is there a raid or something?"

"Something," Robbie replied, as she hauled the truck along the road at breakneck speed towards the island's main airfield, and the only one with a proper concrete runway, where the few remaining bombers had been flying from to attack the German and Italian convoys heading south to resupply their troops in the North African desert. Some of the new Spitfires had also been sent there to stop the island's defences from being wiped out if a single airfield holding all the Spitfires was the target of a particularly heavy raid.

"Why Luqa?" Harriet asked.

"That's where Cas is meeting us," Robbie replied.

"That's not an answer!"

"It's the only one I have. You know what he's like when he needs something done. He needs it done right away. I was in Kalafrana when he called, and it took a while to get to you, so we're already late."

"Late for what?"

"For Cas."

"Give me strength..."

"Where the hell have you been?" Cas asked in an irritated manner, as he met them at the gate and jumped aboard the truck.

"We got here as fast as we could!" Robbie replied. "It's not like Malta's road network is known to be the smoothest, especially not after the Germans have been using the entire island for target practice for the last couple of years!"

"What on earth's going on?" Harriet asked, confused by the high tension between Cas and Robbie.

"We don't have long," Cas continued.

"Is he still here?" Robbie asked.

"Just..."

"Am I even here?" Harriet demanded. "Hello?"

"Here we are," Robbie said, as she pulled up on the runway beside a quirky looking twin engine aeroplane with a long cylindrical nose, which was silhouetted against the glowing pink and turquoise evening sky.

"Where?" Harriet demanded.

"Just come on, we don't have time," Cas said.

"Time for what?"

"Harry!"

"Cas!" Harriet shouted back at him. She was quickly becoming furious at his evasive manner and refusal to communicate. "You either tell me what's happening, or I don't move from this truck!" He put his hand to his head and rolled his eyes, then turned back and leant in through the door.

"Harry, you're going to Cairo."

"Wait, what?"

"I've spent the afternoon getting you a posting to Headquarters Middle East, just across the Mediterranean from here in Egypt, and that Martin Maryland reconnaissance aeroplane is going to take you there. Now, no more messing about. The pilot was due to take off ten minutes ago, and has a schedule to keep."

"Why Cairo?" Harriet asked with a frown as she climbed from the truck, a little dumbstruck by the announcement.

"Because it's not here. Come on, we really need to get you in the air." He picked up her bag and walked her over to meet the pilot.

"I don't understand," Harriet protested.

"You will..." He stopped and looked at her. "Look, I can't tell you how happy it's made me to see you again, but Malta isn't the place to be right now, and the very best thing you can do is get on that aeroplane and don't look back."

"Cas..."

"I'll telegraph you. I'll know where you are, so we can stay in touch. It's not that far away. Now, no more talking; let's get going." She nodded and hugged him briefly, then turned and headed towards the pilot.

"I think you're wanted, Sir..." the pilot said as he pointed behind Cas and Harriet. Cas turned and looked behind to see the AOC's car parking next to Robbie's truck, while Robbie waved furiously.

"Bugger..." Cas muttered.

"What is it?" Harriet asked.

"Give us a minute, would you?" Cas asked the pilot, who nodded obligingly and walked away, leaving Cas and Harriet to face the AOC.

"Cas, you sly old fox," the AOC said jovially as he joined them. "Seems you're one step ahead of me as always."

"Sir?"

"Well, I'm assuming you've brought Squadron Leader Cornwall down here to have a look around the reconnaissance types... Good thinking! It never ceases to amaze me how well a team works together when you have the right people on board. I'm lucky to have you, Cas."

"Thank you, Sir..."

"So, Cornwall, what do you reckon?"

"Sir?"

"Oh... Sorry Cas, I thought you'd already told her. I suppose I've gone and blown the surprise! Shall I continue and spare you the trouble?" The AOC paused, looking uncomfortable as though he'd just spoiled a child's birthday party. Cas nodded reluctantly, resigned to what he knew was coming. "Thing is, Cornwall, your reputation precedes you, especially in these parts, and after meeting you earlier, I got to wondering how we could keep you around. Your skills at the controls of a fighter are legendary in these parts, and quite selfishly, I'd rather have you here than send you to the drudgery of an office job in Cairo, and I'm sure that's something you'll thank me for. I know what you fighter types are like; you'd be climbing the walls in a week."

"Sorry, Sir," Harriet replied. "Are you saying I'm staying in Malta?"

"In a roundabout way, yes! Assuming you'd be kind enough to hang around for a while and lend us a hand? Those Spitfires you delivered earlier today are going to change things around here, we're going to be in business like never before, and we're going to need pilots of your calibre if we're going to get the best from them."

"Then I'm not sure I could say no, Sir." She shrugged as Cas rolled his eyes again, barely able to contain himself.

"Good! That's what I told Cairo when I had your posting changed."

"Which squadron, Sir?" Cas asked. "If you let me know, I'll take Cornwall over in the morning and introduce her to the pilots."

"This one," the AOC replied.

'Sir?" Harriet and Cas replied in unison.

"All of the fighter squadrons already have Squadron Leaders, and it wouldn't do to send them another as a supernumerary, especially not one with young Cornwall's pedigree in the air; it'd undermine them at best. No, the PRU types need the type of pilot that can get the best from an aeroplane, pilots like you, Cornwall."

"Yes, Sir..." Harriet replied.

"Fantastic!" He waved his cigarette holder once again. "Right, better get back to work. It's been a long day; why don't you knock off for the night and get yourselves over to the Mess? You can do introductions in the morning."

"Sir..." they both said, and Cas saluted as the AOC marched away smiling.

"Good to have you onboard, Cornwall. You're going to be good for us!" They watched in silence as he climbed into his car and was driven away.

"I'm guessing you're not going to be needing a ride to Cairo...?" the pilot asked as he returned to join them.

"You'd better get going before I take the seat myself," Cas replied, then gave the pilot a forced smile before walking Harriet back to Robbie and her truck.

"What just happened?" Harriet asked.

"You've been kidnapped," Cas replied. "Along with half the pilots and ground crews on the island."

"He caught her, didn't he?" Robbie asked.

"He did..." Cas sighed. "Sorry, Harry," he continued.

"I've got absolutely no idea what's going on..." Harriet sighed as she leant against the front of the truck, squeezed between Cas and Robbie. The Maryland's engines started, one after the other, then it quickly departed for the end of the runway. They watched in silence as it buzzed past them and climbed into the inky blue evening sky. "What's a PRU?" she asked, after the drone of the Maryland's engines faded into the distance.

"Where did we get you from?" Cas said with a sigh as he rolled his eyes.

"What?"

43

"A highly decorated Squadron Leader fighter ace in the Royal Air Force, and you don't know what a PRU is..."

"There's no need to be like that; it's been a long day! Besides, you know exactly where you got me from. It's you that got me!" she thundered as she switched from defence to offence mid sentence, while Robbie sniggered.

"And I'd have got rid of you to Cairo, if you'd stopped arguing for a minute and actually got on that aeroplane when I told you to."

"Get rid? Really? Well, if that's how it is, I wish I had got on it!"

"Good! So do I!"

"Will you two stop it!" Robbie said as she nudged herself forward from the truck and turned to face them both.

"You should tell her why you were so desperate for her to leave, and stop winding her up!" she barked at Cas.

"Yes! You should listen to her!" Harriet said in the most condescending tone she could muster.

"And you should shut up for once and stop trying to win every single debate! It's not a competition, and as it happens, I think a Squadron Leader should know what a PRU is. Even I know, and I haven't been in the Air Force five minutes!"

"That much is obvious," Harriet replied, choosing to stay on the attack, with mischief glinting in her eyes. "If you'd been in any longer, you'd know it's very bad form to shout at a Squadron Leader, and very bad luck to shout at a Wing Commander."

"She's got a point," Cas said. "I've seen subordinates shot for less..."

"Give me strength!" Robbie said with a roll of her eyes, while Harriet and Cas smirked at each other. "I thought I'd missed you!" she hissed at Harriet.

"Well, we can't sit here all night. I have work to do," Cas said with a sigh. "We need to get you some digs sorted, too," he said to Harriet.

"Anj and Lissy said I could have my old room in Mdina," Harriet replied.

"Not a bad idea, but it's a bit of a drag away from your unit, and you'll likely be called away at some odd times. Somewhere closer would be better."

"You can stay with me at my apartment, if you'd like?" Robbie said with a shrug.

"Floriana is certainly closer... If that's OK with you both?" Harriet and Robbie looked at each other and nodded. "Good. That's it agreed, then. You can drop me off in Valletta on your way home."

"PRU?" Harriet asked, as the truck rumbled into life.

"How are you at taking photos?"

"Please say I'm not being sent to work as a photographer..." Harriet sighed.

"Something like that. Your new boss will brief you in the morning, probably best to get here before sunrise. Report to that small stone dispersal office over there." He pointed as they drove past, and Harriet nodded. "He's a good sort; he'll look after you. Do as he says, and you won't be bad off."

Robbie drove them through the dark, rubble lined streets. There were people about, but not many, and the narrow alleys were pitch dark in the blackout, making them difficult to navigate without hitting a person or a bomb crater. She drove masterfully as if she could see in the dark, and soon they were back at HQ, and Cas was climbing from the truck.

"It really is good to see you again," he said as he stood by the door and looked up at Harriet, the light from the half moon between the

45

scattered clouds making his face visible in the darkness. His smile was warm and genuine, as it always was, and Harriet couldn't help but smile back.

"It's good to see you, too," Harriet replied. "Goodnight."

"Whenever you're ready..." Robbie said loudly and a little impatiently. Cas nodded and grinned, then slammed the door closed and walked off into the night.

Back at Robbie's apartment, Harriet unpacked the few items of clothing she'd brought with her and put them in a small drawer, then changed into a short flowery summer dress that Robbie loaned her, on seeing that she didn't have much. The water was running, so Robbie encouraged making the most of it, and they filled bowls and cans. Harriet washed herself down and tidied her hair before joining Robbie on the balcony. She sank into the chair and was handed a tin cup of gin, which was a little stronger than she expected, and caught the back of her throat.

"That's a bit sharp," Harriet said as her throat scratched.

"I got it from some Navy lads. I didn't ask how they made it..."

"Probably for the best."

"You do know he was trying to do the right thing getting you out of here? It's really not the place to be right now."

"I know..." Harriet smiled. "It's just, well, I've only just arrived, and I'd hoped to catch up with you all a little. A day or two couldn't have hurt."

"You'd be surprised. Almost every pilot that's touched down here since you left has ended up staying, and it's not because we liked their company... Losses have been terrible. Almost unsustainable. Even the best don't last a couple of months; some don't last the end of their first day. When the AOC found out you were here, he was bound to make a play to keep you, especially with your reputation around here, so it turned into a race to get you off the island and out of harm's way."

46

"Is it really that bad?"

"Worse. I'm not sure I can even put it into words. The relief convoys have been hit so hard that we haven't received anything for months, other than that sneaked in by submarines and the occasional small, fast Navy ship. Petrol, aviation fuel, food, ammunition, we're practically out of everything. Even the anti aircraft guns are rationed to how many shots they can fire in a day, so they have to make each one count. Until your Spitfires arrived this morning, we hardly had any air defence at all. We just had to sit and take it, and the Germans just kept on coming. At least in Cairo, you'd be spared."

"At least I can be of some help now I'm here."

"I've missed your annoying optimism."

Chapter 3

Feeling Blue

"Good morning!" the golden haired man said chirpily as he walked into the dispersal hut. He was tall and tanned, with a confident smile, and dressed eccentrically in a cricket jumper, blue shirt with an open collar, baggy khaki shorts, and canvas boating shoes.

"Good morning..." Harriet replied, a little bemused by the sight in front of her. She'd been sitting alone for over half an hour, having made sure she was on duty firmly before first light, as Cas had suggested, without giving any particular idea of what time that would coincide with. She sat up in her chair and looked around as the walking golden haired jumble sale breezed past her, twisting her head to watch as he disappeared into his office. She sat back in her chair, not sure what to do.

"You must be Harry Cornwall?" he asked confidently as he emerged from his office.

"Yes..." Harriet said as she stood from her chair.

"I've heard so much about you." He offered his hand, which Harriet shook while raising her eyebrow a little in confusion.

"You have?" she couldn't resist asking.

"Of course, who in Malta hasn't? It was quite the scoop hearing the AOC had managed to secure your services."

"Oh... Well, that's alright, then."

"Isn't it!" he laughed, just as an airman stepped into the dispersal hut.

"She's ready when you are, Sir," the airman said.

"Any snags?" the tall blond replied.

"Nothing out of the ordinary. She should get you there and back without a problem. Your gunner's already on board."

"Already? Keen... Right, in that case, we'd better get going!" He looked to Harriet. "Grab that parachute, would you? I hope we won't need it, but it doesn't hurt to have one just in case. Besides, it makes sitting more comfortable." Harriet nodded and grabbed the parachute from the floor, and followed him outside. "I'm told you've flown twin engine aeroplanes before?"

"Mosquitos and Ansons back in England, though not for long. Most of my time has been on Hurricanes and Spitfires."

"Yes, I heard you were up giving the Hun a bloody nose shortly after you landed yesterday. Feel good to be back in the driving seat, did it?"

"I suppose..."

"Well, the Martin Maryland, the ship we'll be taking up, is a little different to a Spit. You can't throw her around quite as much, and she's nowhere near as fast, but she's a hard worker and can take a lot of punishment." They arrived at the long nosed twin engine aeroplane. Its dark silhouette looked almost identical against the predawn sky to the one she was supposed to have been flying to Cairo with on the previous evening. "Right, I'll show you around, then get you settled before we set off. Can't hang around too long, though; we need to be there before sunrise."

"Where?" Harriet asked, as she followed him around the large aeroplane.

"Sicily," he casually replied.

"Sicily?" she repeated, as her heart squeezed and tummy flipped. She remembered her last trip to Sicily very clearly, and the one before that when she'd seen Squadron Leader 'Flash' Gordon blown out of the sky right next to her.

"Yes. Ideally, we need to get there before the Germans are out of bed. It can get a bit uncomfortable otherwise." He waved up at the gunner in the rear facing turret at the top of the aeroplane, and received a thumbs up in return. "The Italians are fine, you can rely on them to get up sometime around ten, and they won't go anywhere without having a coffee first. The Germans are a different breed, though. Very industrious, up at the crack of dawn and ready for business. Right, here's you." He led her to a hatch hanging open under the nose. "Climb in, close the hatch, strap in tight and get comfortable. We'll be on the road before you know it." He left her looking gobsmacked as he gave the propellers on the starboard engine a final look over, before walking around and climbing up the wing toward the cockpit, which sat above and to the rear of the nose that Harriet had been left to climb into. "You see, the way it works is that you need to be in the aeroplane before it takes off. Otherwise, you get left behind," he shouted down jovially from the wing. Harriet nodded and waved, still bemused, then climbed the ladder and went up through the hatch into the nose of the aeroplane. A ground crewman appeared and took the ladder away, then pushed the hatch up for her to grab and secure, before putting her parachute into the seat base and strapping herself in. It was dark, except for the glow of a few instruments, and she was very apprehensive of why they'd be flying to Sicily. She looked around and found the connector for her radio and oxygen, and plugged in, just as the first engine spluttered into life, followed quickly by the second, sending vibrations through the rickety looking aeroplane. "How are things down there in the Dress Stalls?" he asked over the intercom. "Harry, that's you."

"All good down here," Harriet replied, after making sure the hatch was secure, and her straps were tight, and feeling embarrassed at not having a clue what he was talking about, or what was going on.

"Good show. Right, here we go. Better hold on until we get up; the runway can be like skiing slalom in the dark." She grabbed the frame on either side of her as he released the brakes and rolled through the dark, taxiing to the runway where he went through his power checks; and without waiting for a second longer than he needed to, released the brakes. The Maryland leapt forward, not with the strength or speed of a Spitfire, but fast enough for her to feel more than a little nervous as the nose swung wildly left and right, so much that she wasn't entirely sure how they were still managing to move forward. She was relieved when the wheels finally left the ground, and the yawing stopped. They climbed steeply, circling over the island as the noisy Pratt and Whitney Twin Wasp radial engines dragged them upwards. The higher they got, the more Harriet could see the royal blue predawn sky as it lit up the many windows surrounding her in the nose of the aeroplane. As her eyes adjusted to the dim light, she could see a half steering wheel control column pinned to the bulkhead, and more controls over to her left, including what looked like a throttle. "Comfortable down there, Harry?" he asked.

"Yes... Yes, thank you," she replied.

"Good. You'll see a set of controls down there, have a fiddle and pull them into place, then you can take the reins for a while if you like?" She did as he said, then got comfortable with her hands on the controls, before letting him know she was ready. "Right, in that case, she's all yours. Keep her on the same heading, but get a feel for her. A few turns and bumps won't hurt." She smiled and took control of the aeroplane. It was heavy on the controls, unlike the Spitfire or the Hurricane, but it was fast and responded relatively quickly to her touch. She rolled left and right, dived, then climbed, all while adjusting the throttle appropriately. It felt easy enough to fly, even from her awkward position in the nose of the aeroplane, where she felt like she was sitting on the floor with her legs out in front of her, and her back against the bulkhead separating the nose from the pilot's cockpit. She focused on her job and smiled to herself as the sky over to the east lit up all shades of blue, from silver to dark navy, with the slightest hint of pink and orange on the horizon. Now she knew why he called her cockpit the Dress Stalls. The best seats in the London Palladium theatre, with the best views. "Right, you'd better let me drive for a while." He took the controls again as they left the island of Gozo behind them, and Harriet sat back and relaxed a little. She had no idea what they were doing, but she was enjoying it. The Maryland was like flying a big old bus, and the pilot couldn't be any more pleasant. Whatever Cas had been trying to get her away from didn't seem that bad at all. "OK, Harry. This is where we earn our rations. Keep your eyes open, and shout out if you see any trouble."

51

"Will do..." she replied as she prepared to swallow her words. He pulled the Maryland around to the west and into the darkness, then quickly descended to just a couple of hundred feet off the Mediterranean. Once low enough for Harriet to see the white tips of the smallest waves, he banked around and headed east and into the dawn. Her heart started to race as she saw land, and then he dropped a little further just before crossing the coast. Laid out in front of them, clearly lit by the encroaching daylight, was row after row of bombers. Her stomach clenched tight, and she felt a bead of sweat on her forehead. The Maryland roared over the German airfield at speed. "Well, that should wake them up!" he laughed. "What did you see, Harry?"

"Ju88 bombers, and Ju87 Stukas," she replied instinctively.

"Good, how many?" She frowned as she thought for a while and raked her memory.

"Forty one."

"Are you sure?"

"Yes..." She counted up the picture she'd just seen in her head. "Four rows of six Stukas. Two rows of eight 88s."

"That's forty."

"I know... Wait..." She searched her memory. "A Ju52 transport aeroplane half hidden under a camouflage net at the back of the airfield."

"Good going, Harry. Let's go see if you're right." Her eyes opened wide as he pulled up into a tight turn, then dropped lower than before as they raced back to the airfield, which by now had most definitely woken up, evidenced by the searchlights crisscrossing the sky searching for them. "Have a closer look at that Ju52, would you," he asked as they ran at the airfield, and this time the reception committee was waiting for them. The air lit up with anti aircraft fire of all sorts, heavy explosions and lines of machine gun tracer wrapping around them but somehow missing the mark, though the explosions were close enough to bounce Harriet in her seat and shake the whole aeroplane. She felt helpless. No guns, no bombs, just a cone of windows surrounding her in the long nose of the aeroplane, presenting her as a literally sitting target for the gunners below. She watched the airfield closely, her mathematical mind spinning in overdrive as she counted aeroplanes, and searchlights, and guns, as she searched out the Ju52. She squinted as she looked closely. It looked normal enough, not that she knew what would be abnormal. Then she saw it. The camouflage net it was peeking out from was actually a series of nets, expertly linked together, almost perfectly hiding the long line of transports at the back of the airfield.

"It's not one transport; it's a whole squadron of them," she said excitedly over the radio. "Ten, maybe more, they're hidden by the camouflage nets."

"Good eyes, Harry! Right, I think that's enough trouble causing for one morning. Let's get ourselves home for breakfast." He pulled the Maryland south, and dropped to sea level until they were out of range of the coast, then started a steady climb into the lightening sky. They slipped over Gozo, and then the Maltese coast. Harriet's adrenaline had just started to ease when a shout went out from the gunner.

"Bandit on our six, skipper. Pull up!" The Maryland lifted, and before she knew it, Harriet was looking at the sky as she felt herself pulled tight against the bulkhead behind her. The big beast of an aeroplane rolled as it climbed, and the engines roared as every last breath of power was squeezed out of them before the nose was pushed down again, and her view of the sky was replaced by one of the ground. Just the ground. No sky, nothing, they were heading straight down, going so fast the whole aeroplane shook. Her adrenaline was flowing, and she was scared. Somebody was trying to shoot them down, and there wasn't a thing she could do about it except hold on and pray. The Maryland levelled out and rolled left and right. "Hold her steady...." the gunner shouted. "Steady... Pull up now!" The Maryland lifted hard again, then rolled. "That got him."

"Good shooting!" the pilot said excitedly as they came into land, bumping down hard, then swaying left and right, so much Harriet thought he'd been hit in the attack. They slowed, and straightened, then taxied to the dispersal, where the engines were immediately shut down. "Right you are, Harry, that's us. See you outside." Harriet unfastened her harness, then breathed a sigh of relief before kicking the hatch open and throwing her parachute out, before swinging herself down to the ground. She composed herself for a moment, then stepped from under the aeroplane and turned to look at it, half expecting to see it looking like a sieve from all the flak that had been thrown at it, but other than a few small calibre bullet holes here and there, it seemed in pretty good condition. It was painted nose to tail in a dusty cobalt blue colour that she imagined fitted perfectly with the many shades of blue she'd seen as the sky lightened. "Not a bad old girl, is she?" the pilot asked as he stood beside her.

"I expected her to be full of holes..." Harriet replied.

"Oh, that? I wouldn't worry too much about that; they can't shoot straight first thing in a morning. Not until they've had breakfast, at least, then they can be pretty handy. Right, better get the shots up to Headquarters." He lifted the three large black metal cartridges he'd been handed by one of the ground crew. "They'll be keen to know about those transports you saw. Coming?"

"I suppose," she shrugged and followed him to his waiting car, which he drove the same way as he handled the Maryland on take off and landing.

"So, how do you like the idea of photographic reconnaissance?" he asked, as he raced towards Valletta.

"It's certainly different to what I have been doing," she replied, then looked away out of the window, and rolled her eyes as she worked out PRU. She knew what it was; she'd heard it enough times. It was the Photographic Reconnaissance Unit, the aeroplanes fitted with cameras that sneaked about taking photos of important enemy positions. There's no wonder Cas had teased her for not knowing that.

"It's not quite as glamorous when compared to the life of a fighter pilot, but it's equally as important, if not more so. Without our aircraft, the top brass wouldn't have a clue what Jerry was up to most of the time, and that can be a dangerous way to live. It makes it hard to fight a war with your hands tied behind your back."

"I've never had much to do with the PRU before," Harriet shrugged.

"I doubt you'd have had the time, what with your exploits."

"What's that supposed to mean?"

"I was here when you were last in town, though our paths hardly crossed. You were rather busy shooting half the Luftwaffe down, as I remember, and didn't frequent the Mess that often, or attend any of the social gatherings in town."

"There were social gatherings?" she asked with a frown.

"Oh gosh, yes, lots of them. I'm not a big one for socialising myself, but I went to a few. There's not so many of them these days, though. The Germans seem to have taken all the fun out of things. Even my favourite places to eat have closed, which is more than a little irritating. Anyway, I suppose I had a little more time on my hands than you. Rumour has it you were up four or five times a day when things got a bit hot."

"Honestly, I lost count. It was all a blur by the end."

"You know, for the longest time, many of us thought it was the end. You and your friend, Delacourt, is it?" Harriet nodded and smiled. "You'd both become quite famous around here, and then you were both gone. Those that knew insisted you were alive and had been evacuated, but that didn't stop the rumours, of course."

"People thought we were dead?"

"Well, yes... There was even a story among the Maltese that the priest had read the last rites over you."

"That part may have been true..." Harriet frowned as her mind drifted back to her last flight over Malta before returning to England, and how the German cannon shell had almost taken her arm off,

55

leaving her hanging lifeless from her parachute which had snagged on the church tower.

"You can put the record straight now you're back." He gave her a wink as they pulled to a halt at the entrance to the underground tunnels. They jumped out of the car, and he pulled on a ragged looking blue RAF service cap, the type worn by officers, which seemed like the only piece of regulation uniform he owned. The Maltese army guards saluted him as he entered the tunnels. He led Harriet through the already warm, and slightly smelly, damp tunnels to the AOC's office. "Got something for you, Sir," he said, as he stepped through the door and interrupted the conversation being had between the AOC, an Admiral, and Cas. They waved him and Harriet in, closed the door, and looked at him in silence for a moment. "You were right; we found about a dozen Ju52 transports hidden under camouflage nets. Would have missed them if it wasn't for Harry's sharp eyes. Anyway, the photos should show everything; I think I got them with the oblique cameras."

"Looks like it's on..." the AOC said to the Admiral, who nodded and shrugged in agreement. "Good work. We'll need to keep an eye on the other airfields; they'll need more than a dozen. Probably good to have a look at the docks over on the Italian coast, too, see what's building up. Do you think you can get your chaps on it?"

"I'll get them up as soon as I'm back."

"Good work. I'm told south of Syracuse may be worth a look." The blond nodded. "How's young Cornwall?"

"Perfect for the job, if she'll join us?"

"Well?" The AOC asked Harriet. She shrugged uncomfortably. She didn't really have much of a say in the matter, and she knew it.

"Love to, Sir," Harriet said confidently, making Cas wince slightly.

"Good show!"

"If you don't mind, Sir, there's something I need to do while I'm here?" the CO asked, smiling mischievously as he did.

"Not at all, but don't hang around too long; we'd like to get a look at Syracuse before it gets too late." The AOC gave a nod of approval.

"I'll meet you outside," the CO said to Harriet before leaving the office.

"I'll see you out," Cas said as he gave Harriet a nod. She followed him out into the tunnel, and walked by his side.

"The PRU penny dropped," she said.

"I expected it would... How was it?"

"Different..."

"Yes, and it can be perilous. PRU types aren't exactly popular among the enemy. Rumour has it they get a week's leave to go home if they bag one, so be careful."

"Aren't I always?"

"No." He looked sternly at her. "Brave, talented, determined, yes. Careful, definitely not. This isn't one of those you can just push on and hope for the best with, Harry. You'll need to be sharp, and smart."

"I'll do my best."

"I know you will. So, what do you think of your new boss?"

"I wouldn't know; I haven't met him yet."

"You certainly have," he laughed.

"Who? Not that scarecrow..."

"Careful, that's Wing Commander scarecrow."

"I don't believe you!"

"You'd better. He's the best pilot on the island, better than you even, and he has an outstanding reputation for bringing back the goods. It's why the brass are content to overlook his uniform choices. Anyway, he reports directly to the AOC, and you'll be reporting directly to him. Oh, and don't let looks deceive you. He's not only an incredible pilot; he's a damn good leader. Listen to him, and he'll keep you alive."

"I will. I promise."

"Good. I'd rather like to keep you alive, if at all possible."

"Which is why you tried to send me to Cairo."

"Yes..."

"I appreciate it, genuinely. I'm kind of happy to be staying, though. It is a bit like home."

"Not quite the same as California, though? Or Hawaii, I'd imagine."

"Well, close, I suppose, but this'll have to do for now."

"I'll come down to the airfield and see you when my shift has finished; if you'll be around?"

"I can be? I can't imagine anywhere else I was planning to go."

"Good. In that case, I'll see you later. Remember what I said, listen and learn. PRU flying is entirely different to being a fighter pilot. You're the student, not the master."

"Yes, Sir."

"So, you do remember how this all works. That's reassuring. See you later." He winked and left her as she stepped through the door, out of the stink and into the morning heat.

Chapter 4

Lazy Days

Six weeks after arriving in Malta for the second time, Harriet had settled into her role as a photographic reconnaissance pilot with relative ease, to the point where she was quite enjoying her new job. She'd flown a few times with her CO to get the hang of the intricacies of the job, such as how to position the aeroplane to get the best photos, and how to fly the Maryland defensively, to avoid getting herself shot down by marauding 109 pilots trying to get themselves a week at home for bagging a PR pilot. She had a crew assigned, a pair of sergeants, Bill Hughes, and Art McShane. Bill was about as Welsh as it was possible to be, and when excited, he was almost impossible to understand, the opposite of Art, a laid back Australian who appeared totally unflappable. Once he was confident she wasn't going to get them killed too quickly, the CO had her flying missions around Sicily, and as far as the Italian coast, looking for enemy merchant ships moving cargo south to support Rommel, the German General busy battling across the deserts of North Africa and giving the Allied forces a hard time. She got her photos every time, sometimes getting a little too close for comfort in her determination to deliver the goods, and having to dodge heavy flak or fight off the occasional 109, one of which she managed to shoot down with the perfect deflection shot, using the Maryland's wing mounted machine guns. Some days they were left sitting and waiting for a mission to come through, or lounging around without an aeroplane because the CO had commandeered theirs and disappeared off on one of his undisclosed missions, which could see him gone for hours at a time.

"Do you reckon we'll get up today, Ma'am?" Bill asked while pacing back and forth, staring at the sky and kicking the stones scattered across the ground.

"I've no idea... Why don't you sit down while we wait and find out? You're getting on my nerves pacing back and forth like that," Harriet replied. She was laid back in a wicker chair, with her feet up on an ammunition box; she had her aviator sunglasses on and had a straw hat she'd picked up in Valletta pulled over her face. She was melting in the summer heat, which was sapping her energy, and at times making her miss rainy old England. At least there, she thought, she'd be able to get a satisfying drink. At the dispersal, she was faced with the choice of petrol and salt tinged water, or something the cooks referred to as tea, which made even the American attempts at England's favourite drink seem like a trip to Fortnum's.

"What do you reckon, Art?" Bill asked as he sat beside the bronzed Australian, who, like Harriet, was trying to sleep through the afternoon sun.

"I reckon you should get lost, and go see if you can find anything to drink that doesn't taste like it came out of a 109's radiator," Art replied.

"Bill, I'll have you transferred to the infantry if you don't shut up," Harriet added, as she wiped the sweat from her neck with her silk scarf, the same blue and white patterned scarf she'd been given by the first German she'd shot down. She looked at the edelweiss embroidered in the corner and smiled to herself. It was all so long ago, or so it felt.

"Ma'am..." Bill said, as he stood and walked off.

"Don't go far; we need to stay close in case we're sent up!"

"Thank God for the peace," Art said after Bill had left.

"Don't you start," Harriet said with a smirk.

"You won't hear a peep out of me, Ma'am." Art pulled his traditional Australian slouch hat back over his face and fell silent. Leaving Harriet to smirk to herself. She'd fallen lucky with a good crew; both were very good at their jobs, and very easy to get on with. Both were in their mid to late twenties, Art slightly older than Bill, and although they were respectful of Harriet's rank and experience, they were very protective of her as though she was their younger sister. They weren't the only ones, either. With the specialist nature of their work, which meant sometimes flying for hours on end to look for a cargo ship, or snap photos of German airfields, they spent a lot of time on the ground waiting. It wasn't like the old days of being scrambled every five minutes, and Harriet found herself getting bored in the long rests between flights, which could sometimes last days, so she'd pass the time helping the ground crews with maintenance and repairs, using the knowledge she'd picked up from Claude back in France to make herself useful. In return, the ground crews looked after her like one of their own, and they were often on edge if she was late back from a mission, something which happened with remarkable frequency when she had to take detours due to heavy flak, or to shake off pursuers.

"Is it this hot in Australia?" she asked after a while, unable to rest.

"Hotter," Art replied. "Go out in the bush during summer, and it's so hot you can't think."

"How do you get used to it?"

"You don't... You just learn to live with it..."

"Great..." she sighed, and slumped deeper into her chair. At that, the air raid siren started to wind up its deep and terrifying wail.

"Ah hell, here we go again," Art said as he dragged himself from his seat. "Come on, Ma'am, we'd better get in the trench."

"You'd think they'd get bored, wouldn't you," Harriet said as she stood and searched the skies to the north. The raids hadn't stopped, though they had eased for a while after the arrival of the Spitfires, which had obviously made the enemy think twice about their visits. Meeting seventy Spitfires had been quite a shock for the Luftwaffe, having enjoyed a couple of years faced with only a handful of Hurricanes and Gladiators. On the day Harriet had flown her last combat mission, the day she'd led the Spitfires in from the aircraft carriers, the Germans had lost over sixty aircraft, and as many again were damaged, while not claiming a single Spitfire. They'd built their confidence over the following weeks, though, and as Malta's supplies ran so short that the Spitfires were only scrambled when absolutely necessary; and the gunners were restricted to fewer and fewer rounds to shoot each day, the raids grew in strength and ferocity. The built up areas were battered, and the docks and airfields flattened. There hadn't been as many raids, but those there were had been large and accurate.

"Don't just stand there!" Art yelled, as he grabbed Harriet by the hand. She looked at his panicked face, then to the four Messerschmitt 109 fighters he was pointing at, which were sweeping towards the airfield so low they had to pull up to miss the boundary fences. As their bullets started zipping up the ground towards the buildings, Harriet turned and joined Art in running to the trench, which they slipped into just seconds before the 109s swept by, shooting up anything that was moving. Harriet stood with her back pressed firmly against the trench wall, and struggled to breathe as the air around her seemed to superheat, but she couldn't move; she just had to stand, breathe, and control herself. She looked at Art and smiled, noticing how uncomfortable he looked. He nodded in reply, right before the familiar scream of the Stukas' sirens filled the air and bombs started to vibrate the ground, filling the trench with dust. They waited patiently, hoping to avoid a direct hit until the all clear sounded, and they could extract themselves from the trench and look around to see if anyone had been hurt. The raid had been relatively light, and not much damage had been done, so they headed back to their chairs, where they were met by Bill, who was holding three tin mugs of murky grey tea. "Is this the best you could rustle up?" Art asked with disappointment.

"You're lucky. I managed to get some extra grit and dust in it during the raid."

"May make it taste better..." Art replied. Harriet took hers with a smile, and took a sip of the gritty tasteless lukewarm tea. The only good it did was wash the dust from her mouth and throat, and try to address her thirst.

"Telephone, Ma'am," the orderly said, as he stepped out of the dispersal. Harriet nodded and followed him inside.

"Cornwall," Harriet said.

"Harry, it's Cas," came the reply. She instantly smiled at the sound of his voice.

"Very kind of you to call and check I'm OK."

"I'm considerate like that... Look, we've got a job for you. Is your aeroplane still in one piece after that last raid?"

"Yes, and I'm fine too. Thanks for asking."

"I had no doubt. I'll have a dispatch rider down there with the details of your sortie in a while. Let us know as soon as you're back, and don't hang around as soon as you get an answer."

"Will do..."

"Harry..."

"Yes?"

"I'm happy you're OK. Make sure you stay that way..."

"Yes, Sir..." she said with a smirk, then put down the phone before walking outside. "OK, time for us to earn our pay; grab your kit." Art and Bill did as she said and followed her to the pen hiding their Maryland, where the senior ground crewman, a Corporal, was waiting for them. "Any snags I need to know about?" she asked.

"No, Ma'am, she's good to go."

"Let's get her ready, then." She climbed up the wing and lowered herself into the cockpit, while Bill and Art got in their positions. She went through the controls and pre start checks, and when she was happy that everything was as it should be, she climbed back out of the aeroplane to do another walk around, and wait for the dispatch rider.

"Going anywhere nice, Ma'am?" The Corporal asked.

"You know I can't tell you that, Smithy," she replied with a knowing smile.

"Doesn't hurt to ask, Ma'am. I've been here in Malta for two years straight, and haven't seen anything but. I like to at least imagine you going somewhere different."

"The places we usually end up going aren't really somewhere you'd want to take your leave. The locals tend to get angry and shoot at us."

"In that case, as long as you bring her back without too many holes, I'll be happy to stay here and wait." He gave Harriet a smile, which was returned. It wasn't the first time they'd had the conversation while they waited for a dispatch rider. Harriet was always deadly serious in telling him he wouldn't want to go where she was going, but she wasn't too sure about him. He'd asked a few times if he could tag along for a flight, or even volunteer to be a gunner, but he was so valuable on the ground that he wasn't allowed anywhere further than half a mile from the Maryland. He was the only member of the ground crew that had trained on them in England, everyone else had been kidnapped or scrounged, and while they were good, they didn't know the Maryland as he did. He'd even found a way not even in the manuals that allowed the throttle to be set in such a way that the pilots could squeeze an extra few valuable knots out of the engines. He was their very own genius and resident expert, and it was on the orders of the CO himself that he wasn't allowed to tag along on the missions. As with the curious arrangement with the CO reporting directly to the AVM, Smithy reported direct to the CO. "Here he comes..." he said as the motorcycle came into view. Harriet nodded and waited, wondering where her orders were taking her.

"Squadron Leader Cornwall?" the Army dispatch rider asked.

"Yes..." Harriet replied, before being handed the sealed envelope from his leather satchel. She nodded and opened the envelope to read the instructions. They were coordinates, nothing more. It wasn't the first time she'd received such cryptic messages, with instructions to destroy the single piece of paper while in the air.

"Italy? Sicily?" Smithy asked.

"Hawaii," Harriet replied, as she often had.

"Good luck, Ma'am. Safe skies."

"See you in a while." She gave him a smile, then climbed back up the wing to her cockpit, and lowered herself in before pulling the roof closed and strapping herself in. Engines started, gauges checked, power run up and eased, and she was happy. Smithy had never done a bad job, but it still made her smile when she knew for sure everything was as it should be. She taxied to the end of the runway, where she went through her final checks, then ran up the power and released the brakes. The Maryland charged down the runway straight and true, making her smile again at the CO's wiggling and wavering every time he took off or landed. He was a master in the air, she'd flown a few sorties with him and could vouch for the almost impossible way he got the Maryland to do exactly as he wanted, but on the ground, he was a menace to himself and others. She pulled back on the stick, and the aeroplane lifted lightly from the ground. The Maryland was a beast, and the big radial engines were noisy, but it was a breeze to handle, not at all like the Mosquito, which had tried its best to kill her with its twitchy handling on the ground due to the mass of power and torque in the twin Rolls Royce Merlins trying to drag it off the runway. She raised the undercarriage, checked her gauges, then set a course east and started a steep climb, determined to get out of sight before the Germans came back for another raid, and shot her down before she'd even got started.

Once they were at altitude and safely away from Malta, Harriet checked the coordinates against her map again. They were taking her into the Ionian Sea, away from land, and almost directly south of Taranto harbour. She had Bill and Art scan the horizon, in the sky and on the sea, watching both for fighters and whatever it was they'd been sent to look for. The sun was low behind them; by her calculations, she estimated she'd be over the coordinates about an hour and a half before sunset, meaning that if they found whatever they were looking for, they'd be back over Malta shortly before last light. If possible, she wanted to be back before it was totally dark, there was every possibility that the Luftwaffe would have paid a visit in their absence, and she didn't like the idea of trying to dodge bomb craters in the dark. A crew hadn't been so lucky a few weeks earlier when coming in at night, and their aircraft was written off, with the pilot suffering a bad concussion and a badly smashed up face. Something she was keen to avoid.

"There she is, skipper," Bill said as they came towards the coordinates. "Right on the nose." Harriet saw it at the same time. A large black blob on the horizon, trailing a long white wake which cut a line north through the shimmering dark blue Mediterranean.

"OK, let's go and have a look. Hold on, and keep your eyes open." She checked her instruments, then nervously searched the sky. It's around this time that she knew things could get uncomfortable if they were going to. They nudged closer and close. She had an idea of what she was seeing, but needed to be sure, so she pushed the stick forward and headed down in a shallow dive, while all the time keeping her eyes on the sky above. As they closed, small fluffy grey balls started to pepper the sky around her, not too close, but close enough to make her adrenaline flow. She pushed on down as the fluffy balls expanded into black and orange fiery explosions, light anti aircraft fire from the ship below. She slipped left slightly, then banked right and circled the giant oil tanker below, firing off her oblique cameras that looked out of the side of the aeroplane, and got a good shot as the machine gunners on the deck started taking shots at her, which were thankfully wide of the mark. "OK, Bill. Let Malta know we've found an oil tanker heading south unescorted, and let them know our position."

"Yes, Ma'am!" he replied hastily, then went about his task, while Harriet scanned the sky. She caught a white trail out of the corner of her eyes, and quickly changed the direction of her turn while pulling the nose up so she could get a better view. She squinted as she searched, then she saw it, a single white streak high in the deep blue sky, vapour trails, suggesting the presence of a single engine aeroplane high above. Her heart raced a little more than it already was when she saw another white streak further north and heading in the same direction.

"How's that message going, Bill?" she asked, trying hard to keep the nerves from her voice, while quickly checking her map and calculating what she thought must be the range of the aircraft above. Assuming they were fighters, and they came from the closest airfield on the Italian coast, she estimated that the fighters would be close to the limit of their endurance, assuming they were regular 109s.

"Message sent, not heard back."

"Send it again, quickly."

"Will do..."

"Let me know as soon as they acknowledge. Art, keep your eyes on our tail. I reckon we've got five minutes at the most until whatever it is up there comes down and has a look." She changed direction again, dodging the flak and keeping the gunners guessing as she jinked and dived, and twisted and climbed around the tanker, which was now altering course as erratically as a huge oil tanker could, clearly trying to avoid any bombs that the Maryland may have been carrying.

"I'm on them, skipper. I'll call them when I see them," Art replied. "Though I'm not convinced we should be hanging around too long."

"Just until we get acknowledgement from Malta..." She watched the vapour trails as they changed direction, first the lead aircraft, and then the second. An anti aircraft shell blasted closer than the others, scattering the wing with shrapnel and almost flipping the Maryland, forcing Harriet to fight to keep the wings level. "Come on, Bill, anytime now!"

"Nothing yet..." His voice was panicked.

"Send it once more."

"Sending."

"Here they come!" Art shouted. "109s!" As he did, another blast sprayed the front of the aeroplane with shrapnel, and Harriet watched as the windows of the nose were knocked out, and the walls turned into a colander she could see daylight through. The aeroplane strained, but she held it.

"Bill!" she yelled. "Bill, are you OK?"

"Yeah..." he replied after a moment of silence.

"Right, that's it, we're getting out of here. Art, keep them off our tail. I'm going to dive for the deck and get some speed!" She pushed the nose down and opened the throttle, knowing full well that she couldn't out dive a 109, but it was all she could do. Climbing would slow her further, and the 109s would get her sooner. By diving, she could at least try and get away, or at least delay the inevitable. She headed south, and felt her forearms ache as she fought to keep the Maryland stable, which due to the holes in the nose and wing was buffeting and fighting against the increased airflow that came with the dive. The engines roared as she squeezed every last drop of power out of them, desperate to escape. She pulled back on the controls and skimmed the surface of the sea.

"Malta acknowledges, and asks if we can keep eyes on," Bill called over the intercom.

"Tell them to bugger off! We're coming home, and we're coming home fast, with fighters on our tail!"

"We're not going to be able to outrun them," Art shouted from his turret in the rear between the bursts of machine gun fire he was sending up at the leading 109. "We're sitting ducks, and there's no way I can keep them both off us."

"OK..." Harriet replied. "Let me know when they're closing."

"They're closing!"

"Hold on!" Harriet closed the throttles and pulled back hard on the stick, slowing the Maryland almost to a stall, and making the pursuing 109 pull left to avoid colliding with the tail. Harriet watched as he passed left of the cockpit, and simultaneously she opened the throttles fully, pushed forward, and kicked the rudder bar left and let the 109 have a blast of her guns as he passed into her sights, making the engine smoke immediately. At the same time, the second 109 opened fire and rattled the fuselage of the Maryland, and a cannon shell ripped through the bulkhead behind Harriet, and passed straight out of the window in front of her. She had a fleeting flashback to the last time that had happened, but she couldn't dwell on it. She turned tight to the left, then rolled right. The 109 kept tight on her, but when she pulled up hard, the 109 made the mistake of waiting a second too long before following, and made himself a perfect target for Art, who fired into the cockpit and killed the pilot outright, sending the 109 splashing into the sea and sending a huge plume of white water into the air. "Where's number one?" Harriet asked as she spun her head in every direction, trying to get her eyes on the 109 she'd hit.

"Running home," Art replied.

"Good, then we'd better do the same!" After checking the instruments again, she turned west and started a steady climb towards Malta. Her heart was pounding so hard she felt sick, and she was dripping with sweat. If it wasn't for the tight grip she had on the stick and throttle, she'd have been shaking like a leaf. "How are you both. Bill?"

"I'm hit, but I'll live," Bill sighed.

"How bad?"

"I probably won't be representing the squadron at cross country any time soon."

"Will you get back?"

"Yes..."

"OK, we need to keep talking, and keep checking in. Art?"

"About the same."

"The same as what?"

"Marginally better than the pilot of that 109 we just splashed, but I reckon I'll be right."

"The two of you keep talking, while I get us back."

"How about you, skipper?" Art asked.

"Better than the pair of you by the sounds of it. Now do as you're told, and start talking." She checked her map and compass, and after turning right to get a fix on the oil tanker again to confirm her position, she set her course and headed home.

It was a nervous ride taking almost two hours, and Harriet's heart was in her mouth for almost every minute. The Maryland had taken a lot of punishment during the attack, both from the 109s and flak, and the rough handling that Harriet had exposed it to in her attempts to get away, and now it was struggling with keeping straight and level over the vast Ionian Sea. There wasn't another soul around, other than the three of them being rattled and shaken through the sky. Bill let out a groan every now and then, usually when the airframe bumped its way through some rough air that Harriet had to fight her way through, overcoming the Maryland's urge to use it as an excuse to fall out of the sky. Initially, she'd been relieved to get into action; flying at almost three hundred miles per hour at twenty thousand feet had allowed her to escape the baking heat of the island, but she was getting increasingly anxious in her desire to get back to the oven of Malta, a discomfort significantly more preferable than being lost in the sea. A moment of relief washed over her as Malta came over the horizon, sitting proudly in the hazy orange and red of the distant sunset they'd been chasing. Unfortunately, the relief ended as quickly as it arrived when the port engine started to cough and splutter. It had taken the force of the anti aircraft blast that had turned the wing into a sieve and peppered her cockpit with shrapnel, creating a mesh of holes that were allowing a healthy flow of air that had kept her cool. To her surprise, the engine hadn't faltered, but now it was showing signs of struggling. A grinding noise rattled through the airframe as the engine coughed again and let out a stream of black smoke. She immediately cut the fuel and shut it down. She instinctively knew there was no pushing it any further, and keeping it going would just lead to it overheating and catching fire, if it didn't seize anyway and cause a fuel leak further back in the system through a build up of pressure. The Maryland dipped to the left, and it took a fight to roll it level again. The one remaining engine had enough in it to keep them airborne, especially with the speed they were already holding, but manoeuvring was going to be limited, and she hoped and prayed they

70

wouldn't arrive in the middle of a raid. The surviving engine started to heat up as they approached Malta, making her even more nervous, if that was possible. She let the southerly wind push the Maryland towards the north of the island, all the time gradually losing height, until they were ready to turn in and head south for the runway. The southerly wind running over the starboard engine helped keep it cool, though it was still running much higher than was good for it.

"Bill, can you see if the landing gear is down?" she asked, having dropped it but not felt the reassuring clunk of it locking in place.

"Both wheels down..." Bill replied. His voice had lost the excitable confidence and charm she'd grown used to, instead sounding weak and tired, and making her all the more desperate to get the Maryland down.

"OK, hold on." She scanned the sky for raiders, not that she could do much if she saw anything; if she didn't land the Maryland in the next couple of minutes, she was convinced it was going to fall out of the sky. She crossed the threshold and saw the dark runway coming up to meet the wheels, then cut the throttles as they bumbled to the ground. The aeroplane rattled and shook as they rolled along the runway. Her eyes were wide as she searched for the shadows indicating the presence of deep craters, but to her relief, there were none. She applied the brakes and slowed, then throttled up the remaining engine one last time and dragged the hulking, shaking aeroplane to the dispersal and shut down. She reached up and pushed the canopy open, then released her harness and slumped for a moment while the airframe around her creaked and hissed, as if to let her know it was as relieved as she was to be back on the ground.

"The extra holes are for ventilation, yes?" The CO asked, as he looked down at her from above the cockpit.

"Something like that," Harriet replied, smiling with relief. "Bill and Art?"

"Are being removed as we speak." He offered his hand, which she took, and he pulled her to her feet. She grabbed her parachute and dragged it out of the cockpit with her, then stood on top of the

71

aeroplane and watched as ground crew clambered over it, checking the damage, removing the cameras, and with apparent trouble removing Bill and Art from their heavily ventilated compartments in the wrecked Maryland. "It's a miracle you got her back," the CO continued.

"Yes..." Harriet replied, clearly distracted. She jumped down onto the wing, then ran around to the long nose of the aeroplane, or what remained of it. The front, and much of the underside, had been blown clean away, and one of the medics was inside trying to release a groaning Bill so he could be passed down to the waiting ground crew. "Is he OK?" she asked. The medic looked down at her from the smoke and blood smeared compartment and nodded. She forced a smile, then headed to the back of the aeroplane where Art was being laid on a stretcher. He was pale and unconscious. She hadn't heard much from him in the last half hour of the flight. She'd asked him to watch their tail as she circled north to come in to land, and he acknowledged her, and gave updates that they were clear right up to them coming in to land. She hadn't imagined he would be in such a bad way. He had bloody bandages tied tight around each thigh, clearly having taken the brunt of the chasing 109's attack. She looked at the medic, who shrugged uncomfortably, before going back to work trying to stabilise his patient. Both of her crew were eventually loaded into the waiting ambulance and evacuated, leaving Harriet standing beside the CO, looking at the broken wreck of an aeroplane in front of her, and desperately hoping both of her crew would make it.

"If it makes you feel any better, that Italian oil tanker is now a lot more damp than it was when you last saw it..." the CO said. She looked up at him. The copper light of sunset reflected off his skin and twinkled in his eyes. He was a striking man, tall, lean, and likened by some to a Greek God. She wasn't sure about that part, not having seen that many Greek Gods, but he was undeniably handsome. His looks didn't take the sick feeling from her stomach, though, and neither did his words. "As soon as HQ received your message confirming the coordinates, they scrambled a flight of Bristol Beaufort torpedo bombers, and they found your tanker about twenty minutes ago."

"They got it?"

"They got it..." He smiled.

"I didn't want to let it go. I know how important it is we stop fuel getting to Rommel in North Africa."

"Vitally important. What you did today is going to save a lot of lives over there. Well done."

"Thanks... I'm not sure my crew will thank me..."

"They knew what they were getting into when they signed up. Besides, you got them home, didn't you?"

"I suppose..."

"Suppose nothing. They have a better chance of survival here than they would bobbing around the sea in a dinghy. They'd both have been dead by sunrise out there, if not sooner." The smile on her face was less forced when she listened to the logic in what he was saying, she'd done her best, and they were in the best hands.

"I wrecked the aeroplane, though."

"True... Still, I wouldn't worry too much about that. Smithy can work wonders with a Maryland. I'll bet you a Horse's Neck he has it flying within a week."

"I'll take that."

"Good. I'll give you a ride home, unless you want to hang around here any longer?"

"No, I think I'm done with aeroplanes for today."

"Funny, isn't it? How what starts off as a lazy day can end so differently," he said thoughtfully as they walked. It was almost exactly what Harriet had been thinking.

"I'm not sure funny is the word I'd use... Sir, I need to do something."

"Yes?"

"They both deserve to be decorated for what they did today. Even badly injured, they both stayed at their stations and made sure we got home."

"You can never guarantee these things, but we can give it our best shot. You write it up, and I'll endorse it tomorrow."

"Thanks, I'll get on it right away."

"They deserve it. Anyway, don't work on it tonight. Why don't you have a sleep in tomorrow, and I'll see you sometime after lunch?"

"If you're sure?"

"I can make it an order?"

"No need..." Her smile was becoming more genuine with every pace she took towards his waiting car."

Chapter 5

Something New

"Get enough sleep?" The CO asked as Harriet walked into his office. She'd been for lunch at the Mess, after spending the morning there writing the recommendations for Bill and Art's decorations. The meal consisted of hard biscuits and jam, with a cup of warm mystery fluid optimistically labelled as tea. It wasn't much, but it was still a little more than most of the population had to eat. The majority now ate at the Victory Kitchens, community kitchens that pooled ration coupons and cooked for everyone, making sure all had equal shares of food, and nobody had to go hungry if there was nothing to be bought to cook at home. It was July, and rations had been cut again. The Governor had given a date in August as when he expected the garrison to reach starvation, which he told the government back in London meant the inevitable surrender of Malta. They couldn't defend the island without ammunition and fuel, and they'd have nobody to defend it if everyone starved to death. It made for very desperate times. Everyone was a skeleton, and the weight that Harriet had managed to put on during her time away had come straight off again, leaving her stone coloured uniform looking baggy at best. She didn't mind, though; at least it covered her bones, which once again were quite prominent.

"Good. Got those recommendations for me?" Harriet nodded and handed him the two sheets of paper recommending the awards, which he quickly read before picking up his pen and signing both. "I'll get these up to HQ later this afternoon. First, though, I've got something for you."

"For me?"

"For you. Don't worry, it's not another medal; you've got far too many of those as it is. It starts to look ridiculous if you get too many." He shrugged casually as he stood, and Harriet couldn't help but smile at the row of medal ribbons on his own chest. "No, this is something much more practical, and I'll bet you a Horse's Neck it puts a smile on your face." He led her from his office and out to the dispersal, then they walked to a nearby heavily camouflaged aircraft pen. "There!

What do you think?" he asked, as Harriet stood beside him under the camouflage net.

"It's a Spitfire..." she gasped, her eyes wide open as she surveyed the big blue Spitfire parked in front of her. It looked glamorous in every way, if not slightly different from those she was used to flying, the colour excepted.

"Of course it's a Spitfire!" The CO boomed while rolling his eyes. "Specifically, she's a Photographic Reconnaissance Spitfire. Long range fuel tanks, cameras, observation blisters on the side of the canopy so the pilot can look out. It'll fly well above thirty thousand feet if needed, and it's stripped of everything conventional to save weight, so it can outfly most you may meet that have hostile intentions, which is quite fortunate, really, as it doesn't have any guns..."

"No guns?"

'No guns. They're heavy, as is the ammunition. By stripping them out, we give the pilot some more fuel and more speed."

"How's the pilot supposed to defend themselves if they're attacked?"

"By running..."

"I'm not sure I like the sound of that."

"Well, that's tough, really, because you're the pilot."

"Me?"

"You... You're a Spitfire ace, Harry. It makes no sense sticking you in an old bucket like a Maryland, not when we have a top of the range Spitfire sitting here wanting a driver. Besides, you can throw a regular Spitfire around like it's part of you; imagine what you can do in this thing?" He gave her a wink, and she felt herself smiling. "Unfortunately, we don't have enough fuel to let you take her up and get to know each other, but that shouldn't be an issue for somebody

76

of your pedigree. We do, however, need a convoy finding. If you're feeling up to it?"

"Why not?" She shrugged, then followed him back to his office for a briefing. "Where do they think the convoy they've lost is, exactly?"

"Naples."

"Naples, as in the huge harbour in Italy?"

"That's the one. You've been there before."

"I remember... It wasn't particularly welcoming."

"That's the Italians for you. No sense of humour. Anyway, there's talk of a large convoy being put together ready for a run south to North Africa. Thousands of troops, ammunition, food, the works. If we can find it, we can try and intercept it."

"Do we know where in Naples?"

"No idea. It could be Naples, could be Salerno or Pompeii. That's why we're sending you for a look around."

"I see..."

"We only need to know which port they're at, so no need to use your radio and draw unnecessary attention to yourself. Get up high and get us some good quality photos, then get yourself back home safely. No messing about."

"I never do mess about."

"You know what I mean." He gave her a wink, and they stepped inside to look at the maps and plan her route.

The blue PRU Spitfire leapt into the sky like nothing else, making Harriet smile as she pulled up the undercarriage, then turned west and headed across the island and out to sea. She'd flown lots of Spitfires, but none were quite like this one. The handling was incredible, she felt she only had to think where she wanted to go, and the Spitfire took her there, rolling and turning smoothly without even a hint of resistance. It climbed like a thoroughbred, too. The Rolls Royce Merlin engine was the latest off the production line, and with its two stage supercharger, it could drag the Spitfire higher and faster than any other before it. The increase in engine size also meant the Spitfire had to be stretched. The nose was longer, and the tail bigger, to manage the torque of the mighty four bladed propeller up front. It was still a Spitfire, but stood next to the mark fives being used by the combat squadrons; it was very different. Despite the need to behave and stay focused on her mission, once she was safely out to sea Harriet couldn't help having a bit of fun and putting her new steed through its paces with a few loops and rolls. The handling and performance were flawless. Gone were the days of failing carburettors; this was a dream. She levelled out again and climbed, the big smile stretching across her face, then she checked her watch and map, and turned north as she climbed towards the high wispy clouds above. As she passed twenty five thousand feet, Harriet turned her attention to the rear of her aeroplane. She checked to make sure that she wasn't leaving a nice long condensation trail behind her aeroplane, giving her position away to anyone watching. The changes in the air were frequent, and she could go from clean to trailing a bright white streak in an instant if she wasn't paying attention, so in addition to checking her map and compass, her instruments, and searching the sky for interceptors, she had the contrails to watch for, too. It was a busy job. She pushed a little higher, watching in her mirror all the time, until she was able to mix with the thin wispy cloud. The blue paint job on the Spitfire was almost perfect camouflage, and would hide her from prying eyes both above and below, but hiding in, or close to cloud gave an extra layer of invisibility. It also gave her a place to hide if she ran into an enemy patrol.

The cloud thickened as she approached the Italian coast. Fifty miles out, and she was flying through murk thick enough to make even the best cameras, which the Spitfire was equipped with, quite useless. There was no flying overhead at thirty thousand feet and taking a couple of snaps, which made Harriet sigh to herself. Nothing was ever easy. She circled a while, then started a shallow descent, unwinding through the clouds and keeping an eye on the altimeter. The cloud was thick, and lower than she'd expected. She was starting to wonder if she should turn back, knowing there was very little chance of getting anything remotely resembling a good photo, even if she could find the convoy. She shook her head. She hadn't turned back on a mission yet, and following the CO's lead she took pride in always bringing back the goods. She kept her descent steady, and took her time, watching the fuel tanks as she did, to make sure the extra flying wasn't going to give her any surprises. She was safe, though; the extra tanks gave the Spitfire plenty of range, so that was one thing at least that she didn't have to worry about. The cloud finally thinned a little below two thousand feet, enough for her to see the Italian coast beneath her and get her bearings. She wasn't far from the first dock, which she overflew while leaning right to look down through the large blister in the side of the canopy, a feature built in to give pilots the best view. There were no ships, at least nothing that could be described as a convoy. There were anti aircraft guns, though, and soon they were barking into life, and littering the pale grey sky with black fluffy puffs of smoke that quickly expanded into glowing balls of fire. The shooting was off, which she expected it would be, the CO had taught her to gauge when the artillery commander thought he had the height, then drop a couple of hundred feet to throw off his aim, knowing that by the time he'd readjusted, which they always did, the aeroplane would be gone and out of range, or could just climb a little again and throw off the aim again. Harriet hadn't been sure at first, but he took her on a sortie in a Maryland just to make his point, and despite being nervous, Harriet was amazed when he was proved to be absolutely right. It wasn't just one battery of anti aircraft guns, either. He demonstrated it in a few different places, laughing mischievously as he flew in a straight line and just jinked up and down at speed to throw off the gunners. He was full of all sorts of tips and tricks, despite his relatively young age, being only a few years older than Harriet, all contributing to him being an excellent pilot. He shared his knowledge with his pilots, and encouraged them to develop and improve their flying, and with Harriet, he'd found a perfect protege. Her instinctive flying and head for maths made it easy for her to put his tips and tricks into practice, and to make them work.

Flying on from the first dock, Harriet made her way up to Naples. Something was nagging at her saying that was where the convoy would be, and after overflying the other docks at speed, with no more than a brief glance below, she set course for the big one and prepared herself for the welcoming committee. The gunners would have already passed the message up the line, and she knew Naples would be waiting for her. The thickening cloud wasn't helping, and she knew he had to stay below it; and the further up the coast she went, the lower the cloud was, making her nice blue aeroplane stick out like a sore thumb as she darted in at almost one thousand feet, right into the thunderous chorus of anti aircraft guns of every size and calibre, all of which were doing their best to knock her out of the sky. The welcome confirmed her instinct, they were desperate to stop her getting through, and as she passed through the curtain of flak, she got the perfect view of a vast convoy of merchant ships and Italian warships, all lined up neatly. She dropped lower to avoid the heavier guns, then circled the harbour to get herself into position to use the oblique camera on the side of the Spitfire. She raced in straight and fast, with no room to dive or climb, and ran her camera as she passed the entire convoy. Then she made another pass to make sure she hadn't missed any ships, most of which were now shooting at her. The merchant ships were low in the water, but not too low. By her estimation, they were maybe half filled. Her adrenaline was flowing, but it was different to combat. If anyone got her, it would likely be luck on their part, and she knew enough from experience that if they were on target, she wouldn't know much about it anyway. No fighting to escape the cockpit, no dodging bullets; she was confident she'd be blown out of the sky if and when it came. Once satisfied she'd got what she needed, she pulled up into the clouds and out of sight, not that her hiding made the gunners any less keen on shooting her down. They continued firing, and the clouds flashed ominously. She pulled her stick left and turned steeply, leaving the trail of flashing explosions behind her as she climbed higher and higher, pushing the engine to the max as she raced to get out of town before company arrived, which she knew was inevitable. She slipped out of the cloud and into the clear blue sky at thirty thousand feet and checked her compass and watch, then set course for home. She knew that in all likelihood, any fighters sent up to intercept her would come from ahead, launched from southern Italy, or Sicily, as anything behind her would be unlikely to catch her; so she sat just above the cloud and watched the horizon like a hawk, while all the time checking her tail for signs of the deadly white contrail.

"Hello, you..." she said, as she saw an arrow of four contrails snaking towards her from eleven o'clock. She'd dropped to twenty thousand feet after leaving the thickest cloud behind, to try and stay close to the light wispy cloud and try to hide. The contrails suggested she had company. A section of four 109s, no doubt, vectored to meet her on her return journey, and stop her getting her valuable photos home. Her stomach squeezed. Sicily was below, and she had about ninety miles to safety, but between her and home were four 109s, and she didn't have any guns. She held her course, watching them keenly all the time as they pointed in her direction. She had an idea, but for it to stand a chance of working, she needed the four to stay together, which they obligingly did as they started their dive on her. She pushed the throttle through the gate as she waited, forcing the engine to the maximum, and getting as much speed as she could out of the big engine, not that the airframe gave anything away. The Spitfire simply absorbed the increase without a rattle or creak. Once she was sure the 109s were committed and just coming into range, she pulled left to face them, then pushed the nose down hard. They had no chance of getting in a half accurate shot, and whizzed a long way past her tail as they turned to try and get on her, but it was too late. The mighty Spitfire was dropping like a stone, and even the much feared 109's dive couldn't get them close. They were left long in her wake as she dived across Sicily, and then Gozo, laughing and smiling to herself as she left them standing. She thought for a moment of the old Japanese samurai she'd met in Hawaii. He'd called her kitsune, a cunning mythical fox, and she smiled even more as she imagined herself like a fox giving slip to the hunt, then backed off the power as she crossed the Malta coast at just two thousand feet, and did all she could to scrub off the speed as she approached her airfield at Luqa. She had a quick check in her mirror to make sure the 109s hadn't somehow caught up with her, and after scanning the horizon for trouble, she dropped the undercarriage as she slipped in to line up with the runway, then kissed it lightly with a perfect landing. She couldn't help but smile, her big blue Spitfire was by far the best thing she'd ever flown, and she couldn't wait to jump out and thank the CO.

The pace and intensity increased over the next few days, on both sides of the fight. The German and Italian raids were stepped up, and the reconnaissance pilots, Harriet included, were sent up, again and again, to hunt for convoys, check airfields for transports, and search for gliders. With the CO's permission, Harriet had an orange fox head painted on the cowling of her Spitfire, and was assigned the callsign 'Vixen'. It made her smile and gave her confidence on her missions, thinking of herself as the sly sky fox, outwitting the overwhelming odds of the chasing pack. Despite the best efforts of everyone in Malta, the numerous heavy raids were wreaking havoc on the island, day and night. Casualties and damage were mounting significantly, and those at the top were quite sure that this was the last big push to knock the island out of the war. Supplies were virtually gone, the general population and the military defenders were starving, and the anti aircraft artillery were down to just six rounds of ammunition per day. It would soon be either invasion or starvation that finished them, and nobody was sure which it would be. While the island was still in the fight, though, it was vital that it continued to be a thorn in the side of the enemy convoys. Even if the island was going to fall, there was still a battle raging in North Africa, and every troop ship or oil tanker that was sent to the bottom of the Mediterranean was time bought for the defending Allied forces. Unfortunately, the same equation was being played by the German high command, who'd ravaged every convoy that had come close to Malta, determined to starve the island into such a weakened state that surrender, or a weakly resisted invasion, would take the island out of the war for good. Allowing the enemy convoys to flood North Africa with men, machines, and fuel. Essentially, it was a race to see who could break the opposition's convoys first, and the combined might of the German and Italian air fleets, along with their surface ships and submarines, were winning.

Harriet did her work to the best of her ability. She found a couple of convoys, and worked with a raid of bombers to photograph the damage after they'd done their work sinking some of the ships. She also spent a lot of time photographing the Sicilian and Italian coasts, bringing back images of damage, ships, stockpiles, and anything else that could influence the war. If she found something particularly appealing, which she almost always did, the AOC would task bombers based on Malta to raid on the same night, often destroying supplies vital to the war effort in North Africa before they even got the chance to be loaded onto the ships. The other photographic reconnaissance pilots were just as busy, but unlike Harriet, who'd had a number of lucky escapes from enemy fighters or flak, using her big blue Spitfire's speed and agility to outrun danger at every opportunity, many of them had been killed or injured. The losses were unsustainable. Highly skilled photographic reconnaissance pilots were hard to find, though not as hard as finding volunteers from combat squadrons to replace the dead and wounded in flying unarmed aeroplanes over enemy territory.

"What's the job this morning, Sir?" Harriet asked, as the CO entered the dispersal office. It was dark out, as it always was when she arrived for early duty. She tried to get there ahead of time so she could enjoy the relative coolness before the baking heat of daylight made thinking difficult, and so she could get her hands on the first serving of tea of the day, before the tea leaves were washed through too many more times and lost what little taste they had.

"Nothing, for you at least," he replied, as he strolled across the room with his hands in his dressing gown pockets. He was about the only military person on the island who could dress any way he liked. Standards had relaxed as the siege intensified, but his had never been high. Cricket jumpers and shorts usually, occasionally pyjama bottoms, boots, and a service shirt, and recently a thin knee length dressing gown had made an appearance. Nobody tended to mind, though, probably because he got the results they needed.

"Sir?" she frowned as she stood.

"I've just been out to have a chat with the ground crew. A chunk of German shrapnel got a little too close for comfort when I was on my way home from Italy last night, and they haven't yet been able to make the repairs needed, so I'm going to have to take your Spitfire when I go up this morning."

"But..."

"Day off for you, Harry. You haven't had one for a while, so it'll be good to kick back and take it easy. May even be worth going up to the hospital and visiting your crew. The AOC let me know yesterday that they've both been gazetted for the Distinguished Flying Medal, on your recommendation, of course. Stitching the medal ribbons on their shirts will give them something to do while they recover." He gave her a wink, and she couldn't help but smile. "Get yourself back here for sunset, though. There's something I need you for."

"Yes, Sir. Safe flying." She felt her smile broadening, and lighting up her face as she left the dispersal office; and it didn't go away for the entire journey back to Floriana on the rickety, creaky, and incredibly uncomfortable solid tyre bicycle she'd managed to lay her hands on shortly after arriving back in Malta. Or, more appropriately, the bicycle that Robbie had laid her hands on, and given to Harriet on the understanding she wasn't to ask where it came from, as with many of Robbie's acquisitions. With petrol in such short supply, it was the best transport that Harriet could hope for, despite the discomfort as it shook her unpadded and protruding bones over the uneven and potholed ground, a journey made all the more terrifying at night.

Back at the apartment she shared with Robbie, she quietly piled her kit in the corner, then made tea from the saved tea leaves she'd bought from Fortnum's. They'd been used lots of times already, but they kept going, and after a morning's use, they were dried out again for the following day, and mixed with a sprinkle of fresh tea they'd rationed. It had been Cas' idea. Something he'd learned in the trenches in the last war, and it was paying off. Despite being wrung out a hundred times, their tea was still better than the so called fresh tea that was supplied by the cooks, which on a good day looked and tasted like weak dishwater.

"What are you doing home?" Robbie asked sleepily, as Harriet sat beside her on the bed and offered her the freshly made tea.

"I was stood down for the day," Harriet replied softly, as the first light of dawn started to brighten the room.

"They've had enough of you already?"

"Something like that..." She smiled, as Robbie took the cup and sipped at the lukewarm tea.

"What are you going to do instead?"

"I was going to visit the hospital to see Bill and Art, maybe. I haven't seen them since they were injured."

"I can take you up there, if you like?"

"You've got enough to do. It's OK, I'll go on my bike."

"I have a few bits and pieces to do, but if you don't mind hanging around a bit, I thought maybe we could head down to St Peter's for a swim..." Robbie shrugged enquiringly, and Harriet nodded excitedly.

"I'll leave you to wake up." Harriet stood and left, and headed up to the roof, one of her favourite places since returning to the island, where she relaxed on a lounger and watched the sunrise. She didn't have long to wait for the morning chorus. As the eastern sky lit up, a large German raid came in and hit the island's airfields. Spitfires were up waiting for them, dropping out of the darkness and intercepting the bombers and fighters, while air raid sirens echoed around Floriana, and the day got underway much the same as it usually did.

"You know we should be in the basement shelter," Robbie said as she took a seat beside Harriet.

"Yeah..." Harriet smiled. "I don't like it down there. If I'm going to get it, I want to see it coming."

"Me either. Those places are like tombs. I'd rather daylight be the last thing I see."

Fortunately, the raids that got through were kept to the airfields, it was clearly their turn, and Floriana, Valletta, and the Grand Harbour would have to wait until later for theirs. When the sun had risen, and the tea leaves had been laid out to dry, they headed off in Robbie's truck for the first visit of their day, the war rooms in the hot, humid, and smelly tunnels. Harriet turned her nose up at the smell as she made her way along the narrow damp corridors. Robbie had to check in with the AOC and a few other people, so Harriet decided to call in and see Cas while she was there. She always made an effort to say hello when she was visiting, and he was always happy to see her; despite them meeting for a drink most evenings they weren't working, which was two or three times a week. He was in the operations room, which appeared more hectic than usual following the morning raid.

"What are you doing here?" he asked, making her roll her eyes in reply. "What?" He shrugged in mock ignorance.

"You always say that," Harriet replied.

"Because I always want to know."

"You could just say hello."

"Hello!" he smirked knowingly.

"Shut up!"

"You said..."

"I don't know why I bother... Anyway, I was here, so I thought I'd say hello."

"I'm happy you did." He smirked warmly, his eyes assuring her he was being genuine, and for once, not teasing her. "I thought you were on duty this morning."

"I was, but the boss' aeroplane is out of action, so he took mine."

"Oh well, I've just seen him off on the map." He pointed to the solitary marker heading in the direction she knew to be Taranto harbour in Italy. "Day off instead?"

"Yes... Though I probably can't make it for a drink this evening, he's asked me to meet him at the airfield around sunset. He's got a job for me, apparently."

"We can push it back if you like? Meet later? If you aren't too tired from flying, I mean?"

"No, I'd like that." Her face lit up with a big smile. She watched as he lit a miserable looking navy issue cigarette that looked like it had seen better days.

"Do you really have to smoke those?" she asked. "They smell revolting, and I can't imagine they're doing you much good."

"They're better than the other smells down here," he laughed. "You'd be smoking as much as the rest of us if you worked down here full time, I can assure you."

"No thanks... I'll stick with my Spitfire."

"Nice for some."

"Oh yes, flying over enemy lines all alone and without any guns is thrilling."

"I'll swap you."

"You're alright."

"So, what else do you have on today? I'm assuming visiting us in the dungeons isn't the highlight of your trip?"

"Swimming," she said with a smirk.

"Swimming?" His eyebrow raised, and he looked a little hurt.

"Yep. Robbie and me are going to have a splash about in the cool refreshing Mediterranean."

"I'm not sure I like you anymore..."

"Ready?" Robbie asked, as she joined them overlooking the map board of Malta and Sicily in the operations room below, which was busy with plotters nudging the few markers of active aircraft around, while others cleaned and tidied the map board.

"Do you watch my aeroplane on the board when I'm flying?" Harriet asked Cas. He smiled in reply, then looked down at the map, then back at her.

"Hello?" Robbie asked.

"Yes!" Harriet replied. "Let's go swim in the nice cool water, and leave Cas to enjoy smoking in his oven. See you later." She smirked, then she and Robbie made their way out of the tunnels, and out into the dusty, smoke tinged fresh air of Valletta, which in comparison to the tunnels was like a mountain breeze. The freshness of the air improved as they got underway, and sped through the ruins and out into the countryside, and then to the hospital where Harriet was dropped off to visit, while Robbie went about her business. The visit went as well as could be hoped. The doctor and a couple of the nurses recognised her from her own stay when she'd been shot down the last time she was in Malta. They were very kind in saying how well she looked compared to when they'd last seen her, and complimenting her flying, which they'd followed closely. Art had struggled since his arrival, apparently, and progressively deteriorated thanks to an infection that had seen him unconscious for the last twenty four hours. He looked hot when she visited, and the volunteer nurses bathed him with cool, wet towels almost constantly to try and keep his temperature down. Harriet talked to him a while, and told him about his medal, despite being unsure as to whether he'd hear her in his near delirious state. She hoped it would help. Bill was much better. He was sitting up in bed and talking to the nurses when she arrived; he was very happy to see Harriet. He was even happier to hear of his medal, more than Harriet expected. She thought of her own standoffish approach to medals, and how she'd never been particularly impressed by them, but Bill's reaction made her stop and think. He couldn't be more proud he'd won the DFM, and couldn't wait to tell his wife and children in a letter he intended to write as soon as her visit ended. He assured her they'd be equally as proud, and he thanked her profusely for recommending him, despite her saying it was all his doing, and she was just the conduit in recognising what he'd done. His pride and excitement were infectious, and after saying goodbye, she found herself smiling warmly, and thinking even more about her own medals. She was proud of them; of course she was; she just didn't like the fuss, or the fake hanging on of others who just wanted to be around somebody with a medal. She remembered why she'd been given each, and the hell she'd been through each time. None had been awarded just for being there. She'd almost died, several times, every time. There were also many thousands of brave souls who never received a thing, most of whom she was quite sure were much more daring and more gallant than she could ever be. She argued around and around in her head as she waited outside the hospital for Robbie. Medals were going to be a lifelong conflict for her. The thoughts made her think and argue with herself, and question herself, and as Robbie's truck rounded the corner, she found herself asking why she was so keen to write up Bill and Art for medals, and why it was so important to her to recognise what they'd done, yet it wasn't important to recognise her own achievements.

Just as they'd done the last time in Malta, Robbie parked her truck at the guard post, and paid the Maltese soldier with a pack of black market cigarettes that had found their way off a Royal Navy submarine and into her possession, somehow, and in return, the soldier assured her they wouldn't be disturbed. They passed through the unofficial gap in the barbed wire defences that had been strengthened over the previous year in response to the invasion threat, and walked along the winding narrow sand tracks until they reached the large sun baked stones they'd previously sunbathed on. They were baking hot under the July sun, so hot that Harriet could feel the heat through her plimsolls. They laid down the thick army blankets Robbie had brought, then threw down their bags and got ready to swim. Shyness was the last thing on Harriet's mind as she unfastened her belt and her shorts fell to the ground, before unbuttoning her shirt and pulling it off, feeling the heat of the sun directly on her skin. She was more concerned about Robbie, who was athletic and curvy when they first met, but thanks to the strict rationing over the previous year, she was now as emaciated as everyone else on the island. Harriet watched her undress. They lived together, they even shared the only bed in the apartment, and they were used to seeing each other in various states of undress, but this was different. Out in the daylight and in the brightness of the sun, Harriet could fully appreciate just how much the rationing had taken its toll. Robbie's tan helped, but she was still painfully thin. Her ribs and collar bones protruded, and despite hanging on to some of her curves, she looked fragile. Harriet then found herself looking down at her own body. She'd had time in

England, and an excess of good food in America, but it had all come off again quickly, and she was in no better condition than Robbie. The powers that be tried to find more food for pilots, knowing they were the only ones facing the enemy day after day in battle and that they needed to keep up their energy, but even then, they didn't get much more. She felt guilty as she thought of the food she'd turned down in America, and how she'd chosen fruit over pancakes, after feeling stuffed and bored of good food, and here they were living on recycled tea leaves, hard biscuits, and tinned corned beef that was so badly melted it poured out of the tin, mixed with the briny fat in a foul tasting soup.

They swam for what felt like an age. The water was ice cold at first, but after a few moments of acclimatisation, it felt warm on the skin, almost the perfect temperature, and a welcome escape from the baking sun. It was bliss, a brief escape from the war; and using the half bar of soap, the remains of what she'd brought from England, she scrubbed the sweat, dirt, dust, and smoke out of her hair and pores, before handing it to Robbie while she dived deep to rinse herself. They swam and sunbathed for hours, talking and relaxing and discussing the war, and America. Neither even flinched when air raid sirens sounded in the distance, or when bombs were dropped in the next bay, or even when an Italian bomber raced overhead at low level with a pair of Spitfires chasing hard and blasting away at it. Harriet smirked as she watched, and rolled her eyes at the pilots and their apparent inability to get a shot on target. She shouted advice noisily as the bomber twisted and turned, much more than it should have been able to, as the Spitfires blasted and blasted without even getting close. She knew she couldn't be heard, but she couldn't resist, and soon Robbie had joined in cheering and jeering. Then, from nowhere, a Hurricane cast a shadow over them as it shot out over their heads and put a short burst into the bomber, before pulling up and over as the bomber's engine coughed out a cloud of smoke and sparks. They cheered loudly, then watched in silence as the bomber disappeared out of sight, heading inland and descending quickly, followed by the lone Hurricane. The Spitfires eventually followed, leaving them in silence. They swam again, and drank tepid water from the bottle they'd brought, and had a wholesome lunch of a hard biscuit each, then sunbathed and swam the afternoon away, before finally, and reluctantly, dressing and heading back to the reality of the war.

Chapter 6

Into the Night

"Thanks for the ride, but you really didn't need to," Harriet said, as Robbie stopped the truck by the dispersal hut. It was just before sunset, and despite Harriet's protests, Robbie had insisted on taking her to the airfield to meet the CO.

"I know, but I needed to be here anyway, so it made sense," Robbie replied with a casual shrug.

"Why do you need to be here?"

"Ah, Kitty, you made it!" the CO said, as he walked out of the dispersal hut to meet them.

"You're not the only one with orders..." Robbie gave Harriet a wink and grabbed a large kitbag from her truck, before walking over to meet the CO, much to Harriet's confusion.

"Got it?" he asked.

"There's a lot... I'm not sure how you're going to fit it all in." She handed him the kit bag, which he playfully almost dropped to suggest how heavy it was.

"Oh, I'm sure that won't be a problem. I'll make sure it pays."

"I don't doubt it," Robbie smirked, and the CO's eyes twinkled.

"Got your flying kit with you?" the CO asked Harriet. She nodded and raised her bag. "Good. We'd better get off. I don't suppose you want to give us a ride, Kitty?"

"Sure, hop in..."

"I feel like I'm missing something..." Harriet frowned, as she followed and climbed back into the truck. The CO gave directions, and Robbie drove them down one of the many winding taxiways that had been

92

built to allow aeroplanes to be parked away from the main airfield, keeping them safer from the bombing raids, and making them easier to hide in the camouflaged pens. Luqa had a few, but it was nothing like Takali, which had miles of taxiways, including a particularly long one called the Safi Strip, which stretched almost to Hal Far airfield, and had Spitfires hidden in pens left and right. The CO stopped them by a darkened patch hidden under a large camouflage net. Smithy was there to meet them, and after saying their goodbyes, the CO had them wait outside and watch as Robbie had driven out of sight.

"All ready?" the CO asked Smithy.

"Yes, Sir. We've done all we can to check it on the ground, so as long as it works in the air, you're good to go."

"Guns?"

"Front and rear. Hopefully, you won't need them."

"Fingers crossed. Right, come on, Harry. Let's get busy. Smithy, you and the boys get that camouflage net out of the way; we need to shift quickly."

"Sir!"

"And Smithy, not a word. Understood?"

"Not a word about what, Sir?"

"Good man!" The CO gave Harriet the nod, and led her into the large pen, where she was gobsmacked to see a Wellington Bomber waiting in the darkness.

"It's a Wellington..." Harriet gasped.

"Yes, I know," the CO replied. "I'm the one that had it built."

"Excuse me?"

"Not now, Harry. We need to get her in the air, and quick. I'll explain on the way." He led her to the hatch, then climbed the ladder. She watched him in amazement, as a small team of ground crew pulled the camouflage nets away and stowed them, showing the Wellington in all its glory. Even in the fading light, she could see that it had seen better days, but it seemed intact, or as intact as she would know, having only flown in the back of one.

"You know I can't fly one of these?" she asked, as she followed him up the ladder and into the dark interior.

"Up here," he called from the cockpit. Harriet climbed up beside him, still barely believing what was happening. "Fortunately, you don't need to fly it," he continued, as he sat in the pilot's seat and flicked switches confidently. "Though you could, if you needed to, so you'd better watch the start procedures just in case..." Harriet nodded and watched, then, when given the nod, pulled down the flight engineer's seat and got comfortable.

"OK..."

"As soon as we're ready to roll, you'd better get yourself back to the rear turret and watch our tail. I'll chat with you over the intercom." She nodded as he started one engine and then the other, then checked the gauges before waving the chocks away and rolling the mighty bomber forward. He gave Smithy the thumbs up, then taxied quickly to the runway while doing his last checks, and giving Harriet the nod. She acknowledged his instructions, and climbed down into the dark belly of the beast, moving as quickly as she could to the rear turret, which she climbed into after stowing her parachute, then got as comfortable as she could and plugged into the intercom and oxygen. She held tight as the throttles opened, and they lurched forward, swinging left and right down the runway as they went. His ground handling skills hadn't changed. As soon as the bomber was at speed, he pulled back on the stick and climbed into the darkening sky. The undercarriage was quickly retracted, and keeping as low as he dared on the failing light, he turned, then pushed the bomber south, while Harriet watched Malta race past below her, and searched the darkening skies for black dots that would suggest a German fighter sweep.

The handling felt smooth once they were in the air, and the Wellington responded instantly to the CO's gentle adjustments. Harriet smiled to herself, it felt strange to be travelling backwards and looking where they'd just been, and she hoped she'd be able to spot enemy fighters as well as she could when driving. She glanced around for a moment as they crossed the coast to the south of the island, and passed over the natural pool in the Mediterranean where she'd spent her day swimming. She couldn't help but smile again. She'd enjoyed her day. In fact, as she half daydreamed, she came to the conclusion that despite the deprivation and the risk, Malta wasn't all that bad the second time around. She'd lost some friends among the photographic reconnaissance pilots, but they weren't that close; they didn't have time to be. PR pilots didn't mix the same as combat pilots. They didn't fly together, didn't work together, they were all individuals with their own individual missions, and they didn't get to spend that much time in each other's company. They knew each other enough to be sad when a face didn't come back, but mostly because they knew the same fate wasn't that far away for themselves. Either killed outright, burned alive, or dying of thirst in a rubber dinghy in the Mediterranean. "She's a bit of a Doctor Frankenstein's monster," the CO said over the intercom as they cruised just above the wave tops, breaking into Harriet's thoughts. She looked down as he talked; his death defying low flying was only made possible by the last light of day catching the white tips of the waves, and she was thankful his handling in the air was better than that on the ground. A flinch and twitch could see them getting very wet, very quick, but she had nothing but confidence in his flying, anyone that flew with him felt safe.

"Excuse me?" she replied, daydreams broken and trying to confirm to herself that she'd heard something about Frankenstein.

"The Wellington. We cannibalised all the spare parts we found from other Wellingtons shot down and bombed since the war started, then used them to put some life into this old girl... The question of why, which I know you're thinking, is that we needed her for sorties like this. Also, nobody knows we have her, which is a bonus."

"Why would we need an aeroplane nobody knows about for a reconnaissance mission?"

"Who said we're on a reconnaissance mission?"

"Aren't we?"

"No..."

"Then what are we on?"

"A mercy mission."

"A what?"

"You'll see. We need to keep low a while longer, so we're not seen on radar, then we'll get up high and comfortable for the rest of the trip to Cairo."

"Cairo?" Harriet repeated. Her eyes opened wide, and her heart immediately pounded hard.

"Cairo," he replied. "Right, you'd better keep an eye out for trouble. We're a sitting duck in this thing, it's slow and cumbersome, but it'll take a lot of punishment. Shout if you see anything, but don't shoot unless you have to, and if you have to, make sure it's not one of ours you're shooting at!"

"Why would it be one of ours?"

"Because a twin engine aeroplane has just flown across the south of Malta and across the coast. An aeroplane nobody knows exists, which means the chances of it being an enemy are heightened significantly. In the minds of those who'll be watching, at least... Anyway, keep your eyes open. I'll give you a shout if I see anything, and you do the same."

"Wilco..." she replied, trying to keep the nerves out of her voice, as she looked out over the sea as the aeroplane started to climb. She checked the guns over, then watched and waited, feeling the temperature drop as they climbed into the now ink blue sky, lit with silver moonlight which danced on the water below. Cairo, she thought. She'd never been, and she had no idea why she was going, but the CO had looked after her since the day she'd arrived, and she trusted that whatever he was up to this time would turn out for the best. Assuming they weren't shot down by their own side before they got there.

The journey was thankfully uneventful, and the only thing Harriet saw, other than the moon and sea, was what she was positive was a surfaced submarine. She reported it to the CO, who acknowledged it, but without anything other than a couple of machine guns to cause trouble with, he decided it was best left alone. Especially as diving on it could have encouraged the captain to send out a report which, if it was a German or Italian submarine, would invite their night fighters to come up from the many airfields along the North African coast, which would make the journey much less comfortable. Instead, they took note of its position and left it alone. A little later, they crossed the Egyptian coast and passed over the twinkling lights of Alexandria, then headed inland to Cairo, where they landed at a well maintained runway, the likes of which Harriet hadn't seen since leaving America.

"Welcome to Cairo," the CO said as they stepped out onto the tarmac, greeted by the heat of the Egyptian night, which was a stark contrast to the coolness of altitude.

"Thank you..." Harriet replied, as she looked around in astonishment at the lights in every building and on every vehicle, something she struggled to accept at first, after the strict blackout in Malta. She followed him to the duty office, where he checked the Wellington in, and made a couple of phone calls, one to report the submarine they'd seen off the coast, and the other almost whispered, making it impossible for Harriet to hear.

"Right, we've got a few hours to kill. Shall we go and get a drink in the Mess?" he asked. He had a mischievous twinkle in his eye as he gave her an excitable smile.

"A drink?"

"We're in Cairo! It'd be rude not to. Besides, the boys need time to load the Wellington, and they don't need us looking over their shoulders and making them nervous. Come on." He led her out into the night, and they walked along the road, heading away from the airfield.

"Load the Wellington with what?" Harriet asked as they walked.

"Cameras, film, fuel, spares, even a few Rolls Royce Merlin engines. All the stuff we need to keep our PR aircraft flying. For a few more weeks, at least."

"Oh..." Harriet frowned. "Why did we need to come in a Wellington for that?"

"Because it wouldn't all fit in a Spitfire." He laughed, clearly amusing himself with his answer, and making Harriet roll her eyes.

"I meant instead of it being sent on a ship..."

"It was..." His laugh faded. "The ship carrying our supplies was sunk in the last convoy attempt. The only way we could keep flying was to come and collect what we needed."

"I see..." Her heart sank as she thought of yet another ship going down while trying to get desperately needed supplies to Malta. She sat in silence as her mind went back to her crossing to New York, when the boat she was on passed through the remains of a recently attacked convoy. She could still see the wreckage floating past, and the bodies, and her stomach turned as she remembered how distressing it was to think that there would be survivors in the water, and being told they couldn't stop to pick them up, through fear of being sunk themselves. She'd been sick with fear the entire trip.

"Best not to dwell on it," he said, instinctively knowing what she was thinking, and making her smile a little. "There's always some good to be found."

"What good?"

"We're in Cairo!" His excitable and positive outlook was back, and she couldn't help but feel lifted by his presence and confidence. He lit a cigarette and blew smoke into the clear night sky. He had a confidence about him that was reassuring, and while he had a presence, he never swaggered, not like quite a few of the fighter pilots she'd met in her time with the RAF. His confidence was needed when they got to the Mess. There were frowns at the worn and threadbare uniforms they both presented in, long past their best from repeated wear and limited laundry facilities. Harriet had washed hers that day in the Mediterranean while swimming, which left salt stains on top of the sweat stains she hadn't been able to scrub out. The CO simply charmed them in, with a few winks and nods to the Mess manager about the secret mission they were on, which seemed to do enough to intrigue and encourage lenience, and led to them being presented with a selection of baklava with their drinks. The small Egyptian pastries, scattered with pistachio and dried fruits, had been left over from earlier in the day, and it was suggested quietly that if they wanted any more, there were plenty left in the back.

"This tastes incredible," Harriet said after biting into the diamond shaped treat, and feeling the many thin, syrup drizzled layers of pastry start to melt in her mouth. She'd never had baklava before, but after one bite, she knew she'd want more. Much more.

"The good of Cairo," the CO said with a wink, then popped the remains of the baklava he'd started into his mouth, and washed it down with a long cold gin, garnished with lime. "Better make sure we eat them all, or they'll think us rude and not offer again." Harriet nodded hungrily, and took another from the plate. The rarity of eating sweet pastries was an opportunity she couldn't miss, not after months of corned beef melted in its own fat, and biscuits left over from the last war, which were hard enough to build a bomb shelter from.

They talked while they ate and drank, mostly about the war, and after a few more glasses of tonic, the CO charmed the Mess manager further, and asked if they might have some baklava to take with them on their next secret mission. The nods and winks returned, and as they left, they were each presented with a neatly wrapped package of wax paper tied with string. The CO rummaged in the pocket of his shorts and pulled out a small, black, Germanic looking metal cross. Harriet had seen them before on the uniforms of the German pilots she'd met. They were referred to as the Iron Cross by the British, medals awarded for bravery. He pushed it into the Mess manager's hand, and gave him a wink. "We took it from a German we shot down just today." The Mess manager looked amazed, and shook the CO's hand gratefully, then wished them both a safe journey.

"Found it near a crashed German bomber a few weeks ago," the CO whispered to Harriet with a shrug as they left the Mess. She found herself smirking, something that continued back to their waiting Wellington, which had been stuffed with supplies by the efficient ground crew, making it a tight squeeze for Harriet to make her way into her rear gun turret, ready for the trip home. Once in, though, she made herself comfortable and prepared herself for the journey back to Malta. She was sad to leave, but very excited to get back and share the package of baklava with Cas and Robbie. She checked her guns, hoping she wouldn't need them, but wanting to make sure she could at least try and defend the Wellington if they were attacked, though the cargo of fuel, oil, and all kinds of dangerous and flammable supplies meant that they would likely go up in flames long, long before she got a shot on target if they were jumped by fighters. She put that particular thought out of her mind as soon as the engines roared into life, one at a time, and the airframe started to vibrate reassuringly. They were quickly taxiing to the runway, and after the final power checks, they were slaloming left and right in the CO's familiar yet terrifying take off routine, something which had Harriet closing her eyes tight, and just hoping he'd hurry up and get them off the ground. Suddenly, the noise changed, then dulled, and the speed noticeably dropped off. She opened her eyes and looked out of the turret to watch as they slowed to a halt. "Bugger!" the CO said over the intercom. "Engine failure," he added, before Harriet had the chance to ask what the problem was. "We'd better get back to the dispersal..." With just the port engine running and whining, he encouraged the creaking Wellington back to the dispersal point they'd only just left, then shut down. Harriet extracted herself and joined him outside, where he was already talking to the Flight Sergeant from the ground crew. "Better grab your stuff," he said, as he looked back at her with a frown. "Looks like we're staying the night."

"Is it that bad?" Harriet asked.

"Well, it's not good. The Chief here is going to get to work on it tonight; fingers crossed it's nothing too disruptive. Either way, I doubt we'll be going anywhere until tomorrow evening at the earliest, so we'd better get ourselves somewhere to sleep." She nodded; feeling a little conflicted, she joined him in heading back to the dispersal office to arrange transport. She felt like she had a job to do, but she really didn't mind a few more hours away from Malta, and the baklava would keep. She paused for a moment. The baklava. She'd left it in the turret. She thought of going back for it, then decided it would be safer where it was. She knew all too well that she'd finish the lot if she were to keep it with her for the next twenty four hours, and she really did want to share it.

Back in the Mess, the manager had kindly arranged for two rooms to be made up for his unexpected guests. Most of the officers who were based in Cairo tended to have accommodation in the city, and away from the airfield, meaning that the rooms in the Mess could be used by those transitioning through, or only there for a brief stay and didn't have time to find accommodation elsewhere. It had been fortunate for Harriet, as she'd initially imagined having to sit in the dispersal office and wait for the Wellington to be fixed. Rooms were an unexpected luxury, and the room she was given was a luxury beyond that. The bed had been made up with crisp white sheets made of finest Egyptian cotton, and there were fresh, soft, fluffy towels hanging in the bathroom, which had a large porcelain bath and running hot water. After visiting the deserted Mess bar, where she was given more baklava and a large Horse's Neck, in addition to an overnight bag that had been kindly donated, she retired to her room, filled the bath, and slipped into the hot water. Her skin tingled with the heat, but there was no feeling like it. The overnight bag was yet another luxury that made her feel the engine failure was a blessing from above. Rose petals for the bath, scented soap, a soft cotton face cloth, razor and blades, even a toothbrush and a small tub of mint tooth powder. Once she'd acclimatised to the heat of the water, she scrubbed herself thoroughly. The water was filthy, despite her bath in the Mediterranean earlier that day, but for the first time in months, her hair felt properly clean, and her pores could breathe. Despite the water turning grey with dirt, thanks to the roses, it still smelled good. She leant back and relaxed, and sipped on the fresh tasting Horse's Neck, savouring the competing tastes of fine French cognac and fresh ginger, which cleansed her palate in such a way that the baklava she snacked on tasted even better.

After the long and relaxing bath had almost sent her to sleep, Harriet climbed out of the grimy water, dried herself off, and wrapped herself in one of the very long and very soft bath sheets so she could hang her uniform on a hanger and leave it outside on the door handle, in the hope that the Mess manager's promise of taking care of the laundry quickly would be kept. Then, after finishing her drink, she slipped into bed. It was the first time a bed had felt so comfortable or clean since England, and it was impossible for her to stay awake.

The next morning, in the most unusual alarm call Harriet had ever experienced, she was woken by the charming and quite beautifully sung call to prayer. The local population were mostly of the Islamic faith, and each morning they were called to prayer at sunrise. It was confusing at first, hearing a voice singing in the distance, but it felt strangely reassuring for reasons she couldn't fathom. After dragging herself from her bed, she wrapped herself in the towel, then checked the door handle outside the room. Her uniform had been washed and pressed, and was the smartest she'd seen it for a while. Even her plimsolls had been scrubbed, and while they'd never be white again, most of the worst oil stains had been cleared, and they were generally a uniform soft beige colour. She cleaned up, brushed her teeth, and dressed, then packed the remaining baklava in her gifted overnight bag, and met the CO for a breakfast of fresh fruit and pastries and fresh testing sweet black tea. Actual tea, made from actual fresh tealeaves. Not the dust they were using in Malta. The CO even took a pack of tea from the cupboard and put it in her overnight bag, while putting a finger to his lips to suggest she kept quiet. Some grapes and figs followed, along with a couple of mangoes. She started to think he wanted her to get caught when she saw that the small canvas overnight bag was almost full to bursting.

Breakfast and Mess heist complete, they headed back to the dispersal. The Wellington had been fixed, much to their relief. Some of the more weary parts that had been scavenged from wreckage to make the Wellington serviceable had given up during their final flight from Malta, and had to be replaced. The ground crew were also mystified how some of the other parts hadn't failed, given their condition, and replaced those as well, meaning the Wellington would be returning in much better condition than when it arrived. After a successful engine test, both on the ground and in the air, they put down again and reported all was working. They just had to wait until sunset before they could head back. The CO was keen not to travel in daylight, or arrive in Malta any time other than in darkness, and Harriet was right by his side in that. A solitary Wellington would be a prize target for any passing fighter, and if they were going to get their much needed supplies home safely, they needed the cover of darkness.

Once again, Harriet's assumption that they'd spend their time sitting around the dispersal was proved wrong, when the CO summoned a car, which first took them to the paymaster, who paid them both with a month's arrears of salary, and then into Cairo to go shopping. If she didn't know better, Harriet would think the CO had it all planned, but she knew he was keen to get the supplies back without delay, so she just went with his ability to casually make the best of any situation presented to him. Cairo in the daytime was like nothing she could have imagined. The streets were busy with civilians, mixed with army uniforms of every type, and soldiers from all corners of the Commonwealth. Australian slouch hats, Indian turbans, Scottish bonnets, everyone was there. Gurkhas from Nepal, New Zealanders, Africans from Kenya, it was like the gathering of the Empire. It felt exciting and mesmerising, as did the vast market they visited, which sold food of all sorts, fine clothing and gifts, practically everything a person could want. The CO taught Harriet the fine art of haggling, which more than once had apparently entered into the questionable realm of whether Harriet was for sale. Fortunately, for her and for most of the stallholders, she knew almost nothing of Arabic, which the CO haggled in primarily. Though one older local who was selling American cigarettes, which Harriet was trying to buy for Cas, had offered half of his wares for Harriet, but unwittingly made the mistake of doing so in French, which she was quickly learning was the language of upper class Cairo. Before the CO could reply, Harriet let rip, taking the opportunity to put her seemingly long dormant French into practice. She tore into the stallholder with a fire that shocked him into dropping his prices and apologising, nervously, much to the CO's amusement. They shopped, and Harriet had more fun than she had in a long time, then they took lunch in a very nice hotel which, despite having a very strict dress code significantly higher than flying kit of shirt, shorts, and plimsolls, bowed to the CO's requests. There were looks of disapproval, mainly from the European women who were clearly part of high society, who looked down on Harriet with disdain. Not only was she a woman in uniform, she was a scruffy, scrawny girl, and she was sitting in their very fine hotel. It was like there wasn't even a war on. It took some of the enjoyment from the day, thinking the English were still behaving in such a snooty way despite all that had happened, and she was happy to leave and head back to the air station, and the Mess, where they intended to sit under the fans and enjoy cool tonics dressed with citrus while waiting for sunset.

"I was told you were still here..." the Station Commander said as he approached them. He was an older man, a pre war pilot and now a Group Captain responsible for keeping Cairo's airfield functioning.

"Sir?" the CO said, as he stood courteously, with Harriet copying just a second later.

"Sit, sit," the Station Commander gestured, as he pulled out a chair and joined them. "Look, I won't beat around the bush. The balloon's gone up, and we need a favour," he said with a frown, while fiddling nervously with his moustache.

"Which balloon, exactly, Sir?" the CO asked.

"El Alamein," the Station Commander replied. "Rommel came charging down the coast road from Libya a few weeks ago, sweeping away all opposition and determined to take Egypt. We stopped him at El Alamein, not seventy miles from Alexandria, and we're holding him, but we're pretty sure he's going to try and outflank us; which I'm sure I don't need to tell you would be disastrous." He paused, while looking first at the CO, and then Harriet. "If he gets in behind our lines at El Alamein, our army will be cut off. He'll be in Alexandria within the week, and Cairo not long after. Suffice to say, we're in a bloody awful position."

"I'm not sure where we come in?" the CO asked, as Harriet tried to work it out. She'd seen the maps of North Africa, and she knew that the war in the Western Desert had been a series of runs back and forth along the coast road. She'd even seen El Alamein on the map, and knew how close it was in terms of Egypt falling if the army was lost there.

"All of our squadrons are tasked flying support for the army. The Luftwaffe are making them pay, too, so we don't have any pilots to spare..." He looked a little more uneasy, and Harriet's heart started to race a little. "The thing is, we think one of Rommel's divisions is out in the desert somewhere north of the battle, working their way around our flank so they can hit us in the rear and close the trap, and we need somebody to go and look for them."

"Somebody like a photographic reconnaissance pilot, for example?" the CO asked.

"Exactly! Look, we're not wanting to keep you; I know you need to get back to Malta and keep the fight going over there. God knows we need you there more than ever to stop their convoys, but if we can borrow you just for the afternoon, we'd be forever grateful."

"Well, I didn't have anything else on, so why not?" the CO said with a smile.

"Two reconnaissance flights have more chance of success than one..." The Group Captain looked at Harriet.

"Squadron Leader Cornwall doesn't know Egypt as well as me," the CO replied. "I can probably get around by myself just fine."

"I'd be delighted..." Harriet replied. She didn't like the suggestion that the Luftwaffe were putting up a fight, but she felt confident that she could outrun even the best the Germans could offer in her blue Spitfire.

"In that case, we should probably get going. The chaps will brief you in Ops, and provide you with the maps you need. Leave your kit here if you like, it'll be safe until you're back." Harriet finished her drink, and pulled the piece of lime from the glass and popped it into her mouth, chewing it and enjoying the burst of fresh juice. It would likely be hot up there, and she needed all the fluid she could get.

Chapter 7

Tombs

Harriet's optimism had started to wane during the briefing with the Ops Officer. She and the CO had each been given an area to scout, all of which looked practically featureless on the map, which didn't bode well for the navigation, but that quickly became the least of her worries. They were told that should they find what they thought was likely to be the German division, they were to make sure. When the CO had asked how they should do that, they were simply told to get a closer look. Apparently, they were looking for large numbers of trucks and half tracks, maybe even some tanks which, as Harriet remembered well from her time in France, didn't usually like enemy aeroplanes coming too close, so they tended to do a lot of shooting. If that wasn't enough, they were ordered to radio the location the moment they were sure they'd found the Germans. This would, of course, let the army know where to move to meet the enemy, while simultaneously telling anyone listening exactly where they were, including any nearby Luftwaffe fighter units. It was all adding up to be much more than having a quick look around, and much more dangerous, but there was more to come. The only thing that had kept Harriet composed through the briefing, was knowing that the photographic reconnaissance Spitfires were faster than almost anything the enemy could put up to catch them, and it was only through poor flying, or poor luck, that a PR Spitfire was shot down. That confidence was dashed when she was shown to her nice blue Hurricane. Stripped of guns, the same as the PR Spitfires, and similarly fitted with extra fuel tanks and cameras, it was just nowhere near as fast. In fact, even stripped down, it would still be slower than a Messerschmitt 109. The odds were stacking up, and not in her favour. The CO went over the plan with her one last time, maintaining his reassuring confidence despite the challenges they faced, then they were off.

Harriet climbed into the Hurricane and strapped herself in. It was full of sand and had certainly seen better days, and it wasn't in much better condition than those she'd flown in France. She thought of AP while she went through her checks. The young engineer would have been furious if a pilot brought an aeroplane back to her in this condition. Once Harriet was sure everything was as good as it could be, she joined the CO in taxiing to the end of the runway. He gave her a wave and a nod, and together they opened their throttles and let off the brakes. For the briefest moment, Harriet thought back to France again, and the first time she'd taken off in a Hurricane. It was big, powerful, and was full of holes, having just been shot up, but she fell immediately in love with it, and had been ever since. She smiled as she pushed the stick forward to lift the tail into the airstream, then felt the Hurricane lift off the ground. It was like coming home, in a way. The Spitfire was a dream, and there was nothing else like it, but the Hurricane had a rugged charm she'd missed. With the undercarriage up, she went through her checks, then settled on the CO's wing as they breezed past the great pyramids, an experience that made her smile in spite of her nerves, before they headed southwest and towards the open desert. They climbed high, pushing up to twenty five thousand feet, where they held. Fortunately, in Harriet's opinion. Her Hurricane didn't seem particularly happy with the altitude, and going any higher risked pushing it out of where it was comfortable. At the agreed point, they separated, the CO taking the flight path closest to the hills and mountains running parallel to the coast, which was where the Germans were expected to be. Meanwhile, Harriet took the route further south into the deeper desert, terrain which was considered to be unsuitable for tanks, but which the powers that be needed to eliminate, ensuring future flights could work between that boundary and the coast. When she reached her patrol line, a long way south of the rugged ridge, she checked behind her to make sure there were no contrails giving her away, then set a course due west. There wasn't a cloud in the sky, and her Hurricane blended almost seamlessly, from below at least. From above, she'd be hard to miss silhouetted against the hundreds of square miles of varying shades of brown below her, and she was careful to keep glancing upwards, while straining her eyes to search the ground below for signs of movement. There was nothing, though, other than desert, desert, and more desert. She thought for a moment she saw movement around a small oasis of palm trees, but having descended to take a closer look, as per instruction, all she saw was a Bedouin camp. Having circled a couple of times, and returned the waves of the children sitting in the shade, she climbed back to twenty five thousand feet and continued on her course. She checked her watch, and smiled as the light danced in rainbows across the pearlescent face. She had another forty five minutes until she reached her turnaround point, and she started to daydream about heading back to Malta. She'd enjoyed her shopping in Cairo, and had lots of gifts to take back. Tea, coffee, figs, dates, and lots of American cigarettes. Not to trade this time, but to keep her friends going.

The turn point came without incident. She'd flown as far south as the operations types expected the Germans to stray, knowing that any deeper into the desert truly would be impassable for tanks, so she turned north before heading east again, following a track which, in theory, would mean that between her and the CO they'd cover most of the area the army suspected the Germans would be. Having found nothing on her westerly leg, she had mixed feelings about the trip home. She wanted to find the Germans, if they were there, and contribute to the war effort, but another part of her just wanted to get back. There'd been no sign of the Luftwaffe since the start, but that didn't mean they weren't out there somewhere. Even though she'd outflown 109s while flying a Hurricane in France, she was acutely aware of the fact that the one she was flying didn't have any guns. As soon as she settled on her bearing, something caught her eye. Glancing in the mirror, she saw white streaks in the sky above her, contrails. She counted, using her rudder to slip left and right to show as much of the sky as possible. There were four in all, flying in the usual Luftwaffe fighter formation. Her heart started to race. They were further north and a few thousand feet above her, and there was no guarantee that they'd seen her yet, so she decided to fly straight and level, and not do anything to draw their attention to her. Besides, she knew she couldn't outrun them, so any chance she had of getting away would be to respond at just the right time. She kept her eyes on them while glancing down below for signs of the enemy, feeling that their presence would mean they weren't far away. Her mind and heart raced as she scanned the sky and the ground, time was about to run out, and she needed to find the tanks before the fighters got her.

As the white lines streaking behind the fighters drew closer, Harriet's mind went into overdrive with strategy. She had ideas about how she could escape one, maybe two, but four would be impossible, and nothing she could think of ended in her getting back safe. Every calculation, every manoeuvre, they all led to the same outcome. She couldn't outrun them; she couldn't fight them. She didn't know how far they'd flown, and had no idea how much fuel they'd have, so she couldn't even hope to try and outturn them for long enough for them to break off. To give herself more time to respond to their attack, she slowly started to descend, putting a few thousand feet more between them and her. She looked at her watch; it was a long way home. She knew she wouldn't make it, but it didn't stop her from hoping they wouldn't see her. Her stomach was starting to tense, and her mouth was starting to dry out. She was becoming impatient. The nerves were getting to her, and she wanted to get on with it, rather than keep waiting. She even started shouting at them to get on with it, but all the time, they stayed up high. Sitting at nearly thirty thousand feet, but moving fast and now slipping out of view of her mirror. Her shouting stopped, and her mind focused, as the frustration and fear of the wait instantly evaporated when the first of the fighters started its dive, followed by the next, and then the other two, one at a time streaking down. The dive was shallow at first, but there was something unexpected. They weren't coming down at her. Instead, they were heading north, and they were moving fast. She looked around, checking for others she'd missed, but the sky was empty. She was confused. She frowned as she watched the fighters head away from her at speed, quickly becoming specks in the distance. She'd thought maybe they'd turn in again and come at her, but they didn't. They just kept going until she couldn't see them anymore. Her heart was still racing, but she closed her eyes for a moment and breathed a deep sigh of relief, then started laughing. It was the closest she'd come to collecting her harp, as Cas would say. There was no way out, no escape, and somehow, for some reason, four enemy fighters had decided to leave her alone. She wasn't going to waste time questioning it; she just wanted to get back to Cairo, get on her Wellington, and get home to Malta. It was dangerous there, but she knew what game she was playing. Flying around the desert, miles from anything, and dodging German fighters in a rickety old Hurricane wasn't her idea of fun. She checked her watch again. As she did, the engine coughed. She quickly scanned the gauges, she'd neglected them while watching the fighters and searching for the tanks, and the oil was at boiling point. She immediately throttled back to take some of the strain off the engine, and pushed the nose down to try and use the air to cool the engine a little. Another cough filled the air with smoke, and a grinding vibrated the airframe and controls, as oil started spraying over her windscreen. She shut off the fuel as the exhaust stubs started

109

to flame. Things were turning bad, quickly, and she didn't need a ball of flames to add to the problems. With the fuel off, the engine eventually stopped its noise, and the propeller slowed and windmilled as Harriet quickly went through all of her checks. There was no way she could glide back, and the streams of oil made it obvious she wouldn't be starting the engine again, leaving her with no option but to descend and search for somewhere to put down.

The windscreen being smeared with oil made it difficult to get a good picture of what was below, and she was left to gently rock the gliding Hurricane side to side so she could look out the side of the cockpit, being careful not to scrub off too much speed and risk a stall, while trying not to get a mouthful of engine oil as it ran over the airframe. For as far as she could see, there was an undulating sea of sand dunes with no clear path to land. There was no other choice. Despite her desperate wishes, she would have to put down on the dunes and hope for the best. While she knew the engine was finished and there was no way it would be flying again, she needed to land as safely as possible if she was going to survive. She didn't fancy a slow death in an upturned Hurricane. She thought of her parachute for a moment or two. If she held level, she could jump, then it wouldn't matter too much where she landed. There was a lingering reluctance, though. There'd been a couple of pilots who'd jumped from their stricken aircraft over Malta in recent times, only to rocket straight to the ground when their parachutes failed. She'd even seen it in combat over Kent, and watched a Spitfire pilot flail through thousands of feet as his collapsed parachute trailed behind him. Then there were those who landed heavily, breaking legs or turning ankles. Another undesirable option that was right up there with sitting in an upturned Hurricane. By the time she'd finished thinking of excuses not to jump, she'd already passed the point of no return. To do so wouldn't give her time to slow her descent enough to avoid injury. Instead, she lined up with the seemingly towering dunes, trying to keep parallel with them to reduce the chance of hitting one head on and flipping, as though she was landing in the water. She pulled her harness as tight as it would go, then braced while trying to keep the nose high, determined not to let it dig in if she could avoid it. The tail wheel caught the sand first, and then the belly. She pulled back hard on the stick, holding the leading edge of the wings above the surface of the sand for as long as she could, until the windmilling propeller blades were caught and dragged the nose down, throwing a tidal wave of sand into the air.

"Oh, God, that hurts..." Harriet gasped, as a shooting pain ran up her neck and stabbed deep in her brain like a searing hot poker. She blinked her eyes open and lifted her head; she was hanging against the straps of her harness, and looking down into a valley of sand. Above her, the sky was a mix of deep reds and dark blues, swirling together as specks of light scattered above them. She coughed and tried to spit the sharp sand from her dry mouth, while trying to make sense of the situation. She shook her head, and the pain sharpened enough for her to focus. She was in her Hurricane, and had been since she'd crashed hours earlier. She braced herself against the rudder pedals and released her harness, immediately easing the pain in her neck and head. With a sigh of relief, she lifted herself from the cockpit and climbed out onto the wing. The nose was buried almost up to the windscreen, along with the leading edges of the wings, leaving only the tail raised slightly above the sand. She walked to the rear of the wing and stepped off, immediately sinking to her knees in the soft sand, a move which started the whole dune moving and rushing downwards, dragging the Hurricane with it. She desperately scrambled to kick her legs free, and crawled as quickly as she could, rolling to the side a split second before the tail hit her across the head and dragged her down the deep gully of sand. She laid flat and dug in her heels, stopping her descent as the Hurricane dropped, and was quickly engulfed entirely by the wave of sand that followed. She breathed deep, her throat scratching and painful, and her head pounding, then rolled onto her front and crawled to the peak of the shifting dune, where she pulled herself onto her knees and looked around. The sun was setting on the horizon, and there was nothing but a sea of sand between her and a small rocky outcrop in the distance. Another scan of the skyline confirmed her isolation and lack of options. It would soon be dark, and the sands were shifting. The outcrop seemed like the only safe harbour, so she quickly stood, and dragging her parachute behind her, she started her slog along ridge after ridge of unstable sand dunes, in a race against the creeping night.

The sand dunes had been deceiving from above, looking like shallow ripples across the surface of the desert, but things on the ground were different. They were steep, some like rolling hills in places, with deep valleys between; and the loose shifting sand made it hard for Harriet to climb and descend as she made her way to the rocky outcrop, which was hidden from view each time she dropped into a delve between the sandy peaks, but never seemed to get any closer each time she crested the next dune. Despite the sun sitting on the horizon, it was still warm, and the hard work going into dragging through the sands was exhausting, made no better by not having any water to quench her thirst. She pushed on regardless, and finally, after what seemed like hours, she let out a groan of relief as she stood on a rock, and then another and another, as she climbed the outcrop to the top, where she sat and looked back at where she'd come from. Footprints stretched into the distance over the dunes, tracing her journey over the barren landscape. She laid her parachute on the warm rocks behind her, then lay back and rested her pounding head, while watching the stars in the darkening sky.

When she next woke, Harriet was shivering. The sun had long since set, and she was lying on the rocks under the cold night sky. She felt so cold she thought for a moment she was back home in England, but she wasn't that lucky. Her mind spun. She was in trouble, she knew that much, but more pressing than being stuck in the middle of nowhere was the cold, which seemed to be penetrating her bones deep to the core. She quickly ripped open the parachute pack and pulled out the silk parachute, which she dragged down the rocks with her to the sand, where she dug a small hollow just big enough for her to slip into, before cocooning herself in the silk and getting comfortable. She continued to shake until her eyes felt heavy again, then despite her best efforts to stay awake and stare at the galaxy of stars above her, she slipped into another deep sleep. She occasionally woke, thirsty, and almost delirious, but each time she dropped back into a deep exhausted sleep, until finally, she woke as the sky was starting to lighten, and she watched as the stars faded, while wondering if anyone was looking for her. She thought of Cas. She was supposed to have met him for a drink the previous evening, but ended up on a trip to Cairo instead. She'd asked Robbie to let him know she was flying a mission and may not get back in time, and would see him the following day instead, but the next day had come and gone, and she was further than ever from a weak and warm Horse's Neck in Valletta. She'd been excited to take him some treats back from Cairo, but now she was wondering if she'd even see him again, and the more she thought about it, the more she doubted. She wasn't injured, that she knew of, other than being sore from the crash landing, but she was thirsty, and without water, it wouldn't matter whether she was injured or not; she'd be dead.

As the sun rose, she pulled herself from her silk cocoon, and hauled the parachute with her to the top of the rocky outcrop, where she looked around and tried to make sense of her surroundings. She'd brought her map with her, but it was next to useless, though she was able to work out that the mountainous ridges that separated the desert from the coast were to her north, and it was them she could just see in the far distance. Not having anything to wait for, she stuffed the parachute back into the pack before slinging it over her shoulder and heading down the rocks into the undulating desert, thinking that in the absence of any better ideas, at least she knew where north was. She walked for hours over more towering dunes which sapped the energy from her legs, while the rising sun made her head pound. She laughed briefly when she thought of German tanks trying to make their way through such terrain, and understood fully why the operations officer thought it unlikely they'd be so far south. The laugh didn't last, though, when she realised that her crash, her suffering, and her pending death were largely pointless. If they knew the Germans couldn't pass, what was the point in sending her in the first place? She became angry, frustrated at the futile stupidity of the decision. The further she walked, the more she cursed the RAF, and the British military as a whole. Only they could make such stupid decisions as to send somebody to look for something where they knew it wouldn't be. The annoyance circled in her mind as she started up yet another dune, climbing and slipping in the loose and shifting sand, becoming more drained with every step, and having to dig deep to fight the urge just to lay down in the sand and give up. Another slip and she was on her knees, crawling and dragging herself to the peak, which she slumped over, gasping for breath and close to tears at the hopelessness of the situation, combined with the pain in her rigid muscles, still tight from the crash, and falling asleep on the hard stone of the outcrop. She looked at the many thousands of grains of sand beneath her face as she thought of giving up. She'd been walking for hours since before sunrise, and she was so dehydrated the pores on her arms were open, but she wasn't sweating. Her mouth had moved from sticky to bone dry, and her head was pounding. She didn't want to give up. She wanted to live; she wanted to see her friends and family again. She just didn't know how. From above, the desert had seemed huge; from the ground, the vastness was unfathomable. She'd been heading north towards the ever distant ridges, in her innocence hoping from there it would be downhill to the Mediterranean where she'd find civilisation, even if it was a German column to surrender to. The reality was different. The sea of sand seemed hundreds of miles wide, without a drop of water to sustain her, or a hint of a shelter to protect her from the baking sun.

A voice from deep inside roused Harriet indescribably. It was loud, like one of the Flight Sergeants who used to shout and ball at the WAAFS she'd trained back in England, while they marched up and down the parade ground. She was confused for a moment. She didn't know where she was, or who was shouting at her, but after taking a minute or two to steady her increasingly slowed brain, she realised she'd fallen asleep on top of the giant sand dune, exhausted and unable to even contemplate another step. She also recognised the voice, it was hers, shouting at her from inside her own mind to get up! She nodded and dragged herself to her knees, then flinched in the bright sunlight as she scoured the horizon. For a moment, she was convinced she was delusional, her mind melted by the heat, but lying half buried in the sand at the other side of the dune was what looked like a Wellington bomber. She stared in disbelief. Not moving, not doing anything, just staring at the apparently fairly intact aeroplane. A thought suggested she should wait and watch to make sure it was safe, not sure of who would be around, but she quickly dismissed it; she was desperate. If nothing else, it was shelter from the baking sun, which was now overhead and burning her skin. She grabbed her parachute and fell over the peak of the dune, quickly kicking her legs to get down through the sand so she could stand and start running towards the Wellington. A hundred thoughts ran through her mind, from the logical of how desperate she was to be out of the sun, to the far fetched notion of the bomber being serviceable and able to take her home. A ridiculous notion considering it was half buried in the sand, but that didn't deter her from dreaming as she dragged her way towards it. If it didn't fly, maybe its radio would work. So many ideas. Her mind was firing more with every step until finally, she was facing the fuselage. The nose of the Wellington was half buried, meaning the access hatch underneath was blocked, not that she needed it. There was a hole halfway down the fuselage big enough to walk through. It looked like anti aircraft artillery had made an almost direct hit, twisting the burned and blackened metal of the airframe. She paused for a moment, then ran at the hole and climbed inside. It was dark, but while it was out of the direct sun, which was a relief, it was like an oven. She looked around. Bolts of light cut through the darkness from the many bullet and shrapnel holes, crisscrossing each other, and bringing some illumination to the inside of the bomber. She looked to her right, towards the tail, and her heart raced as she saw the stowage points for the crew flasks. She'd remembered them from her first trip to Malta; the crew stowed flasks of tea and packages of food there for the journey. She pulled at a flask and shook it, and shrieked with excitement as she fought to open it. Cold tea. Wonderful cold black sweet tea. She slumped down on the sandy floor and drank thirstily. She had to force the tea down. Her body was so dehydrated and swollen it was difficult to swallow, difficult, but not impossible. She gulped, and choked, and spat it out, then sipped between gasps. She was so relieved that she laughed, and then cried, then drank some more before stopping herself and putting the lid on the flask again, knowing that she had to conserve what she had. She closed her eyes and leant her head against the metal airframe and got lost in a mix of sobs and giggles, an outpouring of relief.

She jumped as she opened her eyes again. Staring back at her was the lifeless body of one of the crew. He was sitting further down the fuselage, slumped against the bulkhead, and gripping his stomach with bloody hands. She froze, until the reality dawned on her that he'd long since passed. She hadn't thought about the crew, just the hope of fluid and shade, but having drunk and started to recover her senses, she was able to think through what had happened. Whatever had blown through the side of the bomber had clearly done for the man facing her, probably shredding him with shrapnel. She took another sip from the flask, then put it back in the rack as she stood and looked around. Her eyes had adjusted to the darkness, and she could see the mess of the interior. Sand had half filled the aeroplane from the hole in the side, blocking the doors to the rear turret, so once she'd steadied herself, she headed forward. She hoped that maybe the crash was recent, and somebody up front was still alive, but she knew deep down what she was going to find, and her instincts were soon proved right, partially at least. The pilot was still in his seat, but there was nobody else to be found. She hoped the rest of the crew had got out safely, and as she explored, she saw that some of the parachutes had gone, suggesting at least a couple of them had jumped.

After searching the bomber in its entirety, she'd found rations and a couple of flasks of tea, enough to keep her alive for a day or two, and she quickly started to think of a plan. She was exhausted, she knew that much, and she needed to rest before continuing on her journey, which she thought would be better at night once the sun had set and the heat eased. She pulled the life raft into the centre of the fuselage and inflated it, and threw in the rations and flasks, and an unpacked parachute then climbed in and laid down, packing the parachute around her to try and get comfortable. She lay with her head against the inflated wall of the dinghy and watched the light dancing through the oven like darkness, and catching the face of the dead airman still sitting further down the fuselage. She stared at him while waiting to fall asleep, but something inside her wouldn't stop nagging. Whether it was fear, discomfort, or the unrelenting need to do the right thing, she couldn't rest as long as he was sitting there. She knew he was somebody's son or husband, and they would need to know what had happened to him. The more she thought on it, the more she felt she had to find out who he was. If it were her, she knew she'd want her family to know. Besides, she didn't like the way he was just sitting and staring into space. She climbed from her makeshift bed and made her way down the fuselage, then, after apologising to him, she took him by the shoulders and dragged him outside into the daylight, where she laid him in the sand before searching him for his identification papers. She found some cigarettes and a lighter in one of his pockets, and took them both, along with the couple of boiled sweets she found, one of which she popped into her still dry mouth. She felt bad about it at first, stealing a dead man's sweets, then she thanked him as the sweet quickly coated the inside of her mouth. She needed them more than he did. After reading his name, she used a shovel from the emergency kit inside the aeroplane to scoop a hole into the sand, which she rolled him into before covering him over and saying a short prayer and marking the shallow grave with an ammunition box. Then, as she was heading back into the fuselage, she knew she couldn't rest until she'd done the same for the pilot. She dragged him out of the fuselage, having forced his stiff body from the seat in the cockpit, then dug another shallow grave before searching his pockets.

He was an officer, a Flight Lieutenant who looked like he could be a similar age to her. She thought for a moment how close she'd come to being in his place so many times, and she hoped that when her time came, somebody would do the same for her. In addition to the personal effects she relieved him of before burying him, with the hope she'd get them back to his relatives, she found a small bronze coloured tobacco tin which felt heavier than others she'd handled. She weighed it in her hand for a moment, then pushed it into her breast pocket before heading back into the Wellington, where she slumped back into the life raft and wrapped herself in the parachute. She thought of the pilot again. He looked so peaceful, but so haunted, and she found herself wondering whether he'd still been alive after crashing. He didn't have any obvious injuries, not like the gunner she'd buried, who'd been cut open by shrapnel. She wondered whether he'd sat in his seat and waited to die, his back broken maybe, and unable to move; and she wondered what thoughts he had. Whether he was thinking of home, of his parents, or a girl back home that he'd never see again. They were morbid thoughts, but she couldn't shake them. Her only reassurance was seeing how peaceful he looked when she found him. She fidgeted while she thought and waited for sleep, and pulled off her plimsolls so she could brush the sand from her feet. She hated the grinding feeling of sand between her toes, and she'd been irritated from the minute she started walking across the desert. She laughed at herself for a moment. She wasn't in the best situation, and all she could find to complain about was the sand between her toes. The dusting and the laugh seemed to be what she needed, and after the boiled sweet finished dissolving in her mouth, she closed her eyes. She needed to rest before nightfall and her walk north, and finally, her body and brain were letting her, switching off in unison as she slipped into a deep sleep.

A suffocating cough was the first thing that roused Harriet from her sleep, followed by a howling that whistled through the airframe and pierced her thoughts. She sat up, gasping for breath as she looked around. She was in a murky cloud. Smoke, she thought. She immediately jumped from her bed of parachute silk and ran for the hole in the fuselage, desperate to escape before she was consumed by whatever fire it was that had started. She was blasted and almost blinded by sand as she climbed through the hole and quickly pulled herself back inside. She stopped and tried to focus. There wasn't any heat, or certainly no more than the heat of the desert, and the smoke didn't smell. She stepped back again and composed herself, and quickly realised that the cloud enveloping her wasn't smoke; it was sand, lots and lots of sand, being whipped up into the air by howling winds. There was a danger of suffocating if she didn't act, and after looking around the thick haze of the fuselage while she pulled her silk scarf over her mouth and nose, she grabbed the yellow inflated dinghy, tipped out the improvised bedding, and stuffed it into the hole in the fuselage. The worst of the wind was instantly blocked, and the sand almost immediately began to settle, but the air was still thick, and the wind was still finding its way inside. She took one of the parachutes and started pushing the silk into the gaps around the dinghy, further blocking the blasting sandstorm, she then grabbed what she could and headed up to the cockpit, closing the heavy armoured door that separated it from the fuselage behind her. The cockpit windows seemed intact, and as soon as the door was closed, the air started to clear. She opened the flask and sipped on the cold sweet tea. It cleared the dust from her throat, but as much as she wanted to use some of it to wipe the sand from her eyes, she knew she didn't have enough to spare. Instead, she popped a boiled sweet into her mouth, then climbed into the pilot's seat and looked out, though there was nothing much to see. A murky brown cloud hung over the Wellington, almost blocking all light and making it feel like dusk. Harriet looked at her watch and frowned. It was earlier than when she'd gone to sleep, and she couldn't work it out. She wound it and shook it, but the Swiss timepiece was as precisely accurate as ever. The next thing she shook was her head, she didn't have the brainpower to think, thoughts of how she'd escape were beginning to dominate, and she started to consider whether she'd been hopelessly optimistic in thinking she could get the crew's belongings to their families. She climbed back down to the floor, and after reorganising the second parachute, she sat down and got comfortable, or as comfortable as she could be, and pulled the silk over her before leaning her head on the airframe and staring into space. She tried hard to keep the dark thoughts out, but she couldn't help wondering if anyone would find her body, and whether they'd bury her with the others. It was an upsetting thought, the more she dwelled on it. Being buried in the sand felt lonely, and she wanted to go home. She wanted to be buried where her friends and family could find her, not in a desert thousands of miles from anywhere she knew. She thought of those she'd buried and felt guilty, and she committed to getting them home, then kicked herself for being so stupid, knowing she couldn't even get herself home, let alone anyone else. As a tear rolled down her cheek, forcing her to curse herself for wasting precious fluids by crying, she thought of Malta, and of Robbie checking in at the airfield to see if anything had been heard of her, and of Cas sitting in the bar, still waiting for her to turn up for their evening drink. That was the last haunting thought that went around and around in her mind, before she finally fell into another deep sleep.

Chapter 8

You Are Welcome

The dust storm lasted for two days, or so Harriet calculated from the varying shades of darkness that had enveloped the wreckage of the Wellington bomber, and she'd remained on the cockpit floor for the entire time. Sleep came easily, especially as the few hard biscuits she'd rescued from the rations had been long gone, and she was left with a couple of sips of cold tea every now and then. Tightening her belt was all that was left when the storm had finally passed, with a strict rationing of sticky boiled sweets to try and keep her mouth and throat from drying up altogether. It took a lot of energy to remove herself from the belly of the aeroplane. Sand had infiltrated every crack, and the wind had shifted the dinghy enough to blow a cargo of sand into the fuselage, leaving Harriet with only the emergency hatch in the roof of the cockpit as a means of escape. When finally she emerged into the heat of the late afternoon, she was amazed to see that the Wellington had been almost entirely entombed in sand, with only the cockpit showing. She stood on the roof and looked around, but the view was no better than it had been a few days earlier. Just a sea of sand and blue sky. The distant mountains were still just about visible, reminding her of the direction she intended to walk, though the plan wasn't exactly enticing. The thought of walking off into the desert filled her with dread, but what other option was there? She had maybe a pint of cold tea left and a couple of boiled sweets; that was it. Anything else there may have been to sustain her was in the back of the Wellington, and buried under a mountain of sand. She slipped back into the cockpit and went through her remaining belongings. Some cigarettes, a couple of lighters, and the pilot's revolver. She sat comfortably and tried to sleep while she waited for night, deciding that walking in the dark would be easier than trying to walk in the baking heat.

Cas' navigation teachings had paid dividends, and as Harriet marched slowly through the pitch black of night in the desert, using the stars to guide her journey, she found herself smiling at her memories. He'd spent a long time teaching her to use the stars to navigate, and he'd been very patient despite her insistence that she'd just use a compass if she was ever lost. He'd shaken his head and rolled his eyes, but continued anyway, sometimes taking her flying at night in the squadron hack, and making her navigate by the stars alone. She'd loved learning, though she never let him know. It was much more fun to complain and see how many times she could make him sigh. She appreciated his patience, though, more than ever when marching through the desert, which had become much less rolling, to her relief, and a little easier going, though the big dunes of shifting sand had been replaced in places by hard rocky ground, which made progress hard in different ways, offering new opportunities to turn an ankle or a knee. She continued, though, taking only a five minute rest every hour, during which she'd use the remaining cold tea to wet her lips and mouth only, before spitting it back in the flask, then pushing forward and moving on. Never sitting, despite her feet screaming with soreness and every muscle aching. She knew that if she sat, she'd never get up again. It took remarkable discipline, especially as the only thought in her mind was lying down and going to sleep, but she kept going and marched and marched until the lightening sky signalled the arrival of dawn. This was the signal she'd been waiting for, and as the sun approached the horizon, she stopped and pulled her parachute pack open. In the hours before leaving the Wellington, while waiting for the sun to set and the heat to ease, she'd used the emergency axe by the pilot's seat, and her imagination, to cut and tie the parachute into an overcoat not entirely dissimilar to the white robes she'd seen worn by Arabs in the movies. She'd even made a headdress, which she put on, hoping the white silk would keep her protected from the sun, at least for a while. Before setting off again, she took another sip of cold tea, and to her disappointment, it was the last drop of liquid she had. Enough to moisten her mouth and nothing more. It didn't bode well for her walk. She slung the pack over her increasingly sore back, and started to shuffle forward.

The determined march had long gone from her pace as the sun climbed into the sky, and the soreness, blisters, distracting thirst, and eternally irritating sand between her toes had reduced her progress to a slow, short shuffle. Hardly lifting her feet, not having the energy to do so, and not wanting the pain that came with putting them down again. Everything hurt. The thirst grew to the point where she became delirious, unable to hold a thought or memory, only moving forward in an almost automated state. She passed a flock of birds at one point; they were scattered around the desert and twitching on the ground, having dropped from the sky in their own dehydrated state. She wanted to save them, but she couldn't even stop; she just kept moving forward. Even the five minute breaks had stopped. There was nothing left to drink, and no other reason to stop, other than to lie down and die, a thought becoming more and more welcoming as her open pores itched with dryness, no longer able to sweat. Her heart sank when she was faced with yet another colossal dune. She'd been walking towards it for what felt like days, so she knew she'd have to face it sooner or later, but that didn't make it any easier to accept. A little part of her had hoped her body would have given up by the time she got there, but her stubbornness had thought differently, and once again, she had to drag her limbs upwards through the ever shifting sands that were seemingly determined to drag her downwards again. When she reached the crest, she dropped to her knees and gasped in the hot, oven like air that burned her lungs with each sharp rasp of breath. She composed herself for a minute, not sure what to do next. She grabbed the flask and opened it, and desperately licked at the inside of the lid, imagining she could taste some sort of liquid, but she knew deep down it was an illusion, even when she lifted up and tilted her head back and shook the flask into her mouth. As she did, she noticed something that made her stop and stare. Below the dune was a small green squiggle of lush grasses and palm trees. Was it? She'd heard of mirages, hallucinations in the desert that trick the weary and dying, but this couldn't look any more real. She slowly put her flask away, then pulled herself to her feet, all the time staring at the oasis. The reality was given further reassurance by the presence of horses, two of them tied together in the shade of a palm tree. The more she focused, the more real it all seemed, and she quickly stumbled her way down the sand dune and moved with all haste she could muster towards the horses. She couldn't run, she could hardly walk, but she moved like the wind, staggering and tripping, but set on nothing else than reaching the beacon of safety.

"Thank God..." she whispered as she felt the grass on her legs. "Thank God it's real..." She staggered to the horses and dropped to her knees at the bucket in front of them, and using her hand, she scooped the water into her mouth. It was the best tasting liquid she could ever have imagined. It hurt to swallow, and the coolness shot into her brain like she'd been stabbed with an icicle, but she didn't care, and fortunately, neither did the horses.

Her relief, and her drinking, was broken by a firm boot in her backside, which knocked her flat on her face, overturning the bucket and sending the water seeping into the ground. She desperately clawed at it, horrified to see it quickly absorbed while her mouth was still as dry as a furnace. An angry shout, something she couldn't understand, accompanied a second boot, and she rolled over to see a man dressed in traditional robes and brandishing an old, dirty looking rifle. She instinctively put up her hands while looking him in the eyes, and hoping she wouldn't pass out on the spot from the fear.

"Don't shoot!" she gasped, her voice barely audible from the sore dryness in her throat. "English..." The man shouted again, seeming even angrier than he had been, but she wasn't able to understand a word he was saying. In addition to yelling at her, he looked away and shouted some more, and was soon joined by a second man, who made the first look positively angelic. "English!" she repeated. "English, don't shoot!" She pulled the parachute to one side and showed the pilot wings on her blouse. Their eyes widened, and they mumbled between each other. "English," she repeated, hopefully. They ignored her as they continued talking, then the first reached down and grabbed her by the shoulder, and pulled her roughly to her feet. The angrier of the two kept his rifle pointed at her while her parachute was ripped open. She was relieved of her revolver and then her parachute pack, which was seemingly disappointing to them when all they found was the empty flask.

He angrily demanded something from her, but she still didn't have a clue what he was saying. His demeanour didn't suggest she'd found friends, but she was alive at least. She was scared, but the extreme dehydration she was facing made it impossible for her heart to race, so instead, she stood shaking nervously, with her hands in the air.

"Gold," he said in French.

"Gold?" Harriet replied, confused, and wondering whether she'd understood him properly.

"Give me your gold, English!" he demanded.

123

"I don't have any gold," she shrugged.

"Lie!" he slapped her hard across the face, knocking her to the ground in her weakened state. He turned back to his friend, talking excitedly in Arabic and gesticulating wildly, making her all the more nervous. After their conversation, he roughly pulled her to her feet again and pushed the revolver under her jaw. "Give me gold!"

"I have no gold!" she replied, again in French. "I crashed days ago; my aeroplane is two days that way." She pointed in the direction she'd come from. She was now shaking like a leaf as he pushed the revolver against her so hard that she could almost taste the barrel.

"Gold or I kill!" he screamed. She squared her shoulders and stuck out her jaw. She didn't have a penny to offer, let alone any gold, and instead of being beaten, or worse, she thought it better to take the bullet and be done with. He pushed her backwards in his frustration, and she tripped and fell, reaching out instinctively to stop herself from falling. The sun glinted off her watch, and his eyes widened. He grabbed her wrist and started pulling at the watch.

"No!" she screamed, and wrenched her arm away before he could unfasten the strap. She could take being shot, she could take being dead, but she wasn't giving away the watch that had seen her safe through France, England, Hawaii, and Malta. The watch that had come all the way from Switzerland, that she'd been given as a mark of friendship. He grabbed her again, almost feverishly, as he tried to remove the watch. She swung and punched him hard in the nose, then pulled away her arm, an act of defiance which stopped him in his tracks. In his anger, he pushed the revolver into his belt and pulled out a long scimitar that glinted in the sun, then grabbed her wrist and prepared to swing. Her eyes widened as she realised what was about to happen. A shot rang out before she could respond, stopping his swing before it had even started. A fine red mist filled the air, and he slumped to the ground. As his friend turned and raised his rifle, another shot knocked him onto his back, leaving him staring upwards as a narrow stream of blood ran from a hole in the centre of his forehead. Harriet stood in shock, staring at the figure dressed in flowing black robes, and sitting on top of a brilliant white stallion. With the slightest nudge, the towering horse walked slowly towards her, then stopped to let its passenger jump to the ground. It was another man, another Arab, though he was in much better condition than the two that had accosted her. His eyes sparkled, and his perfectly manicured moustache bristled as he half smiled at her, before looking down at the two dead assailants.

"You killed them..." she gasped.

"They drank water from my well," he replied, almost casually.

"I drank water from your well, too..."

"You are welcome," he said with a big smile. He looked at the wings on her chest. "English airman, yes?"

"Yes..." she replied nervously, and rearranged her parachute modestly. "I crashed south of here, a day or two walk."

"You walked all that way?"

"Yes..."

"You were lucky." He looked at her white silk robes. "Your parachute kept the sun off you; it saved your life." He nodded, then looked down at the dead men. "Though they almost took it."

"They wanted gold."

"They would..."

"I don't have any gold."

"Really?" he gave her a frown of disbelief, which immediately made her fear what would come next. "English pilots usually carry gold to pay for their safe passage if shot down." She shrugged, and secretly cursed the operations officer in Cairo even more. Not only had she been sent on a fool's errand, but she'd also been sent unprepared. "Not that it matters," he continued, before she could say any more. "They'd have taken it and killed you anyway..." He shrugged, then walked towards the slumped corpses. "Come, boy, help me relieve these dogs of their possessions, then we can go home."

"Boy..." Harriet whispered; her throat was so painful she could hardly talk, and her head was pounding so hard it was becoming difficult to focus. "Boy..." she repeated, then tried to take a step, stumbled, and immediately blacked out.

"You're sure he's one of ours?" an antipodean voice asked in the distant darkness.

"Yes, yes, an English airman," came a reply with a distinctly Arabic twang. "I found him walking in the desert."

"He doesn't look much like one of ours, Sir. Look at him; his skin's the colour of a native, and look at those robes," another antipodean added.

"Look," the Arab replied, his voice very close this time.

"No!" Harriet gasped as she opened her eyes and pushed his hand away, just as he grabbed her parachute robe. He jumped back, pulling at the silk as he did, revealing her wings and medal ribbons. She looked at him. It was the man who'd rescued her from her assailants. His eyes were smiling warmly, and he held his hands as if to surrender to her. She blinked and focused, and saw two other men standing a little further away. They were wearing army shorts, shirts, and boots, and both had scruffy beards and Arabic headdresses. They looked at her curiously, but neither unslung the Thompson machine guns hanging over their shoulders. They were tanned, deeply, and the closest had glinting blue eyes, which were all the more piercing when he frowned at her.

"Who are you?" he asked.

"So..." Harriet tried to reply, but instead broke into a fit of coughs. He walked forward and offered her the water canteen from his belt, which she took with a grateful nod. Her swollen throat was sore, and she almost had to force the water down, but it was a welcome relief.

126

"Thanks..." She dried her mouth on her parachute robe, and handed him the canteen. "Squadron Leader Harriet Cornwall, RAF."

"Harriet?" he asked, as he pushed the canteen back into his belt, then offered his hand and pulled her to her feet.

"Harriet..." she replied as she pulled off the parachute robe, revealing herself and making the Arab's eyes open wide in disbelief.

"Looks like your airman is an airwoman," the soldier said to the Arab with a laugh. "Lieutenant Henry Ross, Long Range Desert Group," he said to Harriet, while offering his hand again, this time to shake. "No offence, but you look like you've seen better days."

"I have, and none taken. Not that I'd care anyway, you're a sight for sore eyes." She forced a smile and dusted herself down.

"Were you looked after?" He nodded questioningly at the Arab.

"Yes. Yes, he saved my life."

"Good." He turned to the Arab and put his hands together as though he was praying. "You have our thanks; please come with us." He then gave Harriet a nod, suggesting she followed them out of the tent, which she did, at a slow shuffle that hurt from her feet to the top of her head. They were surrounded by large tents pitched in a lush green oasis scattered with palm trees. It was a beautiful place, though she had absolutely no desire to stay. She'd had more than enough of the desert for several lifetimes. Ross led them to a row of stripped down trucks, where more soldiers were waiting and making tea, while others carried water containers to and fro. The trucks were odd looking, they were pink coloured, with no roofs and heavy machine guns mounted front and rear. Most of the soldiers stopped what they were doing and looked at her as she approached the convoy, intrigued to see a young woman in British uniform. "Did you give him your gold?" Ross asked Harriet as they walked side by side. He was a giant of a man, towering over her, and looking all the more formidable with his full beard and Arab headdress.

"I don't have any gold to give," she shrugged, frowning at the suggestion, not for the first time.

"No worries, we'll take care of it." He waved at one of his soldiers, who instinctively gave him a nod, then went to his truck to collect a box, before joining Harriet and Ross, and handing it over. Ross put it on the front of the truck, then opened it and showed the Arab the contents. "Sugar, with our gratitude." The Arab smiled warmly. A smile that grew as a trooper arrived with a large fuel can. "Kerosene," Ross said, and the Arab nodded, then produced the revolver Harriet had been carrying, and handed it back to her.

"Thank you for saving me," Harriet said. "I owe you my life."

"You are a pilot, yes?"

"Yes..."

"Then you are a warrior sent to rid our country of the Italian and the German, and it is my pleasure to have protected the life Allah gave you." Harriet felt herself blush a little, as the slightest smile made its way onto her face. "It surprised me you are a woman; I didn't believe the English let their women fight."

"They have no choice," she gave him a wink, quite unintentionally.

"You know, the Quran says that any who do deeds of righteousness, be they male or female and have faith, they will enter heaven." He put his hands together in prayer, and bowed slightly, making her smile nervously.

"We should probably be on our way," Ross said.

"Thank you, again," Harriet said to the Arab, then nodded to Ross, who helped her into the back of his truck.

"Alright, get those fires out," Ross shouted to his soldiers. "We need to be moving." The convoy exploded into life, and soldiers quickly buried their fires, poured tea into tin mugs, and loaded their trucks. Minutes later, they were mounted and rolling away from the oasis.

Harriet watched from her place in the back of the truck as the Arab waved them goodbye before heading back to his tent in the oasis. The truck rocked back and forth, in a way that would have been uncomfortable if it wasn't for the remains of her parachute she'd bunched up underneath her. The soldiers in the truck were friendly enough, they gave her water and boiled sweets, and Ross even produced some Kendal mint cake which he insisted she have. It picked her up a little, but the exhaustion got the better of her, and she soon slumped into the bottom of the truck. The soldiers took care of her, and a blanket was stretched above to keep the sun off her as they rolled through the desert, following baked flatlands, and rolling over endless dunes as they made their way east. As sunset approached, they pulled into a dried out riverbed, where the trucks were camouflaged, and sentries were posted. Harriet was finally shaken from her slumber by Ross. He greeted her with a cup of tea, which she took gratefully as she lifted and lent against a box in the back of the truck, feeling aches deep in almost every bone. "Food will be ready soon," he said as he sat on the tailgate.

"Thank you..." she replied. Her voice was still husky, and her throat still sore.

"When did you last eat?"

"I had some biscuits a few days ago."

"Is that all?"

"Yes..." She shrugged casually. "I'm not even supposed to be in Egypt. I was passing through when I was asked to fly a reconnaissance mission to find a German division trying to outflank us, or so I was told. No rations, nothing, just a few hours flying. Then I crashed on my way back to Cairo."

"Sounds bloody unlucky if you ask me."

"I suppose," she shrugged.

"Don't worry, we'll get you back. We'll rest up here tonight, then make our run east in the morning."

"Don't you travel at night?"

"In a rush to get back?"

"Yes," she smirked a little.

"I don't blame you, considering your recent experiences. We do travel at night, though it can be dangerous despite us knowing this area quite well. It gets a bit dark out here, and the ground can be hard going, but not impassable. Though tonight we'll hold and wait."

"What is it you're doing out here?"

"Oh, causing trouble, it's what we do. We've been in Libya bothering the Luftwaffe for a week or so, blowing up aeroplanes and fuel dumps; it really gets up their noses." His eyes twinkled as he talked, showing his passion for his work. "We were heading back to resupply when your Arab friend flagged us down. It's not the first time he's picked up strays from both sides in the past and handed them over to us. We give him whatever spare supplies we have by way of thanks. Sugar mostly, it's like gold out here, sometimes kerosene, ammunition, and any weapons we've picked up off the enemy. We even got him an old Italian truck a while ago, and in return, he tells us what the Germans are up to in this area."

"Which is?"

"You'll see," he gave her a wink as another soldier arrived with a mess tin filled with piping hot tinned Irish stew. She took it with a thank you, the smell was incredible, better than that of the finest restaurants in London. "Jenks is our medic; I thought it would be a good idea to have you looked over after your walk in the sand. If you don't mind?"

"I'm fine..." Harriet replied, feeling embarrassed at being such a burden.

"Yes, well, I saw you walking when we picked you up. Maybe get him to check your feet, if nothing else. You'll be fine out here, but if you have any sores, you run the risk of them turning septic quite quickly when we get closer to the coast, and there's more moisture in the air." She frowned and nodded, and the medic lay down his pack then knelt by her feet. "I have work to do, so I'll leave you to it."

"Thanks..." Harriet said. He nodded and smiled, and jumped from the tailgate, leaving her to bite her tongue as the medic started to loosen the laces of her plimsolls, a light movement which sent burning jabs into her flesh.

"Probably best not to watch," Jenks said when he saw her wince, and gestured at her mess tin, suggesting she should eat rather than think about what was happening. Harriet nodded, and took the donated fork and put a small piece of potato in her mouth. The salt stung, and her mind raced back to the bacon she'd had in hospital back in England, but while it hurt to eat, she was starving. She was hungrier than she could remember being at any time in the past, and salty or not, pain or not, she was going to eat every last scrap of the hot Irish stew she'd been given, and she wasn't going to complain. Instead, she swallowed it down and tried not to make a sound when her plimsolls were taken off as gently and quickly as possible. The pain was instantly relieved, but it returned soon enough when he removed her socks. They'd stuck to her feet in places, and had to be peeled off. She tried to focus on the food and the pain in her mouth, and hoped it'd be enough to stop her yelling. Instead, she gasped and bit her lip, putting the mess tin down for a moment while she clamped her hand over her mouth. "It's OK, nearly there," he said, then pulled off the second sock. She breathed deep as the soles of her feet felt like they were being stabbed with a hundred hot needles, and at the same time, the cooling air was so soothing. "There. I'll give you a few minutes," he said with a smile, then jumped down off the truck. She nodded, and after composing herself, she finished eating her food. She put down the mess tin and laid her head back, the sky was getting dark, and the silver stars were starting to sparkle against the royal blue background. Her head was tired, despite having slept almost constantly since the Arab had rescued her, and now she'd eaten, the desire to drop into a deep sleep was unrelenting. She picked up her tin mug and sipped on the tea; it was cooling already, and gave her memories of the cold tea that had kept her alive. She smiled to herself for a moment, thanking her lucky stars that it was basic army tea that she'd had to keep her alive, and not Malta tea. "Right, let's get you cleaned up," Jenks said as he reappeared at the back of the truck. He climbed aboard and knelt by her feet again. She braced herself as he prodded at her feet with the back of a scalpel. Some places were more sore than others, but it was just about tolerable. "Right, this is the bit that's going to smart."

"This bit?"

"Deep breath." He tipped an iodine bottle onto a large cotton wool ball, soaking it and turning it yellow. She watched with eyes wide as he pressed it onto the sole of her foot, then let out a gasp filled with the hint of a curse. "It'll sting, but it'll clean the wounds and kill any infection. Deep breaths, and it'll ease." She nodded in agreement, and he went to work with the iodine and scalpel, cleaning and cutting away any loose or dead skin. "Unfortunately, we don't have much to give for the pain, but it won't take long," he said, all the time working without looking at her. "We've got morphine, of course, but you don't want that. Not unless you're really hurt."

"That's OK... Keep going," she gasped. He nodded and did as she asked, though she was quite sure he wouldn't have stopped even if she'd begged. After finishing the first foot, he used more iodine before applying dressings, then he moved on to the other. Once done, he produced a pair of fresh army socks, which he put on her as the pain subsided slightly. They felt so soft and comforting, and she wondered just how bad her feet had been. They'd hurt bad, and it had taken him quite a while to sort her out.

"Anything else obvious I need to look at?"

"I don't think so..." she said with a forced smile.

"OK, well, I'll leave you some cotton wool, some dressings, and some iodine. Check yourself over, and make sure you clean and dress any open wounds. Oh, and don't be shy to shout if you need anything. We're all the same out here, all equals, and we all look out for each other."

"Thank you." She smiled warmly, genuinely grateful for the help she'd been given. She hadn't dared look at her feet; they felt so bad.

She'd just hoped they'd be fine in a couple of days. "How bad are they?" she asked, giving a nod to her feet as he got ready to leave.

"I've seen worse," he said confidently. "Though if I remember right, the worse I saw we ended up cutting off. So, I reckon you'll be right."

"Finished?" Ross asked as he appeared at the truck again.

"Probably needs looking over by a doctor, just to be sure."

"Thanks, Jenks. Better get yourself ready; it'll soon be time."

"Time for what?" Harriet asked as Jenks left, and Ross climbed into the truck beside her, and handed her a small silver flask.

"Work..." he replied, giving her a nod to take a sip, which she did. The whisky made her gasp as it burned her mouth and caught her throat, but she was grateful for it. "We carry rum with us, but I thought you'd prefer some of the good stuff."

"Definitely," she coughed and gasped a little, then handed him the flask. "What work?"

"Watch and see..." He pointed to the eastern sky, and Harriet looked just as the distant darkness lit up in a bright flash. She frowned at first, then as flash after flash followed with increasing frequency, her eyes opened wide. Behind the light show came the distant rumbles, rolling over the desert like thunder. She knew immediately what it was; she'd seen it in France during the invasion, the unmistakable display of distant artillery. "That's your German division," he said quietly as he handed her a battle dress jacket. She looked at him in disbelief as she pulled on the jacket. "By the sounds of it, they've just bumped into several thousand angry Australians who've been waiting for them."

"So, they were out here,"

"Apparently so." He looked into the distance and watched the fireworks, while Harriet let a small smile spread across her face. "You should probably get some sleep; it's going to be a long night."

"What about the Germans?"

"Oh, I think they'll have enough to keep them occupied for tonight. We'll keep watch in case any come back this way, then get going first thing in the morning. There's a sentry sitting up front with the guns, so you're safe. Goodnight."

"Goodnight..." She sat back against the truck and watched him leave, then looked up at the cold sky as the distant artillery flashes drowned out the brightness of the stars. It was therapeutic, in a way, and she soon got used to the distant battle as she pulled a blanket over herself. As she settled and her eyes grew heavy again, she thought of how much she wanted to go home. Not in Malta, not England even, home in France. She wanted to go back in time to before the war, when the most she had to think about was being angry at having to go to nursing school, or angry at her teachers. She missed having such things to worry about; they were infinitely more preferable than worrying about how she was going to die, or which of her friends was going to die next. The war had been exciting at first, though terrifying, but it had been two long years of fighting, and she'd had enough.

Chapter 9

Rags & Riches

The battle had raged long into the night, with the distant guns only falling quiet in the early hours and leaving an eerie silence. Harriet had slipped in and out of consciousness throughout, drifting into dreams of being trapped in a sandstorm and dying of thirst, separated only by waking moments of shivers deep in her bones, which made her pull the army blanket tight around her. It felt like an unending cycle, until finally, she dropped into a deep sleep shortly before dawn after she'd woken to the sensation of being rocked back and forth by the movement of the vehicle. She didn't look up; she was too tired, so she just closed her eyes and slept.

Hours later, when the baking heat finally roused her from her sleep, Harriet was handed a canteen of water by one of the soldiers, which she sipped from as she sat up and looked out over the side of the truck. Not a word was uttered as the line of trucks wound its way through the remains of a battlefield. Burned out German trucks and light tanks scattered the hard baked, rock strewn surface that had long since replaced the rolling dunes of the west. Between them were bodies, lots of bodies, some lying silently as though they were sleeping, while others were burned and contorted. Every instinct was screaming at Harriet to look away, but she couldn't. She'd never seen anything like it, and as grotesque as it was, she couldn't help but look. France had been bad, but she'd seen most of the battle from above, and seeing the outcome first hand and in person was chilling. The completeness of the destruction marked by the many dismembered bodies and scattered limbs. She couldn't imagine what it had been like to be part of what had happened, to be trapped in such a large area of death with no way out, and she desperately hoped she'd never find out.

The silence was only broken when the trucks climbed towards the top of the ridge, and a few Australian voices shouted welcomes. As they crested and passed through the rocks, dirty smiling faces looked up, their white eyes and teeth gleaming in the morning sun, and Harriet couldn't help but smile back, knowing that finally she was safe. She couldn't imagine what they'd been through, and tried not to let her mind wander into what hell they'd battled in the night. The other side of the ridge was a hive of activity. Tanks, artillery, aid posts, and supply trucks, the life of an army, all buzzing with action as the Australians prepared themselves for whatever would come next, be that defence or assault. Troops waved as they marched forward, and colourful language was exchanged between the Kiwis of the LRDG she was with, and their Australian counterparts on the ground. Some hours after crossing the front line, they finally arrived in a small walled town, all desert brown apart from the huge white dome of the large mosque that dominated the view, and they came to a halt in a square where other trucks and soldiers were parked. The soldiers she was with were jubilant, and quickly started talking with their colleagues as they shared the news of the night's battle. It had been the culmination of days of assaults by Rommel and his Afrika Corps, who'd been attacking, again and again, supported by the Italians, to try and break through the line and make a run for Cairo. He'd been held back by a multinational force, with his last assault running into a wall of Australians who'd been up for a fight, and then led a counterattack supported by Indians, South Africans, and the British.

"End of the line," Ross said, as he stood looking at Harriet from the tailgate, with a captain wearing a Red Cross arm band by his side. She nodded and smiled, then shuffled along the floor of the truck. She wanted to say something, but her emotions were bubbling just below the surface, and she felt she'd burst at any time with the relief of being safe. "I've got you a ride home." He reached out and helped her down, and the doctor quickly grabbed her as her legs gave way, much to her embarrassment. She felt so weak that even though she was happy to be safe, she felt she'd struggle to stand and drag herself anywhere more than a few paces. Her muscles and bones were sore and tired, and her head dizzy and a little disconnected.

"Thank you," she half whispered as she shuffled a little, trying to take the pressure off her feet.

"You're welcome. The doctor here has a seat in a Cairo bound ambulance for you." Harriet smiled at the doctor and nodded, then with one of them on each side of her and holding her up, she shuffled towards the waiting convoy. "I thought you'd like to know... I spent some time looking at our maps while you were sleeping, and based on

136

what your Arab friend told us, I reckon you must have walked somewhere around seventy or eighty miles before he found you."

"Seventy...?" Harriet frowned. It was impossible to have walked that far in a night and a morning; she knew that much. "I can't have; that's too far," she replied. "I walked less than a day..."

"I doubt that," he laughed. "I've been out there myself, and picked up plenty of lost souls. The state you were in, I'd say you were out there a couple of days at least, maybe more. You were almost dead. Anyway, well done, Squadron Leader, it took a lot of guts and stubbornness to do what you did, and that's what saved your life." They stopped, and she leant against the side of the ambulance. "Good luck." He held out his hand, which she shook weakly. "Get yourself home and get some rest." Harriet half smiled, then laid her head back against the ambulance as a wave of nausea hit her. He waved and smiled as he walked off to rejoin his patrol.

"It's OK, Squadron Leader. We've got you," the doctor said cheerfully. "Why don't you have a sit down before you fall down?" He helped her step up through the doorway into the ambulance cab, where she slumped onto the passenger seat. He quickly went about assessing her as stretcher cases were loaded into the rear. After checking her over, he disappeared for a while, before returning carrying a sturdy glass bottle and a few other bits and pieces. "Well, I've seen people in worse condition after wandering in the desert, though not by much," he continued. Harriet smiled in reply, not having the energy to get into a conversation about it. He hung the bottle from the roof of the cab, then tied a tourniquet around her upper arm until he could see a vein, which he quickly and without warning pushed a needle into, before connecting a line between her arm and the bottle. "Get that in you, and you'll start to feel better," he said. He then gave her a water canteen, which she took gratefully and sipped at to try and hold off the nausea, which was debilitating to the point that she just wanted to go to sleep. She closed her eyes and laid her head against the cab wall, in part to fight off the nausea, and part because the exhaustion kept coming back in waves, each stronger than the last.

The next time Harriet woke, she was looking into the eyes of a young woman, as glamorous as she'd ever seen, despite being in a neatly pressed khaki uniform. Her hair and make up were ready for a night out in the West End, and she looked as far removed from the desert as was possible. Harriet lifted her head and looked around, startled and a little nervous, thinking maybe she was still in a dream, or worse. The young woman was beautiful enough to plant the seed in Harriet's mind that maybe she'd finally got her harp after all, and was dead somewhere in the desert.

"You're awake," the young woman said; she had a big smile on her face, and her words were soft and gentle, and very well spoken. Harriet felt her hand squeeze, and she looked down to see the young woman's hand on hers. She laid back again and closed her eyes, then looked up a few moments later to see the young woman changing the bottle on the drip connected to her arm.

"Coconut water... That's the magic here," she said as she noticed Harriet stirring again. "How are you feeling, Squadron Leader?"

"Hungry," Harriet replied, surprised that she could talk without her throat feeling like sandpaper, or her own voice thundering around her head. She was still gravelly, but she almost felt human. The young woman finished changing the bottle, then checked Harriet's eyes and pulse, and shrugged confidently.

"Here," the young woman said, as she lifted a ration tin and jabbed a metal fork into it. "A little bit at a time; don't rush things." She sat facing Harriet and lifted a piece of pineapple with her fork, then moved it towards Harriet's lips. Harriet nodded and opened her mouth, and took the juicy pineapple chunk. It burst with flavour in her mouth; the juice was so refreshing she felt she really was in heaven. She chewed slowly, savouring both the taste and the moment. As she swallowed, still feeling a scratch in her throat, the young woman gave her another chunk.

"Where am I?" Harriet asked, after swallowing the third chunk of pineapple.

"Not far from Cairo," the young woman replied. "We've pulled over for a few minutes to let an army column pass. They're on their way west to give Rommel another kick in the britches." Harriet nodded and smiled. "We'll be back on the road soon, don't worry, I'll have you back in one piece. You've struck lucky; I'm the best driver in the unit."

"You're the driver?" Harriet asked.

"Yes... Girls drive ambulances and look after patients, you know. Just like some girls fly planes, or so it seems." She pointed to the pilot's wings on Harriet's chest.

"Aeroplanes," Harriet replied with a smile, after looking down at her wings, and then into the young woman's sparkling green eyes.

"If you say so," came the reply. "Rumour has it the LRDG boys picked you up after you'd walked a hundred miles across the desert, when your 'aeroplane' was shot down."

"I'd check your sources..." Harriet smiled.

"I'm sure you don't look this bad normally, so there must be an element of truth in the story."

"Maybe an element."

"Maybe more than. Anyway, what was a girl doing flying about over the desert?"

"Looking for the Germans."

"I don't know why you bothered. It seems all you need to do these days is sit still long enough, and they tend to find you."

"Apparently so..." A horn sounded in the distance, which was repeated down the line.

"Ah, that's us. Time to get moving again. Sit tight, and we'll have you in Cairo in time for dinner. Here, you may as well finish this." She handed Harriet the tin and fork. "Emma."

"Harry."

"Harry... I like that." She started the engine, and the ambulance rumbled into life, and with a double honk of the horn, they were on their way again. "The coconut water dripping into you is clean, and it's loaded with electrolytes," she explained as she drove. "The salts you need to keep you alive. It's the best we've got; the saline ran out hours ago."

"I'm not complaining," she said with a smile, then closed her eyes again and drifted into a deep sleep. The next time she woke, she was in a small, whitewashed room in the hospital, lying in crisp white sheets.

"How are you feeling?" Emma asked, as she looked at Harriet from the doorway. She was in civilian clothes instead of her uniform, a nice sapphire blue dress that made her look all the more glamorous.

"Alive," Harriet replied.

"Good. Put this on, hurry up." She pulled a turquoise summer dress from her bag, and threw it to Harriet.

"What?" Harriet asked, frowning in confusion.

"No time for questions, put it on, and these." She put a pair of pristine white plimsolls on the end of the bed. "I'll keep watch." Harriet's head was swimming with confusion, and in the absence of being able to think, she did as she was told. She pulled off the sheets, then unsteadily sat on the edge of the bed while wearily pulling on the dress and plimsolls, before shakily and briefly standing to smooth the dress underneath her. "Good work," Emma said as she came into the room and produced a brush from her bag, which she quickly ran through Harriet's hair, before tying it back with a piece of lace. "Ready?"

"For what?"

"I'm busting you out of here. Come on..." She took Harriet's hand, and excitedly pulled her up and towards the door.

"My things..." Harriet said, as she stopped and pulled back.

"What?"

"My things. I can't go without my things..."

"They'll have burned your uniform."

"What?" Harriet was instantly furious.

"You weren't exactly winning any spring fresh competitions; it's normal practice when strays come out of the desert."

"But my watch, the things I brought in with me?"

"You're terrible at this; anybody would think that the sun had melted your brain and removed any sense of urgency!" Emma huffed, then let go of Harriet's hand, and prised open the locked drawer on the bedside cabinet. "This?" She handed Harriet a pillowcase which clinked as she swung it. Harriet quickly looked inside, and pulled out her watch from among the tobacco tins, lighters, and identity tags she'd taken from the dead Wellington crew. "You really need to put that on now?"

"Yes..." Harriet put the watch on her wrist and pulled the strap tight, then took Emma's hand again as they made for the door. Her legs were unsteady, but she could just about walk in a straight line. Her heart was starting to race, though she wasn't sure whether that was because she was exhausted or terrified of whatever Emma was helping her escape from. She'd thought she was in a hospital, but the situation suggested it was a prison.

"Look normal," Emma said as they walked side by side, hand in hand, down the long corridors. It was a hospital; Harriet was sure of it. There were patients and nurses, and the more she walked, the more confused she became. A pair of nurses frowned a little as they walked past, looking at Harriet like they recognised her from somewhere, something Harriet simply smiled politely at.

"Hey!" one of them shouted, a minute after they passed. "Hey, where do you think you're going?" Emma pulled Harriet into a quick walk, and then a slow run.

"What's going on?" Harriet asked nervously as she ran, while trying not to fall over in her weakened state.

"Will tell you in a sec; keep up." Emma pulled her down the stairs, and out of the large doors to a large waiting Bentley.

"Go, go, go!" she shouted to the driver, then looked out of the back window at the chasing nurses and sentries, as the Bentley sped out of the hospital grounds.

"Where to, Miss Cain?" the driver asked, as he honked the horn to clear the busy Cairo streets.

"Shepherd's!" came the reply, as Emma leant back in the seat and laughed mischievously. "That was close!" she said excitedly to Harriet.

"I have no idea what's going on," Harriet replied, while trying to slow her pounding heart. "Was I in danger?"

"Were you?" Emma laughed. "They were only going to load you on a ship home, can you believe that?"

"What?"

"I know, ridiculous, isn't it? In your weakened state, the last thing you need is months at sea dodging submarines."

"I don't know that I'm any the wiser."

"Don't worry, you will be," Emma said with a mischievous smile, then looked out of the window as the busy Cairo streets passed in a blur. Harriet did the same, watching the colours pass by as the Bentley roared through the streets, narrowly missing locals and servicemen alike. Soon they were pulling up outside the grandest hotel she'd ever seen, a huge building that wouldn't look out of place in the centre of London.

"Good morning, Miss Cain," the concierge said as he held the door open. Emma dragged Harriet behind her, and quickly they were inside the lobby, which was huge and cooled by large ceiling fans wafting from above. From there, she was taken through the hotel and upwards, to a large and luxurious room that made even the hotels in New York and Washington look like slums. Harriet stood wide eyed as Emma buzzed around. The fan above her was cooling, and she instantly felt her toasted skin, which had tingled constantly since an hour after her Hurricane had crashed, starting to ease. A knock at the door made her jump, and got her a giggle from Emma, who opened the door to a waiter delivering a silver tray loaded with drinks.

"Have a sit down," Emma pointed to one of the elegant leather Chesterfield chairs near the window. Harriet did as she was told, keeping her pillowcase of belongings clenched tight in her hands as she perched nervously, like a guest in a stranger's home. "Gin and tonic, with lots of quinine," Emma said as she handed Harriet one of the tall glasses packed with ice, lemon, and lime. "Cheers!" She clinked her glass against Harriet's, then sipped and relaxed in the chair opposite. "You can put your things down; you're quite safe here."

"Thanks..." Harriet put the pillowcase by the chair, and sipped at her drink. It was cold and refreshing, and she couldn't help but drink some more. "Where are we?"

"Shepherds"

"I don't know what that is."

"Only the best hotel in Cairo, Harry."

"Oh..."

"Don't worry. Daddy's picking up the bill, so make yourself at home."

"I still don't really understand why I'm here?"

"Nobody seemed to know that much about you when we brought you in, but they accepted you all the same. Probably thought you were a boy the way you looked. Anyway, when I called by this morning to check on you, they told me you'd been moved to the women's hospital. The army being the army, they couldn't possibly have you in a men's hospital, of course. Unfortunately, the women's hospital is run by matriarchs who wouldn't have it that you were RAF, and thought you were some poor expat girl who'd escaped Libya and had her brain melted by the sun when wandering in the desert. They meant well, I'm sure, but they'd decided that the best thing for you would be a slow boat back to England." She took another sip of her drink, while Harriet frowned in amazement at the story. "The thing is, the boat they had in mind was a troopship and not a hospital ship, so much for not fraternising with the men. So, long story short, you'd have been stuck in a stinking hold as the boat dragged its way all the way down to South Africa and around the Cape, then up the other side. It'd have taken you a few months, and the reports are that the German U Boats really are snapping at anything at the moment. Anyway, I thought you'd be better off here until a hospital ship is ready to go, they're much safer, and you've a much better chance of making it home in one piece..."

"Thank you..." Harriet smiled. "I don't know how to repay you."

"I'd have done it for anyone. Us girls have to stick together out here; otherwise, the idiots who think they run the show will have us all back in England drinking tea while our husbands are away with the war." Harriet felt herself smiling at her unexpected saviour's rant. "Can you imagine how boring that would be?"

"Yes..." Harriet half giggled, surprising herself. "Is your husband here in Egypt?"

"Husband? Me? Gosh, they should be so lucky! No, nobody's managed to pique my interest quite that much, not yet, anyway."

"Then why are you here?"

144

"Daddy's a big noise in these parts. He tried to send me home when war was declared, and the balloon went up, and all dependents were evacuated, but I wouldn't have it. I volunteered for the Mechanical Transport Corps so I could drive ambulances instead, much to his irritation. Still, it was worth it. All those girls sent home, and all those boys sent over here..." She gave Harriet a wink. "What about you? Why are you here? The last time we talked, I was feeding you pineapple in my ambulance, after a patrol had found your carcass in the desert."

"I'm not supposed to be here..."

"Oh?" Emma sat forward on the edge of her chair with excitement. "Do tell."

"It's nothing exciting... I flew over from Malta on a supply run, and ended up flying a reconnaissance mission over the desert while waiting for an engine to be repaired for the return trip. Unfortunately, that wasn't the only engine having a bad day, the one on the Hurricane I was flying gave up miles from anywhere, and I ended up crash landing in the middle of the desert."

"That's quite some misfortune."

"You're telling me..."

"Yet you survived."

"Somehow."

"Well, you're here now, and the army won't be trying to ship you off anywhere until you're ready, so why don't you make yourself at home?"

"I'm grateful for your help, the thought of being stuck on a troopship for months doesn't appeal, but I really should be getting back to my unit. I can't exactly just go missing."

145

"You already are missing, darling, so I wouldn't worry about that. You get yourself rested, maybe have a bath and something to eat, then we'll talk about getting you back to Malta, if that's where you want to go. Though I can talk to Daddy and see if you can stay in Cairo, if you'd like."

"Thank you." Harriet smiled.

"Don't mention it. Look, I have a lunch date with some Guards Captain who thinks I'm going to be his little wife back on the family estate, and I need to give him some bad news." She drained her glass as she stood. "How do I look?"

"Wonderful," Harriet laughed.

"A nightmare dressed like a daydream," she laughed. "Order whatever you like from room service, make yourself at home, and I'll see you this afternoon." She breezed confidently out of the enormous suite, leaving Harriet looking at her gin and tonic, and wondering what the hell was happening. She'd understood what had been explained, but very little else made any sense. She'd been lost in the desert for who knew how long, and her memory had more holes than a broken sieve. She sighed, accepting there wasn't much she could do about it, then poured more tonic from the iced jug that had been delivered with the drinks, before exploring the suite. It was huge, and Emma was clearly set up in the larger bedroom, so Harriet made her way to one of the others, which wasn't exactly small, and was equally as luxurious; and from there she went to the large bathroom, where a huge ornate cast iron claw foot bath stood on a black marble floor. The temptation was too much to resist, and after filling the bath, Harriet collected some toiletries and lowered herself into the cool water, and with a towel rolled over the back of the bath to cushion her head, she relaxed and almost immediately fell asleep watching the mesmerising fan circling above her.

After a relaxing nap, Harriet sat up and started to scrub herself, turning the water grey with dirt from her pores. She'd been washed in hospital, apparently, but the dirt of the desert had been ingrained, and sand was still everywhere it shouldn't be. After scrubbing her hair, she drained the filthy water and washed the bath, feeling embarrassed by how dirty she'd left it, then wrapped herself in a soft Egyptian cotton robe and went through to the bedroom, where she brushed her hair through, and tied it back with the ribbon Emma had used during her daring hospital breakout. She smiled to herself as she looked in the mirror. The deep tan made her eyes stand out with a bright sparkle, and she liked it, much more than she liked how much her cheekbones protruded, or any of her other bones for that matter. She was emaciated from the starvation of Malta, made even worse by her time in the desert, which had worn her away to almost nothing while tanning her almost mahogany brown. The sun had somehow managed to cut straight through the clothes she'd worn, to ensure an almost even tan all over, except where her underwear had provided an extra layer of protection. At least her eyes looked good, though, she was happy with that much, and she was alive. Once she'd finished in the mirror, she returned to the bedroom she'd chosen, and lay on the bed with the pillowcase, which she tipped out, sand and all. She looked through the collection of bits and pieces, the possessions she'd taken from the Wellington crew, and made a note that she'd return them to the RAF when she went to give them a rocket for sending her into the desert in a bucket of bolts. She couldn't find her own identity documents or discs, though, which made her wonder for a moment. She'd had them when she crashed, and when she left the Wellington, she knew that much, that was a memory that didn't have holes in it, but she didn't know anything else. She sorted through the bits, and looked at the lighter she'd taken from the gunner, the poor soul she'd found sitting in the fuselage of the Wellington with his guts blown through. She thought of him; she could see his face as clear as day, looking at her with his forlorn smile. She'd wondered a great deal about whether he'd died right away, or whether he'd sat and watched his end in slow motion as the sand piled up around his feet. She put his identity tag and other effects to one side, then opened the pilot's unusually heavy tobacco tin, which was filled to the brim with dark brown tobacco, almost to overflowing. She gently brushed the tobacco, moving it enough to see something that didn't belong. A metal disc similar to those she'd taken off the pilot and gunner. She pulled it from under the tobacco, and her heart raced. It was hers. She glanced down at herself, she hadn't even thought that she wasn't wearing it, but she didn't have the first idea why it would be hidden in the tobacco tin. Intrigued, she tipped the tin onto the pillowcase and froze with her eyes wide open in shock. Sitting in the dark tobacco

147

were ten gold sovereign coins, gleaming in the light. She moved them about, pushing the tobacco from them, then picked one up and looked at it. It was like new. Her scrambled memories immediately formed around the oasis, and the Arabs demanding her gold. She didn't even know she had gold; how did they? Then she thought to Ross' explanation that pilots were often issued gold to help them pay for their escape if they crashed in the desert. She couldn't help but smile as the gold reflected the light in her eyes. The pilot had hidden his gold in his tobacco tin to keep it inconspicuous, and she'd had it in her chest pocket all along. Ten gold sovereigns. Her mind raced as she thought of how she could have used it to make her desert adventure easier, maybe to pay for her escape. Then she quickly remembered that the only people she saw after crashing were the two men intent on robbing and killing her, and the Arab who'd rescued her anyway, gold or not. The gold wouldn't have made any difference at all, not to her or the pilot she took it from. If anything, she'd have handed it over when threatened, and would likely have been finished off before her rescuer had the chance to intervene. As she removed each sovereign and dusted it off before placing it on the bed, she noticed something white running around the inner wall of the tin. She pulled at it, and a neatly folded piece of silk came out. She unfolded it to reveal the printed words, three paragraphs in a form of Arabic, which to her uneducated eyes looked similar, but at the same time quite different, then a paragraph in Italian, and one in French. The language she knew as well as English. It read, 'I am a British airman, and I mean you no harm. If you deliver me safely to the nearest British unit, you will be rewarded with riches in the form of payment and goods.' She smiled as she read it, and thought of her Arab friend and how happy he was to receive the sugar and kerosene Ross had given him. Such practical goods were lifeblood to him. He could use them and trade them more than he could a piece of gold. She still felt she needed to thank him, but deep down, she couldn't begin to imagine how she'd ever do that. He was a Bedouin, roaming the desert with his tribe hundreds of miles from Cairo, and as grateful as she was, she wasn't in a hurry to get back to the desert. The thought also triggered her to think of what Emma had said about staying in Cairo. If she stayed, she'd likely be posted to a flying squadron, anything else would be a waste of a pilot, and the very thought of being shot down over the desert again turned her blood to ice, and not in a pleasant way. She packed the tobacco back in the tin, along with the crew's personal effects, then wrapped the sovereigns in the silk note and put them on the bedside table while she fastened her identity discs around her neck once again. She then laid back on the comfortable bed and watched the fan go around and around.

Chapter 10

Debts

"Ciao, Miss Cain!" the impeccably dressed Italian gentleman greeted Emma, as she led Harriet into one of Cairo's leading tailors, a place renowned for making the finest uniforms for the traditionally wealthy officer class of the British military that had made Cairo their home over the years. It was also one of the few Italian businesses that had survived after Italy declared war on Britain, when many Italian nationals had been interned through fear of their being spies, or worse, a fifth column of civilian soldiers ready to rise up against the British occupation.

"I need your help!" Emma said excitedly, skipping over the formalities and getting straight to the point.

"If I can?" he shrugged.

"My friend got lost in the desert, and needs new clothes."

"I'm flattered you brought her to me, Miss Cain, but perhaps one of our friends who specialise in clothing for young ladies?" He smiled politely at Harriet as he talked, clearly trying hard not to stare at the heavily tanned skeleton standing in front of him. Despite her bath and the loan of some very nice clothes from Emma, she still looked like an exhausted scarecrow, in her own mind at least.

"If she were any ordinary young lady, I would!" Emma replied with a mischievous smile. "However, this is Squadron Leader Harriet Cornwall, fighter ace of the Battle of Britain, and she needs a uniform!" His eyebrows raised as he looked at her, then back to Harriet, who nodded shyly.

"Then you brought her to the right place! Christina!" he shouted, and his wife quickly appeared. "Please, measure this young lady for a uniform."

"Ideally, we'd need it today as we have a dinner appointment tonight... Would that be a problem?"

"For anyone else," he said with an encouraging smile. Harriet looked questioningly at Emma, as she was taken by the hand and led through the shop by the owner's wife to an elegantly decorated room, where she was expertly measured, before being delivered back to the front of the shop where Emma was waiting.

"You can put it on Daddy's account," Emma said casually.

"No..." Harriet protested. "I mean, I have money; I just need to get to the RAF pay office... You've been so kind already; I couldn't possibly burden you with the bill for my clothes, too."

"Honestly, Daddy wouldn't know." She smiled and laughed, then turned back to the tailor. "On Daddy's account. What he doesn't know, won't hurt." He gave her a nod and a knowing wink. "Give her the works, and we'll collect later this afternoon?"

"Of course, Miss Cain. It'll be my pleasure!"

"That's it settled, then. Let's go have a drink."

The afternoon was spent sitting in fine restaurants and bars, drinking tonics and talking, and enjoying a luxury that seemed a million miles away from the war in Malta and England, or for that matter the war not a hundred miles down the coast, where the massed army of the Commonwealth was fighting to the death to stop Rommel from rolling into Cairo. It was surreal to Harriet. There was a raging war all around, but Cairo seemed to exist in a bubble safe from it all, where European civilians and military carried on as though nothing was wrong, and the locals continued to trade with them; though Emma had mentioned there'd been a change in attitude among many of the local Egyptian population, who had started to cool towards the British in preparation for the imminent arrival of the German and Italian armies, not that such an emergency seemed a reality in the minds of the British ruling class. Either way, cool or not, Harriet still felt she was living in the lap of luxury, which was a world away from her existence on the edge of death in previous days.

Harriet tried to put her recent experiences out of her tired mind for a while, and instead tried to focus on Emma's engaging conversation. She was a fascinating young woman. Educated and adventurous, she'd been loaded onto a train in 1940 along with many other women and children of the British establishment in Cairo, when it was thought the Italians would invade Egypt. The train was supposed to take her, her sister, and her mother to the safety of South Africa, and it would have had she not jumped off at the first stop and returned to Cairo, her beloved home. Her father was indeed a very big noise in the local British administration, though even he couldn't tame his daughter and get her to leave. He'd even threatened to use the Military Police, which led her to dare him with threats of retribution he'd never stand. So, he let her stay, and had little choice in her joining the MTC and training as a driver and mechanic. Something she'd insisted on doing as part of 'doing her bit', as she was furious that nobody would let her actually fight to defend her home, because 'women don't go to war!' It was that adventurous flare and her desire to fight that had drawn her to Harriet's plight, and when she'd found a young female pilot out in the desert, she was determined to make sure she was looked after when she got back to safety. Harriet found out that she'd been in the hospital for two days before her great escape, slipping in and out of consciousness while the hospital authorities decided what to do with her. As her papers and identity were hidden, nobody believed she was actually a pilot, with many assuming she'd stolen the clothes from a shot down pilot she'd found in the desert, a male pilot, and the resounding opinion was that she was from one of the English families who'd lived in Libya or Tunisia before the war, and that she'd gone mad in the desert while trying to escape her Italian captors. Emma wasn't having any of it. Despite a passing RAF officer saying they didn't have any female pilots, she'd read the newspapers, she knew of the young female pilot's adventures over London, and she was adamant the filthy and sunburned scarecrow was the glamorous young fighter pilot she'd seen in the newspaper a couple of years earlier, standing with the young princess by her crashed Spitfire. Fortunately for Harriet, she didn't have to do much talking. Her head was sore, and she was still struggling to think straight, so while Emma talked enough for both of them, she was more than happy to sit back and drink glass after glass of tonic with ice. She managed to suggest Emma try for pilot training, which her new friend talked through a dozen times while she toyed with the idea, but each time thinking of how that would mean she'd have to leave Egypt, which she wasn't keen to do.

After several hours of talking and drinking, and a trip to a few other shops where Emma insisted on buying Harriet some new underwear and toiletries, they headed back to the Italian tailor, where Harriet was presented with a new uniform, blouses, skirt, shorts, the lot, all in the finest Egyptian cotton, complete with medal ribbons, and new dress shoes and plimsolls, and new headdress. Harriet was gobsmacked by the quality. It was enough to rival, or even better, the clothes that had been made for her in London. They were a perfect fit, made with such precision that not a stitch needed to be corrected, and the soft Egyptian cotton soothed her sore skin. She felt herself crying as she thanked the tailor and his wife, and then Emma. Looking at herself in the mirror, she looked like a young woman again, a smart young woman, and not the scarecrow she'd seen since Malta. She'd lost herself for so long, but new clothes and lots of kindness had made her feel human for the first time in a long time, and it was difficult for her to bear. After looking in the mirror a few more times, she was finally dragged from the tailor by Emma, who had one last stop on her itinerary, something she'd been waiting until the right moment for, a trip to visit the RAF.

The Bentley was hailed to a halt at the main gate, and a Military Police Corporal came forth to check identity papers. After seeing Harriet, and checking her papers, he stood smartly to attention and saluted before waving the car through. A formal process that made Emma and Harriet smirk at each other as they were allowed to pass. Harriet remembered the headquarters building from her visit with the CO. While Emma waited with the car, Harriet made her way to visit the Operations Officer. She straightened her uniform, and despite the still stinging pain in her feet as the soft Italian leather of her new shoes pushed against the more raw spots from her walk in the desert, she marched confidently through the building, getting looks of confusion and appreciation as she passed from men and women, military and civilian.

"What is it?" the Operations Officer asked, as his orderly knocked on his door.

"Squadron Leader Cornwall to see you, Sir," the young airman replied.

"Who?"

"Cornwall, Sir."

"Send him in."

"Good afternoon, Sir," Harriet said as she walked into the office.

"Cornwall..." he said with a frown, as he quickly stood, quite confused. He was a Wing Commander in his mid to late forties, and he looked at a loss as to what to do with the uniformed young woman standing in front of him. "I'm afraid I don't think we've met..." he offered his hand.

"We have, Sir."

"Oh?"

"Not long back, my CO and I came over from Malta, and we met briefly when you discussed logistics and the supplies we were to take back with us." He looked for a moment, then his face warmed as he smiled.

"Of course! Of course, where are my manners? How are you? Did you get everything back OK?"

"Not quite, I'm afraid..."

"Why ever not? Wait..." His frown returned as he looked at her. "My God..." He went quite pale as he stared at her, and the silence quickly became very uncomfortable.

"Sir?" Harriet asked nervously.

"You're supposed to be dead..." he replied, equally as nervously. "Lost over the desert weeks ago... But... How?" He stammered a little,

154

unsure of himself or the situation, and Harriet felt herself start to blush a little.

"I was..." she started. "Lost, I mean. Not dead, of course." She quickly became as flustered as he was. "The Long Range Desert Group picked me up in the desert after my Hurricane came down with engine failure. I've just got back, almost, via the women's hospital."

"My God, girl!" He set out a sigh of relief that let the colour return to his ashen face. "You scared the life out of me; I thought you were a ghost!"

"Sorry, Sir..."

"No, no, not at all... It's wonderful to see you, Cornwall." He shook her hand firmly, smiling like they were long lost friends, and not two people who'd half met in a short conversation with somebody else. "My God, I can't believe it. Your CO is going to be so relieved!"

"I was hoping you could let Malta know I'm OK, and that you'd maybe ask them to come and pick me up."

"I'm quite sure we can do that. You know, your CO went out a few times looking for you when you didn't come back. He was furious we'd lost you. He even delayed his return trip and flew the following day too, but was forced to give up his search when the weather turned, and a dust storm blew up. He'll be delighted you're back."

'Thank you." She blushed a little, then pulled the tobacco tin from her bag and put it on his desk. "While in the desert, I found a crashed Wellington. Two of the crew were with it, dead, I'm afraid, but I brought what I could of their personal effects. I hoped you'd be able to get them to their families, and let them know what had happened to their loved ones."

"Of course..." He frowned as he opened the tin and looked at the small collection inside. "It's very thoughtful of you, especially after all you've been through."

"They saved my life; it's the least I could do."

155

"Saved your life, how's that?"

"I was able to hide in their Wellington through the sandstorm, and the flask of tea they had on board kept me going through the desert. If they hadn't been where they were, I'd never have made it. I almost didn't anyway, so I really do owe them my life."

"I see..." He nodded thoughtfully.

"I don't know if it's allowed, but if I could get the address of their next of kin, I'd like to write. I buried them and said a prayer, and I'd like their families to know."

"I'll make sure it happens, Cornwall." He smiled warmly. "What about you? It sounds like you've been on quite the adventure; I'm pretty sure we can arrange you some leave. I could even try for a ticket home; all things considered, it may well be granted."

"I'd like to go back to Malta."

"Excuse me?"

"It's my job, Sir, and I'd like to go back."

"Are you sure the hospital checked you out for heatstroke?" he asked with a smile.

"Sir?"

"Anybody with half a brain would jump at the chance of a desk job in Cairo, Cornwall. Or take a trip back to England. Anything's better than Malta right now. It could be argued you were suffering from heatstroke to turn it down."

"I don't think I'm made for a desk job. I love flying too much."

"If you insist..."

"There's something else." She pulled the silk note from her bag and laid it on the desk. The Wing Commander unrolled it to reveal the gold sovereigns.

"Ah, yes. Probably best you sign these back in with the pay office now you're back. Bravo, Cornwall. Most having wandered the desert would have sworn blind they paid the gold to Arabs, then pocketed the sovereigns to spend in Cairo."

"Oh, they're not mine. I wasn't issued any. I found these on the pilot of the crashed Wellington."

"They're not yours?" he asked, and she shook her head politely. "You mean to tell me that you walked across the desert to return the gold belonging to a pilot nobody will see again?"

"Well, that wasn't my only motivation, Sir, but it is RAF property."

"Quite..." He picked up the silk note and looked at the gold, rolling a sovereign between his fingers for a moment, before wrapping it in the silk again with the others, and putting them in Harriet's hand. "To all intents and purposes, this gold no longer exists."

"Sir?"

"The crew to whom it was issued are lost, buried in the desert, along with anything else belonging to the RAF." He gave her a wink, which did nothing to ease her discomfort. "Don't worry, Cornwall, it's not a trick. Rommel's knocking on our door; we've got more to worry about right now than something that technically doesn't exist. Besides, having been lost in the desert myself, I can only imagine you had a hell of a time out there, so put that silk note back in your bag, and use what's in it to buy yourself a damned good meal. Anyone asks, tell them you found it in the desert. You wouldn't be lying."

"Yes, Sir... Thank you."

"I'd save your thanks; I'm not about to do you any favours." She frowned nervously as he picked up the phone and talked into it, getting connected from here to there, before confirming details and

157

timings. "Sunset tomorrow night." Harriet raised an eyebrow questioningly. "There's a Sunderland flying boat heading to Malta at sunset tomorrow. Make sure you're at the seaplane base before take off; otherwise, they'll go without you."

"Yes, Sir!" she said with a big smile, and a smart salute.

"Is that all?" he asked.

"That's all."

"Good. I suppose this'll be a lesson in being careful what you ask for." He gave her a warming smile, and she turned to leave. "Good luck, Cornwall, and thanks for your work." She smiled and left, walking confidently through the headquarters.

"All done?" Emma asked.

"All done," Harriet replied.

"Good, so we should go drop your things at the hotel before we head out to dinner. We'll be early, but that'll just give us time for drinks."

They did as Emma suggested, and to Harriet's amazement, they soon found themselves at the fabled Gezira Sporting Club, which sat on a large island in the Nile, and was the seat of all power and luxury in Cairo. Membership was reserved for military officers and the highest order of local society, both European and Egyptian, the real who's who of Cairo. As they sat overlooking the Nile under the shade of trees, Emma pointed out the famous faces as they came and went. Senior army officers, political figures, and high society types. Harriet had heard of the place; it had its own polo stables and hosted regular tournaments, even in wartime, along with horse racing and every other pursuit the upper classes could need to keep them occupied, all while the common soldier sweated in the desert. It sat a little uncomfortable with Harriet. The luxury was excessive, and she couldn't help thinking of the Australian soldiers she saw in the rocks of the desert ridges as she passed, filthy after days and nights of battle, and living in holes scraped in the sand with a thirst that never left them; all while a hundred miles away waiters in smart white jackets

158

were serving iced cocktails to officers in neatly tailored uniforms, and ladies in fine dresses. As uncomfortable as she was, she was also part of the scene, for the time being at least, and it would be the height of bad manners to walk out, especially when Emma had been so kind to her. She could be wearing hospital clothes and on a slow boat to England, dragging its way through submarine infested seas, but instead, she was wearing the finest uniform in North Africa, or so it felt, and sitting in Cairo's most exclusive club. She knew the discomfort was something she'd feel equally if she went back to her hotel, so she pushed it to the back of her mind and distracted herself with the conversation.

"Hello again..." a vaguely familiar New Zealand voice said. She looked up to see a tall and incredibly handsome officer standing before her, with dark hair and bright eyes that had something of a familiarity about them that she couldn't place. He was accompanied by another man, a Captain. He was shorter and not quite as dashing as the young Lieutenant, but had a warmth about him and a friendly smile.

"Hello..." Harriet replied.

"I don't think we've met," Emma quickly added as she stood.

"Lieutenant Ross, Ma'am, of the Long Range Desert Group, and this is Captain Moor.

"Ross?" Harriet said out loud, quite unintentionally.

"You've forgotten already?" he asked jokingly. "I've had a shave since we last met." She smiled and stood instantly, reaching out and shaking his hand.

"Not at all," she said happily. "Emma, this is Lieutenant Ross. He's the one that found me in the desert. Ross, this is my friend, Emma Cain."

"The Emma Cain?" Moor asked.

159

"Unless you know of another in Cairo?" Emma asked nonchalantly. "Would you like to join us?" The officers nodded and quickly sat, while simultaneously ordering drinks from a passing waiter. "So, you're the one I have to thank for saving my friend from an untimely end in the desert?"

"I wouldn't go that far," Ross replied. "She'd already walked most of the way; we were no more than a taxi service for the last stretch." He gave Harriet a knowing nod, which made her blush.

"Ah yes, I remember. How far was it you said she walked again?"

"Seventy or eighty miles, give or take. The maps are good, but we don't know exactly where she crashed, so there's a bit of guessing."

"I say closer to a hundred."

"Maybe," he laughed.

"You must remember," Emma asked Harriet.

"I can't remember any more than a night and day at the most. I still find it hard to believe it was any further." Harriet shrugged, and the group laughed. They talked, and ate, and got on incredibly well as they watched the sun setting over the Nile while the drinks flowed, including a bottle of the finest Champagne. It was all a little too much for Harriet, who struggled to eat more than half of the steak she'd been served. She filled up quickly and became quite nauseous. Something not made any better by the alcohol going to her head and making her dizzy.

"I feel awful having to ask you this," Emma said to Harriet, after Ross and his friend had gone to the bathroom shortly after sunset.

"What is it?" Harriet asked.

"A frightful imposition," Emma replied with obvious discomfort. "The thing is, I wondered how you felt about your man Ross?"

"Excuse me?"

"I know you're getting on famously, and he saved you from the desert and all that, but he's such a dish I can't take my eyes off him." Harriet felt her cheeks start to burn. "Oh, I feel terrible now."

"What? No! No, I mean, don't, please." Harriet was flustered at the suggestion, and between that and the alcohol, words were falling out of her mouth without any coordination.

"Please don't be irritated with me."

"I'm not, I swear. If anyone's imposing, it's me."

"Don't be ridiculous, darling; you're a delight. It's just silly old me wanting what I can't have." At that, the officers returned, with a waiter in tow ready to take another drinks order.

"You're back," Harriet said as she stood. "I wonder if you'd excuse me. I'm still feeling a little tired after my walk in the desert, and I think I'm going to head off for an early night."

"Not at all," Moor replied.

"Are you OK?" Ross asked.

"Yes, I'll be fine after a good night's sleep, I'm sure."

"I'll see you out..."

"Oh, that won't be necessary; I'm sure Captain Moor will be fine walking me to a taxi. Why don't you and Emma stay and share some more fizz?" She smiled at him, and then Emma, who beamed back in reply.

"If you're sure?"

"Positive. Captain, would you mind?"

"It'd be my pleasure," Moor replied graciously, and offered his arm.

"Goodnight," she said to Emma and Ross, then walked with Moor through the grounds of the club.

"That was very gallant of you," Moor said as they walked.

"What was?"

"Giving up young Ross to your friend without a fight." Harriet simply smiled in reply. "Not that I'm complaining, of course. I get to walk through the Gezira club with one of the most beautiful women I've ever seen."

"Please..." Harriet protested, feeling her cheeks burn.

"Second only to my wife back home," he added with a reassuring smile.

"When did you last see her?"

"One year, eleven months, and eighteen days ago."

"Do you write?"

"As often as we can. Though the mail slows up when we're out in the desert, as you'd expect. Still, it's nice to get something. It puts a smile in your heart. You know how it is."

"Yes..." Harriet smiled at the fondness he radiated when talking of his wife. So many officers played by the rules that what happens when away, stays away, and it was nice to hear a person so wrapped up in somebody he cared for deeply, and hadn't seen for so long; wrapped up enough to know exactly how long that it had been since he last saw her, right down to the day. They talked for a while, about her and their two children. He even showed her photos, which made her feel for a moment that she was connected to another world. He put her in a taxi, and they said goodnight, and she asked if he'd say hello from her to his wife and children when he next wrote, and he promised he would.

At the hotel, she ordered a jug of iced tonic and lime, then hung her uniform and took a long cool shower, before lying on the crisp white sheets beneath the spinning fan, and feeling the cool breeze kissing the soreness of her skin. It was nice to be safe, and to be among decent people. She'd enjoyed meeting with Ross again, too, and being able to thank him properly for getting her to safety. She hadn't thought they'd bump into each other again, but their patrol to Libya had lasted over three weeks, and they'd been stood down to repair and refit their vehicles, and find replacements for those men lost through injury or illness before they went out again. It had been fortuitous. She also thought of Emma and Ross. It made her smile to think of them drinking and talking at the club, and a small part of her felt good, like she'd gone a small way to repaying her debt to Emma by delivering her a tall, handsome Kiwi. It was that thought, and the conversation with the Captain about his wife, that sent her off into a deep sleep.

The next morning, she woke with a dry mouth and sore head. What little alcohol she'd consumed the previous night hadn't been welcomed by her tired body, and it took a long cold shower and lots of iced tonic water to make herself feel better. Emma was full of life, though, and talked incessantly as they enjoyed a breakfast of fruits and small pastries. She and Ross had an incredible night, apparently, and had made another date for brunch, much to Emma's excitement and eternal gratitude. She even offered Harriet use of the car and driver for any errands she needed to do, which Harriet readily accepted.

After dropping Emma for her date and giving Ross a wave, she had the driver take her back to the Italian tailor, where she paid him in gold for making some more clothes to her exact specification. She then visited the delights of the markets to pick up some shopping, and had a late lunch before heading back to collect the clothes a few hours later. The gold had gone a long way. She hadn't even spent half of it, and had lots of change given, which she spent on so many treats they were over spilling from her bags when she finally returned to the hotel. Once back, she packed her bags and took another long cool bath while drinking more iced tonic, then prepared herself for her journey to the seaplane base, which both Emma and Ross returned in time to accompany her on. She had bought some proper Scottish whisky while shopping, which was remarkably easy to get hold of considering they were in Egypt, in the middle of the war, and she presented several bottles of it along with several cartons of American cigarettes to Ross; for him to share with his patrol as her way of thanking them. She also gave him one of the remaining sovereigns, and asked him to give it to the Arab if he passed that way again, or buy something useful with it, sugar or kerosene maybe, and he promised he would.

As the sun dropped lower in the sky, Harriet turned to Emma and took her hands. The excitable young woman had done so much for her, and they'd quickly become such good friends. Harriet thanked her for her kindness and her friendship, and gave her one of the sovereigns as a parting gift. It wasn't the monetary value; she knew Emma had no need of that, but she wanted to give something as a memory of their friendship, and it was gratefully received. They hugged and said goodbye, then Harriet boarded the tender boat that was to take her to the Sunderland, and climbed aboard the great white aeroplane just as the sun kissed the horizon. She stood for a moment in the doorway, and looked back and waved to Emma and Ross, who stood on the dockside silhouetted against the colourful sky behind them, then said a quiet goodbye to Egypt.

Chapter 11

Breaking.

It was pitch dark when the Sunderland finally touched down in Kalafrana Bay, the previously beautiful but now bombed and wrecked seaplane base at the south of Malta. The flight had been uneventful, and Harriet had spent most of it with her face pressed against the window, watching the black Mediterranean slip by underneath them on the still moonless night. She thought of what had happened, and how her time in Egypt had been extremes of luxury and deprivation, and despite making new friends, she knew it was a place she didn't want to hurry back to. Malta was in ruins, but everyone was suffering the same. The Governor had decreed that every rank, no matter how high or how low, would be issued the same rations, and they'd all suffer the same as the local population. It was essential, it had been explained by Cas, that the Maltese didn't feel the British were any different, or getting preferential treatment in terms of food. To do otherwise would be to create division and unrest, which could easily be exploited in such a desperate situation. If the British had it better, all the Germans would have to do is offer equality of rations, and the local population would rise up. At least that's what the theory was. Cas wasn't convinced; he thought the Maltese had more about them as they'd been through sieges before. His theory, which was agreed by Harriet, was that it just wouldn't be right to have full bellies and good food, while other people, other humans, starved. The more she thought of it, the more the absurd inequality of Cairo weighed heavy on her mind. She couldn't work out how the Egyptians hadn't risen up and kicked the British out. There were poor and starving people on the streets everywhere she'd looked, yet in the same city, there was the Gizira Club, with its steaks and cakes. The hunger of Malta was painful, but nowhere near as painful as Cairo's inequality.

Her thoughts were disturbed by the Sunderland losing height; the unmistakable sensation in her stomach made her feel excited, despite being tired. She looked into the distance, and saw the white wave crests as they broke off the cliffs of the south coast. She was home. The engine pitch changed as the enormous flying boat bounced along the waves and slowed towards the jetty. Malta was a dangerous place, according to the crew, and they weren't hanging around. Harriet and a few other passengers were to alight first, followed by the stores that had been brought over, mostly medical supplies. She carried her two kit large bags through the hatch and up the walkway to the dockside, breathing in the humid heat of the Maltese night, which was a shock to her lungs after the desert.

"You're late..." Cas said from the shadows. She instantly smiled and searched for him, then walked quickly in his direction. The sound of his voice triggered something, and her emotions were starting to break through the restraints she'd used to bury them deep inside. She ran the last few steps and instinctively dropped her bags, then threw her arms around him and squeezed tight. He didn't say anything, just held her for a moment, happy to have her home.

"I know, I had engine trouble," she explained as she finally let him out of her vice like embrace and tidied her uniform.

"So I'm told."

"Did you only turn up to criticise me?"

"Maybe."

"What?"

"What?"

"Stop it!"

"I came to make sure it was actually you. The message we got just said a pilot was being returned, I was hoping, but there was no way of knowing for sure."

"You were hoping?"

"That it was you."

"That must mean you've missed me."

166

"Oh, don't start that." He picked up her bags and started to walk away.

"You missed me."

"Did you hit your head while you were away?"

"Yes, how did you know?"

"Thought as much..." She elbowed him as they walked, making him laugh.

"You don't need to carry my bags."

"I know. Don't worry, we're not going far." They walked around the corner of the building and were greeted by the sight of Robbie, sitting on the front of her truck.

"You're late..." Robbie said as she jumped down.

"Don't you start!" Harriet replied, not able to keep the smile from her face. She hugged Robbie, then climbed into the truck while Cas put her bags in the back.

The blackout blinds were closed in Robbie's apartment, which she lit with an oil lamp that made the room glow a soft amber. Cas put Harriet's bags by the table, and pulled out a chair for her to sit before sitting himself while Robbie brought them some water. It was lukewarm with a salty aftertaste, just as she was used to, though the iced tonics with citrus fruits in Cairo had helped cloud that memory a little.

"Wait," Harriet said, before drinking any more. "I have something." She collected one of her kit bags, then sat again with it on her knee, while Cas fiddled with a crooked looking painfully thin cigarette. She pulled out a pair of limes and put them on the table. "For the water," she said excitedly. Robbie looked suitably impressed, and pulled out a knife which she quickly used to expertly remove the rind, before slicing the lime over the cup, not wanting to lose a drop of juice. "There's these, too." She pulled out a carton of American cigarettes

167

and pushed it under Robbie's nose, then another for Cas. They were both instantly in heaven. "Oh, and there's this." She put a bottle of expensive Scottish whisky on the table.

"Did you loot all of Cairo?" Cas asked.

"Something like that," she replied, as she added a box of fresh dates. Their eyes widened, and the welcome home party started. Robbie explained how the CO had broken the news when he returned, and how devastated they'd been at her apparent death. It was difficult for Harriet to hear. She'd been living it up in Cairo the past few days, while they'd been upset thinking she was dead, and it didn't feel nice. They laughed and joked, and Cas teased relentlessly, but the room was simmering with emotion. She'd been gone two weeks, or thereabouts, and times hadn't got any easier on Malta. The Germans and Italians had raided every day without fail, hitting the island several times a day, and night, not letting people sleep or feel safe, and leaving the whole population feeling exhausted and drained. The rations had been cut again, and there wasn't a person on the island who wasn't starving, except, for once, Harriet. After drinking a large whisky and enjoying an American cigarette, Cas looked at his watch, then stood with a sigh. "You're leaving already?" Harriet asked.

"Yes... Some of us have work to do, I'm afraid."

"It's night time," she protested.

"And when has that made a blind bit of difference in this war?"

"I know... I'd just hoped you could stay a little longer."

"I'd love to, trust me. Drink after work tomorrow?"

"Done!"

"You'd better turn up this time!"

"Funny..."

"See you both later; I'll let myself out." He gave them a wink and headed for the door. "I'm happy you're back, Harry."

"Wait..." she stood and dived back into her bag, then followed him to the door carrying a large bundle wrapped neatly in brown paper.

"What's this?" he asked.

"Something for you. Don't open it until you get to your room."

"Thank you..." He smiled warmly, then, after a brief pause, he left.

"He was furious at your CO," Robbie said as she turned out the lantern, before opening the shutters and taking a seat by the open balcony. "I'm surprised you didn't hear the argument all the way over in Egypt."

"Really?" Harriet asked, as she kicked off her shoes and sat opposite Robbie.

"Really. I haven't seen him that angry. He tore a strip off the CO for not bringing you home; they haven't talked since."

"Oh..." Harriet felt something twinge in her stomach, a mixture of guilt and nerves, like it was her fault they'd argued. "It really wasn't his fault. It was lots of things, but he couldn't know it would happen. It was supposed to be a quick run out over the desert."

"The CO said you'd both been asked to do a reconnaissance flight, and you just didn't come back."

"That's about it, really. I had an engine failure in the middle of nowhere, and ended up putting down in the desert a long way behind enemy lines."

"Harry... How did you escape?"

"I don't know. Luck, I suppose." She forced a smile as her mind went back to the desert. She didn't want to go back there, in person or in memory. "I'll sort it between them."

169

"I hope so; he's been like a bear with a sore head for weeks."

"Which one?"

"Both of them!" They laughed and let some tension out of the air. "I'm happy you're back, truly happy," Robbie said after the giggles eased.

"I'm happy to be back."

"In Malta?"

"Yes... I'd take it over Egypt any time." She looked over to Robbie, and watched her face light up as she drew on a cigarette. Her eyes were sunken deep, and her cheekbones prominent. She looked unwell. She held her hand out, and Robbie took hold, and they sat in silence as they looked out over Valletta and the docks.

The sleep was uncomfortable, and made more so by the familiarity of the surroundings. An air raid had shaken Harriet from her sleep, but she was so tired she didn't have the energy to move, and instead just went back to sleep and hoped her aching muscles would hurry up and heal so she could lie still without having to roll over every five minutes because of the pain. Robbie grumbled a few times at her tossing and turning, but didn't really wake enough to complain properly. Before sunrise, Harriet had dragged herself from bed, unable to get comfortable, and pulled on her blouse before standing at the open window and watching the sky start to lighten, while drinking tea made with the fresh leaves she'd borrowed from the hotel in Cairo.

"You're up early," Robbie said as she joined her.

"I couldn't sleep."

"I noticed when you spent the night spinning like a propeller."

"Sorry."

"It's OK, it's not like that's anything new. It wasn't the same sleeping in there without you fidgeting."

"I'm taking that to mean you missed me."

"Something like that..." Robbie gave Harriet a smile as the morning sky lit the dark room, revealing both to each other properly for the first time since before Harriet went away. Robbie was thin, more so than a few weeks earlier, and tired looking. Harriet wondered to herself what it would take to get her a few days in Cairo, just to rest properly and eat, and she decided she'd ask Cas when she met him for drinks.

"Are you OK?" Robbie asked, breaking Harriet's thoughts and bringing her back to the moment.

"What? Yes, why?" She followed Robbie's gaze to the dressings on her feet, and then up her emaciated body.

"You look like you haven't eaten in a month."

"So do you."

"You're probably in the right place to fit in, in that case." She smiled, breaking the tension. "Seriously, though, you look a little beaten up."

"I've felt worse."

"Really?"

"No..."

"Why don't you have the day off? Go to bed and get some rest, maybe? The CO would understand."

"I would if I could sleep, but my muscles hurt so much I wouldn't be able to lie still anyway, so I may as well go to work. Besides, I haven't flown for a while; I'm keen to get back in the sky."

"If you say so..."

"I do."

"Well, I'll drop you at the dispersal if you get dressed." They got busy getting ready, and before the sun was up, they were rolling through the familiar ruins of Floriana as they headed to the airfield, where Harriet was dropped and left, despite Robbie's repeated offers to wait around and take her back home again.

"Hello..." the CO said as he looked up from his desk to see Harriet leaning against the door frame. She'd stood there for a few minutes, silently watching as he scribbled his notes, not wanting to disturb him. A smile slowly spread across his face as he looked her up and down.

"Hello..." Harriet replied.

"I knew they couldn't kill you." He stood and walked around in front of her, then leant on his desk.

"It was close."

"I doubt it; you're too good. What happened? 109s?"

"Engine failure..." She shrugged, almost embarrassed to admit what had ended her flight

"No?"

"Unfortunately."

"I felt sure 109s had got you. Four of the buggers came at me from out of the sun, and they gave me a right run around! They dived from the south, and I just assumed they'd come across you first." Harriet smirked a little as he talked, and her mind went back to the 109s she'd been sure were onto her.

"I saw them, but they dived north and left me alone."

"Well, they would, wouldn't they? The buggers were coming after me!" He smiled, making her laugh out loud. "You're OK, though?"

"Yes, I went down not long after seeing the 109s. I must have pushed the engine a little too hard trying to get some speed because something popped, the windscreen was covered in oil, and the temperature shot up. I had to put her down before she fell out of the sky."

"But that was hundreds of miles from safety..." he replied in shock.

"I know..."

"My God, how on earth did you get back? There was nothing but sand as far as the eye could see!"

"Walked," she shrugged.

"Good on you! No wonder it's taken you weeks to get home!"

"I've had more fun."

"You and me both, and don't go blaming yourself for pushing the Hurricane. Mine was just as much of a wreck as yours by the sounds of it; I'm surprised I didn't end up joining you on your trip. Anyway, I had to drop to the deck to try and get away, and that's how I found our German friends we'd been sent to look for, hiding in the sand. They can't have been a hundred miles from you, maybe more. Lucky, really."

"Sounds like we both had a lucky escape."

"Quite... Though I think I had more luck than you. Are you OK, I mean really? Don't take any offence, but you look shocking."

"I'm fine; I just want to get back in the air, so if you've got any work that needs doing..." She looked over his shoulder and at his desk.

"I don't think so."

"Sir?"

"Cas and I have already locked horns about my not bringing you home. I can't imagine things would improve if I sent you up in harm's way the minute you get back."

"I hardly think he has any say in it!" she blustered, forgetting her place a little, and catching herself before she fully let go at him.

"No, but I do. That aside, you truly do look absolutely shattered, understandably if you were stuck walking in the desert all this time. Your muscles must be wasted; I bet they're sore when you sit or lay?"

"A little..."

"You need rest, and salts, and food and drink. Sitting your bony behind on a parachute for hours at a time while riding a Spitfire around the sky isn't going to help the process, I'm afraid. No, that wouldn't do. Take the rest of the week off, and we'll see how you're doing after a bit of rest."

"But..."

"I can make it two weeks and send you back to Cairo on the next flight out of here?"

"A week would be fine."

"I thought so, now bugger off and get yourself rested. I need you at your best when you're back, so look after yourself." He gave her a wink, and she smiled a little.

"There's just one thing."

"Are you still here?"

"I don't suppose I can borrow that old motorcycle you've let me use in the past? It'll help get me out of town so I can recover properly."

"It's in the pen with my Spit. Don't break it!"

"Yes, Sir!" She turned and walked away.

174

"Good to have you back, Harry."

"Good to be back, Sir." She left the dispersal hut and found the motorcycle. After kick starting it, she was off, racing back to the apartment with a plan already starting to form in her head. She raced through the streets, dodging the shell craters and potholes, feeling a little exhilarated at being able to enjoy at least some speed. However, to her disappointment, she felt quite tired by the time she'd made the short trip to the apartment, and her arms and behind were sore. She left the motorcycle outside while she went in and rummaged through the bags she'd brought back, transferring contents until the smaller bag was loaded. She put her arms through the handles, wearing it on her back like a backpack, then went back to her motorcycle and headed out of town to the hospital. She hadn't seen Bill and Art since she'd left, and couldn't imagine they'd moved out of the hospital just yet, and in Cairo, she'd bought some chocolate, two small coconuts, and some other sweets to help them build their strength. She was grinning to herself as she navigated Malta's rolling roads, while planning how she'd give them a hard time for still being in hospital.

"Good morning, Ma'am," the duty nurse at the front desk said, as Harriet entered the hospital with as much bounce as she could, while swinging the bag off her back. She replied cheerily and asked where she could find her crew. "One moment, please." The nurse checked her notes, then left the desk and went into the office behind. A minute later, the Matron appeared.

"Is everything OK?" Harriet asked. Her heart was starting to race a little, and not just from the ride to the hospital.

"Would you come through, please, Squadron Leader?" The Matron was formal, and as hard as almost every nurse she'd met, and despite now being a Squadron Leader, Harriet was still a bit terrified. She nodded and followed the stern older woman into her office. "Could I get you some tea?"

"No, thank you... Matron, what's wrong?"

"There's no easy way of saying this, so I'll just be blunt. Sergeant Evans died of internal bleeding. He seemed fine, then deteriorated very quickly. We can't be sure, but the surgeon thinks maybe a piece of shrapnel had worked its way close to an artery, and nicked it when he started moving around more. There was nothing we could do; I'm sorry."

"I see..." Harriet felt deflated and confused. He'd been sitting up in bed and talking away the last time she'd seen him. It seemed impossible that he'd died so quickly, so unimaginable that she was struggling to think. "And the other? Sergeant Kennedy?"

"Making progress." The Matron gave a hard, half smile, which lifted Harriet temporarily, until she felt something else coming.

"But?" she asked, preempting whatever was coming next.

"But the surgeon had to take his left leg above the knee. The injury was too bad to stop gangrene setting in; if we hadn't taken it off, we'd have lost him." Harriet nodded, not able to find the words. "We sent him to Egypt on an evacuation flight a few days ago, as soon as he was stable enough to move. He's young and strong, and stands a better chance over there than here. At least they'll be able to feed him up a bit and give him the energy to fight. I'm sorry..."

"It's OK; thank you for your time." Harriet turned and headed out of the room; she was deflated and heartbroken.

"Is there anything else?"

"No... Thank you..." She walked out of the hospital, trying desperately to hold herself together, and quickly slung her bag on her back, then kicked the motorcycle into life and rode off away from the hospital and out into the countryside, following roads and then tracks, until she found somewhere secluded where she could stop and cry. Her tears flowed as a deep guilt ripped through her. Try as she could, there was no escaping the thought that it was all her fault, and they'd both be fine if she'd just turned and ran. Instead, it was all about the mission, as always, all about trying to impress and trying not to disappoint. Finally, it had caught up with her. She'd got the goods, as the CO would say, she found the ship and got the location off, and she'd paid for it with her crew's lives. There was no negotiating with the thought that the price had been too high. She'd stopped an oil tanker, but so what? She'd been to Egypt; she'd seen the fighting. The tanker hadn't got there, but still, Rommel was marching east. Besides, all that effort, all that sacrifice, and people were drinking Champagne in Cairo like nothing was happening. She was angry as well as sad. Two good men out of the war, one dead, one almost. What good were medals to them? She'd been so excited writing them up for the Distinguished Flying Medal, more so when they were approved. A medal wouldn't bring Bill back, or save Art's leg. She cursed herself as she leant over the petrol tank of her motorcycle and tried to control her tears. "Pull yourself together!" she shouted at herself, then dried her cheeks and started the motorcycle again, and opened the throttle and raced at the next bend. She skidded as an army truck rounded the corner coming the other way, forcing her to hit the brakes and slide across the road, just managing to miss both the truck and one of Malta's many stone walls. It was enough to get her adrenaline flowing, and to clear her mind for a moment, long enough to know what she needed, and she headed to Mdina.

"God be blessed," Lissy said, as she opened the door and stared at Harriet.

"Hi, Lissy," Harriet said with a simple shrug.

"Thank you, thank you, thank you," Lissy repeated, while looking upwards with her hands clasped tight together in prayer, then she ran forward and hugged Harriet. "Oh, thank you, God. You brought my girl home." Harriet's emotions started to get the better of her, and she felt a tear on her cheek. She shook as Lissy squeezed her tight. The hug was what she needed more than anything. "Anj will be beside himself when he gets home." She pulled Harriet into the house, and once in the kitchen, she paced excitedly, with tears in her eyes, then thanked God again before giving Harriet another hug. "Sit, I'll make tea," she instructed, while pulling out a chair and pushing Harriet down. "They told us you were dead!"

"Who did?"

"Cas. He came to tell us, only last week."

"Sorry..."

"Don't you dare; I couldn't be happier to see you. Never be sorry to be alive."

"I'm not; I'm sorry you were told I was dead."

"He was doing what he thought was right, I suppose. He said you'd been shot down over the desert in Egypt. It was hard to believe at first; we didn't even know you'd left Malta! He explained, though. It was a hard time." She opened the cupboard and frowned into the tea caddy.

"I have something," Harriet said, and pulled a tin of tea from her kit bag. "Here." She handed it to Lissy, who stared at it with excitement.

"I won't use much."

"Use as much as you like; I brought it from Cairo for you."

"For me?"

"For you. I brought gifts for you and your family." She opened her kit bag and started emptying the contents, including the coconuts she'd bought for Bill and Art, and piled the sweet biscuits, fruits, sweets, and tinned meats on the table, as Lissy's eyes opened wider and wider. There was even tinned evaporated milk, and powdered milk and eggs for Lissy's grandchildren. "Oh, and I got you this. I know you were running low." She put a bottle of whisky on the table, and a carton of American cigarettes.

"My dear girl, you can't give us all this."

"I can, and I am. You and your family looked after Nicole and me and made us welcome in your home; it's the least I can do."

"It's your home, too. You are family, you and Nicole. You know that."

"Then you can't say no to the gifts, not from family."

"My English daughter, I am so proud of you, and so grateful to God for bringing you back to us."

"Where is everybody?" Harriet asked, trying to lighten the situation and reduce the emotion. She was already a simmering wreck, and could do with something a little less intense.

"Anj is working, as always, and my daughter and her children are at the school in the town. It's good for them to get out and see other children, you know?"

"Of course." Harriet smiled as they talked; it was a pleasant distraction from the bad news she'd had at the hospital. Even her story of walking in the desert was light relief from the instant dread that haunted her since returning to Malta. She'd been back less than twenty four hours, having been desperate to escape the luxurious surroundings of soft sheets, cold drinks, and all she could eat, so she could return to humid heat, ruins, and the news that she'd killed one of her crew and maimed the other. If it wasn't for Lissy's smiles and hugs, and the warmth she had for the girl she insisted was her English daughter, Harriet thought she'd go mad, and quite quickly. She told Lissy about her crew, after they'd talked for a while, and despite trying to be casual and dismissive about it being what happens in war, she couldn't hold back the tears. Lissy listened, comforted, and pointed out that being in a war didn't make the feelings any less real. She talked with Harriet and helped her find the words for how she was feeling, and as they finished their second cup of tea and a chocolate dipped date, Harriet was starting to feel like some of the emotional burdens had lifted a little. Lissy convinced her that her tiredness wasn't helping, and with some rest, she'd be better able to process what had happened.

"You should come to dinner tonight; Anj and the rest of the family would love to see you."

"Thank you, but I already have an appointment to keep tonight." She smiled as she thought of her pending drinks with Cas. She was looking forward to it, and had been since Cairo.

179

"Can't it wait?"

"It's already a few weeks overdue. Maybe another time?"

"Of course, tomorrow perhaps?"

"Tomorrow it is." They both smiled, then Lissy poured each of them a small whisky from the bottle Harriet had brought from Cairo.

"I shouldn't..."

"You don't have to fly or work; you said already," Lissy shrugged. Harriet nodded in agreement and enjoyed the whisky, and the burn it left in her throat, and she continued to enjoy it through the air raid sirens that cut through the conversation, and led them both to the rooftop terrace to watch as a small hit and run style raid ravaged Valletta and the area around the docks, then disappeared out to sea before any intercepting aircraft got anywhere close. It wasn't much of a show, and by the time they were gone, wisps of black smoke trailed up from the docks, where the bombs had found a target of some sort, beating the odds of finding something that hadn't already been bombed and could still be burned. As all clear sounded, they headed downstairs again, where they said their goodbyes and Harriet set off for home, where she planned to fall into bed and sleep. Her eyes were heavy already, and it was only just coming up to lunchtime.

"Are you ever on time for anything?" Harriet asked while tapping her watch, as Cas joined her in the bar that evening, wearing the new uniform she'd had made for him in Cairo. He was fifteen minutes late, which given the chaos of the war and the nature of his job, was quite unremarkable, except where Harriet was concerned. He rarely arrived on time for anything, usually early, sometimes late, but hardly ever on time. Something which Harriet was sure he did on purpose, as it needled her, and she made sure he knew it.

"Given your recent escapades, you can hardly sit in court over poor timekeeping," he said casually, looking not in the slightest bothered by her chastising.

"That's not fair!"

"Technically, you're about two weeks late..." He smirked as he shrugged. "And stop tapping my watch like that; you'll scratch the glass... More than you already have..."

"Technically, you gave me the watch."

"Technically, I loaned it to you until we could find you one of your own."

"Technically, you can have it back in that case!" She frowned at him, then half smiled as he rolled his eyes and shook his head.

"Drink?"

"Bollinger, thank you," she smirked.

"Bollinger. May as well make it a bottle," he said to the barman, who shrugged in reply, then prepared two Horse's Necks. The drinks they always had there. Everyone in Malta knew there was more chance of seeing a herd of flying pigs than there was a bottle of Bollinger. The only booze on the entire island was whatever could make its way there on submarines and the occasional aircraft, and there wasn't that much space for bottles of fine Champagne. "So, missing Egypt yet?"

"If I never go back there, it'll be too soon..."

"Liked it that much?"

"I don't know what I hated the most. Being lost in the desert without any water, or being in Cairo, surrounded by polo fields and people who'd never even heard so much as a door bang, despite being in the middle of a war."

"Yes... It can be like that sometimes."

"You've been?"

"Oh, yes, and I'm in no hurry to go back. Though the tailor is worth a visit, thank you." He gave her a wink as he looked at his uniform, and she nodded and smiled politely in reply. "Cairo's the last bastion of the fading British Empire, where the rich and shameless mix with career officers who still live to make the world England. Frankly, being there makes my skin crawl."

"At least we agree on that... It just felt so wrong. I saw soldiers in the desert, half starved, thirsty, and burned brown by the sun, living in holes and fighting hand to hand with Germans and Italians, while not a hundred miles away, people were watching horse races and drinking Champagne. Bollinger included! I couldn't wait to get back."

"Yes, that sounds like Egypt..." he sighed. "Still, I can't imagine rushing back to Malta was the smartest thing you've done in your life."

"Excuse me?" She opened her mouth in mock shock at his statement.

"I expect you'd have better odds of staying alive in the desert. You'd probably have more to eat, too. Things haven't exactly got any better since you've been gone."

"They're better now I'm back..."

"They are?"

"Yes, I'm here. My presence instantly improves any situation." She smirked, and he couldn't help but laugh.

"It is good to see you again. I was worried when you didn't come back."

"I heard..."

"Oh?"

"Robbie mentioned you and the CO got into an argument about it."

"Oh..." He looked a little sheepish. "Well, he shouldn't have got you into a situation like that. It's far too dangerous, and you're far too important!" he ranted, then caught himself and gathered his composure. "To the war effort, I mean..." He quickly added, in response to her raised eyebrow.

"You know you can't keep me safe from everything, don't you? I mean, we are in the middle of a war, and I'm a Spitfire pilot. Danger kind of goes with the job."

"Don't I know it! Anyway, how was your day off? Get up to much?"

"Oh, went to the theatre, had lunch with a few friends, went shopping. You know how it is." She smirked and laughed as he raised an eyebrow. "Actually, it finished better than it started..." she continued. "I went to the hospital to see Bill and Art, my crew who were shot up a while back."

"How are they?"

"Dead... Well, Bill is. Art got gangrene, and they had to take his leg off before evacuating him to a hospital in Egypt. They're not sure if he'll make it."

"I'm sorry..."

"Why? You didn't do it. What happened to them was entirely my fault."

"Oh, how's that?"

"I stayed when I should have run. It was only a tanker, and from what I saw in Cairo, they don't seem half as concerned about convoys getting through as we do. I put my crew in danger, put their lives at risk, to try and stop a tanker crossing the Mediterranean in some sort of misguided belief that it matters!" Her eyes glazed over a little as she fought to control her anger.

"It does matter..." Cas said calmly.

"How? How can it possibly matter, when in Cairo they all sit on their arses drinking Champagne while watching horse races? We're dying

183

out here to stop Rommel from getting his supplies, and they couldn't give a damn! They've got it better than any of us; why are we killing ourselves to protect their lifestyles?"

"We're not..."

"What?"

"We're not. We don't fight to keep those pompous dinosaurs sitting on their arses; their time is coming to an end anyway, mark my words. This war will be the end of them, and their way of life, regardless of who wins."

"Then what the hell are we doing?"

"We're fighting for those filthy wretches you saw in the desert going toe to toe with Rommel's best. There's tens of thousands of them out there, all dirt poor, with empty bellies and dry mouths, and as likely to see the inside of places like the Gezira club with its polo and horse track as we are a chilled bottle of Bolly's finest vintage materialising in front of us and doing a dance across the bar." He took a sip of his drink while Harriet fought to hide a smirk that was appearing in response to his suggestion. "Rommel is at El Alamein. A little over seventy miles from Alexandria, our deep water port in North Africa. Home of the Royal Navy since they left Malta, and the gateway to the Nile delta and the Suez Canal. If he seizes Alexandria, he takes our supply routes, he cuts off the Navy, and he's no more than a steady march up the Nile to Cairo with nothing to stop him. Knowing that, as soon as Alexandria falls, Egypt will turn on Britain in an instant. Their government has been looking for an excuse to push for independence for years, and the arrival of the Germans would do it. We'll lose hundreds of thousands of troops, cut off in the desert with no supplies, we'll lose Suez and our supply lines, we'll lose the oil fields, and while the Germans consolidate their position on the south of the Mediterranean and prepare to come and finish us off, the Italians will move south into Africa and wipe out any of our garrisons before heading for Rhodesia and South Africa, and their gold and diamond mines. Regardless of what happens elsewhere, without North African oil and South African wealth, the war in Europe will grind to a halt, even with the Americans in the game now..." He paused for a moment and gave Harriet a smile. "The reason that none of this has happened yet, is that Rommel's supply lines are stretched tight, and intelligence reports suggest that he's only receiving a quarter of the supplies he needs, at best. He wasn't stopped at El Alamein by the fight we put up alone. He was stopped by lack of supplies, and ultimately lack of fuel. You contributed to that. Had that tanker got through, the fuel it was carrying would have been rushed up the supply lines, and Rommel's tanks would be in Alexandria, make no mistake. So, while the loss of your crew is regrettable, and a tragedy to their families, the sacrifice of two men has saved the lives of tens of thousands. When all's said and done, it comes down to the numbers. One loss there saves thousands somewhere else. It's that simple."

"It's a cruel way to look at it..."

"It's a cruel war..." He smiled again, attempting to be reassuring. "If we see the numbers instead of the people, it sometimes makes the horror a little more tolerable."

"I'm not sure I can do that."

"Neither can I, but it's a good theory." He gave her a wink, which made her smile again. "However we look at it, the facts are the same. What we're doing here is vitally important, regardless of how easy some in Cairo have it, and as much as I'd like to see certain classes chased through Africa and forced to experience the deprivation of the common soldier, we can't let our anger at them and their ways jade us."

"You're right, I suppose."

"I'm sorry about your crew, though. It's never easy losing somebody you're responsible for."

"You're right about that, too..."

"Are you OK?"

"I suppose, why?"

"You've said I'm right twice in a row. I'm worried you're sickening for something."

"Must be all that sun in the desert; it did make me a little delirious."

After an evening of conversation, Cas insisted, as he always did, on walking Harriet to her apartment in Floriana. She always protested, pointing out that despite the bombing, Malta was the safest place in the world for a young woman to walk alone at night. She was always grateful when he insisted, though. With the blackout, the streets were pitch black, and it would be easy to fall down a shell crater or trip over some debris, or even be caught in a night raid, which had happened a few times, and she felt better having somebody with her, just in case. They talked as they made their way through the dark streets, and laughed. It was the end to the day that Harriet needed. Regardless of the explanation, or the numbers, the news of her crew had hit her hard, more than losing others had in the past. Maybe because they were actually in the same aeroplane, she reasoned, and her actions had a direct impact on them. Or, maybe because she was exhausted, and didn't have the strength to deal with the emotions as she usually would. Either way, spending time with her Maltese mum, and then having an evening of drinks with Cas, had made the world much more tolerable. Even the wailing of the air raid siren had them laughing as they ran to the nearest shelter, tripping and stumbling in the dark as they did. Searchlights lit up the sky just as they reached the entrance to the shelter, which was packed to full when they got there, mostly with Maltese people who had practically moved in after their houses were bombed. They stood at the entrance with a few others. They watched as the sky started to flash with the explosions of anti aircraft fire, and listened in fear when the rumbling thuds started as the raiders dropped their bombs on and around the nearby Grand Harbour. Harriet clung tight to Cas as the bombs came closer, feeling her nerves start to shake with the vibrations that were now rocking the shelter and showering dust onto the people below, filling the air with dry grit that took her back to the sandstorm in Egypt. He held her tight, and put himself between her and the shelter entrance as the bombs almost rocked them off their feet, determined to keep her safe from any shrapnel that found its way in. They were safe, though, and the thuds and vibrations eased as the explosions became more distant with the raid's passing.

186

"I didn't miss that..." Harriet said, as the noise finally dulled.

"Come on, let's get you home," Cas replied, as he took her hand and led her out onto the street. The darkness was now broken by fires in every direction, particularly the harbour, which once again had borne the brunt of the attack. They walked quickly, staying away from the flames, keeping to the darkness where possible, and letting people get on with putting out fires and saving lives. There were already more than enough volunteers; they didn't need anyone else getting in the way.

"Robbie..." Harriet said quietly, as she rounded the corner and stopped in her tracks. Her heart was pounding as she stood and stared at the remains of her apartment block, burning and smoking, while local people fought their way through the rubble. "Robbie!" Harriet shouted, as she pulled her hand away from Cas and started to run.

"Harry, wait!" Cas shouted, then quickly gave chase. By the time he'd caught up with her, she'd already pushed her way through to the front, and was joining in the efforts to pull at the rubble and hand it to the chain of volunteers that had formed. He joined her, and they worked side by side for hours, until finally a moved slab of masonry revealed a small cavern. Down in the darkness, a wooden beam was laid over Robbie, keeping the heaviest of the rubble from her torso, but she was still covered in stones and dust, which half filled her mouth. Ignoring Cas' protests, Harriet immediately pushed herself through the small hole and into the cavern, then used her hands to dig the pile of dust and gravel from Robbie's face, and with her fingers, scraped the dust from her mouth. While Cas and others moved the heavier rubble from above, being careful not to dislodge anything carelessly and bury Harriet and Robbie together. Harriet moved the smaller rocks from around Robbie, clearing her chest enough to push her head close and hear the faintest of heartbeats. Knowing her friend was still alive, just, she worked even harder to clear the debris, so once the hole above was widened and made safe, Cas could climb in, and help lift Robbie to the waiting hands of the rescuers. Before Harriet could pull herself from the rubble, Robbie had already been loaded into a military ambulance, and was on her

187

way to the hospital. Harriet turned to continue digging, ready to get to work in searching for the neighbours, when Cas pulled her away.

"Get off!" she barked, as she pulled away.

"No..." he replied. "You need to come with me, Harry." He nodded reassuringly and offered his hand. She paused for a moment, then took it, and he led her down the rubble and into the street, away from the rescue team that had arrived, and was busily coordinating the continuing rescue effort. He brushed the dust from her hair, and her tear soaked cheeks, then handed her his small silver flask. She took it, then sat down on a lump of masonry and stared into space, with the flask shaking in her hand.

Chapter 12

Hide and Seek

"Good morning, my dear. How did you sleep?" Lissy asked, as Harriet walked into the kitchen dressed in her uniform blouse and khaki shorts, and the new plimsolls Emma had bought her in Cairo. It was the first time she'd worn her uniform in over a week. Cas had delivered her to Lissy and Anj on the night her apartment was bombed. She'd stayed in her old rooftop room ever since, practically living in the dress Lissy's daughter had given her, and whiling away the days sleeping or helping Lissy around the house. She'd ventured out a couple of times, taking the motorcycle to St Peter's Pool, where she swam in the warm Mediterranean and sunbathed on the rocks, and she'd visited the hospital every day to see Robbie, despite her being unconscious in a deep coma, and she watched while the doctors and nurses fought to save her from the myriad of injuries they'd found. Her skull was fractured, as were her ribs, and her lung punctured. That was just the list of immediately life threatening injuries that they knew of. There was a broken leg, wrist, nose, and a hundred cuts and scratches, too. Harriet talked to her each day, convinced Robbie could hear, but it was heart wrenching. She was starting to hate the hospital. Other than her own experience there, where she and Nicole had been patched up before being shipped out, all she got there was bad news. Visits meant something bad had happened. Cas had visited her a couple of times during her leave to make sure she was OK. The first was the day after the bombing, when he brought what possessions of hers he was able to rescue from the rubble. She didn't know it, but after taking her to Lissy's house, he went back to the apartment and joined the search party, then spent hours raking through the rubble. Remarkably, despite the destruction, he was able to find the kit bags Harriet had brought back from Cairo, and they were surprisingly undamaged; even the bottle of brandy she had stashed among her other goodies was still in one piece.

"Not bad, thank you," Harriet finally replied to Lissy, after thinking about the truth for a moment. She'd had nightmares that had kept her awake, as she'd had every night since the bombing. Cas' words about the importance of their job and the inevitability of losses had helped relieve some of the guilt she'd had for Bill and Art, but it didn't mean she wasn't upset by what had happened. Then, Robbie was the icing on the cake. Harriet had stayed out longer than usual that night; being so relieved to be back from Egypt, she'd got lost in the moment, and she knew that had she gone back at her usual time, she'd have been in bed and under the rubble as well. With the occasional nightmares of being trapped under water or burned alive, the additions of dying of thirst and being buried alive were making it difficult to sleep at all.

"You're in your uniform..."

"It's time to get back to work."

"A few more days rest wouldn't hurt?"

"I think most of the pilots on the island would agree, but I've had a week off already and need to get back before I forget how to fly." She laughed, trying to make light of the situation, but only got a cool smile from Lissy in reply. They had breakfast, then Harriet took to her motorcycle and headed across the already warm and scorched brown island. Her stomach spun a little at the thought of flying again, it had been a while since her last flight, and a lot had happened. The nerves weren't helped by having to hide in a ditch while a morning raid of 109s swept the island at treetop height, shooting up everything that was moving. While unsettling, the fighter sweep was also quite steadying, and helped her focus on what it was she did for a living; and pull her mind out of the gloom that had been haunting her recently.

Two hours later, she was in her trusty blue Spitfire, scouring the coast of Sicily and taking photos of airfields, going in high from the sea, then running home before the defenders had time to send interceptors up to get her. She was back in Malta before they even got close, then back up again to look at some of the other airfields, before racing home again with the goods. She felt better with each flight, like she was in control again. The Spitfire was fast, powerful, and responsive, and she felt confident that the vixen could outrun anything that even tried to get close, even the anti aircraft artillery, which the CO had taught her how to confuse by calculating their firing patterns so they didn't come close. By the evening sunset sortie, a low level run over

190

the airfields further along the coast, and away from Malta, she was smiling again. Having taken the long route out over the Mediterranean, she shot over the land with the large dropping sun behind her, making it difficult for anyone to get their eyes on her, pilot or gun crew. She was gone before a shot was fired, and touching down on Malta just as the post sunset glow was fading from purple to blue.

"Great flying today, Harry," the CO said, as the airmen removed the cameras and film from her Spitfire, while she jumped down from the wing.

"Thanks, it's good to be back at it."

"How's she performing?" he nodded at the Spitfire.

"Like a dream. Better than that rickety old Hurricane they gave me in Cairo."

"Yes... I let their CO know our thoughts about that, in no uncertain terms. Mine was held together with string and goodwill at best, but at least the engine didn't give up like yours."

"Don't remind me!"

"Sorry..." he laughed. "Anyway, good work today, but you'd better get off and get some sleep; we've got an early start tomorrow. I'll need you ready to take off an hour before sun up."

"That is early... What's going on?"

"Something big, at least I think so. I'm being briefed on the details tonight, so I'll tell you first thing."

"I may just hang around here and sleep in the dispersal hut."

"Well, if you're going to do that, you may as well come for a ride up to HQ with me and get briefed from the horse's mouth. We'll see if we can scrounge any tea or biscuits."

"I'll get rid of my flying kit." She ran into the dispersal hut and dumped her kit, then quickly joined him in his car, which he ran quickly through the ruinous streets, making the most of the last light of the day, arriving just as the sky was turning an inky dark blue. They passed through the sentry point and the duty desk, then made their way through the humid stinking tunnels. She coughed a little as the very human smell tickled the back of her throat and made her eyes water a little.

"Everything OK?" the CO asked, as he noticed her watering eyes.

"Yep..." she replied, swallowing hard then trying to breathe without tasting the air. It was her first time in the tunnels since being back, and she'd forgotten how hot and humid they were, and how most in Malta didn't have access to rose petal baths to sweeten them while a laundry worker scrubs the sweat from their clothes. As much as she hated the inequality of Cairo, she was missing some elements. The CO smirked. He knew what she was thinking, and it tickled him.

"Yes?" a voice shouted, after the CO had knocked on the AOC's office door for the second time. He pushed it open and waved Harriet in ahead of him.

"Sir..." she said in shock as she saw the man standing before her. It was her old AOC from England, the man who'd given her the start she'd been begging for in the RAF.

"I see my instinct to put you in a uniform and have you fly for us paid off, Miss Cornwall," he said in his soft yet notable antipodean accent.

"Yes, Sir..." She smiled as she stepped closer to the desk.

"What's the matter? You look like you've seen a ghost!"

"I wasn't expecting to see you, Sir."

"What? Oh, yes... I took over while you were away building sandcastles. I trust you've recovered well enough from your adventures?"

"Yes, Sir. Absolutely."

"She was up three times today, Sir, and she got some bloody good photos of the airfields along the Sicilian coast," the CO added.

"Good, we're going to need them. Right, we'd better get you briefed while you're here. Shall we?" He gestured to the door, then led them out and along the corridor to the operations room. Harriet stood behind him as he took his place behind the duty controller, overlooking the large map table below, and the team of young women poised to track raids. Harriet scanned the table, and was drawn to the markers to the west of Malta. The AOC looked at her, and then followed her eyes before nodding and smiling. "Your instincts serve you well, Cornwall."

"Sir?" She looked back to him, feeling a little surprised.

"What you're looking at is the biggest convoy that's been sent into the Mediterranean yet, and Malta's last hope of salvation. If it gets through, we stay in the war; if it doesn't, we'll be finished by September." He paused for a moment, giving her time to appreciate the gravity of what he'd just said. "They've had a tough time of it already, and lost an aircraft carrier to submarines. To make it worse, the Italian fleet put to sea yesterday, and nobody's seen them since. That's where you come in." He looked at Harriet and the CO in turn. "We need to find the Italian fleet, at all costs... Your reconnaissance pilots need to fly every hour and every square mile until we find them, and when you do, you're to break radio silence and report their position immediately. Understand?"

"Yes, Sir," they said in unison.

"I know that it puts you reconnaissance types at risk, but we have no alternative. If the Italian fleet intercepts that convoy, we've had it. I wish I could give you better news, but there you have it. We're in the fight of our lives."

"You can rely on us, Sir," the CO said.

"I know I can; it's why they gave me the best. Now, you'd better get some rest. I want you up and over the Mediterranean before the sun rises. Speak to Ops, they'll make sure you have the speed and heading of the convoy, and you can work out your likely intercept points from that. If I were you, I'd start at the convoy and work outwards, but be careful! They're not within range of our air cover yet, and without their carrier, they're likely to be a bit twitchy about seeing aeroplanes flying around." He offered his hand to the CO. "Good luck. I know you won't let us down."

"We'll do our best, Sir." the CO replied.

"Good luck, Cornwall," he added, as he shook Harriet's hand. "It's damned good to see you again, and to see how well you've done. You're a credit to the service."

"Sir..." Harriet replied with a nervous smile. It was all she could do to hold the tension in, especially after hearing the 'at all costs' part, which involved reporting the fleet as soon as they found it, meaning breaking radio silence and giving their position away to any unfriendly fighters in the area.

"I'll let you get on, if there's nothing else?"

"I wondered if Wing Commander Salisbury is around?" Harriet asked, then found herself inexplicably blushing.

"Afraid not right now, I have him on an errand. I'll let him know you came by, though," the AOC replied with a smile. "Good luck, and if you put your heads in the canteen, we had some proper biscuits come in on a submarine last night. It wouldn't hurt us if you were to take a handful back for your pilots."

They saluted, and left him to talk with the duty controller. Harriet had a last look around, just in case Cas was hiding somewhere in the Ops Room, but he was nowhere to be seen; so it was back to the dispersal hut, where she helped the CO planning routes on the briefing map for the following morning. He'd sent a message out to all photographic reconnaissance pilots instructing them to report bright and early, even cancelling the leave he'd given a couple who were up at the rest house on the coast, where RAF pilots who were close to exhaustion were sent to relax, sunbathe, and swim in relative peace. Harriet had never gone, instead preferring to spend any time off she'd had in Malta on the south coast or in Mdina. The rest house could be quite a place, according to Cas. Lots of pilots with nothing better to do didn't make it sound like the most restful of places. After working for hours, the CO finally said goodnight and left her to push chairs together and get comfortable. Soon she was alone in the darkness, wrapped in her flying jacket and trying to sleep, which she eventually did after a night raid rattled the airfield, making her cringe and tense, and think about Robbie, until it finally passed and her eyes closed.

It seemed she'd only just closed her eyes when the room started to come alive with arriving pilots. The CO was first, bringing a large urn of tea with him and the biscuits he'd looted from the tunnels the previous night. Harriet poured herself a drink of the still distasteful dishwater and had a biscuit with it, while shuffling in her chair, trying to get comfortable. Despite the time off, she hadn't had that much to eat, mostly because of the rationing. This meant that her muscles weren't growing or recovering, meaning they ached almost as much as her bones whenever she sat or laid for long periods. After a night on the chairs, she wasn't looking forward to a long flight in a Spitfire, which she knew was coming. The other pilots joined her, with a polite nod and hello to each other as they got comfortable. They were very different to the pilots of a fighter squadron, who were boisterous and full of banter, morning, noon, and night. The nature of their job meant there was every chance they'd be dead the next time they went up, and each time they flew, they knew that luck and chance had as much to do with their surviving as anything else. That made them want to live, so every moment was spent living. Reconnaissance pilots were a different breed entirely, and while many came from fighter squadrons originally, they behaved very differently. They knew that what they did took a lot of planning and thinking, and took a great deal of strategy before they even left the ground. They also knew that being unarmed, they had to outthink and outfly any enemy, and that made them very restrained in their outward behaviour. Some called them aloof or arrogant, but the truth was that they flew alone with nobody to watch their back, and they relied on themselves and themselves alone, which made them quite insular.

195

The briefing was delivered, and the seriousness of the situation was imparted on the gathered pilots, who took it in their usual calm and unflappable stride. They were briefed on their routes and search patterns, and given the latest intelligence on the likely locations of the Italian fleet. The orders given by the AOC were relayed in a clear and unmistakable way; they were to break radio silence and report the location of the fleet immediately, with no delays. After asking questions, the pilots were sent off to check their maps and prepare their flights, with the instruction to be in the air within the next hour.

After getting comfortable in her seat, Harriet went through her checks one last time, then pushed her map under her leg and started the engine. It coughed into life, breaking the darkness with flames from the exhaust stubs, as the mighty Merlin engine roared into life. As always, she smiled for a moment as the blue smoke hung in the cockpit. She loved the smell as much as anything else, and the first vibrations shook her muscles and made her heart race. It never got old. She checked the magnetos, and the temperatures and pressures, enjoying seeing the soft glow of the needles on the dials as they responded to her actions. She smiled again; she was ready. She'd prepared her maps the night before, all she needed to do was get herself and her Spitfire ready, and that didn't take long at all. She waved the chocks away, then taxied to the end of the runway, swinging left and right so she could see over the long nose of the Spitfire, and spot any unusually dark patches denoting the presence of shell holes. Once in position, she ran up the engine again; and when she was convinced everything was as it should be, she let off the brakes and was pulled back into her seat as the big blue Spitfire immediately burst into a sprint along the runway. She watched the gauges and the silhouettes outside; it was still pitch black, and she needed to focus without any real visual cues to guide her, but she was confident and comfortable, knowing that the Spitfire would take off when it was good and ready regardless of what she did, and it did. She felt her stomach flutter as the Spitfire leapt into the sky. It was her favourite feeling. She lifted the undercarriage, checked her gauges, then turned onto her first bearing, and climbed hard into the dark sky. The top of the climb made her smile in a way she hadn't for some time; when she levelled out at thirty thousand feet, she felt like she was sitting among the stars. The clear canopy of her reconnaissance Spitfire offered an unobstructed view of the heavens, and for a moment, she just looked up, staring at the millions of stars as they shone and twinkled all around. Just for a second, she felt that all was well with the world, almost like she'd left and was no longer part of the killing and pain thousands of feet below. Her mind wandered briefly, and she imagined if her seat in the stars was what she could expect when she finally got her harp, and joined those that had gone before her. If it was, she was OK with it.

Harriet's daydreaming was interrupted by the first rays of dawn lightening the eastern sky behind her, signalling the arrival of what she knew was going to be a long day. Seconds after the light in the east had caught her attention in her rear view mirror, she noticed an orange glow on the western horizon. It could only be one thing, the convoy, though it wasn't the way she wanted to find them. Dreams of stars and angels faded, and her senses were heightened. It was time to focus, and she started searching the darkness below for signs of ships. The lightening sky provided the contrast she needed to focus her efforts on scouring the sea, rather than trying to work out where it ended and the sky started. She picked out a few more dark shapes with smoke trailing upwards, and then the convoy turned, and she saw the neat muted white lines of the wake behind each of the ships. She'd definitely found them, but she wasn't counting as many wakes as she'd been told to expect. She continued to her calculated turn point, while a few flashes of anti aircraft fire started coming up from the convoy to let her know she'd been seen, or heard at least. She felt confident she was high enough to be safe, but felt sorry for the crews below, who she was sure were thinking she was the enemy. As she turned, she thought of the German Condor reconnaissance bomber that stalked her across the Atlantic, and how nervous it had made her feel, even when she couldn't see it. She watched her compass, and set a course northeast of the convoy's position, then started her search for the Italian fleet. The thinking was that the Italians could be literally anywhere, and could be hiding north or south of the convoy, with the only expectation being that they'd be in front and in waiting, rather than chasing from behind. Heading northeast had another benefit; it would put the Italian fleet between Harriet and the rising sun, silhouette them against the skyline, if they were there. She searched to the limit of her fuel tanks, but found nothing. If the Italian fleet was out there, they weren't anywhere around her search route; and with

Sicily on the horizon, it was time to turn away and head home. As she checked her instruments and switched fuel tanks one last time, she saw something on the low horizon, much closer than Sicily, but nowhere near the water. It looked like a cloud of gnats, which was all she needed to encourage her to hurry up with her turn, and open her throttle. As she banked away, she watched the swarm of Junkers 87 Stuka dive bombers as they headed in the direction of the convoy. Above them were Messerschmitt 110 fighters flying escort, and a trio of them were breaking away from the main body and heading in her direction. She pushed the nose of her Spitfire down and quickly scrubbed off ten thousand feet, while watching her speed wind up way beyond the cruising maximum. It was enough to leave the distant 110s standing. It was unlikely they'd have been able to catch her anyway, she'd seen them and started her turn long before they even knew she was there, and her Spitfire would outrun a 110 even on a bad day; but it wouldn't hurt to put a little distance between them, just in case her engine gave her problems, or something else decided to go wrong and slow her down. She watched them in her mirror; they soon got bored and turned away, knowing they didn't have a chance; and once she was safely away, she started to climb again, watching her mirror to make sure she wasn't trailing a tell tale white contrail. She continued to watch her mirror, and ahead, and all around just to be sure, and over three hours after taking off, Malta came into sight. Smoke was twirling into the sky over Valletta and the airfields at Takali and Luqa, announcing the recent departure of a raid. She briefly felt guilty about the relief she felt, knowing the raid had already been through, and she wasn't going to arrive in the middle of it. She searched the sky for signs of trouble, while descending and scrubbing off as much speed as possible, then she put her blue Spitfire down and taxied quickly to her blast pen, swinging left and right, and avoiding a particularly large smoking crater that wasn't there when she'd left. It was big enough to swallow her whole, and she was happy it hadn't been in front of her when she took off in the dark. She shut down the engine and sat for a moment, listening to the airframe creaking after its long journey, and when she finally unfastened her harness and pulled herself to her feet, she swore she was creaking too. She stood on her seat and stretched, lifting her arms high above her head and stretching her aching muscles and stiff spine, before stepping onto the wing, feeling at least forty years older than she was. Pain shot up her bones as she jumped to the ground, and she had to steady herself against the fuselage for a moment, before heading into the dispersal hut.

"Find anything?" the CO asked. He was in his flying kit, looking like he'd just got back shortly before her.

"A swarm of Stukas," she replied, after clearing her throat. She made for the refreshments table, and he handed her a tin mug of tea that he'd just poured for himself. "They were heading in the direction of the convoy," she continued, after drinking some of the awful salt tinged tea.

"Poor buggers..." He stood and sipped his tea, and pulled a face suggesting he liked it as much as her.

"You?"

"A submarine to the southeast. No idea whether it was theirs or ours, but I radioed it in then made a run for it before trouble arrived." He looked at his watch, then took another sip of tea. "Better get back up as soon as the kites are refuelled. Make sure you drink enough; you're going to need it. I'll ring HQ and give them the news." He took his mug and disappeared into his office, while Harriet walked back outside, stretching her muscles again, and doing her best to stay mobile. Scared that if she sat down and rested, she wouldn't be able to get back up again. She decided to go for a walk despite the baking heat outside; she felt a need to keep moving. She gulped her tea and refilled the cup. It was disgusting, but she needed the fluids. It had been warm on her first sortie, but her next would be over lunch, and it would be all she could do not to melt until she got up high in the cooler air.

She didn't have long to wait. By the time she'd finished her tea and used the bathroom, the ground crews had refuelled her Spitfire, topped up the oil, and checked it over, before reporting it fit for round two. She had a couple of hard biscuits with jam while she looked at her second route of the day. The CO had a theory that the Italian fleet wasn't ahead of the convoy, as was expected by the powers that be, but would close from the rear, picking off stragglers as it used its superior speed and worked its way forward through the slow, heavily

199

laden merchant ships. Harriet shrugged in agreement. It was as likely as any other suggestion, and in the absence of reports coming from any of the other pilots flying a fan to the sides and ahead of the convoy, it felt worth having a look. They agreed that the CO would fly north of the convoy, and Harriet to the south, and after looking at the routes on the map, they headed off to their aeroplanes. Harriet climbed in, and instantly felt uncomfortable as she sat on her parachute and strapped herself in. She forced a smile as the ground crew fluttered around, preparing her for flight, but she knew it was going to be an uncomfortable trip. The soreness alone was enough, but the baking heat was threatening to melt her before she even got off the ground. She checked everything over, then with a shout to make sure everyone was clear, she started the engine and quickly gave the signal for the chocks to be pulled clear and taxied out of the pen, making her way to the runway while checking her gauges. The Spitfire was a beautiful aeroplane, but its only failure was overheating quickly on the ground. Something that didn't endear it to sitting around in the height of the Maltese summer while pilots went through their checks. By the time she was at the end of the runway, she was comfortable that everything was as it should be, and after a quick check for obstacles and raids, she pushed the throttle forward and released the brakes. The Spitfire jumped forward, and she held on as it raced to get into the air. With a push forward on the stick, the tail came up, and the air got under the control surfaces, lifting the Spitfire into the air. She raised the undercarriage and sped out over the island.

The CO came alongside her after a while, and they flew side by side as they headed west in search of the convoy again. She tried to get comfortable, shifting in her seat from one side to the other, lifting and relieving pressure for a few seconds at a time, before bracing herself against the rudder pedals and straightening her legs to lift her behind entirely from the parachute, and releasing the throbbing in what remained of her muscles, at least until her legs tightened and she had to sit again. She looked over to the CO after her fifth time of raising herself, and he gave her a thumbs up and a wave, before pulling away to the north. She checked her map, then sat tight and pulled away to the south. She knew he'd given her the easy route. If the Italian fleet was knocking about to the rear of the convoy, it would likely be to the north, closer to Sicily and Italy, and in range of their air cover. The south was an outside bet, and while she knew he was motivated by doing the right thing in sending her south, she also knew he loved to get the goods, and wanted the northern route so he could find the Italians. He had an instinct and knew where to find trouble, and he was very good at getting out of it. After an hour on her south easterly course, she saw the main body of the convoy far to the north, visible only by the black smoke above it from the funnels, and the fires on the ships below. She frowned as she watched the smoke smudge the blue sky, knowing what the sailors must be going through, and thanking the gods that she was a pilot. Life was dangerous, but at least she felt she had a fighting chance, unlike the sailors on their slow moving ships. She went back to scouring the sea for signs of the Italians, hoping to do something useful. The time passed, and her bones and muscles ached so much that they started to seize, and her back started to tighten, followed by her neck stiffening. By the time she was ready to turn for home, there wasn't a part of her body that didn't hurt, and she started to question her insistence that she was ready to go back to work when she did, instead of taking longer to recover. She banked to her right, as per the CO's plan, so she was able to count the ships as she passed over the convoy, and report on how far back the stragglers were. His instructions were to report on the state of the convoy if she couldn't find the fleet, and that's what she was going to do. She flew until she saw smoke in the distance, which she approached cautiously, all the while checking for signs of enemy aircraft.

Her stomach churned as she arrived at the scene of a sinking ship. She circled a few times, watching the crew floating in lifeboats, as the burning ship rolled slowly onto its side and set fire to the fuel oil that had seeped into the water. She wanted to radio their position, but she knew she couldn't. To do so would put her own chances of getting back at risk, and she had work to do. Even if she didn't find the fleet this time, she had to get back with a status report on the convoy, before refuelling and heading out again. She couldn't risk that. The crew were in lifeboats, and in all likelihood, the convoy knew where they were, and if they didn't, she'd report their position when she got back. She pulled her map from under her leg and marked the convoy's position, according to her best approximation, then descended in a wide circle and passed over the lifeboats and waggled her wings to the crew before heading east, letting them know she'd seen them, and giving them hope that they wouldn't be left to their fates. They waved back, and she watched them as they became specks in her rear view mirror. She felt a sense of sadness for a moment, and hoped they were OK. She thought of the friend she'd made on her Atlantic crossing, Hardy, and somehow that made the plight of those she'd left behind all the more real. She pulled her attention forward, getting her mind back on the job, then climbed again as she chased the rest of the convoy. She was up at height again when the last ship came into sight, though not high enough to avoid the attention of their nervous gunners, who immediately opened fire and gave her a rocky ride as she got closer. She pulled up, trying to show the distinctive shape of her Spitfire's wings in the hope that the crew would stop firing, but all it did was encourage others to join in. She climbed some more and gave them a wide berth, not wanting to make them nervous, or get herself shot down by her own side. She circled away while climbing, and watched the convoy as it dragged slowly across the sea, spread out over miles, with some ships looking in a worse state than others. More merchant ships joined in with taking distant pot shots at her, but the Navy cruisers and destroyers seemed to stay on station, not bothering with her, she hoped because they recognised her as friendly. As she circled, she caught sight of the oil tanker. It was just ahead of the ship that had fired on her, and it was smoking. She took out a piece of paper and made a note of the ship types and their places in the convoy, along with their apparent condition. It looked like they'd been badly beaten, and the biggest convoy the Mediterranean had ever seen didn't look up to much. She continued to circle in a very wide radius, dodging the occasional shots while she got a full appraisal of the convoy's condition. Once she had everything, she descended and headed away from the convoy, in the direction of the sunken ship she'd seen, then turned and headed back again. She approached the convoy at low level, then pulled up and waggled her wings. This time the gunners held their fire, having finally recognised the Spitfire that had been circling and bothering them as a friendly aircraft, and she got a cheer and a wave as she passed each ship, giving them confidence that they were finally within range of the RAF, and eventual safety. She pulled up into a victory roll as she passed the cruiser at the head of the convoy, it made her smile to perk them up a little, but she also felt uneasy that she'd built up their hopes. They were still maybe another day's sailing, at least until they came within range of the combat Spitfires. They still had a long way to go.

Chapter 13

Guns

Having left the convoy long behind her, Harriet climbed up high for safety, but had to level out just above twenty thousand feet when she noticed the giveaway white vapour of a contrail forming behind her as she tried to go any higher. She frowned as she settled at her altitude, and started checking above and behind even more vigorously than she already had been. She didn't like being so low, preferring to have the advantage of height for both visibility and speed to escape, and reducing the chances of being jumped from above. She was still confident, though, unless somebody got in a lucky shot, they'd have very little chance of catching her. As she searched around, something lower down caught her eye, and after dipping her left wing to improve her visibility, she saw a trio of white wakes cutting like arrowheads through the deep sapphire blue of the Mediterranean, pointing in the direction of the convoy. Her heart raced; she knew before she started her descent what she was seeing. Submarines. She dropped like a stone until she could clearly pick out their periscopes, and the dark shadows of their hulls beneath the surface. They were about a mile apart, and ideally positioned to meet the convoy head on and cause chaos. She circled while she thought of what to do. She had no weapons, so she couldn't attack, and it wasn't the full force of the Italian fleet she'd found, but it was just as dangerous to the convoy. There was no real alternative; she hadn't found the fleet anyway, and was on her way home to refuel. She took a deep breath, then after confirming on her map where she thought she was, she called up control. The air was dead, just a faint buzz of nothing in her ears. She called again and again, but there was nothing. She let out a shout of frustration, then pulled up into a steep climb as she tried to get some height, hoping it would help improve the signal, but still, there was nothing. Of all the systems she could check after take off, the radio wasn't one of them. Strict radio silence was the order of the day, and she'd always expected that it would just be there, but now she needed it, it wasn't. She continued to circle at different heights, and continued to transmit, hoping desperately that somebody would hear her, but it was all in vain. The air remained dead, and the only thing she could hear above the roar of the engine was the pounding of her own pulse in her ears as she thought about what to do next. She had about an hour to fly back to Malta, maybe a little less if she pushed the engine hard, but by the time she'd taxied in and got a message to HQ, the submarines could be anywhere, and Malta's bombers would have to rely on luck if they were going to find them, assuming they weren't already among the leading ships of the convoy. The convoy... If she couldn't get a message back to Malta, maybe she could get a message to the ships direct. She checked her fuel gauge. It was going to be close, but if she was careful with the engine, she calculated that she should just be able to make it back to Malta, though she'd be flying on fumes.

Decision made, she set course for the convoy, climbing again so she could squeeze every last minute out of the fuel she had. Her heart was racing a little, she was anxious about whether she'd made the right decision. She continued to transmit for a while, hoping she'd get a response that would turn her back, but none came. The radio was useless and no more than added weight, and if she could, she'd jettison it to save weight and squeeze a few more minutes of flying time in. She scoured the sky as she flew, searching for other aircraft she could catch up with and lead to the submarines, the CO on his homeward trip perhaps, or one of the other pilots who'd been instructed to use the convoy as a point of reference in their search patterns. Nothing came, though, and instead, she was left to feel like the only person in the world, until finally, the smoke from the convoy appeared on the horizon. She checked the sky again, then, when she was getting close, she started to descend, determined to fly low over the leading Navy cruiser and let them get a good look at her markings, and hopefully send a signal to the rest of the convoy not to shoot at her. It seemed that her plan had worked, and as she shot past the cruiser almost at wave top height, the most she got was a few machine gun shots from over keen gunners, all of which were fortunately wide of the mark. She pulled up above the convoy, then headed back to the leading cruiser, before circling it in a wide clockwise arc, keeping her right wing dipped deep, revealing her cockpit, and more importantly, the morse light just behind it, in clear view of anyone watching. Then, once she was sure she wasn't going to be shot at, she pushed her right elbow onto the morse code tapper and started tapping out a hello signal, which flashed through the lamp on top of the airframe. She hadn't used morse code that much, and while she knew it and understood the series of dots and dashes that made up letters and numbers, she wasn't particularly quick in sending messages. She tapped away with her elbow, slowly, while circling and keeping an eye on the cruiser. She smiled as finally a body on the bridge started flashing away in reply with a lamp. She picked out enough of the letters for her mind to fill in the gaps and form whole words, and soon knew she was being asked, quite abruptly, what she wanted. She pulled up and straightened out, while climbing a little before starting her tight turn again, and this time she flashed the words 'submarines ahead'. This caught the Navy's attention right away, and a signal, more abrupt than the last, demanded 'where'. She focused and tapped out the bearing and distance while circling, repeating it three times on circuit after circuit until it was acknowledged with a simple 'Thanks. Run!' She frowned, and signalled to request they repeat. 'Run' came the simple, yet urgent reply, and the sailor with the lamp started pointing furiously to the north. Harriet levelled off and banked around to take a look in the direction he was pointing, and immediately her blood ran cold as she saw the swarm of Junkers 88 twin engine bombers approaching the fleet. She waved at the sailor, and pushed the throttle forward as she headed away from the fleet. She looked in her mirror, and already the 88s were starting to dive. She hadn't seen them; she'd been so focused on getting her message to the ships below, that she hadn't thought to look up. The sky started to fill with the black dots of anti aircraft fire as she raced away, quickly leaving the fleet miles behind her. As she looked forward again, she noticed more aircraft, another squadron of 88s escorted by the equally menacing twin engine Messerschmitt 110 fighters. She was much lower than them, but on a collision course. She considered her options. If she pulled up, she'd make herself an obvious target, and if she turned, she'd be presenting them with her tail. They were still far enough away to hope that the blue of her Spitfire was camouflage enough to hide her against the background of the sea, and that they wouldn't see her if she maintained her course and passed right underneath them. She checked her fuel gauge again. Her calculations had been right; she had enough to get back, assuming she was able to get away from the trouble that was rapidly surrounding her.

To her relief, the bombers passed over, though her heart was constantly racing, and her mouth was as dry as when she was in the desert, while a trickle of sweat ran down her spine. She breathed a short sigh of relief as she passed under them, but the trickle of sweat soon turned to a waterfall as she looked up and saw four of the 110 fighters flip one after the other into a dive in her direction. She'd been seen, and they had the advantage of height. She didn't have much air between her and the waves, and there was no diving to gather speed, so she had to rely on opening up the throttle, pushing it through the gate and forcing the engine to maximum power. The Spitfire responded as graciously as it always had, and soon she was skimming the waves as she raced for home. It wasn't enough, though. Being able to throw their heavy twin engine aeroplanes into a steep dive gave the German pilots the advantage, and soon they were closing on the struggling thoroughbred. The leading 110 fired from a distance, and the cannon shells danced along the water to Harriet's left, remarkably close to hitting her. That was all she needed to know about the type of pilot she was dealing with; to get so close from so far, he had to be good, and that meant he would have her in the next shot if she sat still. She watched her mirror intently, and in the split second that she saw his muzzles flash, she pulled up hard, leaving the shells to splash along the water in the exact place she would have been if she'd stayed on course. The Merlin engine roared as it dragged the Spitfire upwards, almost vertical as she raced to escape. She'd calculated the angle of their dive, and was sure that given the angle, their speed, and the handling characteristics of the 110, which she'd fought plenty of times before, they wouldn't be able to pull up quick enough to get on her tail, giving her time to put some distance between her and them, and hopefully get some height. It paid off, and as she rolled through her climb, she saw them slowly pulling up and around to come back at her, but she was already close to being out of firing range, even for the best shot. They weren't dissuaded by her agility, though, and all four were soon coming back at her, though this time they were having to climb, and their sluggish aeroplanes were no match for the lightweight thoroughbred photographic reconnaissance Spitfire. It had been a narrow escape, but only a temporary respite, as another four 110s peeled away from their escort duties and turned back at her. She was now trapped between eight of them, four diving and four climbing. Whatever manoeuvre she pulled to outsmart one group would present her as a target to the other, and she was quickly running out of options. She started to regret not having any weapons. The extra speed and fuel capacity were great, but not being able to fight her way out of trouble was a tough price to pay. She considered her options. Turning would present the divers with a bigger target, and would slow her enough for the chasers to start to catch her, while climbing would just slow her and get her shot down. She kept on course and kept her throttle open wide; her fuel was being drained much quicker than she'd calculated for, but having the fuel to get home had quickly been relegated in importance by the desperate need to not become a burning fireball. She held her course to ram the 110s head on, and as soon as they started firing, and their cannons started to flash, she pushed her stick down, bringing her just out of the target zone, so she could watch the glowing tracer pass overhead. The divers steepened their dive and fired again, and she pushed forward again, this time steeper to avoid their shots; then, with a little more speed gathered, she pulled up again and aimed for the third diving 110. They scattered, fearing they were going to be shot at from underneath, or be rammed by a maniac, and she was able to pull up high above them all; though the chasers had used the dips and climbs as time to keep on course and eat up the distance between them, and she had to roll out of her climb as tracer started zipping past her canopy again. When upside down, she had a view of them all, but despite scattering, the diving four had quickly got around, and were now coming at her from all directions, while the chasers were coming hard at her right through the middle with guns blazing. She rolled and spun, avoiding more tracer, but it was getting closer, and the opportunities to escape fewer. No matter where she turned, she had one ahead of her, and at least one behind, and the only thing keeping her alive was that there were eight of them and one of her, and they were all getting in each other's way while trying to get in a shot. Her luck could only last so long, and a line of gunfire from a rear gunner cut across her right wing, then she felt thuds in the airframe as cannon shells cut into the fuselage behind her, smashing the radio bay open. She rolled and dived, narrowly missing a collision with a pair of 110s, and aimed for the convoy, which was besieged by bombers and surrounded by a thick ring of anti aircraft explosions, as every ship fired every gun it had. The Navy escort ships were also making smoke, a trick to create a thick dark fog up around the convoy and make it difficult for the bombers to find their target, a reasonably effective tactic, though one of the merchant ships was already on fire and burning fiercely having been hit a couple of times. Harriet held her breath as she dived into the chaos below, and watched as the glowing tracer from her pursuers lit up the smoke enveloping her. She broke through and levelled out just above the water, pulling a pair of 110s right past one of the escorting destroyers, which quickly put all guns to work in knocking one down, and sending the other climbing in flames. Harriet snaked her way between the ships, and through a huge fountain of water where a bomber had planted a near miss, which lifted her Spitfire and almost flipped it on its back. She left the thicker part of the smoke to see the battle raging. The bombers were swarming and diving, while the fighters stayed high above, waiting for interceptors that Harriet knew would never be coming. The only fighters lower down were the marauding 110s which were hunting for her, and soon on her as they saw her blue Spitfire slip from the black smoke. To make things worse, her fuel gauge was quickly winding down. She'd been pushing the engine hard, but not that much; the only explanation was a punctured fuel tank or ruptured line, neither of which were good news. The 110s closed, as she turned to try and head for the smoke. It was dangerous in there, with the crossfire from the ships, the thick smoke, and the bombs dropping all around, but seemingly it was more dangerous out of it. She didn't get the chance to get back to the smoke, though; the 110s were way ahead of her thinking, and had spread out in a line, cutting her off and forcing her to turn away. There was no going over them or around them, so all she could do was try and run. She pulled back on the stick and threw the throttle forward as she desperately tried to escape, but the 110s were on her, and a line of cannon shells clipped the end of the left wing off; then another 110 blasted her tail. She rolled to avoid the next burst, then reversed the roll to dodge the next, but it was no good, they were all over her, and in every direction she turned, she was nose to nose with a fighter or being sniped at by their rear gunner. Soon her Spitfire was so riddled with holes that it was struggling to stay in the air, despite its best efforts, and no matter how hard Harriet tried, there was no escape. A reality sealed by a burst of cannon fire into her engine, which led to flames almost immediately starting to lick from under the cowling. There was no time to think, or to hope. She flipped upside down and pulled back the canopy, then disconnected her oxygen tube and pulled the harness pin. She fired out of the cockpit like a cork from a Champagne bottle, just as the flames started to reach in through the canopy, and she fought desperately to stop herself tumbling, while simultaneously grabbing under her left armpit for her D ring, which she tugged on hard. The parachute deployed, snapping her head back as it checked her descent, sending searing pain through the shoulder that had been put back together following her last airborne exit from an aeroplane. She gasped as she composed herself, then froze as a 110 flew straight at her. There'd been stories of the Germans shooting British pilots while they hung defencelessly in their parachutes, under orders to make sure pilots didn't live to come back in another aeroplane. She hadn't believed the stories; it ran contrary to everything she knew of the Luftwaffe, but believe it or not, the 110 looked like it was coming for her. She closed her eyes and held her breath as she waited, then opened them again as the fighter passed to her side, in time to see the pilot wave, before joining his friends in heading back to the convoy.

With the imminent danger of being shot out of the sky, either in her aeroplane or out of it, passing as the fighters left her, the next danger stepped forward to present itself. The sea was coming up quickly, and she was in the middle of the Mediterranean with what remained of the convoy several miles east of her, and heading further away. Without much time to think, due to her relatively rapid rate of descent, she remembered her experience of landing in the Channel with a parachute, and kept her hand on her harness pin as the surface of the water rushed up to meet her. A few seconds from impact, she released the pin and slipped out of the parachute harness, then hit the water just ahead of the parachute, disappearing under the surface and getting a mouthful of saltwater before kicking upwards and coughing the water from her lungs. She quickly grabbed at the parachute, which had landed to her side, then pulled at the lines until the seat came to hand. She released the dinghy and opened the valve on the black canister of carbon dioxide, which immediately inflated the small yellow boat. The dinghy had been a new addition to parachute packs since earlier that year, only three whole years after the Germans had been using them, and almost two years after many RAF pilots had drowned after coming down in the English Channel during the Battle of Britain, having nothing but their Mae West life vest to keep them alive. They were a welcome addition, and Harriet was relieved, if not exhausted, when her small yellow boat had inflated, and she'd managed to pull herself aboard. She lay on her back and gasped, trying hard to control her breathing and lower her heart rate, before her heart burst out of her chest. The extremes of combat without any guns had drained what little energy she had, and once safe in the dinghy, she almost immediately passed out.

"Anyone home?" a voice shouted. Harriet blinked her eyes open, and for a moment, couldn't work out where she was. She looked around. She was surrounded by water, and the sky was a mix of orange and pink. "Grab hold!" the voice shouted, and she looked up towards it. She was amazed to see the jagged holed grey hull of a huge tanker beside her tiny life raft. It was sitting low in the water and listing a little, and the voice belonged to a sailor standing at the side rail and waving a grappling hook back and forth on the end of a rope. She quickly reached up and took hold as he'd suggested, then gave him a thumbs up. A rope ladder was lowered over the side by another sailor, while Harriet held tight and was pulled along by the hulking tanker. She got a thumbs up in return as soon as she was close, and with one hand, she grabbed the ladder, then with all her strength, climbed the side of the ship, and was pulled over onto the deck, while the sailor grappled her dinghy and pulled it up behind her. "Welcome aboard!" the sailor greeted her. "Ma'am?" he added, surprised to see it was a woman he'd just fished out of the water.

"Squadron Leader Harry Cornwall," she said as she looked around at the ship. It was in a bad way, smoking and blackened from a barrage of attacks.

"We'd better get you up to the skipper," he said. "If you'd like to follow me." He gestured for her to follow him, and she smiled and nodded, happy to be on something more stable than her flimsy dinghy, which she'd been equally as grateful for when she first dropped into the water, but she hadn't fancied spending a night in it. She made her way along the deck, which was scattered with shrapnel and bullet holes, and up the steps to the bridge. "Squadron Leader Cornwall, Sir," the sailor said as he introduced her to the Captain, who was busy staring through his binoculars.

"Thank you for picking me up," Harriet said, when the Captain hadn't replied for a couple of minutes. He moved his binoculars down to his chest, and held in position for a moment while thinking, then finally turned, and looked at her in bemusement.

"Are you the one we just fished from the water?"

"Yes, and I'm grateful for the lift."

"I wouldn't thank us just yet. We've been bombed mercilessly since before sunrise, and had a torpedo put through our middle. Your little dinghy may well be a much safer place..."

"Well, thanks all the same. I'd rather take my chances than die of thirst bobbing around in that thing."

"Touché," he laughed. "That's something we can do for you, at least. Young Mills will take you to the galley; cook will sort you out."

"Thanks..."

"You're welcome. What were you doing bobbing around in your little boat, if you don't mind me asking?"

"I was shot down a few hours ago."

"Shot down?"

"Yes. My Spitfire had more holes than a sieve by the time the Luftwaffe had finished with me."

"Your Spitfire?" he asked in amazement.

"Yes... They let us girls fly them sometimes." She tried not to roll her eyes as she prepared for the ', but you're a girl' moment.

"I'm sure they do, but how the hell did you get this far out in a Spitfire? I was told we're well beyond your range."

"You are," she replied, taken aback by the unexpected course of the conversation. "I fly reconnaissance. I was sent up to find the Italian fleet, which we're told is hanging around waiting to intercept you."

"The Italian fleet? Did you find them?"

"All I found were three submarines, but my radio was out, so I had to let your convoy know by signal lamp. Unfortunately, the Luftwaffe arrived at about the same time, and here I am."

"So, you're the one?"

"Excuse me?"

"We received a flash signal across the convoy warning us of submarines ahead, and the Navy sent a couple of destroyers ahead to get amongst them. I expect there'll be a few drinks coming your way."

"I'll settle for some water."

"Of course. Mills, take our guest to the galley, would you? Better get her a tin hat while you're at it."

"Will do, Sir," the young seaman replied, and gestured for her to follow him.

"Where's the rest of the convoy?" Harriet asked before leaving.

"Up ahead," the Captain replied. "There's a couple of destroyers behind us, and another merchantman, but the main body is up front. We were stopped after an earlier attack and had to get the engines going again." She nodded and forced a smile, then turned to follow the sailor. "Squadron Leader?" the Captain called after her.

"Yes?"

"Don't hang around if there's a raid. Stay above the waterline, and be ready to abandon ship the minute I call it. We're floating on fuel oil and kerosene. If they hit the tanks, we've had it, and it won't do to be anywhere near when she goes up." Harriet frowned and nodded nervously, then followed the sailor into the ship, through blackened walkways to the officer's wardroom. She was given a steel helmet, then left to sit at a table by a small porthole. Without warning or request, the cook brought over a jug of ice cold water, some freshly made tea, and Spam sandwiches in thick cut white bread with lots of butter. She sat and stared at the meal in front of her. Seeing the food quickly reminded her how hungry she was, and her stomach started to growl loudly, enough for her to look around to make sure she was alone. She poured a glass of water and gulped it down. It was painful as it pushed through her dry throat, but it tasted incredible. No salt, no petrol, just nice cold water. She finished it, then took a sip of tea, which tasted equally as good. Even the fresh tea she'd brought back from Cairo was tinged by the poor quality water, which made what was in front of her taste like Fortnum's finest. She found it difficult to contain herself, and went to work on the Spam sandwich. Like the water and the tea, it tasted like heaven, and even though she got full quickly, she continued to eat, making sure she didn't leave a crumb, or a drop of tea. It all tasted so good, but it also made her feel sleepy, and she found herself leaning on the table with her head on her folded arms, and looking out of the porthole until her eyes started to close.

The ship's alarm dragged her from her sleep, with the sound of thumping and buzzing anti aircraft guns of all sorts following close behind, and not giving her a chance to think about the stiff neck she'd developed from sleeping at the table. She grabbed her glass and finished the water, then pulled on her helmet and looked around. She didn't have a clue what to do or where she should be, so she decided the bridge would be as good of a place as any, and started on her way to find it. Men were shouting along gangways, and one by one, large steel doors were being slammed closed and sealed. She sprinted, making her way to an outside door, which she stepped through before pushing it closed behind her. She looked at her watch, it was gone eight, and there was a thin orange glow in the distance from the long set sun. There was another, much more ominous glow in the other direction, one of burning ships. They were in another raid. She looked up as the silhouette of an Italian bomber came low and dropped its bombs into the sea, sending a tidal wave of spray over the deck. She didn't know what to do. She wanted to fight, but she couldn't; there was nothing to do except stick to her plan of getting to the bridge, though she had no idea what she'd do when she got there. Her logic was she'd know on the bridge when it was time to abandon ship, and she'd be surrounded by people who knew what to do. That, and she wouldn't be trapped inside if the ship went down. One of her all time favourite nightmares. She climbed the steps as quickly as she could manage, which was almost two at a time, thanks to the fear raging through her. The Captain glanced at her briefly, nodded, then went back to his business of controlling the chaos of the ship under attack.

"What can I do?" she asked.

"Don't suppose you have a Spitfire to hand, do you?" the Captain asked, in a much calmer manner than the situation demanded.

"Not right now..."

"In that case, you'd better hold on to your hat and stay out of the way." He pointed to the corner of the bridge, where she quickly headed with a nod. She watched as more Italian bombers came down, shooting and dropping their bombs, which miraculously straddled the great lumbering tanker. The gun crews fired continuously, and at least one of the bombers left a trail of smoke behind it in the darkening sky, leaving the tanker unscathed in the long and ferocious attack. Unfortunately, another nearby ship didn't fare as well, and it took a direct hit from a bomb, which lit up the sky with the brightness of the flash, and sent a tower of flames shooting upwards into the sky. Harriet watched, her heart pounding as the ship burned. She was desperate to help, to do anything at all to save those on board, but she was helpless. All she could do was watch helplessly. Her heart raced throughout the attack, as the sky flashed all around from the bombs and bullets flying in every direction, and the explosions as ships and aircraft exploded and burned. It was like being in hell. She didn't have time to think of being tired, or her aching body; every nerve and every sense was consumed by the battle raging all around her. She shuffled nervously, full of energy, most of it wanting her to run for safety, but there was nowhere to go. The deck was covered in smoke and shrapnel holes, and wasn't the safest place to be in the dark even if debris hadn't been falling on it like rain, and below decks was strictly out of bounds. The tanker was already running low in the water, and it wouldn't take much for what was left to be consumed. So, she stood and watched, and held tight onto the railing in front of her.

The battle eventually passed after what felt like hours, but in reality, it was much less. Harriet had counted three separate waves of bombers attacking from different directions. The Captain sent men onto the upper deck to look out for survivors, and detailed a boat crew to stand by just in case. They weren't needed, though, and after leaning over the bridge wing searching the dark waters for signs of life, Harriet returned to the bridge, just in time for cocoa and biscuits that were delivered by the same smiling cook.

"You may as well get some sleep, Squadron Leader. You can use my cabin; I won't be using it." the Captain said as he finished detailing the crews to their stations.

"I'll be fine, thank you," Harriet replied confidently. He nodded and smiled; he could see in her face how nervous she was.

"Well, in that case, you'd better make yourself useful. Why don't you go up top with some binoculars and help keep watch?" She nodded and took the binoculars he offered, then went out and up the steps to the upper deck right above the bridge, where she paced for hours with frequent cocoa deliveries, while searching the murky, fire lit darkness. There was a heavy machine gun at each end of the deck, and a light anti aircraft gun in a position to the rear. She said hello as she paced, and stopped to talk briefly to the sailors crewing each position. They were intrigued to see a woman, especially a pilot, but none were inappropriate or even remotely disrespectful. The story had got around that she was the Spitfire pilot that had been shot down trying to warn the convoy of submarines, and they welcomed her as a member of the crew. Her gender didn't even come into it, much to her relief. She'd had bawdy comments from sailors in the past, until they'd seen her rank and worked out they may get into trouble. In the middle of a battle, though, they had better things to think about. One of them even brought her a stool from below, so she could sit mid way along the deck and search with her binoculars.

Her eyes were getting sore, with both smoke and tiredness, and she questioned herself as to why she couldn't even take an hour or two in the Captain's cabin. It was above water and relatively close to the bridge, and her exhausted mind was quickly overriding her fears, and the lure of a bed was becoming too much to resist. She stood, letting out a groan as she slowly pulled herself up from the stool and stretched her back and arms; then, without warning, she was thrown backwards by the shock of a huge explosion that lit up the sky. She quickly composed herself, then used the railing to pull herself to her feet so she could see what was happening. A ship was burning fiercely, but it was something else that caught her eyes as she scoured the sea around it with her binoculars. A small boat was moving at speed, firing machine guns into the burning ship. She recognised its shape from her reconnaissance flights, it was an Italian torpedo boat, and she knew that where there was one, usually there'd be others.

"Torpedo boat, three o'clock!" she shouted. The call was repeated by the gunners, and everyone she could see turned and looked. The anti aircraft cannon behind the bridge immediately started opening fire, as did the heavy machine gun, scattering the water with shots as they chased the fast moving torpedo boat. Harriet called out their shots, and shouted left or right, higher or lower, until the guns finally found the target, and the torpedo boat burst into flames as the high explosive projectile from the anti aircraft gun hit home. The entire fleet, which they'd come much closer to through the night, burst into life. In the gunnery flashes, she could see the silhouettes of other torpedo boats in amongst the ships. They immediately started shooting back, raking the ships with gunfire as they zipped in and out. Another explosion in the convoy signalled another torpedo hit, and another torpedo boat exploded when a Navy destroyer scored a direct hit. It was carnage. She searched all around the ship for more intruders, then followed another shout as a crewman saw a torpedo boat to the rear, coming in fast. All guns concentrated on it, and a destroyer quickly turned to intercept, but by the time they'd hit the torpedo boat and sent it off in flames, it had launched two torpedoes. Harriet watched in terror as the white bubble trails glowed in the fiery night as the torpedoes raced towards the tanker. She looked around, there was nothing to do, and nowhere she could go, so she just watched and waited. Her heart almost burst with relief as they passed along the right side of the tanker, missing by an arm's reach at the most. She let out a sigh as she looked up and thanked any god that was listening, then without warning, she was lifted from her feet and thrown across the deck as the entire tanker shook, rattling her head as she crashed to the deck, and making her thankful for the steel helmet she'd been given, though she was still dazed. She tried to sit up, but before she could, a stream of tracer bullets rattled the deck, hitting the pair of sailors on the machine gun to the far left, and passing over just inches above her face. She laid flat on the metal deck and tried to claw through it with her fingernails in a panic to try and get away from the bullets. They sparked and ricocheted all around her, then passed as quickly as they started. She rolled over onto her front and dragged herself towards the shot up sailors. One was bleeding badly from his guts, and being dragged towards the steps by the other, who'd been hit in the legs. She crawled past them, through the blood now pooled across the deck, then dragged herself up to the gun and searched the sea below. A torpedo boat was making its escape, and she pushed her shoulders against the padded braces, then aimed and pulled the trigger, firing a stream of tracer after it and clipping the stern and one of the crew, before it turned and moved out of range. She swung around, ready for her next target, but instead was faced with the scenes below. The tanker had been hit amidships by a torpedo, starting a fire which was quickly spreading across the deck, and making the ship list heavily. Gunfire was still rattling in every direction, but she couldn't see anything to shoot at, even when she was able to drag her eyes from the fire. The other gunners were still at their stations, and fire control parties soon appeared on deck and started fighting the flames. It seemed nobody was abandoning ship just yet, so she kept her station, determined to do her bit for as long as she was able to. She couldn't fight the fires, she wouldn't know where to start, though it looked like the crew were already on that, and she didn't want to think about what was happening below decks. The tanker was creaking and slowing in the water. It didn't feel healthy, but she had to think about more than her own fear; for the time being, she had to keep watch for more torpedo boats.

Chapter 14

Dropping In and Holding On

The crew fought through the night to keep the tanker afloat, and Harriet kept her post, watching over the sea for torpedo boats and submarines, in addition to the occasional bombing raid by the Luftwaffe. The convoy was well lit by burning and smoking ships, so they were an easy enough target to find, but the bombing was from a high level and quite inaccurate, so Harriet didn't have much to do other than try and stay awake. The convoy had passed the Straits of Sicily in the night, slipping through the channel separating Tunisia and Sicily, which brought the ships within range of the combined German and Italian forces in both North Africa and Sicily, and made it a miracle that any of the ships made it to daylight. However, as the sky lightened and the sun rose, the convoy had come back together, the best it could, and the remaining ships were almost within reach of Malta.

Breakfast was served as dawn broke, and the crew prepared for the inevitable air raids that would come with the morning sun, as the enemy resumed their determined efforts to sink what remained of the convoy. The fate of both sides hung on the convoy. If it got through, Malta would keep fighting. If not, Malta would be invaded in a month, if surrender through starvation didn't come first. Harriet looked around as she ate the hot porridge with raspberry jam that she'd been given by the ever smiling cook, who was followed by a crewman who brought her another large box of ammunition, a harbinger of what was to come. She tried to ignore it, and kept her eyes on the horizon instead, trying her best to enjoy the porridge while she plotted their position in her head. She knew much of that area of the Mediterranean like the back of her hand, she'd studied the maps over and over as part of her reconnaissance flights along the Sicilian and Tunisian coasts, and she'd crisscrossed the area they were now sailing through many times while searching for enemy convoys. She'd even sat above one or two and watched as the bombers she'd called in from Malta turned the smoking dots in the water below into burning fireballs. She'd seen the flak screens thrown up by the convoys, she'd even witnessed some of the pilots she knew from the Mess blown out of the sky in their attacks; and she'd seen the mess the bombers that got through made of the ships. There was nowhere to run and nowhere to hide, and she'd often watched and felt a deep dismay for the crews of the ships below. They were the enemy, but she never wished it on them to be a sitting duck. It all stemmed from her escape from Dunkirk, where she'd watched helplessly as Stukas dived, again and again, attacking the boat she was on, while there was absolutely nothing she could do except wait for the inevitable. Which, in that case, came courtesy of a submarine. She'd also seen first hand what an undefended air raid could do to a powerful fleet of ships when Pearl Harbour was raided by the Japanese. There were lots of bad experiences to look back on. Either way, she hated ships, and she hated being stuck on them when people were trying to sink them. More ammunition arrived, along with a tin mug of sweet tea topped with evaporated milk, and as refreshing as it was, it didn't make the waiting any better.

"Looks like you've had a busy night, Squadron Leader," the Captain said, as he joined her on the upper deck.

"I didn't feel like sleeping, so I thought I'd be helpful after your sailor was hit."

"I'm grateful. Good eyes seeing those torpedo boats, too. The boys said you'd spotted them."

"I wouldn't go that far," she said as she blushed. "I'm sure they saw them at the same time I did."

"Quite... Anyway, I have a question I think you're better placed than any to answer."

"Oh?"

"How well do you know the area?"

"Reasonably."

"Good." He put a folded chart in front of her and tapped it with his pencil. "We're about here."

"I know..."

"How far until we come within range of Malta's Spitfires?"

"About..." She looked at the chart, then pointed some way ahead of the convoy's current position. "Around here at maximum range with fifteen minutes over the convoy. Or here for better cover." She slid her finger further along the chart.

"OK, well, the good news is we may see Spitfires before the day's out." He gave her a smile, which Harriet returned. "I'll send one of the lads up to relieve you in a while. They've been below fixing the holes in the bulkhead and keeping us afloat."

"No rush, I'll be fine."

"Yes, I don't doubt you will."

He left her to pace and watch the sun dance over the waves, as the August heat started to rise. The food and tea had been good, but they'd sat heavy in her shrunken stomach, and she felt a little nauseous as cramps gripped at her, and after a while, they became about the only thing keeping her awake. The last few days were starting to catch up with her, and adrenaline only went so far in keeping her going. She daydreamed as she paced, and wondered how Bunny and the others were doing in America. She caught herself smiling as she thought of how close she came to being back in Hawaii with them, flying long ferry missions back and forth from California. It would have been a long trip in an SBD, and she'd have enjoyed every minute of having her pancake fed behind aching all the way. Malta had been a roller coaster. She'd enjoyed being a photographic reconnaissance pilot, most of the time at least, but it had brought some harrowing lows, one of which she was still in the middle of, and a large part of her was wishing she'd gone along with the plan to fly to Kauai and hide.

Her daydreams were broken some hours later, when the adrenaline was gone, and she was fighting the urge to sleep, as she spotted a distant swarm of black specks approaching from the north. She didn't need to say anything or do anything. The Navy escort had also seen them, and ships' sirens were sounded across the convoy, including the tanker. She quickly pulled her helmet on and checked the heavy machine gun. It was ready, as was she, and the adrenaline was already beginning to flow again as she pushed her shoulders into the rests and held the grip, ready to fire when the time came. The ships started to make smoke, and funnels across the stretched out convoy started to pump out a filthy brown grey smoke that formed into a large murky cloud around the ships, not that it did any good. The specks came close enough to be recognisable as a swarm of Ju88 bombers, and they didn't hang around in getting to work. The first wave dropped towards the front of the convoy, flying straight down at the cruisers, which were steering wildly while firing an array of guns and forming a layer of anti aircraft explosions. The bombers miraculously passed straight through without even a scratch, and their bombs started to fall. Harriet watched intently, but her attention was soon pulled to the 88s coming towards the tanker. The escorting destroyers threw up a barrage in an attempt to dissuade the attack, but the pilots were fearless in holding their course, and cut through everything that was thrown in their direction. The first stick of bombs hit the water to port, sending white towers of water into the blue sky, then down over the tanker, soaking Harriet in the process. She took aim at the second bomber and fired, using her skills of deflection shooting to hit her target. The machine gun was no match for the 88, though, and her bullets sparked and ricocheted without making the pilot flinch from his path. His bombs fell wide, sending more spouts of water into the air, and Harriet quickly moved her aim to the next, this time rattling the cockpit and making the pilot pull away and drop his bombs a long way from the tanker. Her heart was pounding. The first wave was dropping bombs all over the convoy, and a raging explosion in the distance showed that a ship had been hit. They came almost straight down, one after another, then two and three at a time, with their escorting Messerschmitt 109s and 110s flying low over the ships, firing and mixing with the 88s until it was hard to keep track, and Harriet, like the other gunners, was swinging left to right trying to get in a shot. A 110 came close and ran bullets along the side of the tanker, and Harriet was just able to jump backwards as the metal deck and barriers sparked with ricochets between her and her gun, narrowly missing her and making her sweat more than she ever had flying in combat. She instinctively jumped forward and swung her gun after it, but before she could let rip, the rear gunner sent a stream of bullets

222

in her direction, making her dive out of the way again, this time hitting the deck and watching it blacken and burn next to her face as the high pitched shriek of bullets pinged off the metal and bounced in different directions. When she was sure the immediate danger had passed, or as sure as she could be at least, she dragged herself up again and staggered back to her gun. After reloading, she swung the barrel around, searching the sky for targets, but it looked like the raid was clearing.

When she was sure that the raid was over, and the last of the black dots disappeared in the direction of Sicily. Harriet slumped against the shoulder rests of the gun and caught her breath. Sailors were everywhere, running around checking the damage, while others delivered ammunition, and soon one appeared with a tin mug of tea. She nodded in thanks, then gulped the warm liquid, and felt it cutting through the dryness in her mouth and throat, and quickly hydrating her. She could have done with a bucket full, but she was grateful for what she'd been given. When she'd been able to shake every last drop from the mug, she kicked the brass shell casings away and put it on the deck, then checked her gun over before taking her helmet off and running her fingers through her sweaty hair. She looked at her watch, then glanced around the sky for signs of a raid. It wasn't even nine in the morning, and already it was hot, and they'd been through a heavy raid. She knew the day was going to get much worse before it got better. If it got better. The Germans and Italians knew precisely where they were. There was no darkness to try and hide in, and they were still a good few hours until they were going to come close to being within range of Spitfires, which even then wouldn't be able to stay for long. The Captain had been quite reassured about the prospect of getting within range of Malta's Spitfires, but she didn't have the heart to tell him that when they finally came, there wouldn't be many of them. There weren't that many Spitfires on Malta. There had been a steady stream of losses since her original delivery, and the RAF struggled to keep pace in providing replacements. Those they did have weren't at their best. Engines suffered from the dust and sand, which mixed with the oil and turned into a grinding paste that quickly wore the moving parts down, leaving them in need of regular stripping, cleaning, and replacing. Every serviceable Spitfire on Malta had also been in combat almost daily, meaning they'd been pushed beyond their limits, and the airframes were as ragged and run down as the engines, most with numerous patched bullet holes and mismatched colour schemes from where spare parts had been cannibalised from crashed and written off aircraft.

It was an hour after the raid had left that sirens sounded again, and pulled Harriet back from her daydreams. She casually pulled her helmet back on, then cocked the machine gun and pushed her shoulders in the rests, before peering through the circular spider web gun sights and sweeping the sky to the north. She soon saw them. Stuka dive bombers, escorted by a mix of 109s and 110s, who once again would know they were still out of range of Malta's Spitfires, meaning they'd soon be joining the Stukas in diving and strafing the convoy with their machine guns. She braced herself and tried to plan the track of the raid so she could anticipate their attack lines and pick a target, and it quickly became obvious that the tanker was the focus of this raid. The convoy threw up a screen of anti aircraft fire once again, while the ships made smoke, trying desperately to hide, or at least obscure themselves enough to throw the bombers off their aim. Once again, it was a valiant, yet vain attempt, and the Stukas started their dives one by one, following each other as they tipped over and came down as steep as they could. Harriet lined her sights up with the first of the Stukas to break through the storm of anti aircraft fire and smoke. She fired just ahead of it, zipping around the underside, and then passing over the wings. She fired and fired, becoming increasingly frustrated as her bullets seemed to go everywhere except into the Stuka, and the pilot didn't flinch as he dived closer and closer. Finally, she hit home, and her bullets rattled all over the fuselage around the cockpit. The pilot was clearly startled. He pulled up hard as more guns from the ship followed Harriet's lead, and the Stuka was enveloped in smoke and fire as explosions from the heavier guns rocked and shook it. Harriet watched as it passed overhead and pulled up, while simultaneously releasing its bomb. The black shape flew far over the ship, and Harriet breathed a brief sigh of relief, before quickly turning to train her gun on the next bomber. She lined up, but before she could fire, she was lifted from her feet, and only her tight grip on the gun stopped her from being thrown overboard. An explosion so massive that she felt the entire tanker lift from the sea, then splash back down with such force that she was thrown to the deck. She looked around, startled to see the sky to the other side of the tanker glowing red and streaming with projectile debris rocketing in every direction. The cargo ship that had been there a few seconds ago no longer was, being replaced by an inferno of smoke and flames. She'd seen it through her binoculars at first light when it had come close alongside; the decks were stacked with thousands of tins of high octane aviation fuel for the RAF in Malta, and it was said by other members of the crew that it was loaded with ammunition. The fiery projectiles launched by the explosion rained down on the convoy, and a flaming chunk the size of a Merlin engine rocketed over Harriet's head, making her duck for cover as it screamed by and splashed into the sea. She staggered around, trying to compose herself; it seemed like the world around her was on fire. A scream of 'incoming' cut through the ringing in her ears and the heavy noise of battle, and she instinctively looked up to see another Stuka coming down, aiming straight for the tanker. She ran to her gun and spun it, quickly taking aim with a deep determination not to let this one through. She waited, composed herself, then fired. Her bullets streamed away and passed straight through the propeller disc, shredding the blades, and hitting into the engine with deadly precision, making it flame and smoke as the dive steepened and steepened, far beyond the usual angle of pull up and bomb release, and with a muted thud which rattled the tanker, the Stuka crashed into the deck forward of the bridge. Harriet ducked and pushed herself into a tight corner while pulling her elbows around her face and waiting for the bomb to explode. She eventually opened her eyes, and looked around to make sure she wasn't dreaming. The other gun crews were back on their feet and firing, so she stood and did the same, checking her gun and reloading first, and briefly looking at the wrecked Stuka sticking out of the deck ahead. She didn't have time to think of the miraculous escape, and quickly focused on giving another stream of bullets to a 110, which was skimming the waves and blasting away with its cannons. She clipped the tip of his wing, which was all it took for the pilot to realise it wasn't the safest place to be, and pull up to escape. Presenting the belly of the large twin engine fighter to one of the anti aircraft gun crews to hit it and blow it out of the sky.

The 110 going down signalled the end of the second raid of the morning, and after reloading and kicking the spent brass casings away, Harriet pulled off her helmet and sank down into the corner she'd tried to hide in when the Stuka crashed. She put her head in her hands and closed her eyes. She was exhausted, sweaty, and filthy with smoke. Tea and ammunition were brought up again, and following it came the cook with a large stone jug filled with rum. He splashed a large shot of it into Harriet's teacup and gave her a wink, then rummaged in the pocket of his apron and pulled out a bar of Kendal mint cake, which she took with a grateful smile. She was so tired and shell shocked that she couldn't quite manage words, but the smile was enough. The cook had talked to her briefly when she'd been picked up and sent to the Mess to get something to eat. He was shocked at how lean she was, and fed her with thick cut Spam sandwiches with swathes of butter, and given her some boiled sweets and a small bar of chocolate to try and give her some strength. They hadn't said much else to each other, mainly because every time she'd seen him, she'd been so exhausted she could barely talk, but she felt they'd become friends. It was a thought that made her smile as she sipped on the foul tasting tea fortified with rum, then broke off some of the Kendal mint cake and felt it melt in her mouth, while she tried not to think of whether she'd see Malta again. The ship carrying the aviation fuel had been blown apart by the Stuka's bomb, in an explosion so big she hadn't been able to imagine it's like, even after her experiences at Pearl Harbour, and she couldn't help thinking how the tanker loaded with oil, fuel, and kerosene that she was on would go up if it took a direct hit. She fought hard against the picture in her head, it didn't bear thinking about; and instead, she finished the rum laced tea and mint cake, which to her surprise had given her quite a lift, firing up her brain and body, and giving her the energy to function again. She checked her gun over, and some fresh water was brought, and then it was time for the next raid.

The raids continued through the day, and lunch was served by the cook, who left her some chocolate with her sandwiches, which she managed to wolf down between raids, determined to get the food in her stomach before it was dirtied or lost during a raid. Between attacks, she kicked the brass bullet cases into the sea; they were becoming a hazard and were easy to trip or slip on, in addition to being baking hot to touch under the sizzling Mediterranean sun. The biggest and most deadly raid came in the middle of the afternoon, and once again, Harriet found herself taking desperate shots at anything that came close, frequently missing, but sometimes hitting her target and giving them something to think about. One of the heavy gun crew had talked with her between raids, and his advice was that a ship's anti aircraft fire was as much about deterring pilots as it was knocking them down, and she shouldn't beat herself up if she didn't hit many. It didn't really help. She was frequently frustrated when she couldn't hit the attacking aircraft. She'd developed skills in the sky that had made her a lethal weapon in air to air combat, but it was very different being stuck on a fixed object such as a ship, which she couldn't manoeuvre into position to get a good shot. Effectively she was reduced to hoping her adversary would put themselves in a bad position so she could get in a half decent shot. The thoughts of not being able to hit much repeated as her frustration increased, until she was distracted by the sight of a Stuka bouncing across the water, after the gun crew at the rear of the tanker had hit it mid attack. It skimmed like a stone on a pond, then hopped onto the rear deck and burst into flames, leaving the tanker with two wrecked enemy aircraft on its decks. Then it happened. A Stuka came straight down at them, flanked by fighters that blasted the decks with cannon and bullet fire, forcing gun crews off their aim long enough for the Stuka to release its bomb. The pilot's aim had been perfect, and his nerves must have been ice cold as he dived through the curtain of gunnery put up to stop him, and as he dived away over the ship, his heavy black bomb sailed almost peacefully through the sky. Harriet watched it, mouth open with bemusement and dread as it fell to the deck almost in slow motion. Seconds later, she was lifted from her feet as the bomb passed through the deck and exploded. She just managed to get below the parapet, helped by being knocked over by the blast, as a cloud of flame passed over her station, boiling the air and turning the sky black. She pushed tight into her corner and curled into a ball as the inferno enveloped the ship, and then, as quickly as it had arrived, it dissipated. She looked up through the clouds of smoke; she could see the sky again. Her lungs were filled with black smoke, and she had to roll onto her hands and knees while she coughed to try and get some air, which was still boiling hot. Eventually, she composed herself enough to stand and look around. The deck below her was awash, the sea coming over the sides and sloshing against the fixtures and the crashed Stuka, while the bomb's impact site burned. A fire crew was already fighting the flames, while others ran around doing all the damage control they could, but it was obvious the ship was lost. Gun crews kept their posts, Harriet included, and they watched the skies while their comrades fought the rapidly spreading and expanding fires, as the giant tanker sat helplessly in the water. The battle to save the ship went on for hours, while two Navy destroyers provided protection, sitting either side of the tanker to provide cover from the next raid to come in, which to Harriet's great relief was focused elsewhere on the convoy. She felt selfish for feeling relieved, but she knew that in their perilous state it wouldn't take much to finish them off. She assumed it was that which had spared them. Having seen burning ships from above herself, she knew they can't have looked to be in a good way, and it must have been that thinking which pushed the attacking aircraft to leave them alone, assuming they were already lost. Eventually though, the crew could do no more, and Harriet's heart sank when she heard the order to abandon ship to the destroyer coming alongside.

"You can't," Harriet said, as she made her way onto the bridge and faced the Captain as he briefed his officers. "You can't abandon the ship. Not now, not when we're so close."

"Not now, Squadron Leader," he said firmly yet respectfully.

"Yes, now!" she replied equally as firmly, making the other officers look at her with surprise at the young, emaciated woman shouting the odds at their Captain. "Every other ship in this convoy can sink, but not this one, not the tanker. If this fuel doesn't get to Malta, the island will be out of the war by September. Spitfires can't fly without fuel. Bombers can't fly without fuel. Generators can't run without fuel. We won't be able to attack the enemy convoys, and we won't be able to defend the island, and that means Rommel will march across North Africa, and we'll be finished. If this tanker doesn't get through, we lose the war." There was silence as they all looked at her.

"Gentlemen, you have your orders. Get the crew off as quickly as you can," he said calmly. "Squadron Leader, can we have a talk?" He gestured to the door that led out to the far wing of the bridge, and Harriet followed him out, priming herself for the coming argument. "I'm sorry," he said calmly, taking her a little by surprise as she'd been waiting for a rocket back for her outspoken tirade. 'Everything you said is absolutely right, but the fact is that the ship is about lost. Frankly, I'm amazed she's still afloat. That last bomb to hit us did so in almost exactly the same spot as we were torpedoed, and should in all fairness, have broken her back long before now. The flames have

228

beaten us back, we're dead in the water, there's water washing across the decks, and we could go down any second. Would you have me send my crew down with her?"

"There's nothing you can do?"

"Everything we can do, we have done. The flames and heat will buckle what remains of the bulkheads soon enough, dragging her down, and if we're not off her before the oil tanks breach, we'll be surrounded by a burning sea as she goes, with no hope of escape."

"I see..."

"I'm sorry, Squadron Leader. We tried our best."

"I'm sorry, too. It was wrong of me to behave the way I did. Especially in front of your crew."

"Nothing was said that hadn't been already. We can be a forthright bunch, us sailors, so let's just say that you talked to us in our own language." He gave her a smile, which she returned. "Right, let's get the crew off while we still can, and we still have some daylight. Come on."

Harriet joined the others in jumping across to the destroyer, which had come perilously close to the side of the tanker to pick up the crew, then she was shown to the destroyer's Wardroom with the other officers, and given tea, rum, and sandwiches. Nobody talked. She frowned at how her filthy fingers had blackened the fluffy white bread of her sausage sandwich, and paused to try and wipe the dirt from her hands onto her shorts, which were equally as filthy. She looked around at the others. Every one of them was black with oil and smoke, and every one of them was tucking into their sandwiches without a thought about how dirty their hands were. She blushed with embarrassment that she should worry about such a thing as a bit of dirt on her bread. The men she was with had fought their way across the Mediterranean, and lost many of their crewmates along the way. Then, almost within sight of Malta, they had their ship taken from under them. They had a lot to think about, as did she, so she picked

229

up her sandwich and ate. Then, when she'd finished her food and drink, she joined the others in falling asleep where they sat, exhausted.

"Lads, I need a few volunteers," the Captain said, dragging everyone in the small Wardroom from their sleep. Harriet opened her eyes and tried to focus, she'd been lost in a dream, surfing in Hawaii and having the most wonderful time, and it was a harsh reality check when she woke and realised where she was. "The old girl's still afloat, and the fires seem to have died back somehow, so I'm going to take a small party across to assess the situation, and see if we can get her underway again."

"I'll go," Harriet said, as she stood from her seat.

"I'm afraid I need sailors this time, Squadron Leader. We need to get the boilers lit, and the engines working, if we can, and check the steerage to see if we can make anything of her."

"You'll also need somebody to fight the enemy off if they come back!" Harriet replied firmly. "I'll keep watch while you work."

"OK..." He gave her a smile that suggested he knew all too well that arguing the point was useless, knowing she'd likely do exactly as she wanted regardless of what he said, and soon she was joining him and a small band of volunteers in being helped over the railings of the destroyer, and onto the still flooded decks of the tanker. She quickly made her way to her gun position, and checked the ammunition before leaning against the railing and scanning the dark night sky, full of twinkling stars and smoke. Other than some of the Navy escort, the rest of the convoy was long gone, or at least as far as she could see. There was an orange glow on the eastern horizon which she assumed to be them, while hoping the glow was from the already damaged ships, and not from a fresh attack. The destroyers circled through the night, watching for submarines after dropping more volunteers back on the tanker when the Captain confirmed that they could keep her afloat. Harriet was kept company by a group of American sailors from one of the other ships in the convoy; they'd volunteered to help crew the anti aircraft guns after the previous crew had been either killed or wounded in the final big attack that had almost finished the ship. They were a tough but jovial bunch, and they shared their supplies with Harriet, once they'd got over the shock of finding a woman on the ship. One, an older man, was superstitious to the point that he swore that having women on ships was bad luck, but the others soon pointed out that Harriet had been on board through a torpedoing, a bombing, and two Stukas crashing onto the deck; which in their opinion meant she was more of a lucky charm than anything else. She felt happy to be around them. They reminded her of her American friends, and all the people she'd met over there. The biggest reward, though, was when they produced some bottles of Coke from their supplies, one of which she was given. She hadn't had Coke for ages, and she was amazed that it was still cold, having been in a bag of bottles hung over the side in the water, chilling them below the air temperature. They talked through the night, and by sunrise, a destroyer was ahead of the tanker, trying unsuccessfully to pull it along with a substantial, thick tow rope, while another tried to nudge it along from behind.

A small raid was fought off at first light, forcing the destroyers to break away so they could fight it off, while the American crew threw up deadly accurate fire which knocked down an Italian torpedo bomber, while the others were forced off their track by the destroyers. The destroyers leaving to fight the battle had left the tanker to list a little, and when the fighting was over, one of them came alongside and was attached to the tanker with ropes, giving it some stability and stopping it from tipping over. It was the start of a plan which was rapidly put in place by the Navy escorts, and by mid morning the tanker had a destroyer on each side, lashed to it with a series of ropes and cables, and another had come to support them, nudging from behind and helping steer. Between them, the destroyers were able to move the tanker forward. It was slow, but it was progress. The cook appeared again at lunchtime, having volunteered to come back on board to look after the crew, and with his usual warm smile, wink, and nod, he left Harriet with her Spam and processed cheese sandwiches, tea with evaporated milk, and a stone jug of rum which he left for Harriet to share with the Americans, who she sat with while they ate and took turns keeping watch.

The sirens couldn't have been timed any worse. The raids had been light compared to the previous day, and Harriet had hoped that was the way things would stay, but halfway through her sandwich, the

231

Stukas and escorting fighters returned. She irritably threw down her sandwich and ran to her gun, ready to do her part in trying to fight them off. Her heart raced as they came closer, and the Navy destroyers started firing their heavy long range guns, sending out a loud thud with every shot. Then, as the raid was almost on them, the firing stopped, making Harriet frown with confusion. Then she saw why. Diving down on the Stukas were eight Spitfires, charging out of the sun. Harriet let out a screaming cheer, which the Americans joined in with when they saw her pointing and yelling excitedly. Her heart raced, but for a different reason this time. She'd never been so happy to see a Spitfire. The Stukas didn't know what hit them. They'd been withdrawn from the Battle of Britain because they were no match for the power of a Spitfire, and sent east where there wasn't as much opposition in the sky, and after having day after day of freedom to attack the convoy at their will, they were now in trouble. The Spitfires cut through them, and quickly sent them running, along with their fighter escort, who'd been equally as surprised by half a squadron of Spitfires turning up. Harriet's jaw ached from smiling as she watched the Spitfires chase their prey into the distance. Thirty minutes later, another four Spitfires arrived and circled high above, keeping watch over the stricken tanker as it limped towards Malta, sandwiched tightly between the two destroyers keeping it afloat. More raids came in, and got heavier through the day as the enemy threw everything they had left at the tanker, but now they were in the range of Malta's Spitfires, the battle no longer went all their way. A flight of Spitfires at a time kept watch, only leaving when relieved by another flight, or when their guns were empty from a battle, and their presence emboldened all of the crews below. They still had to fight, and Harriet still had to join the other gunners in fighting off the bombers and fighters that got past the Spitfires, but the tide had turned, and with each passing hour, Harriet felt more and more confident that they'd make it. By late afternoon they were in sight of Malta. They were moving slowly, but now they were in the range of Malta's shore batteries of artillery as well as the Spitfires, and the level of protection for the tanker increased. The fighting continued through the night, and more Navy ships came out to drop depth charges on the Italian submarines that had come out to intercept the tanker, and the shore batteries attacked the torpedo boats that were making one last attempt to sink the tanker, beating them back.

The next morning, the tanker slowly passed the breakwater guarding the entry into Grand Harbour, flanked by the destroyers that had remained by its side and heroically dragged it home. Harriet stood with the Americans and watched in awe at the roaring crowds that had gathered to greet them. It seemed like everyone in Malta, civilian and military, was there lining the waterfront. There was even a brass band playing Rule Britannia. Then, as the tanker passed the breakwater and made its way to the heart of the harbour, the thousands of cheering people fell silent. Men took off their hats, and women made the sign of the cross. Malta had never been so silent, with only the noise of the destroyers' engines and the creaks of the dying tanker to be heard. They'd made it, and everyone in Malta knew the significance of the moment. Harriet felt tears on her cheeks as the moment overwhelmed her. She searched the crowds as they approached the bastions around the Barrakka landing, the civilians and the military, and her resolve finally broke when she saw Cas. He was standing alongside the AOC among a crowd of military personnel up from the tunnels to watch the arrival of their saviour.

Chapter 15

Deliverance

"Alright?" Harriet asked Cas casually, as she walked off the gangway and onto the dockside, where he was patiently waiting for her.

"I would be, if you stopped finding ways of standing me up when we're supposed to be meeting for drinks," he replied with a roll of his eyes.

"Shut up!" She blushed as she tried to hide her smile.

"Welcome home, Harry. It's good to see you safe." A flight of Spitfires roared overhead on a patrol over the harbour, dragging both Harriet and Cas' eyes upwards.

"Thanks..."

"You're welcome. Though I think somebody wants you..." He pointed back to the ship, and Harriet turned to look.

"Oi, Squadron Leader," the ship's cook shouted from the deck. Harriet smiled and waved politely. The ship was a hive of activity, with crews hurrying to offload cargo, and set up ready for the valuable fuel to be transferred to a waiting auxiliary tanker before it sank.

"Friend of yours?" Cas asked.

"Yes..." Harriet replied with a smile, as the cook made his way up to the dockside.

"I think you left your kit bag, Squadron Leader," the cook said with a wink, as he handed her a large sack. "The tanker will be under water by the end of the day, and it'd be a shame if you left this behind."

"I don't think I..." Harriet started with a frown.

"Take care, Squadron Leader. It's been a pleasure sailing with you," he said, cutting her off mid sentence, and giving a knowing nod before turning and hurrying back to the tanker.

"No wonder you ended up in the drink if you were carrying a bag that size in your Spitfire; I'm surprised you could see where you were going..." Cas said.

"Funny..." She rolled her eyes. "I don't remember having enough kit with me to need a bag, though." She frowned, and unfastened the tie at the top of the sack and peered inside. Her eyes widened immediately.

"What is it?" Cas asked, as he stepped forward and joined her staring into the bag, which was stuffed with tinned meats and fruits, and bags of oats and pasta, among other treats, all relieved from the tanker's stores. "Bloody hell..."

"That's what I was thinking."

"You'd better tie that up again before you start a riot." He stood close to shield the bag from view while she hurriedly tied it.

"Welcome home, Cornwall..." the AOC said as he joined them.

"Thank you, Sir," Harriet replied, as she finished tying the bag and stood smartly to attention.

"At ease, Cornwall. At ease," he smiled. "I thought we'd lost you for a while."

"Yes, Sir. It was close."

"Quite. I'm sure Mister Salisbury would agree that it was a huge relief to us all when we heard a pilot had been pulled out of the drink and was safe onboard a ship. You were lucky."

"Sir..."

"Good show, Cornwall. I can't tell you how much that tanker means to us. Well done on your part in it."

"Thank you, Sir."

235

"It couldn't have happened on a more appropriate day." He smiled, and Harriet frowned and shrugged, not sure what he was talking about. "Today's the festival of Santa Maria here in Malta, a historical celebration of the ascension of the Virgin Mary, and the island's deliverance..." He smiled again and gave Harriet a nod. "The Maltese are already swearing that the tanker's arrival was an act of divine intervention. Right, I'd better get back down the hole and start planning for what comes next." Harriet stood smartly to attention again, or as smart as she could manage in her exhausted state, and Cas saluted as the AOC left as quickly as he'd arrived, with a fierce and concentrated look on his face.

"Lucky you were safe onboard that ship..." Cas said as he looked back at the half sunken tanker behind them.

"Yes..." She frowned as she joined him in looking back at the wreck sitting just above the waterline. Its grey hull was burned black, holed, and twisted, with the two crashed Stukas jutting out front and rear. She knew she'd been lucky, in more ways than anyone could have imagined.

"Hello..." he said softly.

"Hello," Harriet replied, blinking out of her daze and looking back at him with a smile.

"When did you last sleep?"

"I don't know... How long have I been gone?"

"Too long. Come on, let's get you to your room so you can lie down before you fall down." She smiled and nodded, and didn't resist when he took the sack from her. "You can take that off, you know." He nodded to her Mae West life jacket. She looked at it for a moment. She hadn't taken it off the entire journey, only tightened it each time she was sure she was going to need it. She looked back to the tanker one last time, then turned back to Cas with a tired smile.

"I'll keep it on for now." He nodded and smiled, and led her through the crowd to a waiting truck, which they quickly climbed aboard. "Is there any news of Robbie?"

"Yes, she's awake."

"Good."

"She's quite battered and got a few broken bones, so they sent her to convalesce with her grandparents. They're about the only ones that can get her to do as she's told." Harriet nodded and smiled. "Are you OK?" he asked, as they drove through the rubble of the bombed cities.

"Yes..." Harriet replied, as she watched the ruins pass by. It looked even worse than when she'd left only a short while ago, but it was a familiarity that made her feel safe. She was exhausted and struggling to think, but she could feel her emotions starting to rise inside, and to her frustration, her eyes were starting to water as she fought to keep everything in.

"Do you want to talk about what happened out there?"

"No... Yes... I don't know..."

"Maybe when you've had time to sleep?"

"Thank you..." She sniffed and wiped an escaping tear as she turned to face him. "I hate boats," she said as she let out a laugh, it was all she could do to stop the tears. They both laughed as they left the ruins behind and headed out into the barren sandy countryside, framed by the crisscrossing white stone walls and the bright blue sky. It was hot, but she didn't care. She was just happy to be on dry land. She leant her head against the door frame as the truck bounced down the potholed road, then closed her eyes and let herself relax, and accept that she was finally on land, and she didn't have to face her fear of drowning. Not yet, at least, and while the enemy wasn't going to ease their attacks on Malta, she took some comfort knowing there were more places to hide than on a ship full of oil. "Drink tonight?" she asked.

"Are you in any fit state?"

"I'd like to think so."

"Maybe you should catch up on your sleep, and push it back until tomorrow?"

"Maybe you just don't want to have drinks..." She looked at him with a mischievous half smile.

"Maybe I'm just used to you not showing up when we agree to meet for drinks."

"Can't we just be nice to each other?" she asked with an over exaggerated sadness, a long practised tactic designed to elicit sympathy when she'd talked her way into a debate she didn't have the energy to get out of.

"You must be tired if you're giving up that easily."

"Honestly, you can win this time. I think I could sleep for a week."

"I'll talk with your CO. I'm not sure I can get you a week off, but I think a day or two should be alright. I'll let him know you'll report in with him tomorrow, and if you're up to it, I'll meet you in the Mess in Mdina tomorrow night for a drink. Pointless you traipsing all the way to Valletta only to come back again in the dark."

"Thanks..." She smiled warmly, then leant her head on the door again and gazed out of the window at the green cacti lining the roadside, standing out against the sea of beige coloured sun baked land that spread as far as the eye could see. Her eyes were heavy, and it was a struggle to even think, let alone talk, and the rocking of the truck as it passed over bumps and potholes became almost therapeutic, especially with the warmth of the sun, which wrapped around her like a blanket.

The next time she opened her eyes, Harriet was in her bed, looking at the ceiling of her room at the top of Anj and Lissy's house in Mdina.

It was a struggle to clear her mind of a fog that made it difficult to think, let alone process how she'd got there. The last memory she had was of being in the truck and talking about meeting Cas for a drink, and try as she may, there was no recalling how she'd got to be lying on her parachute silk blanket, still in her uniform, with her bag, plimsolls, and flying kit neatly stacked on the floor. It took an effort to lift herself from her bed, first to her elbows, and then sitting and swinging her legs off the side before dragging herself to her feet and steadying herself. Everything ached. She poured some water from the bottle on the bedside table, and after drinking down the unique taste of Malta, she looked at herself in the mirror as she started to peel off her new uniform from Cairo, which was stained almost beyond recognition with oil, smoke, salt, and sweat, as was her face and hair. She was as filthy as she'd ever been, almost unrecognisable even to herself, and despite her best efforts to eat what she could, she was little more than a skeleton without her clothes. The months of reducing rations while in Malta combined with her time in the desert had taken their toll, and her bones protruded more than ever through her tightly stretched, tanned, and burned skin. By the time she'd left America, she felt she'd finally reversed the damage of her previous Maltese experience, having managed to gain weight, and get a healthy colour back to her skin, and it was hard to see all of that work undone. The only positive she could find was that the deep tan on her face still made her eyes stand out brighter than ever. It was enough to make her smile, and she took herself off to the bathroom and the waiting shower, so she could scrub herself in the few minutes of water that was available. It wasn't much, but it was enough to get most of the grime from her hair and skin, and she was soon dressing in her spare uniform, which contrasted with her dirty plimsolls. With her hair tied back, she gave herself a final once over in the mirror, and when she accepted she was passable, she turned her attention to the sack the ship's cook had given her. She smiled to herself as she emptied it on the floor and sorted the contents. Tinned sausages, Spam, corned beef, fruit, oats, and even some flour and powdered eggs. It was a heavy load of shopping that would be worth its weight in gold in the Maltese markets, if not more. She sat and looked at it all. She was hungry, and felt she could open the cans and eat it all right away, but she worried that if she did, she wouldn't stop.

After making her way downstairs, an effort in itself, Harriet left a few tins on the kitchen table for Lissy and Anj. The house was silent. Neither of them were anywhere to be seen, nor their family, so Harriet decided to go for a walk and get some air. Mdina was unusually quiet, or so it felt compared to the almost endless noise of raid after raid while onboard the tanker. It was unnerving in a way, but didn't take away from her relief at being back on dry land. The experience on the tanker hadn't improved her relationship with ships in any way. She wandered a while, then found herself at the Mess, and decided to go inside for a drink. It was late in the afternoon, and there were plenty of people about. Pilots that weren't on duty had risen from their slumber and were lounging around talking. Few gave her more than a passing glance or a polite nod. She didn't recognise many of them, only a couple from her journey on the aircraft carrier, but most were strangers to her, and she to them. Harriet hadn't spent much time in the Mess during her second Malta visit, preferring to spend most of her time with Robbie or Cas, or at home with Lissy and Anj, so she hadn't really got to know many of the pilots from the Squadrons. The attrition rate among pilots was high, and many she'd arrived with had been killed or evacuated wounded since, replaced by fresh faces she wouldn't recognise in a crowd. She took her drink outside and looked over Malta and across to the smoke of Valletta. It was a beautiful view, despite all of the terror that had been visited on the island, and she couldn't help but feel a warmth in her heart for the place and the people. She certainly felt more in common with them than the pilots she was surrounded by, which was a thought that made her feel uncomfortable and removed, and out of place in the Mess. It felt like so long ago that she was with her squadron, playing the piano, singing, and playing rough games of Mess rugby. It was a lifetime ago. She finished her drink and left the Mess behind. Gentle strains of classical music caught her attention as she climbed the steps of the city walls, which she'd intended to walk along on her way back home. She frowned with intrigue as she walked, and the music became louder, until the most unexpected scene came into view. At the end of the ramparts, a young ballerina was dancing slowly and elegantly to the music coming from the wind up gramophone balanced on a chair at the top of the steps. Harriet stopped and watched, transfixed by the dancer. It was the last thing she'd expected to see in the middle of a war zone. The young woman moved gracefully, dressed impeccably in tights and ballet shoes, her limbs moving lightly and smoothly, and her head held confidently high as she danced around the ramparts. Their eyes met a number of times as the ballerina spun and turned, yet she carried on regardless, unperturbed by Harriet's presence, until finally the music built to a crescendo, then faded with the young woman's performance drawing to a close. Harriet applauded, still not entirely sure whether she was cheering a hallucination, but she'd been captivated entirely by the experience regardless, and for the first time in as long as she could remember, her mind had been quiet.

"Thank you," the young woman said, without a hint of shyness.

"You're welcome... What are you doing up here?"

"Dancing,"

"Of course," Harriet felt herself blushing a little as she criticised the stupidity of her question. "I just meant... Well, I haven't seen you up here before."

"I live in Valletta, or I did at least, until my apartment was bombed yesterday. I came to Mdina to stay with friends a while, and stay out of the way of most of the bombs."

"Oh, I'm sorry..."

"That's OK, it's incredibly annoying, but nothing almost everyone else in Malta hasn't been through. War's hell, and all that."

"Yes..."

"You're Harry Cornwall, aren't you?"

"How did you know?" Harriet replied, her blush now extending.

"Everyone knows you."

"Do they?"

241

"Of course, silly. How many female pilots do you think we have in Malta? Besides, you made quite a name for yourself the last time you were here."

"Did I?"

"Gosh, you're hard work. Do you live in a cave?"

"No..." Harriet frowned. "I just don't tend to get out that much... Have we met?"

"Not formally," the ballerina said with a smile. "I don't usually dress like this, I just like to dance when I'm off duty, and try to remind myself of what I was before the war got in the way, and I started spending most of my time underground and pushing aircraft markers around a map."

"I thought I recognised your voice!" Harriet said with a smile. "We've talked a lot on the radio when you've been guiding me to targets."

"Nice to meet you in person at last." She held out her hand, which Harriet shook warmly. She looked at Harriet's wrist as the late afternoon sun reflected off the glass of her watch. "I should get going; I'm on duty tonight." She gathered her things and took off her shoes, then with the gramophone under one arm, and her shoes thrown over her shoulder, she ran down the steps barefoot. "Talk to you again soon, Harry," she shouted as she left, and ran down the narrow street. Harriet smiled to herself, then continued on her walk home to see Lissy and Anj, all the time humming to herself and reliving the dancer's performance. It made her feel alive, and before she knew it, she found herself twirling down the narrow street with her arms outstretched and her face turned to the sky. It was the freest she'd felt in so long, and she wasn't even embarrassed when an old Maltese woman walked past, looking at her like she had a screw loose.

After returning home, Harriet enjoyed a warming meal of Spam and tinned potato stew with her adopted Maltese family, during which she was treated like the prodigal daughter once again. They worried about her with increasing frequency, and this quickly became the topic of conversation, with Harriet politely and lightheartedly batting away the concerns in the same way she'd seen the old hands do it in the Mess. She thought back to Max and Archie as she talked, and how they treated almost everything with humour, including their own inevitable ends, and Cas had explained that it was often the only way to get through. Knowing that to think on your end as a pilot would practically guarantee it coming quicker than planned. Second guessing, holding off, trying to stay safe, it all increased the risk of a pilot being shot down. Harriet had thought it, and him, a little callous at first, but she quickly realised he was right. As she got ready to leave and meet Cas at the Mess, Lissy warned her firmly, yet still warmly, that even cats only have nine lives. Harriet's heart squeezed for a moment as she looked into Lissy's eyes, then she smiled and said goodnight.

"You made it..." Cas said, as Harriet joined him on the Mess concourse overlooking Valletta. He stood politely, and half smiled as she took her seat.

"Hilarious," she replied.

"I got you a gin. It's about all they have behind the bar, and it's not great."

"At least it's something," Harriet replied as she took a sip, and fought hard to not turn her nose up at the dreadful taste.

"I'm told it came off a Navy submarine, and I'm starting to wonder if they'll miss it when they need to degrease the engine room."

"Stop complaining, moody. It's better than the water," she laughed.

"That's true. Cheers!" He shrugged, then they clinked their glasses and drank. "So, feel better for a rest?"

"Much. I don't even remember getting home."

"I'm not surprised. I'd been talking to you for twenty minutes before I realised you were hard asleep."

"Talking to yourself again? Must be a sign of your age..."

243

"It becomes a habit when somebody hardly listens to you anyway..."

"I listen to you."

"Do you?"

"Sometimes..."

"Why only sometimes?"

"You only talk sense sometimes."

"Harsh..." He rolled his eyes, and she let out a laugh. "Anyway, your CO sends his regards, and he's looking forward to seeing you in the morning."

"Good, I'm ready to get back to it!"

"Really?"

"Yes, why wouldn't I be?"

"I just wondered if it was maybe time for you to be rested, that's all."

"I don't think so; I'm fine."

"You've had two close calls in a row, leaving you in the sea and sand. It's been a tough time of things, and a break would do you a world of good."

"I had a break."

"Oh?"

"In Cairo, before I got back here. Honestly. I didn't care for it, and I'd rather be flying."

"They call you the fox these days, don't they?"

"I put a fox on the side of my Spitfire, but I prefer to be called Harry. What others call me is up to them."

"Well, either way, I just wanted to remind you that it's cats that have nine lives, not foxes."

"What's that supposed to mean?" she asked with a frown, as she felt her heart squeeze again.

"Nothing critical, I promise. I'm just concerned as to how many of those lives you've used up."

"I'm fine."

"I don't doubt that, but a rest wouldn't hurt. Would it?"

"I told you, I've had a rest..." She felt herself getting tense, as though she was firing up for a huge argument, as she used to when she was at home in France. "Can we change the subject?" she asked, in a desperate attempt to defuse a conversation she felt becoming charged.

"Of course." Cas smiled warmly, welcoming a way out of the conversation he'd recognised was going in entirely the wrong direction to that he'd intended.

"I haven't heard a raid today, unless I slept through it," Harriet said with a smile.

"No, you didn't. A few tried to come in, but with the new supplies of fuel, the AOC can put his plans into action to deal with the raids."

"Oh?"

"He's been able to get the squadrons up early, as he did in the Battle of Britain, and he has the raids intercepted before the bombers even cross the north coast. It's proving quite effective so far. There's been a couple of reconnaissance flights over the harbour, but otherwise, it's been remarkably quiet."

"That's good. It'll have given them time to empty the tanker."

245

"It has, and they got it emptied just in the nick of time. The minute the last drop was drained, the ship's back broke, and it sank into the harbour." Harriet frowned at the news. She couldn't help but think the ship had a life of its own. It had taken everything the enemy had thrown at it and more, and it should have been sunk so many times. Yet, it somehow kept afloat and got its valuable cargo to Malta. It was a hunk of burned metal, and she hated ships, but something unusual inside of her made her feel sorry for it, and love it a little.

"Are you OK?" Cas asked, dragging her from her daydreams.

"Yes... Yes, sorry, I think I'm just still a little tired."

"I'm not surprised. I can't imagine it was easy for you to be on that ship."

"Not really."

"Come on, I'll walk you home." She nodded without a whisper of argument, and they left the Mess and walked through the narrow streets together. "Looks like I spoke too soon," he said, as air raid sirens sounded in the distance. Harriet nodded and smiled. She didn't have much to say, it was like she'd been consumed by a dark sadness, and she didn't like it. "Shows how much I know about things. Maybe you're right after all about only listening to me sometimes."

"Usually more than that," she said as they reached her door. "Thank you for walking me home. Are you going to be OK getting back?"

"Yes, I should think so. They've managed to bomb most things in Malta so far, but I'd imagine chasing around in the dark trying to drop a bomb on me would be a waste of time, even for them," he replied, while looking up to the dark sky.

"I don't know; maybe they've met you." She half smirked, feeling a slight chink in the darkness that'd consumed her.

"Goodnight, Harry..." he said confidently, as he marched into the night.

246

"Goodnight, Cas. Don't let the bombers bite."

"You should be on a stage," he called out as he left. Harriet smiled as she watched him disappear into the darkness, then frowned a little at the dark mood she'd experienced. She went inside, and said goodnight to Lissy and Anj before heading up to her room. She kicked off her plimsolls and hung her shorts and blouse for the following day, then after pulling on a long blouse she'd picked up in Cairo, she took her silver hip flask and went outside and stood against the rooftop wall, and watched the searchlights sweep the dark sky. She sipped on the brandy as she watched and daydreamed, and searched the darkness she was feeling inside. She was angry, and knew it was the talk of her being rested that had pushed a button, but she didn't understand why it had bothered her so much. She'd shut down and been cold from that moment on, and she didn't like how that had made her feel. All she could think of when on the tanker was getting back to Malta and going for drinks, and as soon as she got what she wanted, she'd ruined it. In her mind, at least. She recognised her tiredness, and after taking another sip of brandy, she went into her room and collapsed into her bed, just as the distant thud of anti aircraft fire and bombs started to drift over from Valletta. She didn't sleep right away; despite her exhaustion, her mind was still spinning with a hundred and one questions without any answers, and twice as many competing thoughts. She thought of her friends scattered around the world, wherever they were. The Americans, the girls she'd trained, and her old squadron. She thought of Nicole, and how much she missed her. Nicole always made things OK, even when they were at their worst. She'd swear and complain, and rant about every little injustice until all Harriet could do was smile. She also thought of Robbie and made a vow to visit as soon as she was off duty the following day. With that decision made, her mind stopped swirling a little, and as the explosions eased and the all clear sounded, she finally slipped into a deep sleep.

Chapter 16

Missing...

"Where's the CO?" Harriet asked, as the duty Corporal entered the dispersal hut. She'd been there since before sunrise, as always, having woken early and dodged potholes and bomb craters on her motorcycle, which Cas had delivered the previous day while she slept.

"Squadron Leader Cornwall... Good to see you back, Ma'am."

"Thank you. Where's the CO? He's usually in by now."

"Sorry, Ma'am. I thought you knew..."

"Knew what?" Her heart pounded as the now familiar frown returned to her face.

"The CO didn't come back from his last sortie, Ma'am. We were expecting him back after dark. He went up to take photos of the North African coast and should have been well on his way back before last light."

"I see..." Harriet's heart sank, and her stomach turned. The phone rang, though in her spinning mind, it sounded a hundred miles away. The Corporal walked past her and into the CO's office to answer it, while she thought through the news she'd just been given. If what the Corporal had said was true, she could only imagine the CO had run into trouble somewhere over the sea. Engine failure maybe, or night fighters.

"HQ asking for you, Ma'am," the Corporal said as he came back into the room. "Ma'am?" he repeated, as Harriet continued to stare into space.

"Sorry, what was that?" she replied.

"HQ said you're to report to the AOC, Ma'am. Right away, they said."

"Yes... Yes, thank you." She headed out to her motorcycle, still dumbfounded by the news, then made her way to the underground tunnels as quickly as she could, all the time thinking about the CO. She knew from her own recent experiences that the Mediterranean was as black as oil at night, and even with a moon it was difficult to see where the sky ended, and the sea began. The CO was good, but even he would have struggled to ditch successfully; and if he jumped, there was no knowing what would happen. The Mediterranean was immense, and the only reason she'd been picked up was because she'd crashed near a convoy; otherwise, she'd have been long dead. More than a few pilots had gone out over the Mediterranean and never come back. The handful that did return only did so through sheer luck of being spotted in the vast sea.

"Thanks for coming, Cornwall..." the AOC said, as Harriet joined him in the operations room. She'd seen Spitfires scrambled during her short trip, and now she saw why. A large raid was building over Sicily, and a squadron was being sent to intercept. "We'll have a chat in a minute, but let's see how things pan out here first." She nodded, and stood by his side, watching the plotters, mostly British and Maltese women, as they pushed the markers around the giant map of Malta and Sicily. She looked over to Cas and gave a half smile, which was returned warmly, then she caught the eye of the ballet dancer, who was busy relaying instructions to the fighters. It was a nervous moment waiting for the fight to start, and the heat and stench of the underground operations room didn't make it any less tense. The squadron commander radioed in with a sighting of bombers, his voice booming around the room from the speakers, followed by the inevitable 'Tally ho!" Harriet listened intently with a racing heart as the battle erupted. Pilots calling in warnings and hits, and shouting at each other in a way that took her back to her own experiences flying in combat, almost putting her back in the seat as the words of the pilots painted a vivid picture of what was happening. As she listened, she realised for the first time what a truly difficult job it was to be in operations. Giving instructions and hearing the fight, but not being able to do a thing about it but listen. Then came a genuinely sickening moment which made her vow on the spot she'd never in her life take a job in operations. The Spitfire squadron had made a mess of the assembling German bombers and broken up the raid, but one of the RAF pilots had been hit, a Canadian by the sound of it. He shouted and cursed as he fought with his harness and canopy. He'd been hit, but he was alive and conscious; he just couldn't get out. He fought until the last moments, when his struggle eased, and an air of calm came over the radio, and he simply said, 'Sorry, fellas. Looks like I won't make it this time,' before his radio went dead. There was a moment of silence in the room, but not an inkling of emotion anywhere. Then, as if scripted, the room burst back into life as everyone went about their business. "Shall we?" the AOC asked, and Harriet joined him and Cas in walking to his office, where the door was closed, and she was offered some weak sweet tea from a flask, which she happily accepted. "I assume you've heard the news about your CO?"

"Yes, Sir. When I arrived at the dispersal this morning," she replied, having taken the dryness from her throat with the warm sweet tea which, like all other Malta tea, tasted remarkably similar to wet dust and petrol. "Did you hear him go down? Like we did just now?"

"No... Not a thing. Best guesses are engine trouble."

"That's what I thought."

"He was a good man, the best in terms of photographic reconnaissance, and we'll feel his loss."

"Yes..."

"Anyway, as senior officer, we thought you'd be the right person to replace him."

"Me?" Harriet recoiled in shock.

"You... What's the matter? You've commanded a squadron before, haven't you?"

"I have, Sir. A combat squadron. That is, I've led pilots in combat, but not a reconnaissance squadron."

"Then you won't have any problem with this job. You don't have to fight; in fact, you have to do the opposite, as you well know. Look,

Cornwall, you've done a good job since you've been flying reconnaissance for us, you always bring back the goods, so it's not going to be too much of a stretch to keep on top of the others and make sure they do the same. Besides, we need you in the post, and Wing Commander Salisbury assures me that we can trust you implicitly with the information that accompanies the role." He looked at Cas, who nodded casually.

"Sir?"

"You're taking the job?"

"Yes, Sir."

"Good. In that case, you should know that from now on, you report directly to me. Your orders come directly from me, and your mission reports come directly to me. No deviations, no discussion. Others won't like it, but you'll bite your tongue and follow your orders. Understood?'

"Understood, Sir."

"The only person you discuss any of this with is Wing Commander Salisbury. He works on my behalf, and he's the only one who gives you orders and takes your reports in my absence."

"Yes, Sir." She smiled a little.

"Right, that agreed. I can tell you the next part... The reason for the secrecy, Cornwall, is that we receive intelligence every now and again direct from London, intelligence which lets us know where to find what we're looking for, or in some cases, that there's something we need to look for. It's not right every time, but it points us in the right direction." Harriet's eyebrow raised as she listened; it certainly explained a lot, including why the CO would sometimes take over somebody else's mission without notice or explanation. "The thing is, Cornwall, if the enemy ever finds out about the intelligence we receive, they'll shut it down immediately, and we'll be blind. That means this is a secret you take to your grave... Am I making myself clear?" He fixed her firmly in his stare, and she looked straight at him in return, piercing his eyes.

"Crystal..." she replied, quietly, and with a conviction that made Cas wince a little in discomfort.

"In that case, I have a job for you. There's an Italian convoy at sea somewhere to the east of us, trying to sneak past us the long way around. Based on their time of departure, their heading, speed, and time at sea, we have a rough idea of where they may be, and it's your job to find them. Maximum effort on this one, Cornwall. Our fleet has left Alexandria on the hunt, and we have bombers standing by. When you find them, we want to know about it right away." Harriet nodded to signal her understanding. "The next part of what I'm about to tell you is equally as secret, but you need to know so you can plan your squadron's activities accordingly." Harriet nodded again, while taking another sip of tea, and he continued. "Your CO was lost mapping the Tunisian and Algerian coast. He was running on long range tanks to give his Spitfire the legs to get there and back, but unfortunately, we all know what happened there. That doesn't change the need for intelligence, though, so while you're up looking for that convoy, I want you to detail two of your best pilots to cover the North African job. By sending two aeroplanes, we may just get one back. As you know, your pilots will have a hell of a time if they're seen, so I'd recommend following your former CO's plans and going late in the day. The darkness on your return leg will give you a little cover from chasing fighters."

"I'll do that..."

"Good. Right, that's it. We'd better let you get on. Good luck, Cornwall."

"Thank you, Sir."

"I'll see you out," Cas said, and with a nod from the AOC, he opened the door and escorted Harriet out into the humid corridor. "Are you OK?" he asked as they walked towards the stairs that led to the entrance.

"Yes... Why wouldn't I be?" Harriet replied, doing her best to appear bubbly and cheerful.

"Just look after yourself, Harry."

"I always do," she laughed.

"Harry, I mean it," he said firmly, melting the smile from her face. "No more close calls, OK?"

"I don't get into trouble deliberately... It's the Germans, usually. They've just got it in for me." She shrugged and laughed a little, desperately trying to keep the conversation light, despite seeing the thunder in Cas' eyes.

"Harry!"

"Cas!"

"You're not taking me seriously."

"You're not taking me seriously either!" Harriet snapped, feeling that same darkness building inside her that she'd experienced the night before. "I'll be fine, trust me. I'm good at what I do, and they haven't got me so far, have they?"

"I'm just trying to help..."

"Well, don't! I'll be fine; you don't need to worry about me!" She marched towards the checkpoint at the main doors.

"Harry!" Cas called after her. She stopped in her tracks and turned to look at him. She had a fire in her eyes to match the thunder in his, but she forced a smile.

"I'll be fine, I promise. I'll be back tonight, and we can have drinks in the Mess tomorrow evening after work, if you want?" He nodded in agreement and smiled, then she continued on her way and stepped out into the blinding light of day, breathing in the fresh air, and trying to get the smell of the tunnels from her nose.

Harriet had a furious ride back to the dispersal office, during which she argued with herself angrily about her conversation with Cas. She felt like she was spoiling for a fight, and she just couldn't stop herself. Usually, she was considered and controlled, externally at least, and she was able to identify and intercept when she was about to lose control. It was always Nicole with a short fuse and furious temper, and it was Harriet's job to calm her down, which made it all the more difficult to be like that herself. Unlike Nicole, though, she wasn't able to switch it off with the click of a finger and become a pussy cat again. Instead, she drove herself crazy going over what was said again and again, and continuing the argument in her head long after it was over.

Once at the airfield, she planned the North African trip, then briefed two of the more experienced pilots in the squadron who'd been called in from rest, especially for the mission. They weren't particularly happy at losing a day off, but they had orders to follow, and once they'd got over their initial grumpiness, they engaged in the mission planning thoroughly, and between them and Harriet, they'd agreed one would start at the west, one east, then converge and overlap. The theory being that worst case, they'd get photos of at least half the coastline back, and at best, they'd get two lots of all of it. Once planned, they went off to sleep for the rest of the day, knowing that there was a very long and dangerous flight coming. Harriet then went over her own plans again, checking the coordinates the AOC had given her, and planning her flight, which she memorised the best she could, before having one last mouthful of cold tea ahead of her trip. She grabbed her kit once she was ready, and pushed a half melted boiled sweet into her mouth before heading out to her Spitfire.

"Cas..." she said in surprise, as she almost walked into him at the entrance to her Spitfire pen. "What are you doing here?"

"Apologising," he replied softly, in the tone she knew always put her at ease, even when at her most stressed.

"Don't be silly," she said with a genuinely warm smile. Her planning session had helped her break her thought cycle, and allowed her to come back to herself and appreciate the opportunity to put things right.

254

"I'm not, I don't think. Or maybe I am. The truth is, Harry, I worry about you, and sometimes that worry comes out of my mouth instead of staying locked away in the back of my brain somewhere." He held up his finger when Harriet opened her mouth to reply, and she held in what she was about to say, giving him the chance to finish. "I know that it makes you nervous when I let it out, and I know it makes you feel awkward. So, if you'll accept my apology, I promise I'll try to watch what I say. Basically, I'm sorry, and I want to stay friends."

"It's not that..." she replied. "At least not in the way you think."

"I don't understand."

"I'm not sure I do. I certainly don't want to argue with you, and if you ever said we weren't friends, I wouldn't know what to do." For once, she didn't blush as she talked, but he did. "I'm not myself at the moment, not my best. You were right when you said I'm tired. I know I am. I just don't know how to stop. Everyone expects that I'll perform and do a good job in everything I do, whether it be at school or now as a pilot, and sooner or later, that starts to define a person, and it's conflicting; it's driving me mad. People keep telling me how good I am, and how I can be trusted to do the job, and how they're always depending on me to do the impossible. Can you imagine how that feels, when all you want to do is go home and sleep for a year? The pressure, the fear of failure, the fear of being the disappointment that cracked and couldn't do their job properly. The knowing that I can't stop like anyone else can, because if I do, I become the woman that couldn't cut it, and every other female pilot will suffer."

"I didn't know..." Cas said. "Harry, I'm so sorry. I didn't even think..."

"Please don't be sorry. You're the one person I know who I can rely on when I know things aren't OK. It's me who should be apologising to you. I snap at you and tease you, yet you're always there for me and never bite back." She stepped forward and hugged him, taking him totally by surprise, but he hugged her back.

"I'm not sure officers are allowed to do this," he said, trying hard to use humour to stop his own emotions bubbling over.

255

"I'm not sure I care," she replied, before stepping back and laughing a little, something he joined her in. "Cas, when I get back tonight, I'm going to think more about what you said, about having a break, I mean, and tomorrow I want you to help me plan how to do that properly."

"I will, I promise."

"I have to get going..."

"I know..."

"Drinks tonight in the Mess?"

"Eight?"

"I'll see you there."

"Happy hunting."

Harriet had a spring in her step and a smile on her face as she strapped herself into her replacement blue Spitfire. One of the ground crew had even painted her distinctive orange fox head on the engine cowling, an added bonus that lifted her spirits even more. She went through her checks, and with a wave to the ground crew, she started her engine. The blue smoke hung in the air for a moment, and she breathed it in before the propeller blasted it clear. The smell, the roar of the mighty Merlin engine, the vibrations through the airframe, it all had her smiling like a young girl again. The Spitfire wrapped around her, making her feel safe from whatever lay ahead, bulletproof even. The chocks were pulled away, and she gave Cas a wave as she nudged the Spitfire forward out of its pen. The temperature was high, and she couldn't hang about, or the engine would overheat before she got off the ground, so she taxied as quickly as she could to the end of the runway, weaving left and right to watch for hazards, then turned and ran up her power for her final checks. With a quick look around for marauding enemy aircraft, and others that could be landing, she opened the throttle and let off the brakes. The Spitfire sprinted down the runway like a racehorse, and as the speed climbed, Harriet pushed the stick forward and lifted the tail into the airstream, then felt her tummy flip as the powerful aeroplane leapt into the air. She waved to Cas once again, then raised her undercarriage and quickly set course, racing south across the island and out to sea, climbing to gain height as quickly as she could, before starting her first turn and checking her watch. What was about to happen was one of the specialist skills of a photographic reconnaissance pilot, and one which appealed to Harriet's keen mathematical and logical mind. With no landmarks to be found in the sea, her navigation was all about numbers, timings, compass bearings, and speed. If she kept the right speed, followed the right path, and turned at the time she was supposed to, she'd get to exactly where she should be. With the help of the sun's position in the sky alongside her bearing and time, she could also find her way back home. Or close. As she climbed to her cruising altitude, she checked her mirror for signs of the tell tale white condensation trail, and was reassured to see nothing behind her. It was something else to check, in addition to the navigation and searching for the enemy, but her head was clear, and she felt it computing and calculating as freely as when she was in England flying ferry missions for the ATA.

She flew to the start of her search pattern, then turned and started scanning for the convoy. She flew long zigzags, north to south, searching a large box of the sea for the convoy, while all the time checking for contrails and fighters. She started to think of her time on the tanker, and how the sight of an enemy aircraft struck terror into the crew, and a part of her felt conflicted about what she was doing. For the briefest moment, she wondered if she should just turn back and claim she didn't find the convoy at all, then talk with Cas about taking a break. Nobody would know, and the break would do her good. A week off swimming at St Peter's Pool and sunbathing on the hot rocks, in between sleeping and having drinks in the Mess, would be just what she needed. The other part of her soon took over, though, and she remembered the soldiers of the Long Range Desert Group who'd picked her up, and all the dirty and battle weary Australian soldiers who'd fought Rommel to a standstill, and she knew that she had a job to do. As horrific as being found would be for the crews of the enemy convoy, it was nothing to the terror everyone else would feel if Rommel took Egypt. She focused her mind again, and as she did, she saw the white lines of wakes drawn in the deep blue Mediterranean to the northeast. She'd found them. She prepared herself for a pass; she needed to be sure before she broke radio silence. With another check for enemy aircraft and contrails, she checked her gauges and the compass and marked her position, then set course for the convoy. It didn't take long for the escorting ships to open fire with their heavy anti aircraft guns, and fluffy black clouds that rapidly expanded into fiery explosions started to fill the sky. They weren't close at first, but that soon changed as the Italian gunners got their sights on her, and soon she was having to dive to throw off their trajectory planning, making it difficult for them to hit with the heavy guns, but bringing her into the range of the smaller. She did a pass of the convoy and took photos to be reviewed back in Malta, not that she needed them to confirm what she was seeing. Italian battle flags flew proudly from the escorting ships, and the convoy was quickly zigzagging defensively. She'd certainly found them. She hit the transmit on her radio to report in.

"Hello, Shadow, this is Vixen. Over," she said into the radio, all the while keeping her eyes on the convoy, and the burst of their anti aircraft shells, while simultaneously scanning the sky for enemy aircraft. She was confident they were far enough away from land for regular fighters not to be escorting the convoy, and even if they were, they'd be carrying long range fuel tanks, which meant they wouldn't have a chance of catching her once she started her run home. "Shadow, this is Vixen. Anyone home?" she asked, getting a little impatient as the flak came closer, knowing it would only take one lucky shot to put her in the water, again, and she wasn't in the mood for Cas' sarcastic comments if she missed drinks. At least that was the thought she kept to the fore of her mind, while pushing the image of being shot out of the sky, or worse, having to parachute and being captured, and held onboard an Italian convoy while the whole of the RAF and Royal Navy tried to bomb it out of existence. "Shadow, Vixen! Enemy convoy sighted. Over!" she shouted, as the force of a nearby explosion almost flipped her Spitfire.

"Hello, Vixen. Shadow here, sorry about that. Confirm message."

"About bloody time!" she replied, feeling a sense of relief and frustration. She'd been circling long enough for the Italian gunners to be throwing everything at her and more, and there were less and less gaps in the storm of explosions for her to fly through. "Enemy convoy sighted at my location. Approximately twelve cargo and one tanker, supported by three cruisers, five destroyers, and some smaller ships. Minesweepers, I think. All heading due south."

"Understood, Vixen. Good job, well done. Get yourself home for tea."

"Message received, see you soon." She pushed her nose down and opened the throttle, quickly increasing speed and making herself a difficult target as the gunners started to anticipate her trajectory. She pulled back on the stick, climbing fast and steep to twenty five thousand feet, then levelled out and headed home, leaving the convoy long behind her and out of range. She checked her mirror; no contrails and no fluffy explosions coming close. She smiled to herself. The flak had come close a few times, but there were no fighters, and she hadn't been hit, so all she had to do was set a course and get back home. Something that wasn't going to be easy, as she quickly realised when she looked at her compass and saw it stuck and not moving. She tried descending, rolling, and sudden movements, but nothing would shift it. She hadn't noticed it after giving the convoy's direction to Malta; she'd been too busy trying not to fly into an explosion. She quickly gathered her senses, then searched the mirror for the convoy, and put her tail on it to be sure she was heading in a westerly direction, then checked the time, and the sun's position. Based on her planning and best guesses, she was content that she knew roughly where she was, but she knew that there'd be no turns and timings heading home; she just had to aim west and hope for the best, which is what she did, while doing all of her usual checks, and spinning her head constantly to search for enemy aircraft. To complicate matters, with no compass for her to confirm her heading, and no landmarks to guide her, there was no telling how much the southerly summer winds were blowing her off course. She gave corrections to the south based on those she remembered giving on her outward journey, applying pressure on the rudder pedals gently for short bursts, and all the time hoping for the best. The time passed slowly on the return journey. She'd found the convoy close to the limit of her aeroplane's range, which brought yet another complication in terms of fuel consumption. If she was drifting off course, she'd need more fuel to get to where she was going, in all likelihood, which meant she couldn't run at full speed or at maximum altitude for long. She ran some

259

calculations through her mind, then descended to fifteen thousand feet and throttled back a little, hoping that she'd found the Spitfire's sweet spot of most economical fuel consumption. She checked the fuel tanks; they seemed OK, as did the engine temperature.

After what felt like months sitting in her Spitfire, seeing only blue sea and blue sky, she finally saw land and let out a sigh of relief. Her corrections and calculations had done the job, and she could breathe freely, knowing she'd soon be on the ground again. She went through her checks, then started her climb back to twenty thousand feet, or as close as she could get without leaving a contrail, so she could circle the island and check for fighters, before dropping in and landing. As she climbed, she caught sight of a stream of bombers heading in her direction and smiled, knowing they were on their way to find her convoy, though she was a little concerned as to the time they'd take to get there, and she hoped their navigators were sharp when it came to calculating where they expected the convoy would have moved to. She shrugged; it wasn't any of her business. She'd done her job; the rest was up to them. Suddenly a stream of bullets shot across the nose of her Spitfire in an orange glow of tracer, clipping the cowling, then breezing just above the canopy, as though they were somehow bending around it. She let out an angry scream as she flipped her Spitfire and pulled back on the stick to avoid the gunfire, which was now coming from all directions, while she continued letting out a stream of obscenities at the gunners for shooting at one of their own. It was only when the adrenaline hit and her brain sharpened that she realised the bombers she was approaching weren't RAF Wellingtons; they were an entire squadron of Italian SM 79 Sparviero bombers. Upside down, she also realised she wasn't approaching Malta; she was north of Sicily, almost in Italy, and breezing about at fifteen thousand feet. The target of the cursing moved from the bomber gunners to herself, and she quickly dived away from the enemy formation, her heart racing and mouth drying as she searched for their fighter escort. Soon the ground defences woke up, too, and anti aircraft fire was following her across the sky with increasing accuracy. The Sicilian gunners were good, they were used to chasing reconnaissance aircraft, and their aim was taking a lot of effort to dodge. She quickly recognised the landmarks and got her bearings, then headed back out to sea, dropping and climbing, and changing direction frequently as she raced south, opening the throttle to full power, pushing through the gate to squeeze every last bit of speed out of the engine, knowing all too well that she was now in a race against the southern Sicily based German fighters that would already have been scrambled to intercept her. It was going to be close. As she approached the south coast of Sicily, she could see the 109s circling to the west a couple of thousand feet higher, and as she came level, they saw her and peeled away one after another, four in all, diving after her. She pushed the nose down into a steep dive, and watched as the speed wound up quickly, pushing the needle past the numbers as the airframe started to shake. There was nothing she could do to fight, and after checking the fuel gauge and getting another shock, she knew she didn't have time to play games. She had to get over Malta and land, or jump. Either way, she needed to be clear of Sicily.

"Shadow, this is Vixen!" she called into the radio. "Shadow, this is Vixen; I'm coming in hot, and I'm bringing company!" She looked in her mirror; the 109s were giving chase. Landing was going to be difficult, but if she could drag them down the runway, she hoped her own gunners could get them. It was a plan that was soon pushed off the boil when her engine cut just as she passed the island of Gozo off the north coast of Malta, leaving her with the creaks of the airframe for company as the propeller slowed to windmill over. She quickly looked at her instruments; the fuel tanks were empty. The last push had drained them. She pushed her canopy back; she was going to have to jump low, the second she crossed the Malta coast. The odds were rapidly stacking against her, and it felt that every time she had a solution, an obstacle was thrown in her way. The coast came up quickly, but not as quickly as the 109s, and she fiddled with her harness ahead of her jump. She thought of the radio message she'd heard in the Ops room, when the pilot hadn't been able to unfasten his harness, and she became a little distressed when her own wouldn't move. She looked down as she pulled at it, then whispered thank you to anyone listening when it clicked open. As she looked up, she was greeted by the welcome sight of eight Spitfires charging down on her from the south, on a heading to intercept her pursuers. She watched in her mirror as the 109s turned and ran, chased north by trails of cannon shells and bullets from the angry Spitfires. She breathed another sigh of relief, then lined up with her airfield. There was smoke around the island, particularly around Valletta; a raid had obviously been through not long ago. She scoured the sky for signs of the enemy, not that she could do much if she saw one, then scrubbed off the rest of her speed the best she could and dropped her undercarriage and flaps. A reassuring clunk and flash of lights confirmed the wheels were down; all she had to do was keep the Spitfire in the air long enough to reach the runway, which she just managed, touching down at the very start of the runway and bouncing along at speed. She braked gently, not wanting to lose too much momentum, then turned and took the direct route to the dispersal, where the Spitfire finally rolled to a halt just a few hundred paces from the blast pen. She'd made it. She laid her head against the rest for a moment, then quickly unplugged her sweat soaked helmet and pulled it from her head, before dragging herself upwards and stepping out onto the wing.

"Everything OK, Ma'am?" The Corporal asked as he greeted her.

"Yes..." she replied with a smile. "The fuel ran out just as I was crossing the coast, and the compass has had it. Otherwise, I think everything's the way it should be."

"I'll have a look at it after I've got the cameras sorted, Ma'am."

"As quick as you can, I'll be back in a minute so I can take the photos up to headquarters." She smiled, then walked away confidently. She couldn't help smiling as she headed to the dispersal hut. Despite the challenges, the flight had been exhilarating, and even being chased by 109s didn't dent her confidence. If anything, it made her feel all the more invincible. The desert and the convoy were behind her at last; she was back.

"Sir..." she said, as the AOC stepped out of the hut and watched her approach.

"You made it back safely, I see," he said in his usual warm yet formal tones.

"Yes, Sir. I ran into a squadron of Italian bombers on the way back, and a flight of four 109s chased me home, but our boys saw them off before they could get close."

"Good... Good, I'm happy it went well."

"Did we get them?"

"What?"

"The convoy, did we get them?"

"Oh, yes, yes we did. Our bombers hit the convoy an hour after you found it, and the fleet is scheduled to intercept this afternoon... Look, Cornwall, I need to have a word..."

"Sir?" Her smile turned to a frown, and she felt her heart racing. Immediately she thought to her conversation with Cas before her flight, and she was instantly concerned that the AOC had turned up to discuss her rest. She felt herself getting angry, and questioning how Cas dared talk to the AOC without agreeing it with her first. She'd changed her mind; she wanted to stay. "Sir, if this is about the rest that I'd agreed with Wing Commander Salisbury, I'm not sure you've heard the full story. The thing is, he probably got the wrong end of the stick, and while he probably thought he was helping, he wasn't." She talked fast and excitedly, while trying to remain casual and professional, whatever it took to get her story across and stop whatever was happening.

"Cornwall, I'm not sure what you think I'm here to discuss. Wing Commander Salisbury hasn't mentioned anything to me about you. In fact, he's the reason we need to talk."

"Sir?"

"There's no easy way of saying this, so I'll just say it. I know that you and Salisbury are friends, and I wanted to let you know myself that he was hit pretty bad this morning." He winced a little as he talked, sensing the discomfort in Harriet's frozen silence. Her heart was pounding harder than it ever had in combat, as her mind spun, and a deep nausea took hold.

"I don't understand..." Harriet replied, her voice trembling with shock, and silenced to almost a whisper compared to her previous

263

confident and agitated dialogue. "How could he be hit? He doesn't fly?"

"A raid came in when he was on his way back to HQ, and he was caught out in it by a rogue Stuka that had given our Spitfires the slip."

"I see..."

"We got the message from the hospital a short while ago telling us he'd been brought in, though I couldn't tell you what condition he's in. Would you like to go?"

"Yes... Yes, if I could?"

"Do you have a vehicle?"

"My motorcycle."

"Are you up to it? I can give you a ride over there, if you'd like?"

"No... No, it's OK. Thank you for telling me..." She was totally shell shocked, and while she was able to process what she was hearing, her mind struggled to make sense of anything.

"I'll take care of things here, and make sure your photos get to HQ. You get yourself off." He gave her a warm smile that she could see right through. He was as uncomfortable as she was. She nodded, then walked off towards her motorcycle, quickly gathering pace, then breaking into a run. She urgently needed to be at the hospital. Still wearing her flying kit, she raced along the dusty roads as she made her way across the island to the hospital, riding as fast as she could while staying upright. All the while, her mind spun around the same outcome, 'what if he was dead?' It was a desperate ride, and the empty turmoil in her stomach made her feel dizzy with nausea, and even cold to the touch. She pulled up outside the hospital door, and was off her motorcycle and heading inside before the engine had even stopped.

"Wing Commander Salisbury?" she asked the duty nurse.

"Excuse me?"

"Wing Commander Salisbury, where is he? He was brought in a while ago after being bombed."

"One minute."

"Not one minute, now! Where is he?"

"Come with me," the nurse said, after checking her paperwork. She stood and led Harriet through the hospital to the recovery ward. "We have a visitor for the Wing Commander who came in," the nurse said to the senior Sister on the ward.

"No visitors, I'm afraid," came the stern reply.

"Where is he?" Harriet demanded.

"The patients in here are in a tenuous condition, and we don't allow visitors!"

"Oh, shut up!" Harriet blustered, then nudged her out of the way with her shoulder, and marched into the ward. "Cas?" she called, trying her hardest to pull herself together. "Cas!" She became more frantic as she looked at the beds, until finally she looked into a small side room and found him, and quickly ran to his side. "Cas..." she gasped, then put a hand over her mouth. The left side of his head and face were bandaged, as were his left shoulder and arm, and his chest. The one eye not bandaged was closed, and his face was scratched and cut, as was his neck. "Oh God, Cas..." she grabbed his hand and squeezed it. Her composure broke, and floods of tears ran down her cheeks as she fought to catch her breath.

"Here," a doctor said, as he entered the room and stood by Harriet's side and handed her his silver flask. She took it without looking at him, and took a gulp of whisky, which burned her throat and cut through the dryness in her mouth.

"Will he live?" Harriet asked.

"If he does, he'll have a bloody horrific headache when he wakes up." Harriet simply nodded in reply. "We've done all we can; it's up to him now."

"Thank you..." Harriet half whispered, not taking her eyes off Cas' bandaged and battered body.

"By rights, that explosion should have finished him; it's a miracle he stayed alive long enough for us to get him into surgery. He's certainly a fighter."

"Yes..." She forced a smile and looked at the doctor. "What are his chances?"

"Well, he's alive now, so he's doing better than average. Other than that, I couldn't say. He's pretty badly beaten up."

"Is there anything I can do?"

"Pray..."

"Excuse me?"

"Whatever happens next is out of our hands... I'll have a chair brought over for you, if you'd like to stay a while? I'm sure we can rustle up a cup of tea, too. You look like you could do with one." Harriet nodded, and he left her holding Cas' hand. She felt herself trembling. He looked peaceful, yet defenceless, and for the first time in her life, she was genuinely lost as to what to do. There was no way out of it, no changing it, and nothing she could do would make the outcome any different. She could cry, scream, or shout, and it wouldn't make the slightest bit of difference. A nurse returned with a cup of tea, which she handed over with a sympathetic smile that didn't even register in Harriet's mind. She simply took the cup and sipped the sweetened, lukewarm dishwater while staring blankly, her mind no longer able to process anything other than the awful taste in her mouth. She couldn't think, because she knew if she did, she'd come apart at the seams. She'd got through everything so far, all the fear and loss, because she knew deep down that there was one constant, one person who could pick her up and make things OK, regardless of how bad things got, but now that person was lying at death's door. She wanted to help, to do something to make it right, but all she could do was hold his hand and pray, and that's what she did.

"Harry..." a familiar voice said from behind, speaking in hushed tones and bringing her back from the prayer she'd been stuck in for an eternity, where she'd bargained with any god listening, and made promises in return for Cas' life. She lifted her head and turned to see the CO standing beside her in the dim lamplight of the darkened room. She stared for a moment, unsure of what to think, or what to say. He'd been lost. Was he really there? Was she? Or was it the end?

"Sir..." she whispered in reply.

"I came over as soon as I heard. How is he?"

"In a bad way... I thought you were lost?"

"What?" He smirked a little. "No. No, just a spot of engine trouble. I was able to put down on a Vichy French airfield. Fortunately, I knew their CO from before the war, and he and his squadron like the Germans about as much as they do Churchill; so they helped fix me up and get me back. Unfortunately, they couldn't get word back due to them being under the watchful eye of the enemy." Harriet nodded as she processed the story. "I'm told he was hit in a bombing raid?"

"Yes... They didn't find him for a while."

"I see... How are you?"

"I'm OK." She forced an unconvincing half smile.

"The AOC tells me you've done a sterling job in my absence."

"Hardly."

"Well, regardless of your opinion on the matter, I'm pretty sure you've earned a break. Why don't you hang around here for a while? Keep the old man company until he wakes up, and I'll go take care of the flying side of things."

"He's not old..."

"No. No, he isn't. Are you going to be OK?" She nodded solemnly. "OK, in that case I'll leave you to it. Call if you need anything, you know where to find me." She nodded again, and forced another half smile. "Oh, I almost forgot. Here, I brought you something." He pulled a bar of chocolate from his pocket. "A gift from the French." He smiled, then left her staring at the gift. She pulled back the paper and snapped off a couple of squares, and popped them into her mouth. She gave Cas' hand a squeeze, tighter than before, hoping to stir something in him, but there was no response; so she slumped back in the wicker chair as her mind ran over every conversation she'd ever had with Cas, especially recently, when she'd been snappy and angry at him. He'd taken it all in his stride, even when she'd shouted at him, and the guilt she was feeling was turning her stomach with near unmanageable nausea.

"The Wing Commander said you'll be staying for a while," the nurse said as she returned.

"If that's OK?" Harriet asked.

"I'll make sure you get something to eat and drink."

"I don't really feel like eating, but I am thirsty."

"I'll see what I can do." Harriet nodded, then leant forward and stared at Cas. His chest was slow to rise and fall, like every breath was an effort, and it pained her to watch. Her thoughts circled again, and all she could think was that she wanted Nicole. She needed a hug, and somebody to tell her it was all going to be OK, and Nicole was the expert at that. She talked to Cas for a while, and made all the same promises to him that she'd made to the gods, or most of them at least, and when her eyes started to get heavy, she moved the chair closer before leaning back and slouching down, so her head was against the rest. She closed her heavy eyes and said another prayer, remembering all those she'd reluctantly learned at school, and reciting them in Latin and French, again and again, hoping somebody would hear.

Chapter 17

Darkness and Dreams

"Harry..." Cas whispered, his voice cutting through Harriet's recurring nightmares. She opened her eyes and looked at him. His uncovered eye was half open, and his head was turned to face her. "Harry, is that you?" She froze for a moment, then sat up and glanced around to see a blanket laid over her, and a folded towel tucked between her head and the chair. The room was dark, except for the faintest amber glow of a small candle flickering in the lamp beside the bed.

"Yes..." Harriet replied softly, when she finally found her voice. "Is this real?" she asked. Her head was fuzzy, and she couldn't be sure whether she was still dreaming.

"I don't know..." came his reply. Harriet pulled herself up from her chair and stood beside him, and he looked into her eyes. He was confused, scared even. "Harry, where are we?"

"In the hospital, I think..." She looked around the dark room. He patted the bed, and she took a seat next to him on the soft mattress.

"More comfortable than the chair..."

"Much..."

"I'm so tired..."

"Can I get you anything? Does it hurt?"

"Everywhere."

"I'll get a nurse."

"No... No, I'll be OK. I just need to sleep." He held her hand tight, then collapsed into his pillow and slipped back into unconsciousness. Harriet watched him drift away again, then leant back against the head end of the bedstead and squeezed his hand. He groaned a little and squeezed back, and she briefly smiled, then her own eyes closed.

"What on earth is the meaning of this?!" A firm and quite furious female voice demanded. Harriet's eyes shot open, and she instantly winced at the bright daylight flooding the room. A nurse stood frowning at the foot of the bed, hands on hips and her face turning all colours. "Beds are for the sick, Squadron Leader! If you want to sleep, I suggest you go back to your accommodation and leave us to look after our patients!" Harriet was shell shocked. She'd been swimming in confusing nightmares since she'd closed her eyes, and she wasn't sure what was real. "Come on, get those filthy clothes off the linen!" The nurse demanded as she walked around the bed towards Harriet, who was half laid against the bedstead, and half laid against Cas.

"Steady on, nurse. She was hardly going to sleep on the floor," Cas half whispered in reply. Harriet's heart raced as she sat forward and looked down at him. "Hello..." he said with a half smile.

"Hello..." she replied, hardly able to contain herself, or keep a huge smile from her face. "You're awake."

"Wonderful observation!" the nurse demanded. "If you wouldn't mind?" Harriet nodded and removed herself from the bed, stepping aside so the nurse could examine Cas.

"They're very efficient..." Cas said with a smirk. His whispering voice sounding dry and scratchy. Harriet poured some water from the jug on the bedside table and handed it to him. "Thank you," he gasped.

"You are in my way, Squadron Leader!" The nurse bellowed, not breaking her momentum as she went about checking him over. "Either remove yourself, or I'll have the Military Police do the job for me."

"Are you going to be OK?" Harriet asked Cas, totally ignoring the nurse. She'd met enough of them to know how far she could push, and while she knew she was approaching her limit, this particular nurse was proving to be quite feisty.

"He will be if you move and let me do my job!"

"I think so..." Cas replied, after taking a sip of water and having the glass taken from him by the irritated nurse. "I daren't be anything else with her around." He nodded at the nurse, who rolled her eyes in frustration.

"I'll see you soon," Harriet said with a smile, then left half the chocolate bar on his pillow, and waved before leaving the room. She wandered along the corridor and stepped outside into the warm morning air, then leant against the hospital wall and looked up to the sky. She smiled as she said a thank you, then felt a tear run down her cheek. It was a mix of relief and exhaustion. Things were getting too close, and she knew it. She composed herself as the sound of boots heralded the arrival of a couple of soldiers, who politely saluted before heading inside, leaving her to walk over to her motorcycle. It was right where she'd left it the previous day, and it started right away. She pulled her silk scarf up around her nose and mouth, and put on her sunglasses, then she took off across the island. Thinking through what had happened, and her future. She knew she was close to the edge, but she didn't know what she could do about it. Maybe she did need a break, or a posting even. She even considered the merits of going back to England and teaching WAAFS to march up and down a parade square. She pulled up at the dispersal office and put on her hat, then headed inside to see the CO marking up one of the large maps on the wall.

"Well?" he asked as he turned to face her.

"He's awake," Harriet replied with a smile.

"Thank God," the CO's shoulders dropped as the tension left his body. "Are you OK?"

"Yes, thank you."

"Good. So, what are you doing here?"

"Reporting for duty."

271

"I don't think so."

"Sir?"

"Get yourself off to your digs, you must be exhausted."

"But..."

"That's an order. I don't want to see you back here until tomorrow, understood?"

"Sir..."

"And don't let me hear that you've been doing anything other than resting, or we'll fall out."

"Yes, Sir." She smiled, then headed for the door.

"Harry?"

"Sir?" She stopped and turned to look at him.

"Good news about Cas."

"Yes, Sir." She smiled and headed out to her motorcycle, and after stopping to talk nicely to the ground crew, and share her chocolate with them while they filled her petrol tank with high octane aviation fuel, she headed back home. Air raid sirens sounded as she rode, but no enemy aircraft came. Instead, a swarm of Spitfires leapt into the sky, flying low overhead to intercept the incoming raid north of the island, and keep the enemy safely at arm's length. She couldn't help but smile. The Germans seemed to have had the wind knocked out of them. The Spitfires were being reinforced, and the arrival of the fuel tanker had not only kept Malta in the war, it had turned the tide. The days of a handful of Hurricanes and Gladiators battling to intercept overwhelming raids were long gone. The Spitfires had steadily turned the tide, and while raids still got through, they were no longer the terror they were. The rationing was still bad, and the island was still close to collapse, but the spirit of the defenders seemed stronger than ever.

After collecting her things and packing a bag, Harriet headed down to the pool in the sea at the south of the island. The place Robbie had first taken her and Nicole so long ago, and the place Harriet had spent so many hours sunbathing and swimming. She paid off the Maltese sentry with a pack of American cigarettes she'd brought back from Cairo, then left her motorcycle with him and climbed through the gaps in the wire, then headed down the sandy tracks to the large sun baked rocks surrounding the hollow that made the natural pool. The deep blue Mediterranean was washing in, its white waves crashing against the rocks, and fizzing and bubbling invitingly. Harriet dropped her bag and stepped out of her clothes, then picked up her bar of soap and dived off the small cliff, disappearing under the cool water. It shocked her at first, but she'd acclimatised by the time she surfaced, and she lay on her back as she felt the water cool her skin. She moved to the shallows and scrubbed herself, using the soap to wash the smoke and sweat from her body and hair, then after leaving it on a rock she dived deep to rinse off, before rolling onto her back again and floating. After swimming a while, she laid on the rocks and ate some chocolate and hard biscuits, which she washed down with cold tea she'd made from her own recycled leaves. She thought a lot about her recent experiences while she laid in the sun, and with the words of warning about cats having nine lives rattling around her head, she totalled up her near misses. There'd been enough in Malta alone, that was without France, England, and Hawaii. She was conflicted when it came to what she wanted to do next. Cas was going to help her take a break, or maybe even get away more permanently, but he was in no position to do that anymore; and while she'd been full of bravado and confidence after her last flight, she knew that much of it was fake. She'd been fighting to convince herself she was fine, driven by the dreaded and unshakable drive to not disappoint people, but inside she knew she was burned out. At first, she tried to pin it on the tanker experience, or her crash in the desert, but with time to think she was able to admit to herself that she was done before she even got back to Malta. She remembered how she'd felt on the aircraft carrier when she was told where she was heading, the nausea and sweats, despite being in a ship rolling in the cold and miserable Atlantic. Before that, even. She wanted desperately to stay in America. She'd made good friends and she was enjoying her job, but more than anything she was enjoying being out of harm's way, Pearl

273

Harbour excepted. Now, though, with Cas incapacitated, temporarily at least, she'd either have to keep doing her job and hoping for the best, or ask the CO for a posting. She knew he'd do it for her. He cared about his pilots more than anyone else she'd met, and if they were burned out or struggling, he'd try and get them posted before things took a turn for the worse, always with a letter of recommendation and a warm handshake. He knew that the life of a photographic reconnaissance pilot in Malta was a dangerous one, and he knew the risks increased with every mission, so he never judged. Mostly he arranged postings without the worn out pilot even knowing, having recognised the signs long before they were able to admit it themselves, but sometimes they'd hide it so well that he wouldn't know until they asked.

After dozing and sunbathing, Harriet made her way back to the hospital to visit Cas. This time feeling much fresher for her scrub in the Mediterranean. The nurses showed her through to his room, where he was propped up on pillows and drinking a cup of tea. His face lit up when he saw her, or what of it wasn't wrapped in bandages.

"Harry!" he said with happiness in his still dry whisper.

"How are you feeling?" she asked.

"Better for that chocolate you left me. I bribed the snapdragon nurse with a couple of squares, so she's no longer out to get you."

"I didn't know she was!"

"Apparently you were making the place look untidy."

"Charming... Anyway, you look much better than you did yesterday. Are they letting you out soon?"

"Apparently not... I'm banged up worse than I thought, or so they say."

"Does it hurt?" She frowned with discomfort, remembering her own hospital experience.

"Mostly."

"Where?"

"It'd likely be easier to ask where it doesn't hurt." He forced a laugh, which clearly pained him even more.

"Cas..."

"Oh, don't worry. I'm in good hands. Have a seat." He patted the bed again.

"No chance! If that nurse catches me sitting on a bed again, it'll take more than chocolate to stop her from having me shot!" Instead, she pulled up the wicker chair and took a seat. "I'm thinking of asking the CO for a posting..."

"That came out of the blue." He frowned as he looked at her. "Are you OK?"

"I've been thinking about what you said, and you're right, you know you are, I'm tired and I'm starting to worry that I'm losing my edge."

"In that case you should ask him right away. He's a good man, he'll understand. In fact, I dare say he'll respect you for telling him."

"It's not that easy..."

"Pride goes before a fall, Harry."

"Shut up!"

"I mean it. Just take a deep breath and say what you have to, it's the only way."

"In that case it's not just the exhaustion that's stopping me."

"Oh?"

"I don't want to go because I don't want to leave you here. Not like this." She looked at him, bandaged and bruised. "I'd convinced myself before that you were safer than most, working down in the tunnels and all, but look at you. I can't just leave you here. You're about the only thing that's been constant in my life since the war started, and no matter what I think or tell myself, I can't just go."

"I see..."

"Don't look at me like that!" she blustered, as she felt her cheeks glowing with the fiercest blush.

"Like what?"

"Shut up!"

"If I'm the only thing stopping you leaving, I may be able to help..."

"What? How? And don't tell me to forget about you and get on with it."

"I'm not staying either..."

"What?"

"The AOC was here a short while ago. The doctors want to evacuate me to Egypt, and he's inclined to agree..."

"You didn't say..."

"You didn't give me chance..."

"You could have told me before you let me say what I did!"

"Does it matter?"

"No..." She smiled through her blush. A great weight lifted from her as she realised that she didn't need to worry. She hated Egypt, but it was infinitely safer than Malta. "When?"

"Soon, I think. There isn't the medication or food here for me to recover quickly, or so I'm told, so despite Cairo being my least favourite place to visit, I'm comfortable with the idea. If I'm honest, the only thing holding me back is you."

"Me?"

"I've been worried about you, Harry, as you well know. If I'm honest, it filled me with a sense of dread to leave you here. Something you've eased significantly with what you've just said." She smiled again. "In fact, I was so worried that when the AOC broke the news, I asked him to arrange some leave for you. I thought a few weeks visiting your ambulance driving friend would be just what you needed."

"Cairo?"

"Yes. If I've got to put up with the place, there's no reason you should get away with it. A couple of weeks of rest and I should even be up to going out for a spot of dinner, if you're up for it?"

"But what about the AOC?"

"Well, I'm not sure how he'd feel about joining us for dinner, but I can ask?"

"Shut up! You know what I mean!"

"He said it's a fantastic idea. In light of your fun in the desert, and then again on the tanker, he thinks you've more than earned a few weeks off, should you want it?"

"What? Yes! Yes, of course I want it! When?"

"I don't know, soon, I think. He said to go along and see him later today, and he'll make the arrangements."

"I can't believe it." She shook with excitement, as she almost bounced in her seat.

"Maybe a couple of weeks will give you time to think about that posting. We can discuss it while we're there, if you like?"

"I'd like that!"

"Me too!"

"You again!" the nurse said as she entered the room. "I'm quite sure visiting time isn't until this evening."

"You'd better get going..." Cas said with a wink.

"I'll go see the AOC."

"Good idea."

"See you later!" She stood and smiled. "At visiting time!" she added, as she looked at the nurse.

"Goodbye, Squadron Leader," the nurse replied, once again rolling her eyes. Harriet waved, then left with a spring in her step. She was walking on air again, and smiled the whole way to the headquarters and the tunnel complex. Even the heat and stench of human bodies didn't bother her as she skipped her way to the AOC's office, which he invited her into after he'd finished briefing a group of his officers.

"Come in, Cornwall," the AOC said as the officers departed. She did as he asked, and stood in front of his desk. The room was still overheated from the body heat of the men that had just left, but it wasn't enough to dampen her spirits. "I've been expecting you."

"I've just come from seeing Wing Commander Salisbury in the hospital, Sir." she replied.

"Yes, good news he's awake. Against the odds, apparently, but good news all the same."

"Yes, Sir."

"Despite his best efforts to convince us otherwise, he's still in a bad way, as you know, which is why we're evacuating him to a hospital in Egypt. I'm sure he told you?"

"Yes, Sir." Her smile dulled a little. She knew he was worse than the front he was putting on for her, but she didn't like hearing it. "When does he leave?"

"Tonight."

"Sir..." Her heart jumped at the news. She'd thought she would have a few days at least.

"There's a Sunderland due in on a supply run after dark, and after a quick turnaround Wing Commander Salisbury will be heading back to Egypt with it."

"I see... Sir, he said he'd mentioned to you about some leave... For me, I mean."

"Yes, we thought a couple of weeks off would do you good. You've more than earned it."

"I wonder if I could go on the Sunderland tonight? I could keep him company on the trip."

"That was the plan..."

"Was?"

"Yes. Unfortunately. Best laid plans of mice and men and all that..."

"I'm not sure I understand, Sir."

"We received a communication this afternoon ordering you back to England."

"England?" Her heart was racing, and her head was spinning. It was a shock to say the least.

"Yes, came as a surprise to me, too. I was hoping to keep you around, Cornwall. It was thought a few weeks rest would be enough to get you refreshed and back taking photographs for us. Things are changing out here, we're in the driving seat at last and we have big plans. I could use a pilot with your skill."

"Why England, Sir?"

"Honestly, Cornwall, I haven't got a clue. You're to report to Whitehall without delay, and that's about all I know. I talked with the Air Ministry to see if there was somebody else we could send in your stead, but they were quite adamant. They want Squadron Leader Harriet Cornwall, nobody else."

"Do I at least have time for a few days in Cairo, maybe?"

"Sadly not. There's a supply ship coming in tomorrow evening, and you'll be going back to Gibraltar with it."

"Sir..."

"I've cleared it all with your CO. You're stood down until you leave, time to get your affairs in order."

"Yes, Sir."

"You don't strike me as overly enthused, Cornwall."

"I don't particularly like boats, Sir."

"I wouldn't worry too much about that, the one you're going out on has been supplying us throughout the siege, and they haven't got close to her yet. She's far too quick for the enemy to catch, I'm sure you'll be quite safe... Though I suspect there's something more on your mind?"

"I just wasn't expecting to be going back to England, Sir..."

"No. It's a surprise to us all, as I said. Still, hopefully it'll be a break for you. Better than a couple of weeks in Cairo I'd imagine. Anyway,

I'll hope to see you before you leave, but good luck, Cornwall, and thanks for everything." He held out his hand, which Harriet shook gracefully, before leaving the office and walking through the damp smelly corridors. The spring had gone from her step, and a confused whirlwind raged inside her. She was getting out, getting away, but to England, and despite only just forming the plan, she desperately wanted to go to Cairo. Her emotions were in tatters, and her inability to process the situation just showed how tired she was. As long as things were going as expected, she was fine, but as soon as they changed, she was a mess. She walked out into the daylight and looked around. Soon she'd be leaving Malta again, maybe for the last time, leaving on a boat which would be sprinting alone across the Mediterranean and hoping for the best. The only thing she did know from all the confusion, was that the manner in which she was leaving made her instantly sick to her stomach.

"Did you know?" Harriet asked, as she walked into Cas' hospital room.

"I told you that visiting time is this evening!" the same nurse replied.

"I've spent the last two years flying in combat and shooting down more enemy aircraft than I care to remember, and I did it all without a hint of remorse," Harriet said fiercely, as she stood directly in front of the nurse and looked her in the eyes. "Now wouldn't be the time to cross me."

"How dare you threaten me?" the nurse blustered.

"Try me."

"Matron will hear of this!" The nurse said, as she hurried from the room.

"Good!" Harriet shouted after her, before turning back to Cas.

"Did you know?"

"Know what?" He looked bewildered. "Harry, what's going on?"

281

"I'm being sent back to England!"

"What? Harry, I promise I'd have told you. When? To do what?"

"Tomorrow night, and I haven't got a clue. Nobody has. And to make matters worse I'm being sent out on a bloody boat..." She slumped down on the chair facing him.

"So, Cairo's off..." he said sadly.

"Not for you. You leave tonight."

"Tonight? What?"

"There was a time when you knew everything before anyone else."

"There was a time when I wasn't stuck in a hospital bed. God. Tonight. I thought a few days at least."

"Me too."

"And the AOC can't change things? Or even hold it off until after your leave?"

"Nope."

"I see..."

"Do you? I certainly don't. I don't know what's going on, or what to think. One moment I was happy, the next, well, I don't know..."

"But you were going to ask for a posting anyway, and England would have been the likely outcome."

"After Cairo."

"Yes... That would have been better..." His whispered voice was full of sadness, while Harriet fought to keep her eyes glossy and no more, despite feeling she wanted to cry. "Look, why don't you come back at visiting time and we'll have a drink before they move me? I'll talk with

Matron and smooth things out with the nurses, and we can have a picnic of dried biscuits and bad tea."

"I'd like that." Harriet nodded, but still didn't move.

"Good. Now you'd better make yourself scarce before that snapdragon comes back. If you go to our favourite bar, the owner may even be able to rustle up a couple of Horse's Necks for us?" Harriet nodded, then pulled herself up to her feet.

"I'm sorry I came in with a bit of an attitude."

"Oh, I wouldn't worry. The nurses need somebody to fight back every now and then, it gives them practice and keeps them sharp. I'll see you later." He gave her a wink, and she instinctively smiled.

"I'll see you."

The raids were mercifully light, with Spitfires scrambled to intercept and keep the enemy away from Grand Harbour and the airfields, which made Harriet's trip to Valletta easier than it would have been some weeks earlier. More people were in the streets, moving rubble and trying to go about some sort of life, and despite the depths of depravation they'd been subjected to the civilians were cheerful in their work, and much to her embarrassment they cheered Harriet when they saw her walking through the ruins. She quickly made herself scarce, and ducked into the bar she and Cas had frequented for drinks where, after explaining the situation to the owner, she was presented with two bottles of Bollinger Champagne, much to her amazement. Her protests were rebuffed with a polite smile, the owner had presented Champagne to his regular pilots when they finally left the island as a thank you for all they'd done for Malta. Nobody ever knew where he got it, and nobody ever asked. Though Bollinger was quite a surprise, nobody on the island had seen it for years. He said goodbye, and sent his best wishes to Cas, then Harriet made her way to the General's house to visit Robbie and give her the news.

"Hey..." Robbie said, as she saw Harriet standing at the patio door. Robbie was lounging under a parasol in shorts and vest which showed the bruising and stitched wounds that made up her previously flawless flesh.

"Hey... How are you feeling?" Harriet replied.

"Tired. Still!" Robbie replied with clear irritation. She'd been frustrated since being discharged from the hospital and sent to live with her grandparents to convalesce, mostly because she wanted to get back to work, but her injuries prevented it. As did the word of the Governor, a friend of her grandfather's, and a man whose orders were for her to convalesce indefinitely, seeing as she'd argued not to be evacuated back to England. If she was staying, she was doing as she was told, and that was beyond debate. "How about you?"

"I don't know." Harriet sighed, as she sat on the lounger beside her friend.

"What's up?"

"Cas was hit in a bombing raid."

"Oh, Harry. Is he OK?"

"Yes. Kind of, he's alive, but being evacuated to Cairo tonight."

"I'm sorry... Though I'm relieved he's OK."

"Me too."

"I'll miss him."

"Me too..." Harriet gave a half smile.

"I don't doubt that. It looks like you'll be stuck with me to talk to. It's not the same, I know, but I'll do my best." Robbie gave a smile, and reached out to hold Harriet's hand.

"I don't even have that."

"What are you talking about?"

"I've been ordered back to London. I'm leaving tomorrow night."

"What? No! Harry! Are you sure? I mean, they made a mistake in America, didn't they? They haven't done that again?"

"Apparently not. The AOC was adamant, he even double checked as he wanted to keep me around."

"Heavens knows why..." Robbie winked, making Harriet smile. "I'm sorry you're leaving."

"I don't know if I'm that sorry. I don't know much, really. It just feels kind of strange for it all to end like this. You laid up, Cas broken, and me being summoned back to England. It feels like such an anti climax to our Malta story."

"It could be worse..."

"I suppose. We stopped the Germans invading, so far at least. That's something."

"You're right, but I wasn't talking about that."

"Then what?"

"At least you're going back to England in one piece and still have a job to do." She glanced down to the scars and bruises, and her cast entombed broken leg.

"I'm sorry. I probably come across as insensitive and selfish."

"Not really. I know what you mean. If I was you, I'd probably feel the same."

"It doesn't feel right leaving you here, though. Wouldn't you come to England, too? I'm pretty sure your grandfather could arrange for you to leave with me?"

"On a boat? Not a chance!"

"Harsh."

"Honestly, I couldn't leave. Malta's my home. You know that."

"I know..."

"Besides, what would I do in England? It's far too cold and wet there for me, I like to feel the sun on my skin."

"I'm going to miss you."

"You'll be back. You couldn't stay away the last time you left."

"I'm not sure any of that was through choice!"

"What time do you leave tomorrow?"

"I don't know. Sometime in the night, whenever I'm told, I suppose."

"I'll see you before you go, won't I?"

"I promise, and I'll tell Cas you said goodbye."

"Thank you..."

They talked and had drinks, then Harriet set off to see Cas again for their party in the hospital. It had done her good to see Robbie, and to be able to talk about what was on her mind, it helped a little, but she was still conflicted. She put it out of her mind, and when she reached the hospital again the nurses had agreed to provide a couple of glasses, which she and Cas used to drink the Champagne. It was a little warm, but it tasted good. As did the tinned fruitcake that Robbie had insisted she take, having somehow managed to retain control of her black market empire despite being indisposed. They talked and laughed, as best Cas could. He was tired and in pain, but still able to make conversation and keep Harriet smiling. At his request Harriet took a small piece of cake to the nurse she'd had words with on her previous visit. It was the right thing to do, she knew it and didn't even argue when he'd suggested it, other than to ask if he wouldn't mind doing it to save her embarrassment. There was no avoiding it, though, knowing full well that there was no way he could get out of bed to stand up, let alone walk anywhere to deliver cake, and with a deep breath to steady herself she delivered her gift, and her apologies, and even received a half smile in reply.

As the sun set the ambulance came, and with the agreement of the doctor Harriet was allowed to travel in it with Cas and the other casualty being evacuated, a Spitfire pilot who'd been badly burned a few days earlier. The smell was sadly familiar, an unpleasant air of burned flesh made worse for the stifling heat that refused to yield. It brought memories of past encounters, of lost friends and her own terrors, but like so much else she pushed them to the back of her mind and focused on the moment. At the bombed and battered seaplane base at Kalafrana, down at the southern tip of Malta, she and Cas spent their time on the dockside, talking quietly while looking out to sea, as the sky darkened to reveal a blanket of twinkling stars. He slipped into unconsciousness now and then, thanks in part to the pain, and the medication he'd been given to manage it. It frustrated him, as he wanted to make the most of every minute they had left, but despite his best efforts to convince her otherwise, he was in a bad way. Harriet just smiled and held his hand while he slept, and watched the stars while listening to the waves crash gently against the rocks below. She knew from experience how hard it was to stay awake when injured, and as much as she wanted to talk, she knew he needed rest. There was silence when he was asleep, except for the waves and the occasional voices in the darkness, or distant rattle of a truck, and for a while it was the most peaceful Malta had been.

A distant rumble of engines to the south heralded the arrival of the Sunderland flying boat, and Harriet watched as the ghostly white shape came out of the darkness, circling at first, then skimming the sea as it came closer, heading for the concrete pier. Harriet's heart sank. The peaceful moment was over, and already she could hear a car coming close. She squeezed Cas' hand tight, and called his name quietly.

"Is it that time already?" he asked, as he woke and looked up at her.

"Yes..." she replied with a forced smile. The dockside quickly came to life, with supplies and passengers being hurriedly unloaded, while ground crews got to work refuelling the giant aeroplane and preparing it for its quick turnaround. "I was supposed to be going with you..." she sighed.

"I know. I'd have liked that."

"When do you think I'll see you again?"

"I don't know... Maybe they'll send me back to England when they've finished putting me back together in Egypt."

"Do you think so?"

"Maybe. I expect they'll have a replacement out here for me within the week, so I can't imagine they'll have much need for me here."

"I hope so, though Robbie will miss you. She said to tell you goodbye."

"How is she?"

"Still laid up, but putting a brave face on it."

"I tried to have her evacuated you know, when she was injured."

"She told me."

"She told me, too, in no uncertain terms."

"She's strong minded."

"Yes, not unlike somebody else I know."

"Shut up..." She smiled as she responded, then frowned as the approaching stretcher bearers' boots crunched on the concrete. "I'm going to miss you."

"You're not, I'll be fine. You can't miss me if you know we'll see each other again soon."

"I mean it, I'll miss you."

"I know... I'll miss you too. I'll write, I promise."

"Excuse me, Ma'am," the stretcher bearer said politely as they stood close. "We need to put Wing Commander Salisbury on the plane. They're not hanging around tonight, and they want to get in the air as soon as the fuel tanks are full."

"Aeroplane," Harriet said with a smile as she stood and faced the soldier.

"Ma'am?"

"Planes are for shaving wood, that's an aeroplane."

"Yes, Ma'am." The stretcher bearer replied.

"You're in danger of becoming a proper RAF officer..." Cas laughed, before coughing and groaning as they lifted him from the ground.

"You're delirious."

"Hilarious, did you say?"

"You wish." She smirked as she walked by his side on the all too short journey to the Sunderland.

"Wait..." Cas said, holding up his hand and stopping the stretcher bearers as they reached the dockside.

"What is it?"

"I just want to say that I'm lucky to have met you, Harriet Cornwall." He reached out and took her hand, and gave her a warm smile. "My life's been better for knowing you."

"Shut up!" She smiled awkwardly, hoping the stretcher bearers wouldn't see the blush she knew was making its way to her cheeks.

"I mean it. I want you to know. Just in case I never get to see you again."

"You will, I promise."

"You can't be so sure... I'm on my way to Cairo, and soon you'll be heading back to England. The way this war's going, there's no telling what will happen." He winced in pain again, and laid back on the stretcher, making her wish she could go with him, and at least try to make his trip more comfortable.

"I am sure, and you need to stop worrying. No matter what happens, I'll find you..." She squeezed his hand one last time and gave him a smile, then watched as he was carried into the aeroplane.

She waited patiently as the Sunderland was prepared for flight, and searched the dark portholes for a glance of Cas, but he was nowhere to be seen. Finally, the engines roared into life one at a time, and the propellers started to spin. The noise was deafening, and the vibrations shook the ground as the Sunderland moved away from the dock, then turned out to the sea. As the tail swung around, for the briefest moment she thought she saw his face at the window, and waved excitedly hoping he'd see her and wave back. Seconds later the engines roared, and the giant seaplane started its run south, then the great white ghost climbed effortlessly into the sky. It didn't turn or circle, much to Harriet's disappointment, instead just continuing south as it climbed into the night. She felt empty as the sound faded, and the crews melted away to their duties, leaving her alone on the concrete dock. She couldn't help but think what it would be like had things been different, and she'd been allowed to go to Cairo too. When she left Egypt, she'd never wanted to return, but there was now nothing else in her mind.

After returning home, Harriet spent an uncomfortable night tossing and turning in her bed, not able to sleep through an all consuming feeling of dread which refused to leave her, no matter what she tried. She'd felt it before in the past, usually before something big, but it was

290

never this intense. It was so bad she felt sick, and had to get up and go out on the terrace, where she watched the stars while sipping the last of the brandy she had in her silver hip flask. In the morning, with hardly a minute's sleep all night, she had tea with Anj and Lissy, and broke the news that she was leaving again. They were sad she was going, but unreservedly happy for her; they knew as everyone else did that she was tired, and they couldn't think of anything better for her than going back to England. Things had changed in Malta, though the situation was still desperate, and both told her again and again how they thought she'd be so much safer in England. Something she knew deep down inside to be true. She just didn't want to leave before the job was finished, or at least that's what she told them. The truth, that she'd come to recognize during her tortured sleepless night, was that she wanted to stay with Cas and Robbie, and the CO, and Anj and Lissy; they were all her family, and she didn't want to leave them. That and her experience on the tanker had terrified her so much that she couldn't even think of going home by boat without being so scared she wanted to cry. Every time closed her eyes, she saw the ships in the convoy exploding, and the crews burning alive in the fiery sea. The very thought made her blood run cold. She finished packing her things after breakfast, and took some time to sit on the terrace of her room and watch Malta go by. The blue sky contrasting with the sandy yellow ground, with the occasional flight of Spitfires launching upwards in a hurry to intercept something. An incoming raid, maybe, or a reconnaissance flight. Then, after a final goodbye and promises to write, she loaded her kit and headed to the airfield to see the CO, and hand over the motorcycle she'd been allowed to keep as her own personal toy for the duration of the stay, and say goodbye and thank him for all he'd done for her. He was a proper officer, a leader that cared passionately for those he commanded, not to mention the most incredible and talented reconnaissance pilot. She'd learned a lot from him, and she'd felt privileged to fly with him.

There was a lot of activity when she arrived, with ground crews rushing around several of the aircraft pens. She stood at the back of the dispersal hut and listened unhappily as the CO briefed a handful of pilots on the unfolding situation. A squadron of torpedo boats were reportedly somewhere to the west of Sicily, lying in wait for the fast Royal Navy Mine Layer that was racing to Malta loaded with much needed stores, and was to be Harriet's return ride to Gibraltar. The reconnaissance pilots had been tasked to find the torpedo boats at all costs, the Mine Layer had been Malta's lifeline over the last couple of years, and even though the last convoy had got through and put a huge dent in the enemy's plans, the island still relied on regular short fast supply runs of essentials, such as medical supplies, anti aircraft ammunition, and aviation fuel, which was often strapped to the decks in large pallets of fuel cans. Most pilots had been tasked for the day, and were already on missions when the call came in, so the CO had to scrape together whoever he could find off duty. He gave them bearings, search instructions, and orders to break radio silence immediately if they saw the torpedo boats, so a waiting squadron of torpedo bombers could go and deal with the threat. He dismissed them and sent them to get ready, then walked over to talk to Harriet.

"Harry... Let's walk." He gave her a half hearted smile, and gestured for her to join him.

"I have my flight kit with me..." she said hopefully, as she walked by his side.

"What's that?"

"My flight kit. I have it in my bag if you need an extra pair of hands. I'm stood down and have nothing better to do." She shrugged confidently, while her heart raced at the thought of getting up one last time, and taking her blue Spitfire for a farewell blast through the Mediterranean skies. He looked at her for a moment, and she smiled back, hoping to persuade him it was a good idea. "Besides, if we don't find those torpedo boats, I may be sticking around longer than I expected! I may as well make myself useful, don't you think?"

"Harry, they got Cas," he said bluntly, as he stopped and faced her. She smiled, and frowned, not sure she'd heard him properly.

"What? I don't understand... He left last night; I saw him safely on the Sunderland."

"The Sunderland didn't make it to Egypt, Harry. A distress call was picked up in the early hours, and then nothing. Night fighters, we think. A few of us went up this morning to search the area..." He

292

shook his head and put his hand on her shoulder. A single tear ran down her cheek, while she used every last ounce of strength to stop her legs from collapsing under her. She turned cold as she felt her heart squeeze so hard that she thought it would burst, like somebody had reached into her chest and gripped it tight. She couldn't talk, she couldn't think. "I'm sorry..."

The End.

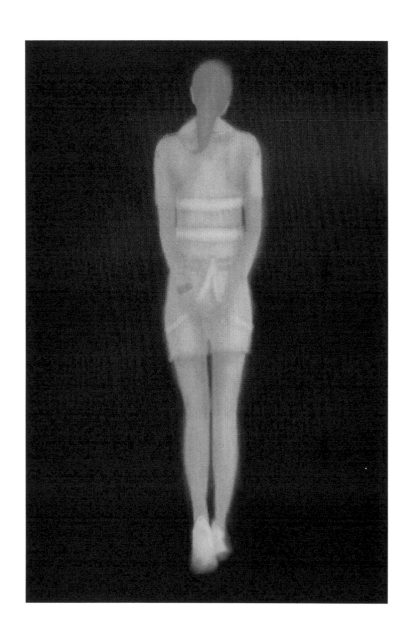

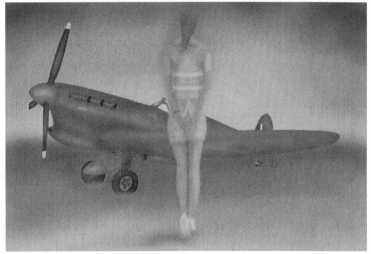